HIGHLAND
BETRAYAL

ALYSON
McLAYNE

sourcebooks
casablanca

Published by Sourcebooks Casablanca, an imprint of Sourcebooks,
Inc.
P.O. Box 4410, Naperville, Illinois 60567-4410
(630) 961-3900
Fax: (630) 961-2168
sourcebooks.com

Printed and bound in Canada.
MBP 10 9 8 7 6 5 4 3 2 1

*To my dad, Jim, whom I admire and respect
more and more every day. You are living
proof that we get better with age.*

One

MacDonnell Castle—Loch Lòchaidh, Scotland, 1452

MAGGIE MACDONNELL CROUCHED IN THE DARK, cramped tunnel, her candle by her side, and slowly, silently lifted the stone slab above her head until a sliver of light seeped under the edge.

She peered into the laird's solar through the legs of a chair she'd carefully positioned over the tunnel entrance weeks ago. A pair of men's feet, shod in dirty shoes, rested on the floor in front of her—someone sitting in the chair. From across the room, she heard the sound of a quill scratching on parchment.

That would be Irvin, of course. No one else would be so bold as to sit at her brother's desk.

Wedging a stick between the ledge and the stone so it would stay open far enough for her to eavesdrop, she picked up her own quill and parchment, ready to write down whatever was said. She had pages of notes and had spent hours poring over them, but it wasn't in her nature to plot or deceive, and she had a difficult time piecing the various bits of information together.

She tended to be as direct and sharp as her daggers.

The clink of the inkwell closing reached her ears, followed by the pungent perfume of melting sealing wax.

"He's at Clan MacPherson."

Aye, that was her cousin's nasal tone, and she scowled.

"Lachlan MacKay killed the laird there and then married a MacPherson lass. I hear the rest of the clan lairds came for the wedding. I doona know how long MacLean will stay there, but if he heads home when the others do, you should be able to intercept him along the way."

Maggie stopped writing and barely held in a gasp. Was Irvin talking about *Callum* MacLean? Were they somehow in league?

Betrayal and hurt raged through her at the thought, and she clenched her hand around the quill, smearing the wet ink from the parchment onto her skin.

"Aye, Laird," the man sitting in the chair responded. The voice was that of Irvin's man, Blàr. "And if I miss him?"

"Then carry on to Clan MacLean. Deliver the letter and speak to our friend inside about the other matter we discussed."

"And Ross. What do ye want me to do about him, Laird?"

Maggie held her breath. Normally, she would have been irate at Blàr calling Irvin "laird," but this time, she ignored it.

What do they intend for Ross—their real laird?

"Naught. He's doing it to himself," Irvin said. "He's near dead already with the drink. I give him less than a year, and I can wait. 'Tis the other two we have to plan for."

"You'll kill Maggie, then?" Blàr asked from right above her. "Can I do it? 'Tis the way she looks at me. As if she's stepped in something foul. I want to see her face change when I shove my dagger in."

"Nay, I willna kill her. She has value. I'll take her bairn instead."

Her brow creased in confusion. *Bairn? Is he addled?* Then a growing horror bloomed as she realized his meaning.

Blàr's feet danced in front of her. "She's with child? The wee besom."

Irvin snickered. "You havenae any imagination, Blàr. *I'll* get Maggie with child—or someone else will. She'll marry me and stay with me to protect the first bairn and the rest after that till I'm done with her. The clan will be happy to have Donnan's beloved daughter as their lady, and 'twill seal my lairdship with rightful heirs."

Blàr's ankles sagged dejectedly. "Well, what about the other brother, John? Can we kill him?"

"Aye. But first we have to find him."

Maggie grasped the hilt of one of the daggers that was tucked into a sheath on her forearm. Three of them, all perfectly balanced and as sharp as the day they were forged. She considered striking out right then, slicing first through the tendons above Blàr's heels and then charging through the passageway like an avenging angel. But then what? Kill her cousin in cold blood? The man was a weasel. He'd never fight back.

She'd have to put a dagger in his back as he ran.

She sighed softly. Nay, she couldn't do it, even

though she might soon find herself locked up and tied
to a bed for her cousin's—or someone else's—use.

It was a grim imagining, and she shuddered.

A chair scraped across the floor at the desk.

Blàr quickly stood and stepped forward. "Should I
take the letter with me, then?"

"Nay. Pick it up at first light. Less chance of it falling into the wrong hands. Maggie's been curious of
late—asking too many questions about my business—
and she's been trying to interfere with Ross's drinking.
We canna have that."

"Nay, Laird. But I hardly think anyone could pull
Ross from his cups. He loved your sister verra much."

Irvin laughed. "Aye, he did. John, too, the wee
ablach. And my sweet, dull-witted sister loved them
both. 'Tis a shame she had to choose just one."

Irvin made grunting sounds followed by squeals,
simulating sex, and they laughed raucously. Maggie
swallowed the bile that rose in her throat. That he
should speak so about any woman, let alone his dead
sister, sickened her.

"It worked out well for ye, though," Blàr said as they
walked toward the door. "I always wondered if ye had
shoved things in the direction ye wanted them to go."

Aye, Maggie had wondered that too. She heard
what sounded like a hand clapping a shoulder, then
Irvin said smugly, "I don't e'er shove, Blàr. I nudge."

The solar door opened, and after a moment, it
closed and was locked from the outside. Maggie
pressed her palm to her brow and breathed deeply to
calm her anger. She had to proceed with a clear head. If
they caught her snooping, she'd be locked up for sure.

Lifting the stone slab, she pushed it to the side so it lay on the solar floor, then grabbed the leg of the chair and moved it out of the way. When she stood, the floor came to her waist, and she climbed out, taking her candle with her.

She was relieved to escape the tunnel. She hated being confined—had since she'd fallen into a well as a young lass…and her mother had fallen in after her.

The dying fire cast only a dim light about the room, but Maggie knew the layout of the laird's solar by heart. Crossing to the desk, she put down her candle. She searched the wooden surface until she found the letter that had been recently sealed, the wax with the imprint of her brother's ring still warm. She carefully peeled up the seal and placed it in her pocket.

She paused then, dread filling her stomach like a lead ball, before opening the folded parchment and reading her cousin's small, perfect script. It barely filled the page. Her jaw trembled at the words, and relief weakened her knees.

Callum was innocent…in this at least.

Not that it mattered. Nothing about him was of interest to her anymore. Although when the time came, *she* would be the one to tell him that. Not her lying, scheming cousin.

She reread the letter—informing Callum that the marriage contract between him and Maggie was broken. Since no goods or land had been exchanged and both of their fathers, who had originally arranged the marriage, were now dead, the MacDonnells were withdrawing the offer.

A cascade of emotions washed through her—ones

Maggie thought long dead: anger at Irvin for presuming to end her betrothal, but also anger and hurt that Callum had never returned for her.

At one point, she'd had high hopes for their future. She'd respected him—*liked* him—and he'd made her laugh, which her father had always said was important in a marriage. And when Callum had kissed her, she'd more than liked him. Aye, those feelings had stayed with her for a long while.

Not anymore.

She drummed her fingers on the desk. She could write Callum, explain the situation, and ask for his help. It would please her to finally get a message out, all the more if it went tucked inside Irvin's own sealed letter.

Or she could let the letter stand, let their betrothal officially end. For all she knew, Callum would be happy to hear that he was a free man. Maybe his whispered words of affection three years ago had all been a lie—the same as his pledge to return for her.

And if he did come to fight for her, insist the contract was still valid, what would happen? He'd have no idea of the danger he would be riding into. She imagined a dagger or arrow piercing his heart, and her chest tightened. Nay, it would be best if he carried on with his life far away from the MacDonnells and never learned of her plight.

She was a strong Highland lass. She didn't need saving.

Lifting her hand to the silver brooch on her breast that held her arisaid together, she opened the clasp. The brooch had been a wedding present from her father to her mother on their wedding day, passed down to her upon her mother's death thirteen years ago. She'd sobbed in her father's arms when he'd given it to her.

He had too.

Maggie had worn the brooch every day to keep her mother close and to remind herself how quickly things could change.

She unpinned it, and her arisaid sagged. After looping the material under her arm, she wedged her nail into an almost invisible crease in the silver and tugged the top off the brooch. A small hollow appeared. Maggie fished inside and snagged another piece of parchment with her fingernail. Pulling it out, she slowly unrolled it.

Two holes pierced the center of the dirty, ragged parchment—dagger holes—and a third hole pierced up top where the parchment had been pinned to a tree. Under the two holes, Callum had scribbled a *C* and an *M*.

She remembered the look in his eyes when he'd pulled out their thrown daggers, a contest to see who had better aim. He'd written their initials on it before giving it to her. For a lass like Maggie, who preferred daggers to flowers, it was the sweetest love note she could have received. At the time, she'd carefully rolled it up and fit it into her brooch, so it would always rest next to her heart.

Now she would include it in the letter to Callum, and he would know she was done with him.

Before she could change her mind, she placed the parchment in the folds of Irvin's letter. She resealed it with hot wax, then found her brother's ring on the desk and pressed it into the hardening liquid.

She set the letter in its place, ignoring the melancholy feeling that rose within her. Callum MacLean was better off without her. And she was certainly better off without him.

What were the chances he would come back for her now?

Two

CALLUM MACLEAN LEANED AGAINST THE TREE, LEGS stretched out on the ground in front of him, eyes closed. His mind raced. In his sporran, tucked away for safekeeping, was a letter from Maggie and her brother, Ross. It ended Maggie and Callum's betrothal and had been handed to him by a shifty-looking man named Blàr.

Callum had been on the road for four days with his foster brother, Gavin, laird of Clan MacKinnon, Father Lundie, and ten of their men. He'd had the letter for three of those days, yet he was still no closer to making a decision about Maggie than when he'd first received it. As always, when it came to his *betrothed*, Callum's heart and head were not aligned.

He heard riders approaching, and from the warning whistles of some of the watchers, he knew it was Gavin and several others who'd been out scouting after seeing wolf tracks. Callum didn't move and continued to mull over the problem.

"Laird MacKinnon," he heard Father Lundie whisper to Gavin. "Laird MacLean is still sleeping."

Callum cracked an eyelid to see his foster brother bearing down on him, the priest hovering by his side.

"I don't know what *you* see, Father Lundie," Gavin said, "but *I* see a man stuck. Like a wee lad forced to choose between sweets."

"Nay, Laird," Father Lundie said. "He hasn't risen since you left. I think he must be ill to be sleeping during the day. 'Tis unlike him to sit so still."

"'Tis exactly like him to sit still when he's trying to solve a puzzle. But this isna a puzzle. He just needs to get his head out of his arse."

"Is there a problem I can help with?" Father Lundie asked. "Perhaps I can assist—"

Callum didn't wait for the priest to finish. Instead, he kicked out his feet just as Gavin came into striking distance. Gavin jumped up just in time—expecting it, of course—but when he landed, Callum scissored his legs and knocked him to the ground.

"You wee shite," Gavin said as he pushed himself up onto his elbows.

"Oh, were you there? I couldnae see you with my head up my arse."

Father Lundie stared down at them, looking startled, before he hurried away.

Gavin crawled up beside Callum and leaned back against the tree next to him. "Give me the letter and the other parchment from Maggie. We'll talk it through."

Sighing, Callum fished out the messages from his sporran, then handed them over. "I've already assessed them from every angle."

"No doubt."

"The first is from Ross, or so it says. But 'tis not Ross's script nor manner of speaking."

"So someone else wrote it for him. His steward perhaps? 'Tis not uncommon."

"But what would compel Ross to cause such a breach? The marriage is a good alliance for Clan MacDonnell, and it's only improved since the original contract was agreed upon. My allies are his allies. If he was upset I havenae returned for Maggie, then he would demand the marriage take place, not terminate the contract. And from all that I've heard, Ross has not been himself since he lost his wife and bairn. I was at their wedding. I saw how much he loved Eleanor."

"You think it's someone else's doing then? Someone pulling his strings?"

"Aye."

"Maggie?"

"Nay. Maggie wouldnae pull strings. She'd throw daggers."

Gavin lifted the second parchment. "Isn't that what this is?"

Callum ground his teeth and nodded. "I've no doubt Maggie sent that. And the message is clear. She's ending our betrothal—and making a point. The day I wrote our initials on that parchment was the first day we connected as a man and a woman rather than as a lad and lass staring bemusedly at their future wife and husband, 'Twas the first day I knew she was mine. We were competing, tossing daggers. We tied on every round. I gave her that parchment and, afterward, kissed her for the first time."

"So she kept it, and now she's throwing it back at you."

"Aye."

"She's hurt."

"Aye."

"And angry."

"Aye."

"Well, 'tis obvious you have to go and win her back. And find out what's going on with Ross."

When he didn't answer, Gavin looked at him. "I said—"

"I heard you. How could I not? You bellow like a rampaging boar." His words were sharp—sharper than if they'd just been said in jest. And they were untrue, of course, but Gavin understood the frustration behind them and didn't take offense.

Callum sighed. "If I go there and win Maggie back, which willna be easy, what do I do then? Marry her? There's a good reason I havenae returned for her."

"Your father's murder."

"Aye. I canna in good conscience bring her to Clan MacLean and put her in danger."

"Well…marry her, and then she can come home with me until you find the murderer. Although Isobel will want to learn Maggie's skill with the dagger, and that will cause trouble."

The corners of Callum's mouth twitched, despite the fact that he hadn't smiled in days. "I'd like to see that. Kerr will have a fit."

"What about me? I'm her brother. She'll start tossing knives at me every time I suggest it might be time for them to wed."

Callum shook his head. Gavin and their other foster brother, Kerr, had been trying to convince Isobel to marry Kerr since she'd turned eighteen. She was dead set against it, even though Callum suspected she'd be devastated if he married someone else. "The two of you have it backward. Isobel likes being defiant. She'll stay unmarried simply to spite you both."

Gavin made a disgruntled sound in the back of his throat. "So what do you want to do about Maggie, then? We canna stay here forever."

Callum drummed his fingers on the ground. "She wouldnae have included the parchment if she wanted me to come. So she knows the letter was sent, and knows what was inside it, but the circumstances surrounding the letter are troubling."

"If she's no longer your betrothed, then maybe 'tis not your problem. You can ride away with an easy conscience."

The argument was logical, but Callum knew his brother had said it only to push him into action. No matter what Maggie might want him to do, he couldn't ride away knowing something wasn't right at Clan MacDonnell.

What if she needs help?

She didn't want him to come. But he couldn't stay away. Not until he knew for sure she was safe.

He grimaced, scrubbed his hand through his hair. "We'll head north to Clan MacDonnell."

Gavin rose to his feet, grinning, then reached down to help Callum. "'Tis a good thing I'm here to get you moving; otherwise, Father Lundie would have ended up performing last rites on your prone body."

He almost tugged his foster brother over for that, but Gavin had planted his feet in anticipation. It would end up being a tug of war.

Callum took the offered hand and, after rising, was brushing the dirt from his plaid when a wolf howled in the distance. The eerie cry was quickly followed by several others. He straightened slowly, the hair on his neck prickling, as he and the other men listened closely.

The pack was hunting.

Better a stag than one of his men. But then a horse screeched far away, and he heard a woman scream.

"God's blood!" he shouted. "MacLeans! Mount up!" He ran for his horse as Gavin rallied his own warriors.

Callum's second-in-command, Drustan, a lean, hardened warrior who'd been his father's best friend before he died, wheeled his mount toward him. "Should we light the torches?"

"Aye. And leave two men with Father Lundie. Have them build a fire and stay near the trees. Tell them to push the priest onto a branch at any sign of trouble."

Drustan nodded and rode away.

It wasn't the first time Callum had faced off against wolves, and God knew it wouldn't be the last. Knowing the wolves had no malice toward you—they were just hungry, and you were prey—made it terrifying. Far worse than coming up against another man.

Callum would do what he could to help their target, pray he and his men weren't too late, but he had to prepare himself for the worst. He'd seen the carnage left behind after a wolf pack attacked a family. The images had stayed with him for months.

Another scream sounded.

Callum's man Gill tested the wind with a single strand of his long black hair, then pointed his arm to the northeast. "She's over there. Maybe a half mile?" Callum didn't doubt he was right. Gill was the best marksman he had.

"We'll go straight through the brush," Callum said. "I'm afraid we'll miss her if we follow the trail."

They spread out in a line, distanced far enough apart to cover as much ground as possible but close enough to be safe, although the wolves were unlikely to approach the men as long as their torches were lit.

When they heard another yell, they homed in, invigorated to know she was still alive. After what seemed like an eternity, they entered a clearing, riding hard.

They reined in at the sight of dead and injured wolves on the ground, cut and bleeding, and a woman's skirt torn to pieces. One of the wolves had a familiar dirk sticking out of its ribs.

Callum's heart pounded as he looked at the dagger, and he slowly raised his head to follow the trail left behind—more blood, another dead wolf, crushed grass and flowers. And bits of plaid in the blues and greens favored by the weavers at clan MacDonnell.

Someone had run across the glen, the wolves at their heels.

His gaze reached the base of a lone tree where three more wolves lay dead—all with daggers in them. The pine tree didn't look sturdy enough to sustain someone's weight—much less the weight of wolves clawing at it, as indicated by the scored bark—but he caught a glimpse of bare feet and legs tucked up on the first bough. The rest of the woman's body was hidden by pine needles...but he knew.

He urged his stallion, Aristotle, forward, the others fanning out behind him, and tried to quell his rising panic. *God, let her be safe.*

When he rode beneath the branches of the tree and looked up, relief washed through him so intensely, he nearly fell from his horse. A lass glared down at him—very much alive—her auburn hair as wild as he remembered and her hazel eyes just as bright.

Maggie MacDonnell—*his* Maggie MacDonnell.

No matter what she might think.

"For the love of God, lass," he croaked, "what are you doing up there?"

"I would think that was obvious, Callum MacLean. I am attempting to stay alive."

He ground his teeth together, trying to rein in the storm of emotions that blew though him. Her hands and clothes were splattered with blood. Wolves' blood, hopefully, from when she'd stabbed them. "Are you hurt?"

The words came out harsher than he'd intended, sparked by his fear of what could have happened.

Her chin trembled, and she thrust it out belligerently. "'Tis not your concern, Laird MacLean. Nothing about me is your concern anymore."

Beside him, Gavin gasped in recognition. "Is that Maggie? *Your* Maggie?"

"Nay," she said, directing her attention to Gavin. "Just Maggie. *My* Maggie."

"Aye, it's her," Callum answered. He heard a murmur pass through the men, and his tension rose another notch. She might insist she wasn't his, but as he looked at her, noted everything from the freckles across her cheeks and nose to the dark sweep of her lashes, he remembered what it was like to be in her presence. The quickening of his blood and heightening of his senses. How she felt, how she smelled. How she kissed.

He glanced over his shoulder and tried to catch Drustan's eye, but his second-in-command stared up at Maggie with a strange look on his face. "We'll stay here tonight," Callum said, and Drustan, his skin pale and lips tight, finally looked at him. "Set fires at regular intervals in case the pack returns, then go back for the others."

"Aye, Laird." Drustan's voice was hoarse. He signaled to the men, and they retreated.

Callum shot Gavin a look, but his foster brother ignored him as he was wont to do. Instead, Gavin smiled up at Maggie gently. "Hello, lass. It's been a long time. Do you remember me?"

She switched her gaze to him, and her eyes widened. "Is that you, Gavin MacKinnon? What have you done to your bonny blond hair? 'Tis even shorter than Callum's."

Gavin raised a hand to his bristly, ravaged scalp. "I know. 'Tis how I feel now. When I find my son, Ewan, I'll let it grow."

The hardness left her eyes. "Aye, I heard about your loss. I'm so sorry. Last year, wasn't it? At the spring gathering?"

"Aye." Then he smiled again, although this time, it looked forced. "And you, Maggie? Other than being up a tree and chased down by wolves, are you all right?"

A small laugh puffed from her lips. "Well, I'm not dead, am I?"

Callum's mouth firmed, and he urged Aristotle past Gavin. He stopped directly beneath Maggie and positioned the horse sideways to the tree. Rising onto his stallion's back, he placed one foot on the horse's shoulders, the other on his rump. He reached his arms up to her. "Come down, Maggie. I'll catch you."

"I doona need your help."

"Aye, you do. I'll tend to your wounds before they fester, and then I'll see you home."

Her eyes flashed, and she reached for one of her daggers, but the leather sheath strapped to her forearm was empty. Her mouth set mulishly. "You can give me a horse, naught more. I'm going to find John."

The last he'd heard, Maggie's other brother was off fighting skirmishes against the English for whoever would pay his wage. Even if he still lived, it was unlikely she'd find him easily. "But what about Ross? He is Laird, aye? Doona tell me he sent you away?"

"And why should I tell you anything? 'Tis not like you're my husband."

Callum ground his teeth at the deliberate provocation. When they'd parted ways, Maggie had been more than eager to marry him.

He tried his most conciliatory tone. "Maggie—"

She jerked her arms in displeasure and pine needles showered down on him. "You are a lying scoundrel, Callum MacLean, and I doona need you or anyone else. I can take care of myself."

He brushed the needles from his hair. "And that's why you're stuck in a tree, half-naked, with no horse and a wolf pack on your heels. How many were there, Maggie? Do you think they'll return? I'm assuming they've run down your horse by now."

Her bottom lip quivered before she firmed it. Regret washed through him, taking his anger and fear for her along with it. He dropped his arms. "Och, lass. I'm sorry. For everything. I meant it when I said I'd be back in the spring. Things…changed. It grieves me to see you up there, knowing what you went through. Please, come down so I can help you."

Maggie stared at him, a gamut of emotions running across her face. He used to love watching her— whether she was dancing or laughing or scowling at him. Wild Maggie MacDonnell, who was more interested in daggers and arrows than pretty curls or a swishing walk.

He knew without a doubt she was meant for him. He felt it with a certainty in his bones, the same way he knew his father had been murdered, despite what everyone said. The same way Gavin knew his son was still alive.

"You want me to come down?" she asked.

"Aye." A wariness tinged his words, and beside him, Gavin snorted.

Maggie shrugged and moved closer to the edge of the bough. "Catch," she said, then she jumped from the branch and kicked out with her feet, hitting him squarely in the chest. He fell backward over Aristotle's flank and landed hard on the grass.

He heard Gavin hoot with laughter and looked up to see Maggie seated on the big stallion, her legs bare from midthigh to her toes, her skin scratched and bloodied. She wheeled the stallion around and urged Aristotle into a gallop.

Callum jumped up and whistled, loud and shrill. His horse came to a jarring halt, almost knocking *her* off this time. She rounded to glare at him, a sight to behold with her flushed cheeks and flashing eyes, her tangled hair cascading over her shoulders.

Gavin had rushed to her aid, and she reached over and pulled a dagger from his belt, then hurled it at Callum. It landed in the tree trunk just above his head. Exactly where she'd intended.

Callum smiled. It was a start.

Maggie MacDonnell does not want me dead.

～～

Maggie stared at Callum as he stood in front of the tree, Gavin's dagger still vibrating in the wood above his head, a tight smile creasing his face.

She wanted to knock his smile off. Hard.

She could pull her daggers from the dead wolves around the tree and attack him again, but she didn't think she'd succeed this time. An unprepared Callum was formidable; a Callum who anticipated her next move would be near impossible to beat.

Besides, no matter how much she wanted to hurt him, she didn't want him dead.

Sniffing dismissively, she turned Aristotle and surveyed the glade and the soldiers setting up camp. Could she get away with stealing another horse? The warriors were quick and efficient and took care to choose defensive positions, but they wouldn't be expecting her to break out from the inside.

Irvin would come after her, she had no doubt about that, and if he caught her now, he'd lock her away for good. Her only option was to leave her beloved Highlands.

Her chest squeezed suddenly, and she found herself blinking away ridiculous tears. It wasn't like her to give up, but she knew when she was beat. If John could turn his back on his clan and run away—Ross too, lost in grief and darkness at the bottom of his cups—she could do the same.

They had all abandoned her, Callum included.

Movement caught her eye, and she looked down to see Callum rummaging in the leather pack that lay across his stallion's haunches. Her breath caught as she watched him—his straight, dark hair cropped short as usual, his skin tanned and face angular. Dark eyebrows slashed above the piercing green gaze she remembered well, surrounded by thick, dark lashes. He was tall with sculpted muscles, not just mass, and while he was the leanest of his foster brothers, he was also the fastest and most agile—and just as strong.

His hands working so near her bare legs caused a tremor to run through her muscles. Other lasses might feel embarrassed to be so exposed to a man, but a part of Maggie wanted Callum to see her like this, to know what he'd given up.

She was of average height, but her legs were relatively long and supple. Callum had kissed and touched her when they were younger, squeezed her breasts, even, which she knew he'd liked—she had too—but he'd never seen her naked. Did their proximity affect him as it did her?

Not that it meant anything. Not anymore.

He pulled out a blanket and handed it to her. She hesitated before taking it. She needed the warmth, but the last plaid she wanted to be covered in was Callum's. Those dreams were dead and buried.

"Thank you," she said, the words sticking in her throat.

Callum nodded as he retied the pack. "I've imagined our reunion many times, Maggie. Not once did I think it would happen like this."

Her brow lifted in surprise. "You thought about me?"

"Of course I did."

"There's no 'of course' about it. Why would I think otherwise, when you broke your promise?"

His hands stilled. "I wrote to you. Not as often as I should have, and not in the last six months, but... I haven't heard from you in two years."

She stared at him, trying to discern the truth in his gaze. Aye, she'd stopped writing, but if what he said was true, someone had withheld his letters from her—most likely her cousin.

She sighed and lifted her hand to rub her tired eyes—she hadn't slept for a day and a half—wincing as her shoulder protested the movement. "It doesn't matter if you wrote a hundred letters, Callum. You didn't return like you promised, and I have other plans now. Besides, you'll gain nothing from marrying me."

"I'll gain you."

He slid his palm along the stallion's flank and gently but firmly wrapped it around her bare calf. A shiver raced over her skin.

His gaze lifted to hers. "There is no other lass for me, Maggie. Not before, and not now."

He released her, strode to the front of his horse, and grasped the reins. "I'll see to your wounds by the fire."

Maggie was too stunned to protest, and she let Callum lead her mount across the glade to the fire that had been built in the middle of the camp, stopping on the way to collect her daggers from the three dead wolves under the tree. The blanket almost tumbled from her lap, and she shook it out and placed it over her bare legs, still feeling the imprint of his hand on her skin.

He dropped the reins, saying, "Aristotle, stay," then he clasped her hand before she could pull it back. He helped her down and led her to a stump in front of the fire, passing her the daggers.

Returning to his pack, he brought back a small bag as she cleaned her knives and reinserted them into the leather sheath. A pot had been placed over the fire, and he dropped several small cloths into the boiling water inside.

"Your stallion is named Aristotle?" she asked, searching for something to talk about as the tension between them thickened.

"Aye. It's fitting, don't you think?"

Maggie thought about it and found herself smiling. If Callum hadn't been born to be a warrior and laird, he would have been a scholar. He was logical and exact in his thinking. So yes, it did fit. "Aye."

Callum smiled too. "Lachlan named him, and it stuck."

"I heard he recently married. I ne'er thought that day would come."

"Neither did I. He married a MacPherson lass named Amber. She's the clan healer and a fighter. She reminds me of you. She told me I'd been an idiot to stay away from you for so long."

Well, she wouldn't argue with that.

He pulled out his knife and placed the blade in the water.

"What are you doing?" she asked. "Don't you have a salve you can give me?"

"Aye, but Amber says 'tis better to wash the wounds with boiled water before putting on the salve. She says it'll help with the healing."

He lifted his dagger by the leather handle, then fished out a steaming cloth.

She pulled her legs away. "You're not putting that on my skin."

"We'll let it cool first."

She didn't know why she was allowing him to do this. If she'd learned anything over the last three years, it was to rely only on herself. But when Callum knelt in front of her and lifted her right foot onto his lap, it felt like a butterfly took wing in her chest. She couldn't catch her breath.

He gently pulled the blanket from her leg, inspecting each cut. Most were superficial, but a puncture wound at the top of her knee looked and felt deep. She'd thrust her dagger into the neck of the wolf that had done that and another into a wolf that was tearing at her skirt before scrambling up the tree.

Her shoes and hose were gone, torn right off her feet.

"Your skirt probably saved you," Callum said, his thoughts on track with hers.

"My daggers saved me. And my ability to climb a tree."

"Aye, but the wolves would have clamped down on your skirt first. If you'd been a man, they'd have gone directly for your leg."

"Well, thank the blessed virgin I'm a lass, then."

"Aye. Thank God for that." His tone was grave, but his eyes danced.

She felt a blush stealing up her cheeks and scowled. Nobody made her blush. Ever. Except she remembered those long days with Callum, when her cheeks seemed to be perpetually flushed, when she could hardly wait for morning to come so she could see him again—before he'd left her waiting and never returned.

Lying scoundrel.

"Do you think my horse survived?" she asked. "She was a good mount."

"Nay, lass. Probably not."

Maggie sighed, sad for the horse but glad to be alive. Looking over her shoulder at the skinny, lone tree she'd climbed, she considered her survival a miracle. She'd barely been able to pull herself out of range of the wolves' snapping teeth before they'd started jumping against the tree, trying to knock her off. She'd had to squeeze her thighs and arms tight around the trunk or she'd have slid down.

She'd used her toes and fingers to dig in, to keep pushing herself upward. When she'd wrapped a hand around a bough thick enough to support her weight, she'd cried out with relief.

She hadn't escaped the danger in her own clan only to become dinner for a pack of hungry wolves.

She reached for the warm, wet cloth hanging from Callum's knife. "Here. I'll do it."

"Nay, let me…please."

She hesitated. There was something in the way he knelt before her, the gentle way he held her foot, the soft plea in his voice…and she nodded.

Callum started at her toes and worked his way up, being meticulous in his ministrations as if to make up for the last three years. After cleaning each wound, he applied the salve and a bandage where necessary. It hurt in places, which was good; otherwise, she'd have been a quivering mess, begging him to slide his hand all the way up her leg.

"I think I should stitch this one, Maggie."

She nodded, suspecting as much from the way the wound on the outside of her thigh throbbed and the blood still oozed.

"Three should do it. I know you're a strong lass, but it will hurt. Do you want me to get Gavin to hold you down? 'Tis one thing to run from wolves; 'tis another to sit still while someone pokes you with a needle."

She shook her head, staring him straight in the eye.

His lips firmed, but he nodded, then rummaged in the bag and pulled out something wrapped in lamb's wool. The needles and thread, most likely. She looked away and squeezed her eyes shut.

Callum was quick and efficient, but by the end of it, tears streamed down her face, and she was hard-pressed not to beg him to stop. But she refused to look weak in front of him.

"I'm done," he said, smearing salve on top and

wrapping the wound with a bandage. "Let's look at your other leg."

He covered her right leg with the blanket and carefully exposed her left one, which wasn't as badly scratched. This time Callum was able to dress and bandage her wounds with only one stitch.

After she was covered, he said, "What about the rest of you? You may not like it, but I should look at your—"

"Nay."

"Maggie, to be safe, I need to—"

She whipped out her dagger and notched it under his chin. "You are not looking at my arse, Callum MacLean."

A corner of his mouth twitched up. "Never?"

"Never."

He wrapped his hand around her wrist and lowered her dagger from his throat. His gaze held hers. "I still intend to marry you, Maggie MacDonnell."

She raised one brow, a spurt of anger mixing with longing. Apparently, he hadn't received Irvin's letter. "And I still intend to leave the Highlands."

"Why, Maggie? Can you tell me what's happened? What has Ross done?"

"He's done naught. That's the problem."

"What do you mean? Are you in disagreement with him?" His jaw suddenly hardened, and his eyes stormed. "Does he intend to marry you to someone else? Is that it?"

"What? Nay. He doesn't intend anything. He's drunk, Callum. All the time. E'er since Eleanor and their bairn died." Her voice broke at the end, and she looked away.

Callum gently turned her face back toward him. "If you need to get away, Maggie, then come with me. We doona have to decide about marrying just now—about anything. I'll write your brother and let him know you're with me. You canna go haring off by yourself. It's too dangerous."

She took the cloth and salve from him and cleansed a shallow wound on her shoulder. "Nay, staying in the Highlands at all is dangerous. You canna keep me safe at your castle."

A strange look crossed his face, and he scrubbed a hand through his hair. "'Tis safer than a woman alone on the road to Edinburgh. Especially as you've no idea where to find John. Maybe your leaving will be enough to raise Ross from his cups."

"Maybe. But I canna count on that. I canna count on anyone. You taught me that, Callum. And my brothers. I will continue on my journey tomorrow. Alone."

Three

CALLUM STRODE ACROSS THE GLADE, CARRYING THE remnants of his and Maggie's dinner. A stream trickled through the north end of the clearing, and he crouched at its edge to rinse the bowls and cups. He'd tried to get Maggie to talk more about Ross, about what she was running from, but she refused to divulge any further information. And when he tried to get her to talk about their betrothal, she shot him a glare that ended the conversation before it began.

She'd wanted to wash afterward, so they'd strung up blankets near the stream to give her some privacy, then she'd stretched out by the fire on the bedroll he'd provided and covered herself with his plaid, his pack under her head for a pillow.

Gavin approached with Drustan to wash their dishes, and they crouched beside Callum.

"Did she tell you what the trouble was? Why she was running?" Gavin asked.

"Nay. The only thing she said is that Ross has turned to drink since his wife and bairn died two years ago."

Gavin rubbed his hand over his short, bristly hair,

a gesture Callum had noticed he did whenever he thought of his lost son—almost as if to remind himself.

"Och, I can understand that. But not for this long."

"Who's leading the clan, then, with John gone?" Drustan asked.

"I don't know, but she implied she was in danger." Callum whirled and threw the wooden cup into the woods in frustration, and it crashed against a tree. "I shouldnae have left her alone for so long. I thought she would be safe—safer there than with me—but all I did was leave her to fend for herself."

"She's with you now, Laird," Drustan said. "Alive and fighting."

Gavin looked over to where Maggie slept by the fire. "And covered in your plaid. Marry her tomorrow, Callum. Father Lundie's here. He knows the two of you are betrothed. You don't have to tell him about Ross's letter. You don't have to tell anyone you received it. Even her."

"You're already betrothed," Drustan added. "All the two of you need is mutual consent and carnal knowledge. 'Tis how my wife and I were married. We ne'er said vows in front of a priest."

Callum looked at him, his brow raised. He'd known Drustan his entire life, trusted him like an uncle or much older brother, but he never knew Drustan'd had a wife.

"When were you married?" he asked. "And how come I ne'er knew about it?"

Drustan turned back to his dishes. "'Twas a long time ago and short-lived. Not many people remember."

"What was her name? Did my father know? What happened?"

"Abigail. She…she had freckles like your Maggie. Although she didn't have red hair, but her eyes were similar, and the shape of her face—small and fine boned. And yes"—he paused, and Callum saw his jaw clench and release before he continued—"your father knew. He liked her verra much. She…died"—Drustan took a moment to clear his throat—"after being kicked by a horse. 'Twas the saddest day of my life, and I doona talk about it because it still hurts." He'd placed a hand over his heart while he spoke, a gesture Callum had never seen him do. Then his hand fisted, and he said, "Your da kept me sane and helped me through it, or I wouldnae be here today. 'Tis why I know he ne'er would have committed suicide—not after working so hard to keep me on this earth."

Callum clamped his hand on Drustan's shoulder. It was only the second time he'd seen such emotion from the man—the first being when Callum's father had been murdered.

"And you ne'er wanted to marry again? Ne'er wanted bairns?" Gavin asked.

"Not if I couldnae have them with my wife. I havenae been chaste for twenty years, but I've always been careful ne'er to leave my seed behind. The women I've been with feel the same. And if they doona, I stop seeing them."

Callum wondered who Drustan was seeing now. He was a private man, so he would never tell, and Callum would never ask.

He looked over at Maggie. If she had died, would

he have felt the same? Judging by the way his chest squeezed and his pulse sped up just thinking about losing her before they'd even begun, the answer was yes. Which was a problem if she didn't feel the same.

"Maggie says she willna have me," he said gruffly. "That she's leaving the Highlands for good."

Gavin followed Callum's gaze to where she lay sleeping by the fire. "She canna just leave."

"And how do you propose I stop her? Should I dose her with herbs as was done to Darach's Caitlin until she canna protest the union?"

"Nay, of course not. But…have you talked to her? Explained about your father?"

"I've talked to her, aye, but she's made up her mind against me. And until she's my wife, I doona think I should tell her about my da. At least, not yet."

"I agree," Drustan said.

Gavin raised his brows. "You think she'll tell someone?"

"I think the fewer people who know, the better my chances are of finding my father's killer. And the less chance someone will target her for what she knows. If we're married, I can keep a guard on her. Protect her. But if not, and she continues to Edinburgh to find John, she'll be vulnerable."

Gavin laid a commiserating hand on his shoulder. "So what will you do then?"

"I'll try to talk to her in the morning, and if she still insists on leaving, I'll make sure she gets there safely."

"I'm sorry, Laird," Drustan said. "I know you've always held Maggie dear—"

A scream sounded from the campsite, followed by

a sob, and Callum sprinted across the grass to Maggie's side. She'd rolled onto her back, still asleep, and thrashed her head back and forth on his pack, clearly agitated.

Pulling her into his arms, he rubbed his palm over her hair. "Hush, sweetling. 'Tis all right. I've got you. You're safe."

She whimpered and turned her body fully into his before settling down, her cheek on his chest. He lay back and tucked her into the crook of his arm.

It was a sweet kind of sorrow, knowing he may never hold her like this again. He closed his eyes against the pain, regret a sharp knife in his heart.

He'd done this, driven her away. He had no one to blame but himself—and whoever had killed his father. Still, if marrying him then had meant her life might be forfeit, he'd make the same choices all over again.

This single memory—finally holding Maggie— would have to last him a lifetime.

༺ঌ৹༻

Maggie woke with the bright morning sunlight in her eyes. The first thing she saw was a fire with a pot of boiling water over it. Callum's knife handle poked up from inside, reminding her of her injuries. Not that she needed reminding. Her whole body ached.

She sat up slowly, looking for him. She knew he'd slept with her last night and helped soothe her fears. She'd been half awake at times, but instead of rolling away or stealing a horse and sneaking off like she'd intended, she'd curled into his protective warmth.

She made a disgruntled sound in the back of her

throat, annoyed by her own weakness. Maybe the salve had some kind of sleep aid in it, or she'd been too hurt, too exhausted, to pull away. Or maybe she'd just wanted to be near Callum.

It bothered her to realize she'd needed him like that, and she scowled. She wouldn't stay. Couldn't stay. He'd lied to her. Betrayed her. She could not trust him.

"Thinking about my foster brother, are you? About how you'd like to drive a dagger through his heart and twist it? Then maybe bash his head in with a rock? Aye, me too. Especially when he spits logic and reason at me. 'Tis most aggravating."

She looked over her shoulder, brows raised. Gavin stood there with a grin on his face, two cups in one huge hand and a couple of bowls in the other.

"You've gone and lost your mind as well as all that glorious blond hair," she scoffed.

"Aye, I did for a while. Just like your brother. Grief is a terrible thing. Mind you, I didn't grieve my wife's death. 'Twas a most disagreeable marriage. But it cut out my heart to lose my son, even though I'll get him back some day. Soon, I hope."

He sat down beside her and handed her a steaming bowl of cooked oats and a cup of watered-down mead.

"Thank you." She drank deeply then dug into the oats. "What makes you so sure you'll find him?" she asked, then cursed her wayward tongue. She should never have questioned him about something like that.

"I talked to the survivors from the spring gathering. Nobody remembers seeing Ewan with Cristel before people became sick. And I checked the charred remains the day after they were burned—none of them were bairns."

"So you think she left him somewhere else? Or someone took him?"

"Maybe. But he has my eyes and white-blond hair. He canna stay hidden for long. I've sent men to every part of the country looking for him."

Maggie stared up at Gavin's eyes. Aye, they were remarkable—the most astounding blue-green color she'd ever seen. He fluttered his lashes at her, and she laughed.

"'Tis good to hear you laugh, Maggie. It took me a long time to do so after Ewan disappeared. It sounds like things have been tough for you and your brother the last few years."

"Aye. Ross has been lost to us for a while."

"But why run? Shouldnae you have stayed to help the clan if your brother canna? And what about John? Did you write to him? Tell him the problem?"

"Aye... He may not have received my letters. I'll ask him when I see him."

"There's no need for you to go yourself. We'll send men to find him and give him the news. If Callum is to be your husband—"

"He's not. And I doona need his help to find my brother."

"Maybe not, but in times of need, it's good to rely on one another. 'Tis something Gregor MacLeod taught us."

"How can you say that after the way Callum left me? After both my brothers left? The only one I can rely on is myself."

Gavin gave her an assessing look, and she found herself wanting to squirm—so she frowned instead.

"Life is hard enough without friends and family, Maggie. Callum made a mistake, but he still wants to marry you. He would have done so sooner, but he faced his own difficulties after his father died. He had good reasons for leaving you with your own clan."

"Like what?"

"I canna say anymore. 'Tis his story to tell. But he knows he shouldnae have left you for so long. Let him set things right."

She put her oats aside, her stomach twisting at the idea of allowing Callum back into her life. There would be no escaping the hurt he could cause. But it did the same at the idea of riding away from him. "I canna trust him, Gavin. How can I marry someone I doubt?"

"You doona have to marry him right away. Come with us. If not to his clan, then come stay with me and mine. Let Callum visit you. Rebuild your bond. You'll like my sister Isobel. She doesn't let anyone tell her what to do either."

He smiled then pointed across the glade. When she followed his gaze, her eyes landed on Callum, and that twist in her stomach became an ache in her heart. He led a strong-looking mare toward her, with full packs strapped on either side of its flanks.

"Just look at him… Is there a more handsome man in all the Highlands? Other than me, of course. He's all broody and protective. And laird of a prosperous clan."

She couldn't help laughing, even though her words were serious. "I doona need protecting."

"Well, he'll do it anyway, because he's a great laird and a good man."

She couldn't help staring as Callum drew closer. He was perfectly formed with hard, defined muscles, a big cat's deadly grace, and the face of an avenging angel dispensing justice to the wicked.

Could she trust him not to leave again?

She heard Gavin pick up her dishes then rise to his feet. "Let him in, Maggie. He is the best of us. I promise you willna regret it."

She didn't say goodbye or even watch Gavin leave. She was too intent on staring at Callum. And he at her. He looked grave but determined, as if he faced a heavy task. Stopping at the other side of the fire near Aristotle, he tied the mare's reins to his stallion's, then circled the fire and crouched in front of her.

"The horse is yours, Maggie, and the supplies. I willna stop you if you decide to leave, but I will send a guard with you—five men. They will see you safely to your brother."

Instead of feeling grateful, disappointment crashed through her. What was wrong with her? She pinned a smile on her face, hoping he read it as a sign of thanks. She opened her mouth to tell him she'd leave immediately, but he waylaid her with a raised hand.

"Nay, I have more to say. Let me finish, please."

She closed her mouth and nodded. Her heart beat faster. That flutter returned in her chest. When he grasped her hand and held it in his, palm to palm, her throat tightened.

"Maggie, when I left you before, I meant to return in the spring. 'Twas my true intent to marry you, I swear it. I could hardly wait to make you my wife. But…things changed after my father died that winter. I kept thinking I would fix it by the next spring or next summer, until suddenly, three years had passed and I'd barely written, let alone come to see you."

"Why didn't you come?" She had to squeeze the words past the lump in her throat.

"I knew I wouldnae be able to leave if I did."

She frowned, her anger boiling up all over again. "And why would you want to? I was of age."

"'Twas not the right time."

"And now is? When I've decided to leave? When I no longer trust you?"

"'Tis not ideal, I know—"

"Aye, you have that right."

He clenched his jaw, and his chest rose as he breathed deeply. "We both have secrets. You don't want to talk about yours, and I canna talk about mine. Not yet. I'm sorry, lass. But…if you can, I'd ask you to put that behind you. I told you I'd help you get to Edinburgh, to wherever John is, but there's another option. I doona want you to leave. Father Lundie is riding with me. He'll marry us, Maggie. Now."

She gasped. Married? Now? "But…but…"

He lifted her hand and squeezed tight. "Stop thinking of the past and everything that stands in our way. Just think of the present. With me. You're frightened of something, and this will give you protection. Not just mine, but my foster brothers' and Gregor MacLeod's too. We'll help you with Ross and whatever else it is you're running from."

"So you'll marry me to protect me? That's all?"

"Nay. I'll marry you because I want you. As my wife, as my lover, as the mother of my children. I will create a safe and happy home for you. You doona need to leave the Highlands, and I promise ne'er to leave you again."

She stared at him, barely able to catch her breath. Then he wrapped a strong hand around the nape of her neck under her hair and pulled her toward him. "Please," he said before pressing his lips to hers.

They'd kissed before, and she'd never forgotten the feel of him against her mouth. But the reality of him was so much better than her memories.

His lips were soft, warm. He didn't push or thrust his tongue inside; instead, he gently caressed it against the seam of her mouth. She shivered, a gasp echoing through her and parting her lips. He waited a moment, as if to make sure she wouldn't shove him away, then stroked through the opening just far enough to touch her tongue, to play lazily against it.

She felt scorched from the inside at the contact. Heat built heavily between her legs and in her breasts. She wanted his hands on her, squeezing, like he'd done before.

She'd only just leaned into him, needing contact down the length of her, when a shrill whistle sounded in the distance—or it seemed far away to her passion-drugged body.

"Callum!" Gavin yelled just as Callum set her away from him and stood up.

She blinked and looked around to see the men, including Gavin, running for their horses, weapons drawn. Then Callum grabbed her hand, tugged her up and over to the other side of the fire where their horses stood together. Aristotle had his ears forward and eyes on Gavin. The mare stamped and whinnied nervously at all the sudden noise and activity.

"Someone's coming?" she asked, her breath coming in short bursts.

"Aye," Callum said as he practically tossed her on the mare before mounting his horse. "A lot of some-ones. Do you have your daggers?"

"I always have my daggers."

"Of course you do. Smart lass."

"Callum, if they're MacDonnells, doona trust them. They've come for me, and if I have to go—"

"You're not going with them."

She didn't answer, wishing it were that simple. He tugged her mount closer and looked directly into her eyes.

"You are not going with them, Maggie. If you do, we all go. Gavin and I are lairds of strong clans, allied to even stronger clans. If Ross thinks—"

"'Tis not Ross coming for me. It's Irvin," she blurted out.

He frowned. "Your mother's cousin?"

"Aye, and Eleanor's brother."

"I remember. I did not like the way he watched you at Ross's wedding. He's sly."

"Like a fox."

He squeezed her hand, a muscle jumping in his cheek. "And I left you there with him all this time. I'm so sorry."

She squeezed back. Fear for him tightened her throat. "I doona want you hurt. If anyone's going to put a dagger in your heart, it'll be me."

He puffed out a laugh. "I'd welcome it."

"Nay, you wouldnae. If I were mad enough to stab you, I'd make it hurt."

Gavin charged up on his stallion. "They're coming. Fifty or more men on horses. What did you do, lass?" he asked her. "Steal your clan's jewels?"

Callum lifted his hand and cupped her cheek. "She *is* the clan jewel."

Four

THEY RODE TO THE TREE LINE, ABOUT HALF THE MEN out front, half hidden so the enemy wouldn't have a clear count of their number. The MacDonnells could still surround them, but it would be a more difficult fight in the forest. Callum had sent Gill up a tree for additional coverage, if it came to that.

Maggie didn't intend to let it come to that. Surely Irvin wouldn't be so addled as to start a war with Callum and his allies? Attacking them meant attacking Darach, Lachlan, Kerr, and Gregor. Six clans against one.

She expected treachery and cunning plots from Irvin—not outright war.

"Callum," she said.

"Aye, lass."

"If anything should happen—"

"Nothing's going to happen. Not now, anyway."

"Aye, but if it does, you need to know that Irvin has a spy in your clan. Someone he called 'a friend.'"

Callum turned to her. "He told you this?"

"Nay. I've been spying on him for the last two months." She reached inside her arisaid—what was left of it anyway, Callum's plaid belted over the top—and pulled out a sheaf of crumpled parchments. She handed it to him. "'Twas only last week I learned he'd infiltrated your clan. I wrote down everything I heard, but 'tis complex, and I canna sort it all out. I want you to keep it."

He scanned the pages, disbelief etched on his face. "Does Ross know about this?"

"I've told him, aye, but he's too far gone to do anything about it."

Finally, he lowered the parchments and raised his eyes to hers. "Maggie, why didn't you come to me sooner?"

Her throat tightened, and she swallowed to loosen it. "You broke your promise, Callum."

He opened his mouth as if to speak, then closed it. When he finally spoke, she knew he was choosing his words carefully.

"Aye, lass, I did. And I'm sorry. But you need my help now, and in this, I need you to trust me. I will keep you safe, and the rest of us too."

She pressed her lips together, knowing he spoke the truth but not liking it. "I'll trust you for today. And if you get us out of this, Callum…all will be forgiven between you and me. But I still willna marry you."

He stared at her, then tucked the papers into his plaid and nodded. Once.

The pounding of horses' hooves reached her ears, and moments later, a large number of MacDonnells rode into the glen—at least fifty strong, exactly as Gavin had said. Riding in front was Ross's second-in-command, Alpin. He was a good leader and strong warrior, but he belonged to Irvin. She'd heard Irvin and Blàr talking about it. Laughing. Alpin's daughter was sick and was dependent on medicine that only Irvin had access to. If Alpin didn't do as Irvin asked, Irvin would withhold the life-giving herbs.

She felt terrible for Alpin, but there was no way she could ever trust him. He had too much at stake.

She searched for Blàr but didn't see him, and again wondered if he'd delivered the letter to Callum. From the way Callum was behaving, she didn't think so. It had been a shock to see him, and a jolt to her senses—especially during that kiss. Her lips still tingled and her body still hummed, even though her heart pounded at their present danger.

The advancing MacDonnells stopped on Alpin's command, and he rode forward alone, eyes widening when he saw Callum and Gavin on either side of her. He scanned the trees, looking for more men and any archers, no doubt.

Reining in his horse about twenty paces away, he returned his gaze to her. "You gave us all a scare, lass. We've been searching for you."

"I'm sure you have, Alpin, but as you can see, I'm in safe hands."

He nodded to Callum and Gavin. "Laird MacLean, Laird MacKinnon."

Callum reached out and stroked a hand down Maggie's hair, letting his palm rest on the small of her back. "Good day to you, Alpin. I appreciate you searching for my betrothed, but as you can see, she's safe with us."

Alpin shifted his eyes to Maggie. She could almost see his mind sorting through all his options. This was not a complication he'd prepared for.

"Your brother has been indisposed, lass," he said. "He hasn't risen from his bed for several days. 'Tis your cousin Irvin who sent us to look for you. He's concerned for your welfare."

"You can report that you've found her," Callum said. "And tell him Gregor MacLeod has asked after Ross. We've been told he's inconsolable since losing Eleanor and the bairn. Gregor understands his grief, having gone through it himself, and has taken a personal interest in Ross's well-being…and that of your clan, of course. I understand he may come for a visit soon."

Gavin smiled—more a baring of teeth, really. "Aye, all the lads are planning a visit—Lairds MacKenzie, MacKay, and MacAlister. We were recently together at Clan MacPherson. Perhaps you heard that Lachlan MacKay married the MacPherson healer?"

"I did," Alpin said. "Please offer our congratulations."

"'Twas a lovely wedding," Gavin continued. "Of course, we weren't there only for his nuptials. Lachlan had to kill the MacPherson laird as well."

Silence lay thick in the air. Finally, Alpin cleared his throat. "I heard he was a blackheart."

"Aye," Callum said. "He used deceit and treachery to kill the true laird and take over the clan. Lachlan dispensed justice that day. 'Tis what all of us would have done."

Maggie knew what they were doing—reminding Alpin of their allies, of their dedication to seeing justice done, and of their ruthlessness when needed. She almost felt sorry for the man.

His gaze shifted to her. "My lady, Irvin has requested that I return you to the castle. He wants to make certain you're well—with his own eyes." He raised his hands in almost a pleading gesture. "He has charged me with this task, and I canna fail him…you understand."

Aye, she understood. If Alpin didn't bring her back, Irvin would let Alpin's daughter die. He was a desperate man backed into a corner. He would attack, and while the battle would be hard won, the sheer number of his men would eventually overrun Callum's and Gavin's forces. Everyone would have to die, including Father Lundie, to keep the slaughter a secret.

Except her, of course. Irvin had other plans for her.

Callum's hand tightened on her spine. She looked at him, and he must have seen in her eyes that she intended to go with them. "Nay," he said softly.

"They will attack. He has no choice."

"There's always a choice."

"If he doesn't do as Irvin asks, his child will die. I doona wish that on anyone. He isna a bad man. Just… trapped."

"I willna allow you to go back alone."

"But, Callum—"

"Nay. Whether you accept it or not, lass, we are betrothed. Where you go, I go. I willna leave you to suffer alone again." He looked across her to Gavin. "Are we agreed?"

"Agreed," Gavin said. He shifted his hand behind his thigh, and his fingers touched his palm in an odd way. A signal to his men behind them?

She wondered what he'd said, wanted to turn around and see if there was any activity; instead, she held herself still and listened for movement…but all she heard was the babbling of the brook and horses shuffling.

"Father Lundie," Callum called out.

She did turn her head this time, and when the priest crawled out from the supply wagon where he'd been hiding, Alpin gasped in dismay. Aye, so he knew of Irvin's plans to marry her.

The priest straightened his brown robe and stepped forward. "Laird?"

"Will you accompany us to Clan MacDonnell?"

Maggie gritted her teeth at his words even as relief flooded through her, knowing she wouldn't be returning to the castle alone. She just prayed it didn't result in their deaths.

Alpin frowned and opened his mouth to protest, but she waylaid him. "Aye, Father, it would please me greatly if you would come. My brother could use some spiritual counsel to help ease his mind and soul. He is heartsick, and our priest died several years ago. He hasn't been replaced."

Father Lundie nodded gravely. "I will accompany you, lass. Perhaps through God's grace, I can bring your brother some peace."

"And Maggie has expressed the desire to be wed in front of her brother as well." Callum raised her hand to his mouth and kissed it, a smile on his lips. But when his eyes met hers, they glinted with determination. "Haven't you, love?"

She wanted to scowl at him but had enough control to keep up the ruse. Were those her only options? Married to Irvin or married to Callum? It was not a difficult choice, but it was one she didn't wish to make.

"I doona think that's a good idea, lass," Alpin said.

She gazed at Alpin, her hands on her daggers. "Well

now, 'tis not for you to say, is it, Alpin? Or my cousin. The marriage contract between Laird MacLean and myself has been in place for eleven years. We've waited long enough. We will go with you, all of us, including Father Lundie, or we doona go at all. Those are my terms."

He looked grim, and he ran an agitated hand over the nape of his neck. Finally, he nodded.

Callum whistled to his men. They moved as one into the glen on their horses. A warrior stopped to lift Father Lundie onto the back of his mount. It looked like they would leave the supply wagon behind.

Maggie counted their men—they were three short. Where had the others been sent? Perhaps to Gregor and the other foster brothers with messages to hurry.

"Stay next to me the entire way," Callum said softly to her.

Gavin rode on Maggie's other side, and the remaining MacLeans and MacKinnons positioned themselves in front and behind them, Drustan taking point. It was little protection, but it at least afforded them some privacy. Maggie could talk to the two lairds without being overheard.

They should reach MacDonnell castle by late afternoon, just in time for Ross to be thirsting for his cups. He wouldn't usually rise until noon and would start the day with watered-down wine that quickly progressed to mead, then whisky. It was a pitiful existence, especially as he used to be such a strong, virile man—quick to laugh and as big as a bear.

She hated for Gavin and Callum to see him like this. There had been a time when he'd bested them both at games like the hammer throw and tossing the caber. It had taken Callum and two of his foster brothers together to beat Ross on the tug-of-war.

The heartache she tried so hard to contain beat at her, and she lowered her head.

Callum sidled up to her and reached for her hand. She hesitated, then reached for his too, and he twined their fingers together. "All will be well, lass," he said. "I promise we'll get you out of there safely. Irvin willna act immediately, and before he does, Gregor and my foster brothers will be knocking at his portcullis. It'll be four days at the most before one of them arrives. Surely Ross can hold it together for that long—for your sake and the sake of his clan."

"Ross canna hold it together for five minutes. Eleanor was his reason for living. He's killing himself over her and their lost bairn."

Gavin grunted and ran his hand over his bristly hair. "If we canna rely on Ross, then we have to rely on ourselves. You'll need to best Irvin at his games, Callum."

"Be as sly as him?"

"Aye. You're far more capable of figuring out puzzles and finding answers than the rest of us."

Callum sighed, and she heard the frustration behind it. "Most of the time."

"That's a puzzle we'll sort out too," Gavin said.

She wondered what they were talking about and was about to ask, but the concentration on Callum's face deepened, and she held her questions for another time. He still clasped her hand, and his fingers tapped her knuckles as his mind worked on the problem. "Irvin wants to be laird, and he wants to marry you.

You would refuse, obviously, so he would have to hold something over your head. Ross?"

Her stomach clenched as Irvin's plan for her came to mind. "Nay. He thinks Ross will have drunk himself to death within the year. And he's right."

"Who then? Certainly not me, or he wouldnae have sent me that letter."

She gasped and turned to him. "You received his letter? And my note too?"

"Aye."

"And you came anyway? I thought my note would dissuade you."

"I knew you'd sent the second missive…and meant it. 'Twas troubling. But Irvin's note troubled me more for a different reason. If naught else, I had to make sure you were safe. Obviously, you weren't."

"I would have been if those blasted wolves hadn't come after me."

Both men scoffed at her claim.

"And if you'd come up against some brigands?" Gavin asked.

"Or worse?" Callum added.

"You seem to forget I'm not defenseless. I escaped a wolf pack. I could take out some unsuspecting men."

They fell silent, and Maggie thought the discussion was over, until Callum said, "You're not a murderer, Maggie, or you would have taken Irvin's life to spare your own. You're capable of killing, but only as a last resort. And by then, it might be too late."

They spent much of the ride to her home discussing Irvin's plans, the layout of the castle—including the crawl space under the laird's solar and any other secret passages of which she was aware—the guards' rotations and any weaknesses in the castle's defenses. They also discussed possible escape routes once they were out of the castle.

She added what she could, but mostly, she just listened to Callum and Gavin as they talked through different options and scenarios, more in awe of Callum's quick mind than ever.

When her home came into view, the castle built within the last hundred years and looking so bonny with the afternoon sun warming the stone, she felt both a lift in her spirits and a drop in her stomach. Her jaw set in anger that Irvin had made her feel that way. He'd taken away the home she loved.

When they passed under the portcullis, it closed and locked behind them like the clanging of a cell door. She prayed they wouldn't all end up in the dungeon.

They crossed the bailey, and more than half their guard peeled off toward the barracks. She looked up and saw the door at the top of the stairs that led to the great hall, open.

Irvin ran out, wearing a crumpled plaid, his hair unwashed and sticking up in places, and a few days growth on his chin. Maggie let out a surprised gasp. He'd always been as neat and precise as his tiny handwriting.

He barreled halfway down the steps, his loathing-filled eyes on her, looking almost crazed—before he caught sight of Callum and Gavin. Irvin came to an abrupt halt.

It was almost fascinating to watch as his eyes widened, his mouth twisted—before he gained control and pulled himself together. Drawing in all his pincers and poison like a bug, so he no longer looked dangerous.

"Therein lies cunning and madness," Callum said to her, staring at Irvin, who had folded his hands benignly at his waist and appeared perfectly contained. "We doona have four days. We'll be lucky to get four hours."

"Aye," Maggie said, sliding off her horse. "Let's make the most of it."

She handed the reins to a groom and marched, chin high, shoulders back, up the stairs toward Irvin, knowing Callum, Gavin, and the rest of their men would follow.

Irvin stood unmoving in the middle of the step, obviously expecting her to stop, but Maggie glared at him and kept going, until he finally jumped against the railing, sputtering in protest.

She waved him off and said loudly, "We're going to see my brother, Laird MacDonnell."

⟡

Callum's eyes darted around the great hall, knowing surprise was on their side but it wouldn't last. They moved swiftly in a tight group toward the stairs leading to the upper chambers and the laird's solar. Callum and Gavin stayed close to Maggie without taking the lead. Drustan brought up the rear.

Irvin would kill every single one of them, despite their alliances. And from the look of hatred on his face as he'd stared at Maggie in the bailey, he would kill her too. He'd have done it already, Callum was sure, if he didn't need to marry her to confirm his claim on the lairdship.

He still hadn't figured out what Irvin would hold over her head to make that happen—unless Maggie wasn't telling him everything. But he was fair certain that if she did have a lover or a friend she couldn't live without, she would have taken them with her when she ran away the first time.

He considered that perhaps Irvin had John locked away somewhere. If that were the case, though, she wouldn't have been running all the way across the Highlands to find him. Not alone, subject to abuse at the hands of robbers, the elements, and—as she'd already encountered—wild animals.

She'd been clear that she wouldn't marry him, despite the deception he'd begun with Alpin. If he couldn't provide a secure, happy place for her to live, she would run at the first opportunity.

His chest tightened at the thought, and he pushed it to the back of his mind.

Now was not the time to wallow.

In order to outsmart Irvin, he had to throw out his other plans and start afresh, come up with a new strategy that didn't rely on Gregor and the rest of the lads. The goal was to keep everyone safe, but if the angels smiled on him, maybe he could reclaim Maggie's castle at the same time.

He still hadn't examined the documents she'd given him. He'd had her recount what she could remember, but he didn't want Irvin tipped off that he had a document of interest on him. He'd hidden it inside a secret pocket in his plaid, but if they searched him for it, they would find it.

He needed to get that information to Gregor.

Of course, he'd thought about who the "friend inside" his clan might be, and whether he or she had had anything to do with his father's murder. It was the first clue he'd had in a long time. When all this was over, he would search through Irvin's parchments and talk to his accomplices—starting with Blàr. According to Maggie, he was Irvin's most trusted confidante.

"Do we have a new plan yet?" Gavin asked softly as they entered a passageway that led to the spiral staircase. "Irvin will kill us at the first opportunity."

"Aye." Callum tapped his fingers against his thumb as his mind whirled. "We need to put him at ease, give him some breathing room. And also let him think we'll be walking into his trap, while we lay one of our own…and then maybe, just maybe, we can recapture the castle for Maggie."

Gavin let out a huff that Callum took for a silent, disbelieving laugh. "That doesn't sound difficult at all," he said. "Any idea how to accomplish it?"

"I'm working on it." They reached the stairs just after Maggie, who'd lifted her skirts to sprint ahead. Callum hurried after her. "First, we need to talk to Ross, but I'm sure he's as badly gone as Maggie says. And we'll need to lock Irvin out for that, which will send him into a rage."

"He'll try to kill us as soon as we come out."

"Not if we give him good news first. He'll be worried about Maggie marrying me, but we'll say Ross has delayed the ceremony. That'll give Irvin hope and make him feel smarter than us—he'll think we haven't discovered his deception."

They reached the upper passageway and were

almost at the solar door when Gavin whispered, "Whate'er you do, doona tell Maggie the plan. Her temper's too hot, and she's too easy to read. She'll give us away."

Callum's heart sank. He suspected Gavin was right, but Maggie would be furious if she knew they'd withheld information from her. He rubbed his hand across his jaw. He had to weigh their lives against her feeling betrayed—again.

Unfortunately, it was no contest. All of their lives, including Maggie's, depended on it.

"Aye. But I'm going to tell her it was your idea."

"I doona mind taking the blame," Gavin said, clapping him on the shoulder. "What are brothers for?"

When Maggie knocked and opened the solar door, Irvin pushed his way up from the back of the crowd. The men had formed a barrier in the hallway against the approaching MacDonnells, led by Alpin, and Drustan caught Callum's eye before letting Irvin through.

Irvin reached them, his demeanor frantic. "The laird is indisposed. You canna speak to him."

Callum stayed quiet. He wanted Maggie to continue leading on this, let Irvin's men—who used to be Ross's men—see her in charge.

Maggie frowned at Irvin. "I can speak to my brother and laird any time I want, Cousin. And I intend to speak to him with my betrothed and his men—alone."

"He isna well," Irvin yelled, his face turning red with anger.

"Aye, perhaps seeing Callum and Gavin will rouse his spirits. 'Tis with great mirth I remember him pulling both lairds over in a tug-of-war during the summer festival. None could best him."

Gavin nodded. "Not even Kerr, and he's as big as a bloody ox."

Maggie smiled proudly. "Ross also won the caber toss three years in a row."

Callum saw some of the MacDonnell soldiers grin.

"Well, he's not that man anymore," Irvin said. "Your brother needs quiet, Maggie MacDonnell, and I forbid you from disturbing him."

Maggie grasped one of her daggers. Callum stepped forward to stop her using it, but she didn't pull out her blade. Instead, she straightened her spine and looked down her nose at her slightly shorter cousin. "'Tis not for you to say, Irvin Sinclair. We stand within MacDonnell castle, surrounded by MacDonnell land, which was claimed hundreds of years ago by the MacDonnell clan—not the Sinclairs."

Some of the men grunted in agreement, but Callum also heard at least one blade being drawn. They needed to get inside the solar before fighting broke out.

He stepped forward and grasped Irvin by the arms and moved him to the side. "Excuse us, but we doona want to keep Laird MacDonnell waiting."

They slipped inside quickly, all eleven of them. Drustan, who'd entered last, shut the solid wood door and slid the bar across to keep them out.

Shouts erupted in the hallway before slowly fading away.

Drustan crouched down and stared through the key-hole. "They're leaving, but not for long, I'd wager." He rose, his eyes sliding past Callum, before he froze.

Callum turned to see what Drustan had seen. Maggie stood sideways to him behind the desk, her hair tucked under her plaid, her hand on her brother's shoulder. Ross's face was bloated and his skin sallow, his eyes bleary from drink. The once muscular body that had bested everyone in the tug-of-war had wasted away, other than a round, protruding belly. He slumped in his chair, an open jug of whisky in front of him, and stared in confusion at the men who'd entered his solar.

Aye, it was a disturbing sight, and Callum felt a profound sadness. He may not be able to save Ross, but he could damn well save Maggie.

He dragged two chairs over to the desk. Ross watched him with a bewildered expression on his face before reaching a shaking hand toward the whisky. Callum waylaid him, gently pulling his arm away before sitting down. Maggie perched in a chair on the other side.

"Ross. Do you recognize me?" he asked.

Ross lifted bleak, tortured eyes to his. "Aye. Have you married my sister, then? 'Tis good you've come for her. She'll need taking care of. I'm done with this life. I will go see Eleanor and our bairn soon. I hear her calling to me sometimes."

Maggie pressed her fist to her mouth.

"I'll take care of her, Ross. You doona have to worry about that. And I'll find John for you. Bring him home."

"John loved Eleanor too. He willna want to return."

"I'll find him anyway."

Again, Ross reached for his drink, and Callum stopped him. "Ross, we have to talk about Irvin. Eleanor's brother."

Ross lifted a hand and rubbed his eyes. "Aye, Maggie told me. He's…done something."

"He's stealing the MacDonnell land and castle. He plans to kill John and marry Maggie—except Maggie willna have him. So he plans to force her. Do you understand what that means, Ross?"

A spark flamed in Ross's eyes, and he pushed himself upright. He withdrew his hand from the whisky. His gaze quickly returned to the jug, however, and Callum feared Ross's resurgence was too late.

"He canna have Maggie. Or my home." He licked his lips, and his hand trembled with the effort to not reach for his drink. "Find John. He ne'er liked Irvin. He'll force him out."

"You force him out," Maggie said through gritted teeth. "Hold on and fight him, Ross. Fight for me, and for John. Fight for Mother and Da's home, for our clan."

But his shoulders slumped, and the light died from his eyes. "I canna. I'm done, Maggie. I'm sorry. I doona have your strength."

"You're as strong as a bloody bear!"

"Not that kind of strength." He lifted his hand and tapped Maggie's chest. "The strength inside. It was always Eleanor for me. When I lost her, I lost everything. I'm sorry, love. Let me go. I doona want to stay."

"Irvin's right outside—with *your* men—ready to cut down everyone and take me."

Ross shifted his gaze to Callum's. "You canna let that happen."

"I won't. I'll be dead before he hurts her, I promise you that," Callum said.

Ross nodded and reached for his jug, then poured

some whisky into an empty cup. Maggie looked stricken, and Callum wanted to go to her, hold her, but he knew she wouldn't welcome his comfort. She'd see it as pity and mistakenly believe he thought her weak.

She couldn't be more wrong.

Gavin stepped forward and Ross looked at him, confused.

Maggie put an arm around her brother's shoulders and leaned in. "It's Gavin MacKinnon, Ross. He's here to help us. He lost his wife and bairn too—during the pestilence that hit the summer festival two years ago."

Gavin's eyes were filled with understanding and pity. He'd spent many nights lost in drink when Ewan had first disappeared.

"Good day to you, Ross," he said. "'Tis a long time since we wrestled together as lads. Although I think I did all the wrestling and you just held me down."

Ross nodded, and a glimmer of light filled his eyes. "That I did. I barely recognized you, Gavin. You no longer look like a lass."

Gavin rubbed his spiky hair and smiled. "Even without my long locks, I'm still as lovely as a girl, aye?"

"I'm sure some men think so," Ross said, and Gavin laughed.

Reaching across the desk, Gavin placed a commiserating hand on Ross's head. Ross closed his eyes and leaned into his touch. Callum could almost see the pain radiating from both men, and his heart hurt for them.

"I am sorry to see you so distraught, old friend. I know that state well. But right now, we need to attend to the living." Gavin's voice broke when he said "living," and he cleared his throat before he continued. "Can you still write, Ross?"

Ross looked down at the pile of parchments in front of him and picked up a quill. His hand shook. "Aye, if I press hard enough."

Callum placed a piece of parchment in front of him and helped Ross dip his quill in the ink. "Will you help Maggie by writing a letter? I think you should state that upon your death, the lairdship passes to John. And that if John dies or canna be found within two years, it passes to a MacDonnell of age who has the majority vote from your clan. That'll eliminate Irvin altogether and protect Maggie." He looked at Maggie. "Is that agreeable to you? Or do you want your sons to be next in line?"

"Nay. I want naught to do with the lairdship. But maybe give me some land in case John is killed." She stroked her knuckles across Ross's cheek. "How about Nan's old farm? 'Twas our favorite place when we were small."

"Aye, lass. 'Tis yours. Da meant for you to have it anyway. In this, I willna fail you."

Maggie pressed her forehead to Ross's, then she whispered something in his ear before wrapping her arms around his neck. When she let go, she walked briskly to the window and looked out. Callum suspected her face would be wet with tears.

Ross concentrated on writing the decree that would in effect become his last will and testament. Callum saw that he included all the personal wealth of their family in his bequest to John and Maggie. And if John was already dead or died without issue, his wealth passed on to Maggie in turn.

When Ross finished, Callum, Gavin, Maggie, and Father Lundie all witnessed his signature.

"One more," Callum said as Ross reached for his drink. "Irvin terminated the marriage contract between myself and Maggie—and he did it in your name. To be safe, I'd like you to reinstate the contract."

He could see Ross was fading and they had little time—especially after he took a big swig of whisky. The wretch couldn't hold it together much longer, but he managed to write another letter, stating he wanted Callum to marry Maggie, as their fathers had wished for them so many years ago.

Father Lundie and Gavin witnessed the signature this time, and then the priest took Maggie's chair and sat down beside Ross to give as much solace and guidance to the grief-stricken man as he could.

"We'll have to leave without Maggie," Gavin whispered in Callum's ear, "and by the grim look on your face, you already know that."

Callum squeezed the bridge of his nose and nodded. "I fear she'll ne'er forgive me." But he couldn't see any other way.

Maggie straightened from the window and called out to him over her shoulder, "Callum, they're coming!"

He and Gavin rose and strode to her side to look out. MacDonnell warriors had gathered in the bailey below. Alpin walked to the front of the ranks and signaled them into the keep.

Time had run out.

Five

MAGGIE CROSSED TO THE DOOR AND LISTENED. Drustan stiffened beside her, but he didn't move over to give her room as she would have expected.

The sound of heavy feet on the stone stairs reached her through the wood, and a strange kind of euphoria filled her. It was time.

She was going to fight and triumph, or it would all end here.

A hand on her shoulder startled her, and she spun around to find herself nose to chest with Callum. He looked pinched and worried, with lines slashed deeply in his forehead and his jaw clenched.

"We canna fight them all, Maggie. There's too many. We'll die, and everything we've done so far will have been for naught. We have to give Irvin what he wants. At least for now."

"What he wants is all of you dead and me wed to him in unholy matrimony with a bairn in my belly so he can steal the lairdship!"

"I know that. But our options are limited." A muscle twitched in his jaw before he continued.

"Gregor and my foster brothers will be here within a week, and men have already been sent to find John. Once we have the manpower, we will fight to take back the castle and to save you and Ross."

"Ross doesn't want saving."

"Aye, but at least he can die with you and John by his side—and see Irvin hanged for his treachery. We will set things right for your family."

He was trying to tell her something without saying the words, and a shiver ran up her spine.

Then she understood. He was abandoning her too. "You're leaving," she said.

Callum's mouth tightened, and he nodded curtly.

Bleakness engulfed her, and she crossed her arms over her chest. "Irvin will kill all of you as soon as he can make it look like an accident."

"Aye, but he has to catch us first."

She crushed the hurt that rose within her chest. It didn't matter what Callum or Gavin did. It only mattered what she did. How she was going to get out.

"Go to your bedchamber, Maggie, and bar the door. Or hide in the tunnel."

"Doona worry about me, Callum MacLean. I know what to do."

He opened his mouth to say something, then closed it and shoved his hand through his hair. "It willna be for long. Doona come out until I or one of my men returns for you."

A loud banging sounded on the other side of the solar doors, then Alpin said, "Laird MacLean, Laird MacKinnon. Open the door. 'Tis imperative we speak to Laird MacDonnell."

Callum looked at her brother. "Are you ready, Ross?"

To her amazement, her brother put his hands on the desk and pushed himself up, with only some help from Father Lundie. He was still a big man and dwarfed the priest. After a slight wobble, Ross walked slowly but steadily to the door. Callum clapped him on the shoulder, then nodded for Drustan to pull back the bar.

The door opened, and a row of armed MacDonnells faced them. Alpin stood in the second row, and he gasped when he saw Ross.

"Lower your weapons," Alpin said to his men.

Ross looked out over the sea of warriors that filled the hall. His eyes landed on Irvin, who stood at the very rear, open-mouthed in alarm. "Have we been invaded by an enemy that you feel the need to bring warriors and weapons into my keep, Cousin?"

Irvin shifted on his feet, and a tic jumped in his cheek. "We needed to know you were safe, Laird."

"From my sister and her betrothed? My boyhood friends and a priest? Have you lost your mind?"

Even from the distance of the passageway, Maggie could see Irvin grimace. He was indeed coming apart, and one wrong glance or word would send him over the edge. Why had nobody killed him before now?

Firming her lips, she stretched out her fingers to loosen the joints. A steadying breath, then she reached for her dagger. Callum's hand got there first.

"Nay," he said under his breath. "He isna stupid, Maggie. Look at the men he's chosen to kill us. They doona fit together as a unit. He has something on every one of them. And if he dies, they'll go down with him—even Alpin." He grasped her hand and raised it to his lips. "We have to talk our way out of this."

He looked out to the men and raised his voice. "Maggie and I have agreed to delay our nuptials. Laird MacDonnell wants a proper wedding for us with both John and himself by her side."

The men looked at one another, confused. Some looked to Alpin for guidance, others to Irvin.

"It grieves me to leave Maggie so quickly, but now that our wedding date is set for next spring, I have important matters to attend to. I've lost too much time already coming here."

Hadn't she always known she'd be alone in the end? Callum could ride off and meet up with Gregor MacLeod and the rest of their allies, return, and take the castle for John, but she was leaving tonight. She would not be Irvin's hostage for even one minute, let alone however long a siege might take.

And if the opportunity presented itself, she'd kill her cousin before she left.

Irvin moved slowly toward them, his keen gaze searching their faces. He kept returning to Maggie, as if trying to read the truth in her expression.

He must have seen something reassuring—her anger, perhaps?—for he turned to Callum with a sycophantic smile that belied the smugness in his eyes. "Allow us to escort you to the edge of MacDonnell territory, Laird MacLean. We can talk through the details of your marriage, so everything is as you wish it when you return in the spring."

"Nay, 'tis not necessary, Sinclair. I shall leave the details up to Maggie. Also, we'll be riding too hard to talk. We are intent on reaching my foster father and brothers before they begin to worry that we havenae arrived home. I wouldnae want them dispatching men unnecessarily."

"Aye, 'twould be most unfortunate," Irvin said.

Ross's knees suddenly buckled, and Gavin caught him around the waist. "See them off," Ross said to Irvin, his speech becoming labored. "And no more than that. I doona want any trouble with Gregor MacLeod."

Irvin ducked his head. "Aye, Laird."

Ross reached out for Maggie one last time. She hesitated, then stepped into his embrace and held him tight.

"I love you, Sister," he whispered. "I would do more for you if I could. Trust that Callum will see you safe."

"I love you too. Rest now, Brother. Dream of Eleanor and your wee one." She pulled away, and Ross shuffled to his desk with Gavin's aid.

Turning to Irvin, she said, "I'm going to my room. I doona wish to be disturbed." Callum caught her hand, and she glared at him, throwing daggers from her eyes since she couldn't do so from her fists. "Safe travels, Laird MacLean. As *always*, I'll be waiting for spring with bated breath."

Then she pulled her hand free, marched through the men to her room, and barred her bedroom door behind her.

❧

Callum, Gavin, and their men strode briskly to their horses. They all knew the plan and the different roles each man would have to play.

Irvin wasn't a warrior, but he was a strategic

thinker. He would know that if the MacLeans and MacKinnons made it back to their allies alive, they'd either return in force and take the castle, or they'd come back in the spring expecting to see Maggie and Callum married.

Neither option worked for Irvin, so there would be an ambush along the way—of that Callum had no doubt. They just had to avoid the ambush, circle around, and wait for Irvin to send the rest of his men after them—which he undoubtedly would when he realized they'd avoided his trap. Then they would sneak back in, take the castle, God willing, and throw Irvin in the dungeon.

"Are you sure you didn't come up with this plan to impress Maggie?" Gavin asked as they mounted their stallions and headed to the portcullis.

Callum's lips quirked, despite the trepidation that twisted his stomach at the thought of leaving her here, even if only for a few hours. "Maybe. Can you blame me for trying?"

"Aye, if it gets us killed."

Twisting on Aristotle's back, Callum smiled and waved goodbye to Irvin, who returned his wave. "I canna think of a safer place to wait for Gregor and the lads to arrive than inside the castle."

"Aye, but first we have to get inside—with just nine warriors and a priest who can barely ride."

"Six. Doona forget we need to plant some decoys."

Gavin cursed as the group fell into formation and hurried under the portcullis. The quicker they moved, the less time Irvin and Alpin had to plan their demise.

Father Lundie shared a horse with one of Callum's

men. The priest's lips moved fervently, eyes closed and arms squeezed tight around the warrior, as he prayed for their safety, no doubt. And probably for strength to get him through a hard ride.

They galloped across the open field to the tree line in the opposite direction from their original course. The key to avoiding an ambush was to keep Irvin and Alpin guessing as to their next move.

When they were finally under cover and out of range of the castle's archers, Callum released his breath and glanced back. Two groups of MacDonnells had emerged in the distance, one from the castle and one returning from the direction Callum and Gavin were supposed to have left by. Another group was probably farther down that trail.

"The chase is on," Gavin said, his eyes glinting excitedly.

"Aye. And the more men following us the better. I make it about fifty warriors so far." Callum also felt the rush of excitement and anticipation—and the heightened acuity that went along with it. If he wasn't so worried about riding away from Maggie, he would be grinning just as wildly as Gavin.

"As long as we can shake them," Drustan said.

They hit a stream, crossed to the other side, and up a muddy bank to a game trail that ran along the top of the creek. After a few minutes of riding, they slowed to a canter.

Callum pulled up beside three of his men, one of whom shared his horse with Father Lundie, and stopped. "Ride as long and as hard as you can. Alpin will keep after you until he realizes we've split. He canna afford to lose track of any of us. Go to ground if you have to."

"Aye, Laird," the men said together.

"Laird MacLean, are you sure you doona want me to come with you?" Father Lundie asked as he peered around the shoulder of the man he clung to. "I canna believe Irvin Sinclair would cause you harm in front of me."

"It wouldnae be in front of you, Father. You'd be on your back, dead. Maybe looking up at your soul knocking at the pearly gates, asking for entrance into heaven."

Father Lundie crossed himself and shuddered. "I pray it willna come to that. May the lord bless you in this fight, Lairds, and Michael the Archangel battle by your side."

"Thank you, Father," Gavin said. "Saint Michael would be a welcome addition."

"The path turns to the right ahead," Callum continued. "It follows the stream for another hundred paces or so, then enters the forest as the land rises."

He clasped each man's hand, one after the other. "Good fortune and Godspeed to you."

"Same to you," they replied.

Callum watched as they followed the path and turned with the stream. When they were out of sight, he urged Aristotle faster.

"Doona hesitate," he yelled over his shoulder to Gavin and the four remaining men—Drustan, Gill, Artair, and a young warrior named Finnian. Aristotle picked up speed, and when he reached the point where the bank turned, Callum squeezed his heels into the stallion's flank and yelled. "*Gearr leum!*"

The horse obeyed and leapt off the trail and into the stream. Callum held on tight, his plaid getting soaked as water sprayed up from Aristotle's hooves. He kept going against the current, thankful the creek wasn't higher than the horses' fetlocks and the stones were small and round. The running water would hide their tracks. Hopefully, the MacDonnells would follow the two men and Father Lundie west into the forest, while Callum and the others circled back to the castle.

It would all be for nothing if one of Irvin's men saw them. They needed to be around the bend and far enough upstream that their enemy could neither see nor hear them when they got close.

By Callum's calculations, they had about a fifteen-minute lead on the MacDonnells, which should be just enough time to get them safely hidden.

Behind him, he heard the other men land, one after the other, with various splashes. Frantic curses reached his ears, and he looked over his shoulder to see the last warrior—Gavin's man, Artair—barely holding onto his mount. The horse struggled to keep upright with the huge man hanging off his side.

Artair pulled himself upright, and the belabored stallion carried on. Gavin had said the man would be an asset, and Callum trusted his foster brother's judgment, but they needed speed right now. Brawn would come later.

After finally rounding the bend with no MacDonnells in sight, Drustan signaled Callum to slow down.

"We've been going full speed for almost two hours. Let the horses rest," he said.

"They can rest when we're there." The need to

keep going and return to Maggie drove Callum like a demon torturing a sinner in hell.

"I agree with Drustan." Gavin looked up at the sun, only just beginning to lower in the sky. "Why push them so hard when we canna move on the castle until dark anyway? Keep them rested, so if we need a burst of speed, they'll have it in them."

Callum rolled his head, trying to loosen his tense muscles. "Aye, you're right. I just…"

"You just want to be as close as possible. I under-stand," Gavin said. "If it was Ewan in that castle, I'd be hard pressed to wait."

They slowed to a walk, and both men and horses caught their breath.

Or Callum tried to, but his chest squeezed tight. "I canna imagine what she's thinking. How betrayed she must feel—again. She'll hate me for leaving this time, if she doesn't already."

"Maybe. But she'll be alive. You canna give her a greater gift. Even her castle will pale in comparison to that."

"If I'd just told her—"

"Nay. I watched Irvin's face. It was Maggie's fury—at you—that convinced him to let us go. I'll tell her that tonight when we see her. All is not lost, Brother."

Callum wasn't so sure. Once Maggie had made up her mind, it would take an act of God to change it.

He signaled the men, and they picked up the pace.

When the water deepened, Callum knew they were almost there and they would soon lose the conceal-ment of the trees.

After directing Aristotle out of the water, he

dismounted. The others followed. He signaled Gavin, and the two of them continued on foot for a better look.

Callum pushed a branch aside when they reached the edge of the forest. Ahead of them, on their side of the stream, a cliff rose upward.

On the other side of the stream stretched an open field that encircled the castle about a quarter mile away. A single large tree stood halfway between the creek and the castle.

His heart rate increased as he looked upon Maggie's home, the sun's dying rays turning the gray stone a brilliant reddish-gold. He peered up at her bedchamber window and prayed she was safely inside—behind barred doors.

"Let's go up before we lose the light," Gavin said.

"Aye, I wouldnae want you to lose your footing and tumble o'er the edge like you did before."

Gavin huffed. "I didn't trip, Kerr bloody well pushed me. 'Twas fortunate the water was deep enough to break my fall."

All five of the foster brothers had climbed this rock face several times as lads, alongside John and Ross. The creek was deep enough in early summer to safely jump from the cliffs, but someone invariably got hurt, and Maggie's father and Gregor had threatened dire consequences if they ever did it again.

So, of course, they'd done it again—at night after sneaking out of the castle through a back way. Callum intended to use that same route, the one Ross had shown them years ago, to sneak back in. According to Maggie, the breach in the MacDonnells' defenses was still there.

"Do you think Gregor knew?" he asked. Callum fit his foot in a crevice and crawled up the rock, staying behind scraggly bushes as much as he could.

"That we jumped?"

"Aye."

"Most likely. Not much got past that old buzzard." Gavin said it with affection, and Callum smiled. Hope grew in him now that he was here and Maggie's window was in sight. He knew they were far from safe, but the plan was a good one. And it might just win Maggie's appreciation, as Gavin had suggested, for its daring and audacity.

They were up high enough that they could see into the bailey over the top of the tree and across to the land beyond. Men on horses rode in groups to and from the castle through the portcullis, on the opposite side from them.

"The guard on the wall has been thinned," he observed.

"Aye, it looks like. 'Tis a good thing we doona plan on riding out of MacDonnell territory. They'll have every trail and pass blocked."

"I'm afraid Gregor and the lads will have to go to war to get through to us."

"Maybe. But the MacDonnells willna fight for long. Our combined forces will outnumber them at least four to one. And once they know the castle has been taken and Maggie is on our side, they'll surrender."

They pulled themselves up over the highest ledge and lay flat, looking out over the land. The gloaming was upon them, and it was a glorious view, the sky painted in brilliant shades of orange, pink, and purple.

Callum looked down at the stream. The cliff didn't seem quite as high as it had when they were lads. Still, he had no desire to jump.

They were at equal height to Maggie's window, and he tried to imagine what she was doing inside. Pacing, probably, or curled up on her bed, crying, feeling betrayed, scared, and abandoned.

Well, not for long. The sun had just set, and he would be able to go in soon and get her, rescue her from her cousin.

She would be grateful he'd saved her, wouldn't she?

He'd just decided to climb down and set the plan in motion when something white flew out of Maggie's window and unfurled down the side of the castle.

His heart skipped a beat before it raced to catch up, and he squinted in the failing light, trying to get a better look.

"Did you see that?" he asked Gavin, his voice sharp.

"See what?"

"Look at her window."

Gavin circled his hands in front of one eye to see better. "God's blood, I think that's a rope."

Callum clenched his teeth to stop himself from yelling at her over the distance, telling her to stay inside. A muscle twitched frantically in his jaw when her red head popped out the window.

"She's climbing down," Gavin said, his voice filled with astonishment.

Callum unclenched his jaw just long enough to let out a string of curses. Why was he surprised? Of course Maggie wouldn't wait.

"Didn't Lachlan say Amber climbed out her window too?" Gavin asked.

"Aye. But we were told about it after she was safe, and it didn't seem that bad—or to me it didn't." But he remembered how Lachlan's face had turned a dark shade of red and his eyes had stormed when he'd told Callum about it.

Callum dropped his head in his hands and groaned, his heart racing fiercely. "I canna watch."

Gavin nudged him with his shoulder. "I'll tell you when she's on the ground. If anybody can do it, Callum, it's her."

He didn't respond. He *couldn't* respond.

But on Gavin's sharply indrawn breath, he lifted his head. He could barely make out Maggie in the twilight at such a distance, other than the fiery beacon of her red hair.

She hung from the rope just below her window, and he willed her to keep going or to pull herself back up. Surely her arms would tire quickly. But Maggie would not be Maggie if she did anything Callum wanted.

Instead, she began to swing.

Six

MAGGIE HUNG FROM THE ROPE ON THE OUTSIDE OF THE castle, one floor down from her bedchamber window and one room over. Although "hung" wasn't entirely accurate. She'd slid down the rope partway, then unhooked her feet and wrapped the rope several times around one leg so she could "walk" across to Ross's bedchamber window.

It was much more difficult than when she'd practiced on the cliff above the creek they used to climb as children. The castle wall was fairly smooth, and she had a hard time pushing herself far enough to one side so she could swing back the other way. She'd also misgauged the length of the rope, and all she'd managed to do was hook the heel of her free leg around the stone opening before she ran out of line. If she let go now and tried to pull herself inside, she'd fall.

She needed to start over, but her hands and arms burned, and she was afraid to release her grip for even an instant to give herself more rope.

Unfortunately, she didn't have a choice. If she fell into the bailey now and survived, how would she get over the curtain wall without alerting the guards? Nay, she needed to lay a false trail so Irvin's men would search for her within the castle grounds. And while they did that, she would be using the pulley system she'd stolen weeks ago to get over the wall.

It was a dangerous escape, which was why she hadn't gone this route the first time. But now she had no choice. It was either get out this way or hide within the castle, avoiding Irvin until Callum returned with all the might of his allies behind him. And she *definitely* didn't want to do that.

Callum MacLean was not her future, and she wouldn't depend on him for anything.

She was just about to unhook her heel and start over, praying she could find the strength for a second attempt, when a hand wrapped around her foot and grasped tight...then yanked her through the open window. She yelped as the rope dragged through her hands and along her leg, burning as her skin scraped and her knee wrenched, but before she knew it, she was straddling the windowsill.

Safe.

Tears blurred her vision. The last person she'd expected to come to her rescue was Ross, but there he stood, swaying with drink, eyes bloodshot and hands shaking. Ducking her head and coming all the way in, she quickly unwound the rope and threw her arms around him. He fell against the wall and slowly returned the embrace.

How had he been able to help her? He could barely lift his arms—as worse for drink as she'd ever seen him.

"Thank you, Ross. I doona think I had the strength to loosen the rope and try again without falling."

He stared down at her, confused. "Eleanor?"

Maggie stilled, and then her heart squeezed. "Nay, it's Maggie. Your sister."

He nodded vaguely and glanced around the room with a bewildered frown. "Where's Eleanor? Have you seen her? I thought I heard a bairn crying."

She closed her eyes, took a deep breath, then cleared her throat. "If she's here, Ross, you go to her. Doona fight it, do you hear me? You go to her and your little one and be happy."

He mumbled something and stumbled to the bed across the room. A low fire burned in the hearth, lighting the way. He fell facedown onto a pile of messy quilts and didn't move.

She glanced around his chamber, thankful they were alone, then gathered up the end of the rope from the floor and leaned out the window to drop the line. It bounced and swayed at first before settling in a straight line down to the bailey, ending about three feet from the ground.

Someone yelled above her, and she yanked her head inside, her heart racing. More raised voices—coming from her room, she was sure. She slowly peeked out, staying in the shadows, peering up at her empty window. *Did someone see me?*

Then suddenly, a man's head appeared, and she ducked down.

Lord help her—she'd gotten out just in time.

She rose and faced the room, her eyes darting from her brother to the door, then to the stone beside the washstand. The entrance to the tunnel that led to the laird's solar.

Surely she had some time. They would be looking for her in the bailey, not in the keep. But shouts sounded throughout her home, and she heard feet pounding down the passageway toward Ross's room.

She ran halfway across the chamber to the door, intent on putting the bar across and locking them out. But if she did that, they would know she was here. So she changed direction and headed for the washstand and the tunnel entrance, her breath rushing though her lungs, only to realize it was too late—she'd never make it in time.

She heard the key in the door and, at the last minute, lunged at Ross on the bed, scrambling under the mess of covers and tucking in as close to his big body as possible. He roused a bit, and she prayed he wouldn't get up and leave her there. Instead, he rolled onto his back, almost completely covering her, and snored loudly.

"He's still here, Laird," she heard Blàr say, getting louder as he moved toward the bed. She knew he wasn't talking to Ross, his real laird, which meant Irvin must be in the room too.

"Is he awake? Find out if she told him anything."

Aye, that was Irvin, sounding half crazed, yelling and gasping for breath at the same time. She tried not to make a sound, which wasn't hard. Ross was heavy and squeezing the air out of her lungs.

She heard a loud, hard slap, and her brother jerked above her. "Wake up, ye sack of shite," Blàr said before he slapped Ross again.

If Maggie could have moved, she would have drawn daggers and defended her brother, but she couldn't lift her arms, let alone breathe. When she saw black dots from lack of air and feared she would suffocate, Ross lifted partially off her. She sucked a breath deep into her lungs, trying desperately to control her breathing, fearing they'd hear her. But Blàr was too loud, yelling and shaking her brother before throwing him down on top of her. She quickly wedged her arms between their bodies so she could continue to breathe.

"He's out cold," Blàr said.

"Search the room," Irvin ordered. "I'm going down to speak to Alpin." His footsteps echoed on the stone floor as he exited the bedchamber.

She heard Blàr curse, and then a crash sounded as if something had been kicked over. The stool in front of the fire, perhaps? She scowled and wished she had her daggers in her hands. If Blàr were to drag the covers off her right now, she'd be mad enough to gut him for beating Ross and for kicking the stool her mother had covered with embroidery just months before she died.

It was a family treasure.

As she listened for any noise that might indicate where Blàr was in the room, she played out in her mind what she would do if he found her. How she would untangle herself from the blankets first, so she wouldn't be restrained, deciding if she would stab him or throw her dagger—and where in his body she would bury the blade.

She heard the big chest in the corner open, and the wardrobe next to it. More muttering and cursing as Blàr moved around to the other side of the room.

Through a tiny slit in the covers, she saw him look behind a tapestry that hung against the wall, then kneel and look under the bed.

He rose with a groan, leaning heavily on his hands as if his knees hurt, and moved to a side table where Ross's jug of whisky perched. After pouring himself a full cup, he sat on the edge of the bed, his back to her, and slowly drank the *uisge-beatha*.

She had a clear path to his heart now—from behind—and could kill him with very little risk to herself. But what would she do with the body? Leaving him here would expose her whereabouts and set them on her trail. Also, she might hesitate to kill him, regardless of what he'd done, and then she'd be done for—locked in the dungeon or even worse, being raped by whoever Irvin chose until a bairn was in her belly.

"Blàr!" someone yelled from down the passageway. "Laird Sinclair wants you."

"Aye, I'm coming."

Laird Sinclair? She hadn't heard that one before. Usually, Irvin was careful to keep his clan name forgotten. Maybe it was good she'd reminded everyone that her cousin was not, and never would be, a MacDonnell.

Blàr hefted himself up from the bed and swayed on his feet before he steadied. Most likely from the whisky. Then he crossed to the entrance, kicking the stool one last time on his way out, and locked the door behind him.

Maggie forced herself to count to twenty. She imagined Blàr walking down the passageway to the top of the stairs and making his way down to the great hall.

Finally, she tried to shove Ross off her. He was as heavy as an ox, and she despaired she would never escape, but then he rolled to his side and she was able to sit up, pull the covers away, and get some air.

She examined Ross, who was still breathing but otherwise looked dead to the world. She could see Blàr's handprint on his cheek and now wished she *had* stabbed him, despite the consequences.

"Thank you, Brother," she whispered, tears forming as she stroked his brow. She'd like to believe that in some corner of his mind and heart, he knew he'd saved her.

Inhaling deeply to clear the sorrow, she wiped her cheeks and pulled her legs all the way out from under him. Without looking back, she crossed to the washstand, lifted the sharp, thin razor that Ross hadn't touched since Eleanor had died, and knelt to lift up the stone—something she'd done almost daily over the last three months as she'd spied on Irvin. She tucked the knife into her belt when she was done—she might need it later—and lowered herself into the tunnel. Then she carefully slid the stone into place.

It was dark without a candle, unrelentingly so, but within a minute, she was at the other end below the laird's solar. She lifted the stone slab quietly, finding the room empty and lit only by a low-burning fire, and moved it—and the chair—to the side. It seemed like days ago she was here with Callum and Gavin, but really, it was only hours.

Her heart hurt thinking about them, Callum especially, and she crushed the feeling. It did no good to dredge up those memories. Most likely, she'd never see him again. Certainly not in a week's time when

Gregor MacLeod arrived to help Callum take over the castle, and most definitely not in the spring when he'd said they were to be married.

She felt around for the big canvas sack she'd stored in the tunnel weeks ago, and when her fingers gripped it, she looped the heavy bag over both shoulders and climbed out, putting everything back into place afterward. She quickly found a candle, lit it in the fire, then hurried to another hidden passage behind a colorful tapestry that depicted a field of flowers.

Her mother had embroidered it before Maggie was born, and she stopped for a minute, despite the urge to hurry, and laid her hand on her namesake's work. Closing her eyes, she pictured Margaret sitting in front of the fire with her yarn, re-creating the splendor of the flowers while her father sat at his desk. Her red hair had been just as wild as Maggie's, and her hazel eyes filled with love. Unlike Maggie, however, the only sharpened metal her mother had ever wielded was a pointy embroidery needle.

Finally, Maggie pushed the tapestry aside, careful to keep the candle away from it. A dark, spiral staircase rose upward on the other side, and she ran her fingertips along the cold stone wall beside her as she mounted the steps. The difference between this passageway and the tunnel beneath the solar was that several people knew about it—including Irvin.

When she neared the top, breathing heavily and legs aching under her load, she slowed and placed the candle in a holder mounted on the wall. Taking the light outside now would make her a target.

Feeling with her hand, she found the latch that

bolted the door from the inside, opened it, and stepped as quietly as possible into the night. The moon had just started to wane, and the sky was surprisingly bright—too bright for her comfort. Drifting clouds scattered the heavens, and if she timed it right, the moon should be covered when she made her descent.

She secured the door from the outside with a piece of wood she'd left there and strode to the edge of the turret—the keep's highest point, on the southwest corner directly above the curtain wall. She carefully lowered her bag to the walkway so the metal inside didn't clink. Although there was so much activity going on in the bailey right now as they searched for her that no one would have heard.

Again, she thought of Callum and Gavin and wondered if they'd escaped, wondered if they were safe. With a frustrated sigh, she returned her mind to the task at hand. She didn't want to think about Callum MacLean right now.

Preferably not ever.

Opening her bag, she took out a thick, strong, tightly woven hemp rope. It had been soaked in glue and then dried to prevent stretching. After securing one end around the merlon, she very carefully wound the rest into a pile beside her. Next, she took out a custom-made bolt for her crossbow. She fed the other end of the line through a metal loop on the bolt, then knotted it—just like she'd done in the woods when she'd practiced with the rope and perfected her aim.

She'd have only one shot at it. If she missed the huge tree that stood about three hundred paces from the castle wall, she couldn't imagine she'd have the strength or time to drag the bolt and rope all the way up to try again. Or that Irvin's men wouldn't notice it as it scraped across the stone.

So she'd made sure to come up here during the day whenever she could, playing the shot over and over in her mind, knowing exactly where she had to stand, the precise angle of her arms and turn of her hips required to hit the trunk—directly above a small platform built into the tree that had once been a lookout. She knew the trajectory of the bolt as if she was standing there in broad daylight.

She could make this shot with her eyes closed. She had to.

It was a dangerous escape route, but it would take her the farthest away from the castle in the least amount of time.

And she prayed it would work—without killing her in the process.

Finally, she pulled her crossbow and windlass from the bag. Pointing the bow down, she slid her foot into the metal stirrup at the bottom, then attached the windlass at the top, its rotating handles and cords hanging down. After hooking the cords over the bow's string, she cranked the handles, which winched the cords and drew back the string.

When the bow was set, she lifted it onto the merlon in front of her and laid the pointed bolt, rope attached, in a groove on the top of the stock. Ready, Maggie looked out into the darkness.

She'd planned meticulously over the last few months: she'd planted daggers all around the keep, the dungeon, and the bailey; she'd packed bags of clothes,

weapons, and food, so she could run at a moment's
notice; she'd hidden ropes in several rooms, including the one she'd used to escape from her bedroom
tonight; and she'd cultivated relationships with a few
people she thought she could trust.

But if she missed this one shot, that would all be
for nothing.

She stepped into place, closed her eyes, and
breathed deeply to calm herself, then raised the crossbow. She knew the right position the moment she
felt it. Without hesitating, she pulled the trigger. The
cross bolt flew into the air with a loud twang, the rope
trailing behind it.

Stepping out of the way, she gripped the stone in
front of her, eyes still closed, and listened. She didn't
actually hear a thud as the bolt hit the tree, but the
rope slowed its drag before it started pulling again—
but downward this time, instead of across.

Grabbing the remaining rope, she yanked as hard
as she could, straining to take up the slack until the
rope was as taut as she could make it. She wrapped it
around the merlon several times, then knotted it firmly
in place.

Her heart had begun to race as she anticipated the
next step.

She'd practiced launching off the cliff with the
heavy bag on her back, and she knew how to compensate for the extra load. Still, she'd fallen two out
of twenty times. And this was a much higher drop
without the water below to break her fall.

*What if the bolt isn't embedded deeply enough and my
weight pulls it free?*

She shook her head, exasperated, and tested the rope. It stayed taut. If she was going to go, she needed to go now. The longer she delayed, the closer Irvin's men would be on her heels.

Go or stay? Choose her own fate, or wait for Callum?

She rolled her head and loosened her shoulders. A part of her wanted to wait, she realized. And not because she was afraid of falling to the ground, but because she *wanted* to fall…for him…

…all over again.

It set her teeth on edge, and she scowled. She'd done enough waiting.

Crouching, she picked up her bag, light now compared to before, and fished out a simple wooden pulley. It was nothing more than a wheel with a deep groove around the circumference where the rope would fit. The pulley had handles on the bottom, and it would hang suspended over the rope until her weight set the wheel in motion. She'd ride the downward-sloping line all the way across to the tree.

At least, that was her plan.

She'd never ridden this great a distance before, and it was quite possible she'd either go too fast and smash into the tree or too slow and lose momentum halfway there. Now she was wishing she'd built a harness of sorts in case she needed her arms and hands free—to either pull herself along or slow her descent.

She looked down at her extra rope and decided to make a seat that she could hook over the handle. She pulled out her knife, measured, cut, and knotted the rope, then put everything away. After pulling up her skirts and tying them between her legs, she swung her bag over her shoulders and sat on the wall, her heels hanging into the abyss, admonishing herself: *doona look down!*

She refused to acknowledge the ground below as she looped the harness over her legs all the way up to her backside, wrapped it under her arms, then slid it onto the handles.

Now all she had to do was hold tight, push herself off the wall, and hope for the best.

She snorted. *All I have to do.*

She waited another second, watching for cloud cover, then grasped the handles as tightly as she could and leaned forward until she fell off the wall.

The jolt was almost enough to pull her hands free, and the makeshift harness slid up beneath her arms, which were still aching after her descent from her window—not to mention the scrapes and stitches she had from the wolf attack. She picked up speed at an astonishing rate, racing through the darkness. Tears streamed from her eyes and into her hair, causing her vision to blur so she couldn't see a thing. Her body dangled dangerously below the pulley, and she had no idea where the tree was or when she should lift her legs and try to brace herself for impact, let alone slow down. The wind in her ears was so loud, she couldn't hear anything, and she didn't know if she'd been seen or if Irvin's men were giving chase.

That was the least of her worries. She needed to slow down...*but how?*

She couldn't reach the cable above her with her hands, and even if she could, the friction would cause terrible damage. She pulled her legs up to her waist and tried to put her leather-clad foot on the rope. It bounced off right away, but she slowed down just a little, wobbling as the pulley threatened to come off the track.

Then leaves smacked her leg, and she knew she'd run out of time. She jammed her foot up hard this time, and the wheel came off the line, slowing and jerking as the rope caught between the axle and the side arm. Branches whipped her legs, and she covered her face and body by raising both feet and hooking them over the rope.

She'd have burns on her ankles, but she'd also slowed enough that the damage wouldn't be permanent. All she could do now was close her eyes and wait for impact.

When it came, it was little more than a bump on the arse, and she thanked God for the extra padding that would leave nothing more than a wee bruise, if that.

The breath she'd been holding came out with a whoosh, and gales of relieved laughter bubbled up from her throat. Clamping a hand over her mouth, she tried to contain them, but some still squeaked through.

She'd just unwrapped her legs from the rope, cursing the pain that burned across the tendons of her ankles, when a furious voice whispered to her from beside the platform, "Maggie MacDonnell, if I e'er find you up a tree again, lucky to be alive, I swear I'll lock you in my bloody castle and throw away the key!"

Seven

CALLUM STARED AT MAGGIE, A FEW FEET FROM HIM IN the tree—safe—and he sagged against the trunk, his muscles suddenly weak. His heart still raced, and his jaw hurt from clenching his teeth as he'd watched her descend on the pulley, helpless to do anything but pick up the pieces afterward. Only a few minutes ago, he and Gavin, plus their men, had been under the huge tree on their horses, about to approach the castle and sneak inside. He'd heard the cross bolt hit the trunk up high and had thought they were under attack.

"Find cover," Callum had whispered harshly, not wanting to give their position away to any hidden marksmen. They'd tucked in closer to the tree—the only cover between the cliff and the castle—drawn their weapons, and searched for their enemy in the dark, but no MacDonnells appeared.

The delay had chafed at Callum; he wanted to push forward and get to Maggie as soon as possible. The idea of her alone and vulnerable in the castle ate at him.

When no attack came and he couldn't hear anything out of the ordinary, he said, "I doona know what we heard. It must have been something else. Who would use a crossbow in the dark? Let's move on."

Drustan shook his head. "'Twas a cross bolt."

Gavin whistled softly to their youngest warrior— agile, blond-headed Finnian. "Finn, go check it out. Fast as you can."

"Aye, Laird." The lad jumped from his horse and practically ran up the tree. He poked his head out from the leaves above them less than a minute later and whispered, "There's a lookout up here, a wooden platform with a railing, but I canna see anyone. And I found the bolt. It's attached to a rope that's stretched toward the castle. Shall I cut it?"

Callum and Gavin both replied, "Nay!" just as Callum heard the whine of the pulley on the rope.

His stomach dropped as he stared at the curtain wall, rooted to the ground in disbelief and fear. Only one person he knew would be forced to escape the castle like that.

When the clouds drifted from the moon and the shape of a woman appeared from the darkness, barely hanging on to a rickety pulley, he knew it had to be Maggie. Her wild hair streamed behind her as she streaked toward them from high above.

"Lord have mercy," Artair said. Beside him, Gill made the sign of the cross.

"Christ Almighty, she's going too fast," Drustan croaked, sounding as helpless as Callum felt.

She was bare-legged again, her skirts tied up between her legs, and when he saw her lift them up to the rope, it propelled him into motion.

He jumped from his horse directly to the tree and

climbed as fast as he could, passing Finn on his way down. Dread tightened Callum's chest. He wouldn't make it in time to catch her or soften the impact. Then he heard a bang and the sound of the pulley dragging on the rope, and he knew she'd popped it off the track to slow herself down.

By God, she might make it after all if the rope didn't fray.

Resourceful woman!

He drew even with the lookout and saw her glide into view and bump arse-first into the tree. Seconds later, a gust of laughter burst from her lungs before she clamped a hand over her mouth. All his fear turned to relief, then boiled into anger over what *might* have happened—just as it had when she'd been chased up the tree by the wolves.

He had to squeeze the words past the tightness of his throat and clenched jaw. "Maggie MacDonnell, if I e'er find you up a tree again, lucky to be alive, I swear I'll lock you in my bloody castle and throw away the key!"

She yelped in surprise and almost fell, but her harness held, and she tipped halfway over instead. "Callum?"

He hauled himself up beside her on the platform as she scrambled to right herself. Her skirts fell back to her ankles. He steadied her as he lifted his knife above her head and sawed viciously at the rope. Moments later, it gave way, fell to the ground, and slithered back to the castle.

His emotions careened inside him, all tangled up and whipped into a frenzy like her hair from the pulley ride. Without any thought, consumed by raw need and want, he tucked the knife into his belt and hauled her against him, tight and hot.

Her startled breath fanned his lips as his hand squeezed high on the back of her thigh, pulling it around him.

"Callum MacLean!" She sounded shocked and breathless but not admonishing. Her fingers curled into his waist, anchoring herself instead of pushing him away.

He sank his other hand into the mass of curls at the back of her head and held her in place. Her eyes met his for just a second, and he knew she wanted the same thing he did—wanted him to devour her, to reaffirm that she'd made it, that she was alive!

He caught her mouth without warning, lips open, tongue stroking in, tasting her, savoring her, until neither one of them could breathe. He nibbled down her throat, his hand sliding along her thigh to her knee.

"I've dreamt of this, of you, every night since we've been apart." Voice rough, he sounded almost feral.

She answered with a groan as he slipped his hand under her skirts and cupped her thigh, trailing his fingertips along the sensitive inner muscles. They quivered against his palm, and her breath rasped through her lungs. When he reached the top, she gasped, rocked her hips toward him, her heel lifting higher to push into his backside.

He pressed closer and inhaled her scent—the smell of fresh air and sunshine and that unique bouquet of Maggie that he would sometimes wake to even though she wasn't there.

He knew he should stop, that they weren't safe yet,

but his need for her overwhelmed rational thought. His body was so filled with lust, with feelings, that he could barely reason and strained to sink into her warmth.

He lifted his head and watched her in the moonlight. Her eyes had closed, her mouth had parted. When he skimmed his fingertips along the crease at the top of her leg, her throat arched and lips quavered on her sudden inhalation.

She released his waist and slid her hands up his back to tangle in his hair, pulling and twisting in the short strands.

"We are betrothed, Maggie," he ground out. "All we need is this final intimacy, then before God and man, we'll be married. We doona need a priest. Let me join with you, sweetling."

She groaned and opened her eyes. "I canna believe you've asked me this. We're in a bloody tree, surrounded by our enemies. Your men are just below!"

The low, rough timbre of her voice sent shivers up his spine. "We're alive. When I saw you flying down that rope, knowing you could fall at any moment, going too fast to land safely…" His throat tightened, and he couldn't continue.

She pressed her cheek against his, her breath huffing past her lips in warm bursts of air. Every puff sent a jolt down to his groin, tightening his stones. When her teeth dragged over his stubble, he knew it was with a mix of desire and anger, and he wanted to bite back.

"You left me," she accused, her voice filled with hurt, with fury.

"Aye, and I'm sorry. My father died, Maggie. They

whispered he committed suicide, but I knew it was murder. I couldnae keep you safe at my home until I had answers."

He released her leg and cupped his hands around her face, brought her gaze to his. "But *this* time, I came back. I left so I could return to the castle and save you."

"I didn't need you to save me. I needed you *not* to leave."

"I promise I'll ne'er leave again."

They stared at each other, tension and want thick between them. Finally, she shook her head. "Nay, Callum. I doona trust you, and Irvin's men may be heading our way as we speak. 'Tis a fool's request."

He clenched his jaw to stop the curses on his tongue from flying free—at himself, not her. Aye, he *was* a fool. Stepping back, he sighed. He had so much more he wanted to say, wanted to explain to her, but he'd have to wait.

"I'm sorry, lass. You're right. I lost my head." He released her and moved to the edge of the platform, swinging his legs over the railing to stand on a sturdy branch. She quickly followed, and he helped her over.

"What was your plan after you got me out of the castle?" she asked.

"We didn't have one. The idea was to take over the castle from the inside once most of Irvin's men were out, then wait for Gregor and the lads to arrive."

Her eyes widened. "And Gavin went along with it?"

"It could have worked." He heard the defensiveness in his voice.

"How would you have manned the walls? Stopped Irvin's men from climbing over?"

"I thought you could convince the remaining men to pledge you their allegiance."

"I doona think so. Not if someone like Alpin MacDonnell was rallying forces on the other side."

"Well, maybe Ross then, but it doesn't matter now. You're out, we're together, and we need to get to safety."

"Aye."

She sounded reluctant, and it grated. He wanted to drag her back into his arms so she was pliant, needing him again.

"Let me go first," he said brusquely. "Your arms must be spent."

When she didn't resist, he knew how tired she truly was. The slump that followed the exhilaration of survival could be crushing, and the force it took to hold on to first the rope and then the pulley would have pushed her strength to the limit.

After his feet crunched the leaves and twigs on the ground, he lifted his arms and grasped her waist to bring her the rest of the way down.

She sagged against him, and he felt a tremor run through her body.

"You'll ride with me," he said.

He whistled for Aristotle, who came forward eagerly. Callum lifted her and placed her on his horse before she could protest. He swung up behind her, her rump tight against his groin. His cock was as hard as the tree they'd just climbed down, and he felt just as big.

She squirmed against him, then said dryly, "Well, that's comfortable."

Gavin huffed out a laugh while Gill coughed into his hand.

Drustan grunted before turning away.

"You can sit on my blanket if you like, Lady… MacLean?" Finnian offered, misunderstanding her jest and eager to help.

"Nay, it's still MacDonnell," she said. "I assure you, the ride would be much more comfortable if I *were* finally a MacLean."

Finnian made a sort of strangled sound when he realized her meaning, and the older warriors laughed into their plaids. Callum was sure the lad's fair skin had turned a bright shade of red, even though he couldn't see it clearly.

Oh well. 'Tis something the lad can laugh about later.

The men were excited and invigorated by Maggie's dramatic escape from the castle, and Callum noted a few gazes resting on her in wonder as they readied to leave. Gill, Callum's marksman, looked astounded. Aye, he of all people would understand the difficulty of the shot Maggie had just made—and in the dark.

Pride surged through him, and he kissed the top of her head.

"What was that for?" she asked.

"You're a wonder, Maggie MacDonnell." He looked up and saw the moon had clouded over. "Now, lead us to shelter. You wouldnae have planned your escape without thinking of somewhere safe to go."

"Nay, that would be daft, now, wouldn't it? Much like storming a castle with no way to keep it."

He heard Gavin and Drustan snort, and Callum had

to smile. How could he do anything else? Maggie was safe in his arms, and he wasn't letting her go ever again.

"But it won me points for bravery, aye? I was coming back for you, Maggie MacDonnell. Doona e'er forget that."

"This time," she said, as stubborn as ever.

He pressed his lips to her ear and she shivered. "Every time from now on, lass."

Eight

THEY TRAVELED SOUTHWEST FROM THE CASTLE, toward her grandmother's farm. It had been a slow journey of several hours in the dark, and once they were close, she wouldn't allow them to proceed farther on the horses until the sun came up. Now it was time.

On her orders, the others fell into line behind her and Callum to avoid the snares and traps she'd set earlier in the month. She'd worked hard to make the pitfalls seem like natural deterrents found in the forest and the snare seem like a trap that had been set long ago and forgotten.

She'd also hidden the trail as best she could under fallen trees and piles of rocks—anything to dissuade someone from continuing onward.

"'Tis dangerous here," she said, and took the reins from Callum to steer Aristotle to the side of the game trail.

Callum wrapped his arms around her waist, and she bit her lip to stop from groaning. Earlier, she'd been brought to the brink of something she'd been craving for years, ever since Callum had first touched her.

Then, as now, he'd left her mind a mess and her body in need. And sitting so intimately in front of him for the last few hours, her legs spread, his fingers rubbing tiny circles over her plaid, his hands touching her but not touching her, was enough to drive her mad.

And she was sure he knew it too, the wee ablach.

He dropped his head beside hers and spoke gravely into her ear. "Maggie."

"Aye."

"I figured out what you didn't tell me. What Irvin could possibly hold over your head to make you marry him."

She glanced to the side and met his eyes but didn't say anything.

"When I lay on the cliff, watching the castle, I saw you climb out your window and into Ross's room. I was sick with worry you'd fall, and I thought, 'when Maggie and I are married, I'll get her with bairn immediately, and she'll have to stop putting herself at risk for the sake of our bairns.' Because you would do anything for your bairns—the same as your mother did for you, aye?"

Pain stabbed through her at the mention of her mother, and Maggie drew in a sharp breath.

"That's what Irvin intended too," he continued, "but in a different way. The blackheart would rape you and then threaten the lives of his own bairns if you didn't marry him and hand over the lairdship and clan. Is that right?"

She licked her lips and cleared her throat before speaking. Still, her voice sounded thick. "Aye, Irvin would blackmail me with my own bairns, but I doona think he would care who fathered them. He intended to let whoever pleased him have a turn with me until I conceived."

Callum cursed and crushed her in his embrace. She resisted at first, holding herself stiff, unyielding, but he didn't relent, and finally, a shuddering breath exhaled from her lungs, and she leaned against him, allowed his warmth, his strength, to comfort her.

He rubbed his cheek against hers. "I'm sorry I left you in such danger, Maggie. I thought you would be safer in your home than in mine. But we're together now, and I willna let him have you. Say you'll marry me, love."

"I doona want to marry you just for safety's sake, Callum."

"Then marry me for every other reason that people marry. For intimacy, for children, for companionship. Let's build a life together."

She hesitated. "And if I say no? Will you agree to end our betrothal?"

He took his time answering. "Aye, but not immediately. I reserve the right to woo you properly. If, after a certain amount of time, it becomes obvious you are steadfast in your desire to end our betrothal, I will do so. But only if I know you're safe."

She rolled her eyes. "I fought off a pack of wolves, outsmarted the most conniving man I know, and successfully shot a cross bolt three hundred paces in the dark so I could ride a rope to freedom. Do you really think I need someone to keep me safe?"

"I think you need someone to stop you from killing yourself in the process," he growled.

She twisted in his arms and frowned at him. "I take my safety verra seriously. I practiced in the woods for months before I executed my plan. I would think you of all people would appreciate that."

"I do. And I'm proud of your skills and determination—you've done an incredible job surviving all this time. But…"

"But what?"

"Maybe I doona want you to just have to survive. Maybe I want you to be happy…to let me make you happy."

Her gaze clashed with his. How could he make her happy? She didn't trust him. Didn't trust he wouldn't leave like he'd done before, like her brothers had done, and everyone else in her life.

She dropped her eyes as pain blossomed in her chest. She knew she was being unfair, but the emotions wouldn't let her go, twisting her up inside and clogging her throat. How could she fix that feeling of being…left behind?

"All right," she finally whispered, so low she wasn't sure he'd hear her.

He leaned closer. "All right…what? You'll marry me? Let me make you happy?"

"Nay. I meant that I'll agree to your bargain. I'll let you…woo me…for a while. I willna fight you on it. But if, by the time it comes for us to part, you doona willingly let me go, I'll…I'll…"

"You'll what?" he asked, and she heard the underlying amusement in his question.

She grunted and wedged the sharp point of her dagger beneath his chin. "I'll sharpen my knives and give you a shave." She trailed her knife down his chest and over his plaid until the point pressed against his sporran. "Down there."

He puffed out a laugh, his eyes lighting up like the morning sky around them. "You may shave me there any time you like, lass. 'Tis in much need of my betrothed's...steady hand."

She huffed and turned back around. She needed to focus on the task at hand—for all their sakes—not on how annoying Callum could be. "My grandmother's cottage is down this trail. 'Tis the land Ross willed to me. I've stocked it with food and supplies. Its location isna a secret, but I don't e'er remember Irvin coming here when we were kids. My grandmother was verra solitary."

"You've hidden it well," Callum said.

They passed through a thick copse of trees, careful to disturb as little of the foliage as possible. They came out at the edge of a pretty glade with a sturdy yet abandoned-looking cottage on the far side.

Callum took the reins from her and pulled them to a stop. He whistled, and Finnian and Drustan rode around them and into the glade, scanning it carefully as they approached the cottage. Gill dismounted and drew his bow. She knew from how he held himself that he was a marksman, and her interest sparked.

"I want to set up some watchers before we settle in," Callum said. "Are there any other traps or pitfalls we should know about?"

"Aye, several." She was tired beyond belief, and sore, but this had to be done before she could rest. "And there are a few around the cottage too. Your men should wait."

Callum whistled again, but the warriors didn't stop as she'd expected. When she looked at him and raised her brow, he said, "They've been warned. They'll know what to look for. We need to check the cottage before we expose ourselves further by riding into the glade."

"And we'll need to see your escape routes too," Gavin added, who'd reined in beside them. "I'm sure you've planned those as well."

"Aye. You can enter or exit the glade through the forest at any point, of course, but Irvin's men will most likely come by horse, as we did, on one of the trails. This is the main one, and some will still remember it—perhaps even Alpin—but there are two other game trails we can follow where I've set some traps." She pointed to her right behind the cottage. "One heads north and joins up to a trail going west from Castle MacDonnell."

"Does it connect with the same trail we sent Father Lundie and the rest of our men on?" Callum asked.

"Most likely. 'Tis the only trail I know of going in that direction." This time she pointed to the left side of the glade. "The other trail heads south, which is the direction we want to go."

"Maybe not," Callum said. "Irvin would expect that."

"True, but you're relying on Gregor and your foster brothers rescuing us. What if we wait...and wait...and they ne'er arrive?"

"Doona doubt their loyalty, Maggie," Gavin said. "We've sworn a blood oath. We fight as brothers, not just allies."

"But what if your brothers and Gregor ne'er know you need help? You canna say for sure your men will reach them. If we wait, and your brothers doona attack the castle, we've lost our advantage. Irvin will have had time to formulate another plan, and we'll still be deep within MacDonnell territory. Irvin's men will have to return to the castle and regroup in a day or two. I say we rest here, plan, and then leave after that."

Gavin looked doubtful, and she shrugged. "Well, 'tis what *I* plan to do. You may follow me if you like. I'll do my best to keep you safe."

Gavin let out a surprised bark of laughter.

Callum sighed. "She's right. We canna wait on them. For all we know, our men may be stuck up a tree surrounded by the same wolf pack that attacked Maggie or captured by Irvin. We need to get to my clan—and get Maggie behind my walls—as soon as possible. As long as she's alive and not under Irvin's control, she's a threat to him. We can return in force and take the castle for John after that."

She twisted to look at him, her brows drawn together. "You plan to lock me up and guard me behind stone walls so I'm *safe*?"

He tensed before answering. "I said naught of locking you away. Doona put words in my mouth. What I meant was we *all* need to get to safety. Then we can deal with Irvin from a place of strength rather than weakness. Right now, he's controlling us because we doona have enough men and we're on the run."

She harrumphed and turned around. He'd chosen his words wisely this time, but she still knew what he'd meant. He'd keep her under guard in his home while he went to steal back her castle without her.

She'd had no intention of returning to her castle—at

least not for a while—but it still burned that he never once considered she'd be an asset in an attack.

She gritted her teeth. "I'm not a helpless lassie, Callum. If Irvin or his men e'er catch me, I'd make them pay. As I would anyone who tried to harm me or mine."

"Well, let's hope we're all safe soon so that notion isna put to the test."

She didn't say it out loud, for she knew Callum would try to talk her out of it, but she wasn't going anywhere near MacLean lands. Once out of MacDonnell territory, she would stick to her original plan—heading straight to Edinburgh to find John.

She'd stay with Callum as long as it suited her but no longer.

And during that time, she'd promised he could try to woo her. She didn't know why she'd said the words; they'd just…come out. And now they hung like a sweet treat just in front of her, tempting her to his side, wondering just how and when he might whisper sinful suggestions in her ear or let his hands drift farther down her body.

A tremor shivered through her, and she closed her eyes. Maybe she would stay with him a little while. Just long enough to experience that pleasure at least once.

When a shrill whistle sounded from the cottage and Callum urged Aristotle forward, she hurriedly opened her eyes and straightened in her seat.

Daydreaming with Callum at her back wouldn't lead anywhere but to trouble.

It took them several hours to go through all the traps and diversions she'd set in the bush around the glade, as well as to set some of their own and determine the best places for the men to keep watch, which they would do in shifts so everyone could rest.

Gavin crouched on the ground in front of Maggie and marked the trap she'd pointed out so his and Callum's men could see and avoid it; but it would still be hidden from enemy eyes. It was the last trap in the woods and on the trails around the cottage, and she could barely sit upright on the horse any longer. She was sure Callum knew it; his arms had tightened around her until he practically held her up.

It galled her to be so weak in front of him, but seeing as she could barely lift a hand to pull the reins away from him, there was nothing she could do about it.

And if Callum knew she was so weak, Gavin knew as well. The rest of the men too, no doubt. Next, she'd be closing her eyes and falling asleep against his chest. It's not like she'd done *that* before. Like a wee, needy bairn.

Weak-willed lass.

She forced her eyes open wide, straightened her spine, and scowled for good measure. Callum grunted behind her and kept a tight hold on her. Finnian was in her direct line of sight, and he paled at her scrutiny.

She sagged again and rubbed her thumb and fingers over her eyes. "'Tis the last one. We can go in now."

Without a word, Callum turned Aristotle and urged him across the glade to the cottage. She hesitated, then placed her hand over his and pulled on the reins until the horse stopped.

"Did you forget a snare?" Callum asked.

"Nay…" She pushed a hand through her heavy hair and pulled it over one shoulder. She didn't like revealing any of her secrets, but…

"Have you decided where you'll put the horses?" she asked.

"Not yet. Artair and Drustan are looking for a place close enough so we can reach them in time but still hidden should anyone come looking. Why? Do you know of such a place?"

Aye, she did, but she didn't know if she wanted *him* to know. What if she decided she wanted to leave in the night? Or wanted a place to hide until he gave up on her and left? She may have agreed to Callum's wooing her, but she hadn't said for how long.

She gnawed on her lip for a moment, then pointed to the hill that rose at the far end of the glade behind the cottage. The dwelling didn't butt up against it, but it was close enough that they could make a run for it and still stay hidden.

"There are several caves in the hill. They're hard to find unless you look closely." A memory rose of her grandmother working in the caves. She'd been wearing only her shift, her long, gray hair, as wild as Maggie's in her youth, sticking out in different directions. Maggie smiled despite her exhaustion. "My grandma used to make her whisky there."

Callum whistled, and Gavin and Drustan rode to his side. Drustan's gaze fell on her, his eyes burning like brands on her skin as she slumped in Callum's arms, and she shifted uncomfortably until he transferred his stare to his laird.

Aye, now Drustan knew how weak she was too.

And there was something about him that made her want iron in her spine.

She couldn't see Gill, Artair, or Finnian anywhere, and she wondered where they were. When she peered around Callum's shoulder on the other side, he said, "They've gone to their posts. Between them and your traps, we should have plenty of warning if someone approaches."

To Gavin and Drustan, he said, "Maggie says we can hide the horses in caves behind the cottage. She'll be happy to show us where they are. Right, lass?"

There was an edge to his voice, and she glimpsed the glint of anger in his eyes. And it was aimed at her. Most likely, he'd guessed she'd considered keeping the caves a secret and was irritated by it. In his mind, they were in this together. To Callum's way of thinking, Maggie was already his wife.

Maggie wasn't nearly so sure, although parts of her were more than willing.

She squirmed in her seat, unable to stop herself from pressing her bottom backward against Callum. His forearm locked around her hips and held her tight.

Verily, it was her own fault.

She huffed out an irritated breath. "Aye, I'll take you there."

⁓

Callum sat on the steps that led to the cottage's front porch, the parchments Maggie had given him only yesterday in his hands, and tried not to listen to the sound of splashing water inside. He could have closed the inward-swinging door, but now that he had

Maggie with him—safe and sound—he was afraid to let her out of his sight. Or in this case, his arm's reach.

So he sat outside her door, attempting to make sense of her notes, while she stood inside, naked in front of a basin of cool water. She was washing away the dirt and grime of their travels despite her obvious exhaustion—which was another reason he kept the door slightly open. She could barely stay seated on the horse; how could she bathe without falling?

Aye, he should go in and make sure she came to no harm.

He stood without thinking, then his brain caught up to his body and forced him back onto the step— for the fourth time. With a resigned sigh, he gave up and shoved the sheaf of papers inside his plaid, knowing he fought a losing battle. All he could think about was Maggie.

He'd given his word he wouldn't go inside until she was dressed, but God's blood, he'd never before made so difficult a promise. He was a mass of need. Ever since touching and kissing her so intimately in the tree, then riding with her so close to him, her body rocking against him, her legs spread in front of him... It was all he could do not to go into the cottage and push the basin aside so he could kneel in front of her and feast on her—on his woman.

His *wife*.

If she allowed him to do that to her, surely she would allow intimate congress too, and then according to canon law, they would be married.

Married.

The word reverberated in his heart and through his

body, and he realized how desperately he wanted to be married to Maggie. He'd wanted it for nigh on four years and had almost given up on the idea it would ever happen. And now here they were, so close to it, he could practically feel the warmth of her hand in his as he slid his ring on her finger, hear the whisper of her words as she promised to love and honor him, if not obey.

The corners of his mouth twitched. Maggie was not a woman to blindly obey anyone, nor would he want her to…most of the time.

In their marriage bed, however, he would very much like her to acquiesce. He'd been thinking for years about telling her what to do during their intimate play. And he thought that perhaps she might agree.

Aye, he liked her spirit, but in that, at least, he would love her submission.

When he'd watched Lachlan marry Amber, knowing how right they were for each other, how much they loved one another, even if they didn't know it yet, he'd felt a fierce longing in his heart for Maggie. For the rest of his life—with her—to start.

Now they were finally together…but not yet together.

He was known for his patience, for making the right decisions wisely and carefully. But that was before the woman who should be his wife stood naked inside her cottage just a few steps away. He'd never been so tempted. Not in the four years he'd waited, forgoing all other women in the hopes he'd soon feel his wife's touch.

A knife thudded into the door behind him, a sound he'd know anywhere. It snapped him out of his reverie, and he jumped to his feet, heart pounding in expectation, sword out, eyes narrowed. He didn't see anyone attacking, and none of his or Gavin's men had sounded the alarm. *What was going on?* Glancing at the door, he saw that it was still almost closed and no dagger protruded from the wood.

Where was it? He knew the sounds of attack, and a dagger thunking into something solid was one of them. He quickly backed up to the door, opened it, and stepped over the threshold. That's when he saw the dagger—Maggie's dagger—embedded in the wood on the *inside* of the door. And when he heard her shriek, he spun to her, charged forward, thinking the attackers were within the cottage—with Maggie— and came to an abrupt halt.

Oh dear heaven.

His wife-to-be stood wet and naked on a mat in the middle of the room, her wild red hair falling over her bare shoulders, and her breasts, high and plump, jutting out at him. Her nipples had hardened into tight nubs, and he couldn't take his eyes from them. He wanted to roll his tongue around them, suckle them until they stood bright red against her soft, cream-colored skin. He'd known she was well endowed, had felt the mounds pressed against his body and even squeezed his palm over them when they were younger, but he'd never *seen* them before. Now he knew how they would flow over his hands when he cupped them, lifted them to his mouth as he tupped her.

Her body was lean and lithe with a tucked-in waist and a small patch of wet, red curls guarding her womanhood, where he'd nearly stroked her just hours ago. She'd jerked her hips against him then, wanted his fingers on her, all over her. Aye, she'd *wanted* him.

He took a step forward, his body like a rock, cock hard and straining toward her. Her eyes widened and her lips parted. He wanted to put his cock in there too. When he took another step, she jumped.

"Turn around!" she yelled.

He came back to himself with a jolt and quickly scanned the room, seeing she was truly alone. Which meant he'd broken his promise.

He spun to the door, breathing hard, but for a different reason now. Interestingly, she hadn't told him to get out or tried to cover herself. Nay, she'd liked him looking at her.

His eyes landed on her knife. "I heard a dagger," he said by way of explanation.

"Aye, 'twas my dagger."

"I thought you were under attack."

"Nay, I was closing the door. The wind had blown it open."

"So you threw your dagger at it?"

"My feet were wet. I didn't want to walk across the dirty floor."

"Why didn't you just call me? I was right outside. I would have closed the door."

"I didn't want to chance you coming in."

"God's blood, Maggie! I gave you my word I would not."

"Then why are you standing right in front of me?"

"Because. I. Heard. A. Dagger!"

He huffed out a frustrated breath and dragged his hand down his face. She would be the death of him, surely—either from unrelieved need or from his head exploding during one of their arguments. He needed her under him, soon, where he knew she would submit, all her fight draining away as her body turned compliant and agreeable with her own need.

As it should. She may not want to admit it, but she knew as much as he did they were meant to be together. He'd seen it in her eyes, heard it in the hitch of her breath whenever he touched her.

But he needed her to ask him for that final embrace. It didn't have to be in words, but he had to be sure she wouldn't regret it. She had to be certain. Until then...

He set his jaw and sheathed his sword before marching toward her. This time he kept his gaze locked with hers. She still hadn't covered up, her chaotic thoughts and emotions careening across her expressive face.

"All in good time, love," he said brusquely upon reaching her. Then he picked up her shift from a nearby chair and pulled it over her head and body. She swayed into him, a soft sob breaking from her lips. His body twitched in response, like a stallion anticipating his mare, wanting to alleviate her need, soothe her uncertainty, and take her under his control.

He grasped her head in his hands and pressed his lips to her forehead, resisting the urge to kiss down her face to her mouth. He could; it was open and waiting for him, her breath puffing erratically against his throat.

Releasing her, he walked to the bed that filled the nook in the corner of the small, bare cottage. It looked like it had been recently restuffed.

He pulled the sheet off the bed, shook out the dust,

and refitted it over the mattress, then he shook out and plumped up the pillow. He turned to find Maggie, her plaid wrapped loosely around her body, tossing the water from her basin out the door. They hadn't lit the fire in the stone hearth, but the shutters had been left open enough to let in the light and air, and her hair gleamed in the midmorning sun.

She retrieved her dagger, then turned back into the cottage, her eyes getting bigger when she saw him watching her. A flush crawled up her cheeks, and he knew she was mortified, either at him seeing her naked or at her failure to cover herself as soon as he'd come in.

The latter, most likely. She'd wanted him to see her, no matter how much she might deny it.

A grin burst out on his face. She scowled at him and tossed her dagger. It went wide and landed in the wall a hand's span to his left.

A joy-filled laugh burst from his lungs, and he sauntered toward her. "What is it with you throwing daggers in the cottage, lass? Didn't your grandmother teach you anything? If you'd wanted me to see you naked, all you had to do was ask."

Her brow lifted. "I did not want you to see me naked."

"Aye, you did, Maggie MacLean, or you wouldnae have thrown the dagger in the first place."

"I explained that. And the day I become a MacLean is the day I…"

"The day you what? Make me come running in on you bathing? Tempt me to touch you? You're a smart lass. You knew what would happen." He stopped right in front of her, trailed his fingers lightly down her cheek and along her jaw to her lips. "Can I kiss you, Maggie?"

Her chest rose and fell quickly, and the color had risen in her cheeks. "Nay."

"Even though you want me to?"

She scowled at him, but she'd twined her fingers into his plaid. "Count yourself fortunate I doona have any more daggers on me."

"I do count myself fortunate, but not because you're without your weapons. I'm fortunate to be standing here with you, lass." He nudged a bit closer, until he could feel her heat. "Can I kiss you now, Maggie?" he whispered.

She swallowed, and her mouth parted as she inhaled. Then the tip of her tongue darted out to touch her bottom lip. His eyes narrowed on the movement, wanting to capture her tongue with his.

"The last time you kissed me, you didn't ask my permission. Why do so now?"

"Because I want you to say yes."

She dropped her gaze from his, fidgeted her feet on the packed-earth floor for a moment. "I'll admit, Callum, that I'm drawn to you. The same as I was when we were younger." She raised her chin and squared her shoulders. "But 'tis not something I want to pursue. So I'll be saying nay."

She dropped his plaid and stepped around him, but he stopped her with a light hand on her waist. "For now, Maggie. You'll be saying nay for now."

Nine

CALLUM SLUMPED IN THE CHAIR ACROSS FROM WHERE Maggie was sleeping and rubbed his fingers over his eyes. God's blood, he was tired, but he was too wound up to sleep. And he needed to talk with Gavin about the notes Maggie had given him. And since they didn't know how long it would be before they were forced to run, that meant doing it now.

He'd briefly glanced through the papers while he'd waited for his foster brother to join him, this time able to concentrate. The sheaf of parchments now lay in an orderly pile on the table in front of him, far different from the folded mess Maggie had first handed him when Alpin's troops were bearing down on them.

Once he'd organized the pages into what he thought was the correct order, he'd numbered them with ink and a quill retrieved from his pack. Not that that had helped much. The notes jumped all over the place—from names of people, to clans, to different schemes Irvin was involved in, including many of the secrets he held over peoples' heads. Much of it was confusing and illegible. He wanted to go over it with

Maggie, but she lay on the bed, under his plaid, fast asleep.

The door pushed open, and Gavin, looking as tired as Callum felt, stepped inside. Callum whistled softly to tell his foster brother to be quiet and pointed to Maggie on the bed.

Gavin nodded and moved to the basin of fresh water that Callum had filled for him after he'd had his own wash. Maggie had slept through all of it, much to Callum's disappointment. He'd rather wanted her to feast her eyes on him the way he had on her. But he'd also been relieved. She obviously needed the rest.

Gavin finished at the basin, which sat on a stool near the cold hearth, and after stopping to retrieve a leather flagon from his bag, he walked across the packed-dirt floor and sat in a chair across the table from Callum. His short, ravaged hair and the shirt under his plaid were damp, his face a far cry from that of his youth. Dark shadows circled his eyes, lines were etched deeply into his forehead, and his cheeks looked almost concave.

Lifting the flagon to his lips, Gavin took several swallows, then passed the rich mead to Callum. "Does it say anything about Ewan in there?"

"Nay. I'm sorry, Brother. At least, nothing I could decipher. We'll ask Maggie when she wakes up."

Gavin nodded, his mouth pulling down at the corners, before he reached for the pages. "Let's have a look."

Several hours later, they'd made copious notes on the parchments, fitting pieces together from what was written but also from what they already knew and what they had guessed. Callum felt sick from reading about some of Maggie's clansmen's and clanswomen's secrets. And not only them, but people from other clans as well—even a laird he knew. Some of the secrets were serious, but most of them were just sad and unimportant in the overall arc of one's life. Callum felt like he'd been subject to too much harmful gossip, like he'd showered in filth.

It was unfortunate that so much damage had been done out of fear and deception. A secret should stay a secret as long as was necessary—but not at the expense of other people's lives.

Letters needed to be written and lairds informed when the treachery involved their clans. Irvin had various men and women spying for him in more than just the MacLean clan. The rot needed to be dug out.

More worrying, though, was the sense both he and Gavin had that something more was going on than just Irvin's desire to take over Maggie's clan. Too many clans had been mentioned, and too many secrets intertwined. It almost felt as if Irvin was just one of many arrows in the quiver rather than the archer himself.

Once this was over, Callum would question Irvin and then punish him for the crimes he'd committed, especially now that Callum knew the horrors he intended for Maggie.

He hadn't realized he was staring at his betrothed's sleeping form, nor how tightly he was clenching his fist, his eyebrows drawn together, teeth gritted, until the quill he was holding snapped in two.

"Are you mad at her, then?" Gavin asked dryly.

Callum looked over at him, surprised. "Of course not. Why would you ask such a question?"

Gavin counted down on his fingers. "She says she doesn't want to marry you, she didn't tell you about the caves straight away, she keeps trying to escape on her own, and she's thrown how many daggers at your head now? That's four reasons. Do you want me to go on?"

Callum scowled, but at his foster brother this time. "I should ne'er have told you about the second dagger. If she really didn't want to marry me, she wouldnae have missed."

"Or she didn't want to murder you."

Callum grunted dismissively and returned to perusing the parchments, but he couldn't focus on the task at hand. After a moment, he said, "I was thinking about Irvin and what he had in store for her. How he'd planned to abuse *my wife*."

"Nay, not *your wife*, Callum. You canna think like that. Maggie's a smart, capable lass, and she's stubborn. You say that Isobel likes being in opposition to Kerr and me—and will therefore ne'er consent to marrying Kerr, no matter how much I might want the match for my sister—but I could say the same about Maggie. She's dug her heels in. You may not win this one."

"How can you talk about me losing when the game's barely started?"

"'Tis not a game," Gavin said. "If you make a poor choice like I did, your wife can make your life a misery. Even in death, Cristel had the power to drag me down to hell with her. She didn't care that she hurt me. That she hurt Ewan."

"You canna compare Maggie to Cristel. She would ne'er treat anyone so callously."

"Nay, but I can compare her to Isobel, and you'd be wise to heed your own words."

Callum drummed his fingers on the table, not wanting to fight with Gavin, but he couldn't let it go.

"So you think I should just ride away? Ne'er see her again?"

"I didn't say that. I think you should be together—and I told Maggie that."

"Then what exactly are you saying?"

They'd been speaking in hushed voices, so as not to wake Maggie, but still, it was heated.

"I said that she's not your wife, which she isn't. And from everything she's said, she doesn't want to marry you, which she—"

"—does," Callum finished for him. He knew it wasn't what Gavin was going to say, but Gavin didn't know Maggie, didn't understand the pull that existed between them. He'd never experienced it with Cristel—not with anyone, as far as Callum knew. The closest he could relate to it was the bond he had with his son.

"Would you e'er give up on finding Ewan?" he asked.

Gavin stiffened. "'Tis not the same. Ewan was just a baby. He had no control of the situation. Cristel and I were meant to protect him. We failed him. *I* failed him."

"What I meant was that in your heart, you know that someday you'll find him. That you canna give up on him, because he is meant to walk this earth by your side—father and son."

Gavin swallowed before answering. "Aye. That I believe."

"'Tis how I feel about Maggie."

Gavin leaned over the table and clasped his forearm. "Are you sure, Callum? Or is it just...habit? How old were you when you and Maggie were betrothed?"

"Sixteen. She was only nine. But I didn't feel that bond with her as a man does with a woman until we were much older. I'd always liked her. I felt protective of her."

"I remember. She'd seemed so fierce yet...lost. You calmed her when we visited."

"She needed to know I was there for her." He looked across the room at her sleeping form, her hair bright against the blanket. "Maggie's mine, Gavin. And I'm hers. It's in her eyes every time she looks at me, every time she leans against me. Her body remembers our connection even if her mind refuses to. She's hurt, and she has every right to be. She's scared that I'll leave her, like her mother did when she died, like her brothers have abandoned her."

Gavin sighed, scratched his fingers over his bristly beard. "Aye. I would find it hard to trust a woman after what Cristel did. Especially a lovely lass. That's all Cristel cared about—people being enamored with her face, her body. I told her not to take Ewan to the festival, that there had been rumors of plague. I explained the danger. She said she wouldn't and then she did it anyway. I've ne'er hated anyone the way I hate her. It fills every inch of me. I'm glad she's dead."

Callum's heart grew heavy, filled with pain over Gavin's transformation from the lad who had the loudest laugh and brightest spirit to a man ravaged by hate and loss. "You canna blacken all lasses with Cristel's failings. Look at Amber and Caitlin, even my Maggie. Lovely lasses, all of them, and all of them protective and caring for those they love. If Ewan is alive—and I believe you when you say he is—we'll find him."

Gavin nodded, then leaned closer to Callum. "All right then. What's your plan for wooing her? If, as you say, her body recognizes the bond between you, canna you just make love to her? Then she'll be your wife. Surely she wouldnae refuse you then."

"I've thought about that, but as you say, she's stubborn. She wouldnae think twice about riding away to Edinburgh, no matter if she were my wife or not. And she's not afraid to leave on her own. She's as capable as any man when it comes to defending herself—even better than some. *She* needs to choose *me*. Like Amber had to choose Lachlan. 'Twas not a decision that could be forced upon her—or on Maggie either. Nor would I want it to be."

"So, you need to make her fall in love with you. If she did, she would ne'er leave, aye?"

"I would hope not. I can ne'er imagine Caitlin leaving Darach, or Amber leaving Lachlan."

"Well, then…do that."

"Do what?"

"Make her fall in love with you!"

Callum shook his head, and he slumped in his chair. "Have you lost your mind? 'Tis not such an easy task."

"Pick her some flowers. Write her some sweet words."

"Do you really think that will work on a lass like Maggie? She would slice off the tops of the flowers with her dagger and use my poems for target practice."

Gavin grinned. "Aye, she would. And she'd best every single one of us. Well, maybe not Gill, although he was mightily impressed that she made the shot from the castle wall in the dark. I think he's halfway in love with her on that basis alone."

Anger erupted in Callum. He leaned over the table, a scowl on his face. "You tell him to keep away from Maggie."

Gavin *tched* and rolled his eyes. "I guess that answers my next question, then."

"Which is what?"

"Are you in love with her?"

Callum's heart began to pound, and he slowly straightened. "What does that have to do with anything?"

"A lot, I'd think, if you want her to love *you*."

He rubbed his hand over the nape of his neck and looked at Maggie—*sleeping under his plaid*. "I want her in every way a man wants a woman. And only her, no one else. I want her safe and happy and healthy. I ne'er want to be parted from her." He returned his gaze to Gavin. "Is that love?"

His foster brother smiled, his face softening and bringing to Callum's mind the Gavin of old. "I think so, Brother." He lifted his flagon of mead in the air—a toast. "Aim your arrow for her heart. Strike true." He took a swig and passed the drink to Callum. "Keep it. I've had enough. 'Twas sobering to look on Ross and know how easily that could have been me."

"Aye. Thank you," Callum said before he took another sip.

Gavin rose quietly from his chair. "I'll go take over from one of the lads. And I'll tell them not to come into the cottage. Maybe Maggie will wake with her mind sleepy and ask you to make her yours."

Callum shook his head. "I need her fully awake when she asks me that—in word or in deed." He eyed his brother with concern. "You should sleep too, Gavin."

"I canna, not really. I'll sleep when I find my son."

Gavin crossed the room and left the cottage, closing the door behind him.

Feeling a little broken under the weight of Gavin's despair, Callum gathered up the parchments and returned them to his pack. He then tidied the cottage, closed the shutters, and replaced the chairs, so it looked exactly as when they'd first arrived. If they did have to make a run for it and someone came inside the cottage to check, he didn't want to give away that they'd been here.

He looked at Maggie sleeping on the bed, indecision making him hesitate. If anyone came in quickly enough and the bed was still warm with body heat—if it smelled sweet like Maggie, or even, God willing, held the musky smell of sex—then that would give them away too. But she needed her rest. Aye, he did too, especially if they had a hard ride ahead of them. He decided against disturbing her.

Nay, he'd let her sleep, preferably with him beside her.

She'd barely moved in the last three hours as the sun reached its zenith, and it pleased him that she felt safe enough with him there to let her guard down to such an extent. He couldn't imagine that she'd slept well the past few years, with all the turmoil and upset in her clan. Certainly not since she'd discovered Irvin's treachery and had to escape—twice—during the night.

It was yet another tie being woven between them. A bond of trust and care. Aye, care. He would show Maggie he had her best interests at heart.

As if his thoughts had roused her, she rolled onto her back, thrashing her head on the pillow. Callum quickly crossed to the bedside and stroked his hand through her hair, and she settled immediately. He looked one more time around the cottage, stifling the yawn that wanted to crack open his jaws, then shed his boots and plaid and crawled onto the bed beside her, wearing only his long shirt. She curled instantly into his side when he rolled onto his back, her head on his chest and hand over his waist. It was the same way they'd slept at their camp after she'd been attacked by the wolves.

Callum wrapped his arm around her shoulders and squeezed her close. He yawned again, this time letting his jaws stretch wide, then shook his head in exasperation. He had Maggie on a bed beside him, soft and warm and smelling sweet. She'd let him look on her naked, every lovely, shapely inch, and she'd missed when she'd thrown her dagger at him. Twice. Yet here he was, going to sleep. And despite the ache in his body, he knew he would slumber soundly until Gavin woke him.

Never would he have guessed it was possible.

∽

Maggie opened heavy eyelids and blinked slowly. She felt cocooned in warmth and safety, enveloped by a smell so delicious, it made her toes curl—hints of fresh air, wood smoke, and horses. The smell of fresh petals too, and clean water. But mostly, she smelled the slightly musky scent of…of…Callum.

She sighed in sleepy contentment, knowing she was exactly where she was meant to be. She pulled his arm farther around her waist from behind, weaving their fingers together at her navel, just like she'd wanted to do when they were on Aristotle.

She closed her eyes, let sleep begin to pull her under, then a thought surfaced in her mind. *Why is Callum in my bed?*

She opened her eyes, fully awake now, and stared at the log wall of her grandmother's cottage just a few feet away. Pressed up behind her, warming her, was a hard, male body. Her heart sped up. She looked down at their linked hands to confirm that it was indeed Callum. She'd been riding with him for hours on the way here, had been touched by him, kissed by him, even slept with him through the night on one other occasion, though that time, he'd been gone when she'd woken. She knew the feel of him, the height and breadth of him.

She knew his scent.

He released a heavy breath, and the hair on her crown stirred. *Is he awake?*

She hesitated, then unlinked their hands and turned to him, only to find him fast asleep. Her breath caught as she stared at his face, so handsome. When she'd first seen him as a lass, she'd thought he was an angel come straight from heaven. Sent by her mother to comfort her. When she'd found out he was just a regular lad and that she was meant to marry him when she was older, she'd felt a confusing mix of disappointment, excitement, dread, anticipation, and resentment. A lot of resentment.

Why couldn't he have stayed her angel? He was supposed to have been her last gift from her mother.

Maybe he is and I just can't see it.

Her throat tightened, and she found herself blinking back tears. She should get up. She wanted to get up, but her body refused to move. Just like earlier when she stood in front of him without a stitch of clothing.

Aye, he was right. She had wanted him to see her naked. Not that she'd tell him that.

A lock of hair fell over his forehead, and she lifted her hand to sweep it away before stopping herself. If she woke him now, what would happen? How would she say no if he wanted to tup her, when she longed for his weight on her, wedged between her legs, pressing her into the mattress?

Instead, she drew her fingers down his face, just a hairsbreadth from touching him. She traced the sharp angles of his eyebrows and cheeks, softened a bit in slumber; the perfect formation of his lips, neither too full nor too thin; the dark sweep of thick lashes against his tanned skin.

She wanted to press closer, get inside his skin. Have him reside in hers. She wanted to crawl on top of him, roll around on him like a foal in a field of clover.

God's blood! At this rate, she wouldn't stay a maid much longer, and she would find herself married to Callum by way of intimate congress. She should leave now before that happened. Before she was forced to make that decision…or she gave up and let her body decide.

But she couldn't make herself move. She couldn't stop staring at his face and seeing the boy she'd once thought an angel.

It pleased her the sky had not darkened yet and she could drink him in to her heart's content. The light coming through the partially open shutters had the tinge of late afternoon, perhaps early evening, which astounded her. How long had he been here? And how long had she been asleep? She hadn't stirred once since she'd lain down.

When was the last time that had happened? Maybe before Eleanor had died, or before John had left the castle. Perhaps as far back as when her mother was still alive.

Aye, that was probably it. The last time she'd felt… safe. Truly safe.

Until now. Which made no sense, as Irvin's men were nipping at their heels like a pack of ornery dogs.

Yet somehow, Callum took it all away—the worry, the uncertainty. *The loneliness.*

She closed her eyes and pressed her face into his chest, not wanting to let the emotions free. She had to hold herself together or she might just fly apart. She worked to control her breathing, stop her heart from pounding.

It wasn't working. Then Callum's arm slipped beneath her, pulled her into the crook of his arm as he rolled onto his back. He muttered something under his breath, and she looked up to see that he was still sleeping.

Slowly, she laid her head on his chest and crept her arm around his waist, inch by inch, until she squeezed him tight. She breathed in his scent and felt warmed from the inside out. Finally, the jagged emotions inside her softened, subsided.

She drifted then, thinking vaguely about her plans—how she should climb out of bed, sneak out of the cottage and into the caves. Steal one of the men's horses. She should make her own way to John as she'd first planned. Far away from here, from Irvin and Ross, from the memory of her mother. From Callum.

Aye, especially from him.

She was still thinking that—about how she didn't need him. She was a capable lass. She didn't need anybody. She could take care of herself.

When she fell asleep.

Ten

"MAGGIE!"

Maggie's eyes opened wide, and she shoved herself up in the empty bed, the linen cold where Callum's body had once lain beside hers.

It was dark, but she sensed him near, standing at the edge of the bed. His big hands cupped her face, and he leaned forward, his lips pressing close to her ear. "Hush. Someone's coming. We have to get behind the cottage and out of sight before they enter the glade."

"I see a light, Callum. Torches at the head of the trail where we first came in. Let's go."

It was Gavin's voice coming from the cottage door, and a sliver of moonlight streamed through the opening. All the shutters must have been locked tight, for it was the only light coming in.

Callum released her and placed something in her lap. "Your shoes, daggers, and arisaid. Put them on quickly while I strip the bed, so they doona know we were here."

"Aye," she said, her heart pounding with the need to hurry, to escape. She moved out of his way and propped herself against the wall while she pulled on her shoes, secured her daggers in their leather sheath, and loosely pinned her arisaid. In the dark, she heard Callum stripping the linens from the bed to leave the mattress bare. Then she heard him inhaling. Deeply.

Confusion creased her brow. "Are you smelling the sheets?" she whispered.

"Aye. Smells like heaven. Like you." She heard the grin in his voice and didn't know if he was teasing her or not.

She chose to ignore him, but she couldn't stop the blood from warming her cheeks. "Where's my bag?" she asked, glad he could not see her flushed face.

"I have it," Gavin said. "Hurry, lass. They're getting closer."

Callum grasped her arm. "Let's go."

"Nay, Callum. This way. There's another exit that leads behind the cottage."

He stilled, and his hand on her arm tightened. "I didn't see another door." His voice had taken on that edgy tone that she'd come to recognize—a telltale sign he was restraining some strong emotion.

"It's hidden behind the chair in the corner. My grandmother had it built right into the cottage. The big log at the bottom pushes out and can be reset from the other side. That way, they'll ne'er know we were here."

He inhaled—sharply. But this time, it was not to smell the sheets. His hands wrapped around her head like they did before, tipped up her face. She couldn't see him in the dark, but anger radiated off him, and she felt it invade every pore of her body.

"You will ne'er leave me without telling me you

are going, Maggie. Do you understand? You willna sneak out—in the dead of night or any other time. Promise me."

She hesitated. "Callum, I doona think—"

"Promise me!"

She wanted to stamp her foot, to hit out at him. Instead, she hissed, "I promise, but it doesn't mean I willna leave. On. My. Own."

He grunted, then pressed his lips to hers. Hard. She barely resisted biting him...before she began to melt.

"For the love of God," Gavin exclaimed in a harsh whisper from the door. "We doona have time for that."

Callum pulled away, but he kept one arm around her as he picked up his pack. "Come inside and shut the door, Gavin. Lock it, but doona put the bar across. There's another exit over here. Maggie was just about to show it to me."

She heard the door click shut, and the room fell into total darkness.

"Do you need light?" Callum asked. "We can crack the shutters at the back."

She could dislodge the log by feel alone, had practiced in the dark several times, but even a sliver of light would be welcome. "Aye, thank you."

Callum left her side, and for just a moment, she felt bereft. Then she straightened her shoulders and shook her head. *What a daft, needy lass I've become.*

She reached out and felt for her grandmother's old chair, knowing it by the worn pillow on the seat. Her hand curled around the smooth wooden arm, and she pulled it away from the wall just as Callum silently opened the shutter to let in some light.

Shouts sounded in the distance, followed by a loud crash. Maggie jumped, her heart rate accelerating. That was one of her traps. How close were Alpin and his men?

She hurried now and crouched in the corner, her movements quick and efficient as she reached for one of the short, fat logs.

Gavin crouched beside her. "Just push?" he asked.

"Aye." It was a tight fit and the log heavy, but with Gavin's assistance, it was shoved out of the way in no time.

Gavin whistled softly to Callum, then pushed his bag through the hole. The room went dark, and she heard Callum bar the shutter.

"I'll go first," Gavin said. "When I'm through, hand me your bag and follow behind me."

Stress sharpened her tongue. "You doona need to tell me what to do, Gavin MacKinnon. I've practiced this escape several times. Now quit blathering and go!" She watched as he lay on his belly and crawled through the hole. He was so wide across the shoulders, she half expected he'd get stuck halfway through. She breathed deeply to release the tension as she waited, keeping her hands clenched in her lap.

Finally, he reached the other side and dragged his feet clear of the opening. His hand reappeared, and she passed him her bag. She hesitated, waiting until she sensed Callum kneel behind her, felt his hand on her back. "Your turn," he whispered.

She wasted no time scooting through the hole on her belly, barely restraining a squeal as another loud crash sounded at the edge of the woods. She reached back for Callum's bag. "The chair," she whispered. "Come through feetfirst and pull it into place as you go."

She heard shuffling, then his feet appeared, soles facing upward as he made his way out of the opening. It wasn't quite as snug a fit as when Gavin had worked his way through, but it was infinitely more heart-pounding for her as Callum's plaid pushed up his powerful legs and over his arse.

And what a fine arse it was—tight and muscular in the moonlight. When his waist appeared, she reached up and reluctantly pulled his plaid over the glorious sight, resisting the urge to smack it—or bite it, even. Although she may have let her fingers trail over it just a bit.

He gave her a searing look after he pulled his head free, and despite the knot in her gut, she couldn't help smiling. She rolled the log toward him so he could fit it into place.

"Look good?" he asked, referring to the log after it lay snug in the wall.

"Aye, verra good." Her voice held just enough amusement for him to know she wasn't talking about the log.

He grabbed her hand as they rose and pulled her close for a quick kiss, their bags in his other hand. "'Tis only fair, lass, since I've seen every bare inch of you. Oh wait… I havenae seen your arse, yet, have I? Something to look forward to."

"Let's go!" Gavin said as the sound of horses and men shouting rose in volume.

Callum tugged her after him, and they sprinted to the hidden caves, praying they couldn't be seen.

❧

Callum stood in the dark near the cave's opening and looked out onto the glade below. He kept one hand on Aristotle's reins, his signal to the horse—who stood behind him—to stay silent. His free hand clasped tight around Maggie's. Gavin stood on his other side, also holding his stallion's reins. Behind him, Drustan held the reins of the remaining four horses. Finnian, Artair, and Gill were still out there, on foot, hiding in the forest.

Callum was not worried the men would be found; they were too well trained for that. He was worried, however, that one of the MacDonnells would come snooping around the caves. Then Callum would either have to dispose of him or leave the horses and retreat through the rear of the cave and proceed up the mountain on foot. Which wasn't really an option.

A tremor passed from Maggie's hand to his, and he squeezed tight, trying to transfer his strength to her. Not that he didn't think she was strong—just the opposite. But having to be strong all the time came at a price. Everyone needed support. He had his foster brothers and Gregor, even Drustan to lean on.

Now he would prove to Maggie that he would be her unwavering support too.

Alpin and his men had entered the glade slowly, their torches lighting up the night. He'd done as Callum and Gavin had done, secured the area first, then sent men ahead to scout the cottage. Now they'd surrounded the dwelling and were preparing to go inside.

Callum couldn't see the front of the house as Alpin approached it, but he knew the MacDonnells would break the lock soon. Upon entering, they'd be met with an empty, barren room. But their leader was smart. He'd look for signs they'd been there and might find something Callum had missed in their rush to get out—a hair on the pillow that Callum hadn't seen in the dark, the chair not replaced quite where it should be, the ground still damp where water had spilled.

So many things could hint at their presence, and Alpin could come searching.

Beside him, Gavin tapped the fingers of his free hand against his leg, his thoughts most likely similar to Callum's.

"If they come this way, Gill will draw them off," Callum whispered, wanting to reassure Maggie. "'Twill be a difficult shot, and hopefully they'll think 'tis you and give chase."

"But then how will he get away from them?" Her voice was pitched high—nerves, no doubt.

"He'll go to ground. They all will," Drustan said. "Doona worry about our men, lass. They know how to hide."

"Aye. If they don't want to be found, even we couldnae find them—and that's saying a lot with a man as big as Artair," Gavin added.

"Alpin's a good warrior, and he's smart, but I doona think his heart's in it. Were you friends with him?" Callum asked. It would do Maggie good to focus on something other than their capture.

"Nay, I wouldnae say we were friends. He was always reserved, a private man. With everyone, not just me. I ne'er knew his daughter was sick." Maggie sighed. No doubt feeling sorry for Alpin, despite the fact that he was hunting them.

As if he'd been summoned by their talk, Alpin

appeared in front of the cottage. He walked forward several steps and then slowly turned in a circle—taking in the lay of the land, by the look of it. Pondering all the different routes Maggie might have taken.

When he stopped and stared at their hiding place in the caves, Maggie's hand clenched Callum's. He gently loosed her hold and tucked her into his side, his arm wrapping around her shoulders, hoping to ease the trembling of her body.

"He willna come up here, Maggie. The caves are well hidden. We didn't see them until you told us they were here, and we were looking at them during daylight. Trust me. He'll choose one of the trails. South, I'd wager."

"Maybe both," Gavin said.

Drustan squeezed up beside Maggie and patted her arm. "Which will leave us with a conundrum."

He stood a little closer to Maggie than Callum liked. He knew what it was about—everyone wanted to protect her. Still, it rankled, and he pulled her in front of him so she rested within his arms, back to his chest.

In the glade, Alpin returned to his horse, giving orders as he mounted. The men split, half the horses heading for the south trail, the others to the north.

"Hell's blood," Callum cursed under his breath.

"'Tis not so bad," Maggie said. "As I see it, we have the advantage. We know where they are going, but they doona know where we are. It couldnae be better."

When the last man disappeared into the forest and the glade was clear once more, Maggie smiled up at him. "Do you want to know what I'd do?" she asked.

He stared down at her, unable to see her face in the dark. It was not needed; he knew her gamine features by heart—her pert nose and small chin, thickly lashed hazel eyes, and a bowed mouth shaped for kissing. He caressed his hand down her cheek and imagined he could see every one of her freckles.

"Aye, tell me what you'd do," he said.

She raised her hand and pointed her finger up.

He looked at the ceiling of the cave—not that he could see much of it in the dark. "You'd die and go to heaven?"

"Nay!" she said, and he loved hearing the laughter in her voice. "Although that would certainly ruin Irvin's plans. We should take the horses and climb over the mountains rather than follow the trails around. 'Twould be a longer and more difficult journey, for sure, but we wouldnae have to face off against a host of men trying to kill us."

His gaze shifted to Gavin's, and even though he couldn't see his foster brother clearly, he knew he agreed with her. It made Callum's jaw clench.

"Maggie, do you have any idea how hard that journey will be for a lass? And 'tis late in the summer; we may even encounter snow. The cold, for certain. 'Tis not practical to think you could make it."

Maggie stiffened in his arms, and she took a step away. His heart sank, knowing he may have just made a grave mistake. But it's what he believed, and it had to be said. Maggie's safety was more important to him than her hurt feelings.

There was no laughter in her voice this time when she spoke. "Then I shall have to take extra plaids. You may do what you want, Callum MacLean, but I am going o'er the mountain."

❧

Maggie hunched down in her plaid, a cold wind blowing through the weave even though she'd wrapped an extra blanket from her bag around her shoulders. The sunrise hike up the mountain, by horse and then on foot, had been invigorating. She'd relished the climb, and it was a wonderful way to burn off her anger at Callum's dismissive remark. But by late afternoon, she was beginning to flag.

The first few hours weren't that hard. The trail progressed upward at a comfortable rise, and the vistas of the valley below were breathtaking. It would have been most pleasant except that Maggie was riding with Callum, and she refused to let herself lean against him, which was hard to do when they were going uphill. She still burned with indignation at what he'd said—as if she wouldn't be able to make the journey because she was a lass!

Idiot man.

So after a short break, she sat behind him instead. But then she kept sliding backward over the rump of the horse. She had to hold on tight to Callum from behind and squeeze her legs around him, causing her anger to mix with a burning desire.

Idiot lass.

But as the hours progressed and the trail became rockier, the horses began to labor, and she and everyone else had to continue on foot, the men pulling their horses behind them. Which was a huge relief… at first. Without Callum's body pressed close to share his warmth and his arms squeezing tight to hold her steady, she found herself getting colder and even more exhausted. It didn't help that the sky had clouded over and the wind had picked up the higher they went.

Or that Callum kept throwing her concerned glances.

None of them were as winded as she was—not even Drustan, and he had to be twice her age. He'd stayed by her side, leading his horse, and not once had she heard him puffing for air like she had. She ground her teeth and tried to catch her breath before speaking so she wouldn't give the men any more reason to think her incapable.

"I swear, Callum MacLean, if you look at me like that one more time, I'm going to pull out my dagger and fling it into your arse."

Gavin snorted behind her, and Callum threw her another look. But this one did not hold concern. "Are you sure you'd be able to, lass? Your fingers must be frozen. I doona know how you'd grip the knife."

"I wouldnae need that tight an aim. 'Tis a verra large target."

Everyone laughed this time, including Callum. "Aye, you canna seem to keep your eyes off my arse today, starting with my crawl through the cottage wall."

Heat flushed Maggie's cheeks as an image of Callum's naked arse—firm and well-shaped—filled her mind's eye. Her only saving grace was that she was probably already red from the wind and the climb, so no one would notice.

"I had no choice then, did I?" she said tartly. "You were waving it at me like a wee bairn on his birth day."

"That I was. And I wouldnae have minded if you'd spanked it."

Her brows shot up, shocked that he'd said that, but also warmed. Her blood rushed to all those sensitive spots she wanted him to touch, and they started to tingle. She sputtered, trying to think of something to say, but her mind had turned to mush.

Gavin laughed. "Didn't I tell you Callum was the best of us, lass? I doona think anyone can best him in this game of words. Well, maybe when we all have a go at him at once—but even then, he ends up slaying us with his wit."

"Believe me, Maggie will have no trouble slaying me."

"Aye," Gavin said. "You have the advantage of being a woman, lass."

"Nay, she has the advantage of being Maggie. My Maggie."

Maggie didn't want to melt at his words—especially as she was still mad at him—but the way he said it, *my Maggie*, made her want to lift her arms and beckon him over.

Instead, she kept her eyes forward and looked up at the mountain—and almost groaned out loud at the steeply inclined, rocky path. Not that it was an actual path, just the best route to take compared to all the others. Nay, their trail had dwindled away with the trees, the same time the wind had picked up.

"Do we even know where we're going?" she asked, coming to a complete halt. The men slowed down around her.

Callum pointed southwest to a high, rocky pass rising in the distance. "We'll cross over there. We should be able to ride the horses for a while tomorrow, but at this elevation, they're flagging too."

"We need to preserve their strength in case we have to sprint for any reason," Drustan said.

"Surely no one else would be mad enough to follow us through there?"

"Nay, we're the only ones addlepated enough to climb o'er the mountain," Callum said.

Gavin grunted and pushed past her. "'Twas our best choice at the time."

Maggie was tempted to grab on to Gavin's plaid and let him pull her up the incline. She snuck a glance at Callum and saw he had that same concerned look on his face as he watched her.

God's blood, she was tired. It no longer seemed to matter what the men thought of her. "Are we planning to reach the summit tonight then?" It irked her that she sounded whiny, even to her own ears.

"That will take several days," Callum said.

"Maybe even more at this pace," Finn chipped in, and Callum shot him a stern look.

"What do you mean, *at this pace?*" she asked. "Are you saying we're going slowly, Finnian MacKinnon?"

Finn's smile faded, and he looked uncertainly from Maggie to Callum, then back to Maggie. "Oh, well, I wouldnae say that exact—"

"Yes!" Gavin shouted from ahead of them. "You are the weakest of us in this, lass, and we're walking to your pace. And you canna get mad at me for saying that, because it's the truth."

"I doona think that will stop her," Gill said with a smile, which surprised her, because up until now, he'd barely spoken two words to her. "Our Maggie doesn't have a problem telling us how she feels."

Our Maggie? A minute ago, she was *my Maggie*. Had she been claimed by *all* these rough warriors?

"Aye," Artair said with a laugh. Then he handed his horse's reins to Drustan and grabbed one of Maggie's hands. Gill did the same and grabbed the other. Finnian pushed from behind, and her feet couldn't help but follow, even though she tried to tug free of their grasp at first. They started up the mountain with her in tow. "'Tis just the way it is, lass," Artair continued without even a hitch to his breath. "I am the biggest man here, and when we have to hide, I'm always afraid I'll give us away."

She scrunched up her face as she looked him over. Aye, he was huge, with a big, bushy beard. "The lairds said earlier that even they couldnae find you if you had to hide." She huffed heavily as she said it. She had no choice—they wouldn't let her stop or even slow down. Of course, it was a much easier hike when she shared her weight with someone else.

"Did they, now?" Artair's voice rang with pleasure, and Maggie was glad she'd told him. "Well…there are other times I'm a hindrance."

"A hindrance? Is that what you think I am?" she exclaimed, feeling mad and hurt all over again.

"You are *not* a hindrance, Maggie," Callum said from behind them. "And for the love of God, Finnian, get your hands off her arse or you willna live long enough to push her all the way up to the top of the mountain."

The hands that pushed on her backside, over several layers of thick blankets, quickly moved up to grasp her waist. They were not as helpful there, and Maggie felt the extra burn in her legs. She looked up, hoping they were near the top, but they were barely halfway. She would have cursed, but she couldn't afford to lose any more air.

She'd noticed before that Artair liked to talk, and he continued with his chatter. "I misspoke, lass. You are ne'er a hindrance. Nay, you are the reason we are here. Like I heard Laird MacLean say at the glade where we found you, *you are the precious jewel*. We are just the metal that surrounds the gem. Sometimes we're gold or silver, or wrought into intricate designs like Lairds MacKinnon and MacLean, I suppose, but our job is to keep you safe."

She glanced up at the huge warrior, trying to decide if he was trifling with her or not. "Such pretty words. Are you a poet, then, Artair?"

He looked at her, his brow furrowed in confusion, and she decided he was completely in earnest.

"Nay, I'm a warrior. Before that, I was a blacksmith. But I had to follow my heart and leave the smithy, aye? To do otherwise would make me dissatisfied with my life."

Now *that* she understood and could fully support. "I agree. Like a bird must fly, a woman—or man—must follow their heart's desire. Or they'll stay in the nest, unhappy, wishing for something else…until they fall out and break their bloody necks."

"'Tis you who are the poet, lass," Gavin said, turning around and dabbing at his eyes with his plaid, his mouth downturned and bottom lip quivering. "Your words almost brought a tear to me eye." Then he sniffed loudly for good measure, and Gill snorted in amusement.

She frowned at him, the ablach. If she'd had a free hand, she would have picked up a rock and thrown it at him. That'd give him something to cry about.

An object whizzed past her head and smacked Gavin in the middle of the forehead. He clapped his palm over the injury and swore loudly. "That hurt, you wee shite."

She looked over her shoulder at a smug-looking Callum, who said, "You should have ducked. Doona make fun of my betrothed, or I'll throw a bigger rock next time."

Gavin spun around, still swearing, and the men burst out laughing. Maggie was sure Gavin was plotting his revenge on Callum.

"So, back to my earlier point," Artair continued, and Maggie sighed silently inside, done with this conversation. "Because I'm bigger, 'tis natural I'll be the best at some things and not so good at others. When we sprint the horses, like we did after leaving your castle, my horse always tires first, and I fall behind. 'Tis not easy for the beast to carry such a heavy load. In that instance, I hindered our escape. But other times, my skills have been what saved us."

"'Tis true," Finnian added, sounding sincere, but she detected a hint of something else and waited for the jest to follow. "His arse *is* the biggest arse I've e'er seen. As big as the biggest sow at Aulay MacKinnon's farm."

"And I'll sit on you with it, ya wee ferret," Artair said as everyone laughed again, her included. "You'll ne'er take another breath."

"First you'd have to catch me, and by your own admission, you're as slow as cold honey."

Maggie gasped for air as she laughed—which wasn't a smart thing to do, as she was already winded from the climb. Poor Artair, he was so earnest in his attempt to explain things.

She supposed there was nothing she could do about slowing down the men. It wasn't like she could go any faster—as it was, she felt like she'd already run the whole way. She had no fear of heights or speed, and she knew she was strong and quick compared to most people. Just not *as* strong or *as* quick as the men traveling with her.

"I have ne'er seen anyone land as good a shot as you did with your crossbow the other night," Gill said quietly, almost reverently, after everyone calmed down and refocused on the rigors of the climb.

Heat bloomed in her chest at his regard and at the round of ayes that followed from the other men. At the admiration and respect they were showing her.

Well, maybe not Callum. She hadn't heard him agree. Did he not think she was good at anything? He always seemed to be yelling at her for something.

"Or ride such a distance across a pulley. Or fight off a pack of wolves," Finnian added eagerly. "How many were there?" he asked.

She closed her eyes and tried to block out the sights and sounds that had filled her mind and ears. They flooded back anyway. The wolves chasing her mount through the woods, the gentle breeze and sunshine on her skin in sharp contrast to her gut-wrenching terror. Their teeth snapping at her heels as she ran across the glade. The warm blood pouring over her hands as she made contact with powerful bodies, tearing through flesh and bones with her daggers. The smell of the animals—their musky coats, their hot breath making her gag.

Her desperate climb up the skinny tree that had barely held her weight, the sounds of their howls and snarls sending shivers up her spine even now.

She had to clear her throat before speaking. "Seven, I think."

Finnian's hands left her waist as another set cushioned her arse and took almost all her weight. She recognized Callum's hands immediately, his presence a steady force behind her. "One last push, lass, then we're at the top of this ridge, and we can rest for a bit," he said.

She nodded, even though he couldn't see her, glad for his support and suddenly feeling all done in. If she were on her own, she would have lain down on the rocks and stayed there for God knows how long.

Artair and Gill were breathing heavier now. The incline had increased and the land roughened. They took their time finding the right path and making sure their feet were steady on the sharp rocks.

She assumed Drustan was still behind them leading the horses. The only mount ahead of them was Gavin's stallion, which was just nearing the top.

"Does Drustan have the rest of the horses?" she panted.

"Aye," Callum said. "Finnian's gone back to help him lead them up this steep part." He gave her arse a squeeze through the blankets. "We're almost there, Maggie."

With one last heave, the men pushed and pulled

her to the top. She almost toppled over in fatigue and relief, but Callum steadied her as she caught her breath, her lungs heaving, her legs shaking.

"Callum," she wheezed softly.

"Aye, Maggie."

"If you let me go, I'll fall." She did not want the others to see her collapsed on the ground, a dirty, rumpled heap unable to even crawl away from the edge of the drop-off.

He pulled her in tight and put his lips to her ear. "I'll ne'er let go again, Maggie."

Eleven

CALLUM ADDED ANOTHER STICK TO THE LOW-BURNING fire and leaned against the rock overhang, the wind tugging at his hair and nipping at his skin. Maggie sat beside him, wrapped in her extra plaid, shivering. He'd tried to pull her close, to share his warmth and blanket with her, but she'd refused. She was still mad at him, obviously, despite asking him to hold her up when they'd first made it to the top of the ridge.

His belief that the journey across the mountain would be too difficult for her might have been unfounded. Aye, she was sore and tired, but she'd done far better than he'd expected. And even though she'd been exhausted upon cresting the ridge, she'd insisted they keep moving after a brief rest. They'd ridden the horses for another hour or so, mostly to give Maggie a break, but then the ground had become too rocky, and they'd had to dismount. By the time they found a suitable place to camp that offered some shelter from the wind and hid the light of the fire, the sun was already low in the sky.

Callum had checked behind them continuously

throughout the day for anyone who might have followed and hadn't seen a soul—but they stayed hidden just in case.

It looked more and more likely that they would escape the MacDonnells unscathed. As long as they could make it over the mountain without mishap.

"Maggie," Gill said quietly from across the fire.

Callum looked up at his marksman, who huddled deep in his blanket just like the rest of them. They'd finished eating, a fresh rabbit that Gill had shot with his arrow earlier in the day and some oats cooked with apple that Finnian had boiled—a task that always fell to the newest member of the group.

Maggie looked up and gave him a wan smile. "Aye?" She sounded drowsy, which caused warmth to spread through Callum's chest and down into his groin. He wanted to reach out and tuck her up tight beneath his chin. Instead, he rubbed a frustrated hand along his scruffy cheek and over the nape of his neck.

"How did you make the shot?" Gill continued. "You knew where the tree was, of course, even if you couldnae see it in the dark. But you only had one chance to land the bolt with the rope attached. It's a big tree, but the odds against hitting it securely were completely against you."

"I practiced," she said.

Gill's brow wrinkled at her answer, and Callum understood his confusion. If she'd practiced with the rope from the castle wall during the day, the guards would have seen her. On the other hand, if she'd practiced at night, how could she have seen the target to adjust her aim?

"But how did you do it without your cousin knowing?"

It was her turn to wrinkle her brow. "I ne'er practiced where he could see me. 'Twas in the forest to learn to compensate for the weight of the rope, or up on the turret with no one about."

"At night?"

"Nay. During the day. I had to be able to see my target in order to hit it when the time came."

Gill looked more perplexed than ever. "So you practiced using the bolt with the rope tied to it in the forest and then on the turret. Did you shoot at the tree with just the bolt?"

"I ne'er shot the bolt into the tree until last night."

Everyone's eyebrows shot up at that, including Callum's.

"But...but...that's impossible," Gill sputtered, sitting forward, forearms on his knees. His blanket fell to his elbows, forgotten.

"Apparently not. She made the shot," Gavin said dryly.

"Maggie, how did you practice in the turret if you ne'er shot the bolt?" Callum asked. "And how could that have helped you anyway, when it was almost full dark last night?"

She raised her arms in front of her as if she held the crossbow. "Shooting the bolt was the least of my concerns. I had to practice raising the bow and getting my position exactly right with my eyes closed. As you said, it would be dark, and I wouldnae be able to see a target. There was no point in practicing to shoot a bolt into a tree I probably wouldnae be able to see when the time finally came. I had to be able to *feel* my shot. So I would close my eyes." She closed her eyes, her hair blowing away from her face as a gust of wind puffed through the opening in the rocks. "Get into position." She raised her arms a little higher. "Then open my eyes and see if I was lined up properly." She opened them and looked into the distance over the fire. "My muscles and my mind had to learn the shot. Not my eyes. I had to remember the exact position of my feet, my body, my arms—every time. Not see it."

The men sat quietly, staring at her, eyes wide with wonder, and Callum could see she was suddenly self-conscious. Her cheeks flushed, and she raised her hand to push back her hair. "It really wasn't that hard."

Gavin scoffed, and Gill looked at her like she'd lost her mind. "I'm the best marksman in Clan MacLean—in any clan I know—and I couldnae have made that shot. I wouldnae have even tried."

"Well, that's your first problem right there. You're defeated before you even start. Aren't there things you do in the dark, using your hands, that you doona even think about? You just do by feel?"

Silence fell, then a swath of bright red filled Maggie's cheeks. "Other than that!" she yelled.

They all burst out laughing, and he suspected if they hadn't been sitting, they would have fallen to the ground. Finnian did flop over and actually rolled back and forth, his stomach heaving so hard, Callum could see the rise and fall of his belly through his blanket. Gill and Artair leaned heavily on each other as if their laughter had drained their strength, and Gavin had his head in his hands as his shoulders heaved, which pleased Callum to no end. Even six months ago, his foster brother wouldn't have cracked a smile—just a baring of his teeth when he felt it was necessary to make people feel more comfortable. It gave Callum hope that even if they didn't find Gavin's son, his foster brother would still be able to live a happy life.

Callum sighed contentedly, warmed from the inside out. His heart was full as he watched Maggie, who was looking down into her empty bowl, still flushed but with a small grin on her face.

Movement caught his attention, and he looked over to see Drustan shed his blanket and rise from his seat. It struck Callum that his second-in-command looked about as grim as he'd ever seen him. His mouth flat, jaw clenched, his eyes hard and bright.

Callum rose too, alarm ringing though him. He strode to Drustan's side, his eyes scanning the darkness surrounding them. "Is everything all right?"

The others fell silent, feeling the change in the air.

Drustan took a moment to answer, moving to his mount's head and adjusting the bridle. When he finished, he rubbed his hand over his stomach. "Aye, 'tis naught to worry you. I have a wee pain in my belly, that's all."

He smiled at Callum, but it was the same false smile Gavin had given his foster brothers for so long after Ewan had disappeared, and a chill ran up Callum's spine.

"Are you sure, Drustan? If something's troubling you, you must tell me."

"'Twill pass by the morning. I'll go for a walk and feel better after that." He squeezed Callum's shoulder—hard—then walked out into the dark.

Callum looked after him, then turned to the fire and met Gavin's gaze.

"We can follow him, if you want," Gavin said. "But if his gut's bothering him, he'll not want to be disturbed."

"Agreed. Let's give him some privacy. Who's on watch first?"

Artair rose with his weapons and his blanket. "I am. I'll keep an eye out for him."

"Good. Let me know if he hasn't returned within an hour or so, and I'll go look for him."

"Nay, let me know, and I'll go look," Gavin said. "Maggie will freeze otherwise." He nodded at Maggie, who leaned against the rock overhang with her eyes closed.

Suddenly, her eyes popped open. "I'm awake!"

"Of course you are," Callum said as he crossed to her side of the fire. It would have been easier to just lie next to Maggie once she was asleep, like he had last night, but she was determined to be just as strong as the men, which wasn't possible. They'd trained most of their lives for circumstances like these.

He placed another stick on the flames, then moved his bedroll and extra blanket toward her. She frowned at him, but he could see that her lips were blue from cold, her fingers stiff as she held the blanket. He gave her a direct, no-nonsense stare to match her frown and kept moving until his roll was right beside hers.

She was probably tired enough to sleep despite being cold—fitfully, at least. But it was his job to take care of her, to see to her needs, and it was a task at which he'd failed for too long. As long as he was by her side, she would never be cold again.

"We'll all be sharing heat, lass," he said, nodding to Finnian and Gill who were also moving their bedrolls closer together. "To do otherwise would be foolish and dangerous. Which means you and I will lie together side by side—like we did last night, and the night in the glade. If you hope one of the others will share with you, think again. They willna sleep beside my bride-to-be."

She opened her mouth to protest, but he lifted his hand, saying, "And before you say we're not betrothed, know that in their eyes, and in mine, we are—whether you accept it or not. You promised me time to woo you," he added.

She sat up on her bedroll and crossed her arms over her chest, her mouth set mulishly. He placed his pack at the top of the roll to use as a pillow, then spread his extra blanket over both their sides and slipped underneath.

"Come here, Maggie. Please. Let me warm you."

He'd made sure she had the side closest to the fire, and eventually, she lay down and faced the flames, allowing Callum to warm her back. He wrapped his arm around her waist and pulled her in tight, but she stayed stiff in his embrace, the occasional shiver wracking her frame.

"I'd wager Gill isna holding Finnian this close," she said tartly, loud enough so only Callum could hear.

He laughed. "Maybe not. Although Finnian *is* a bonnie lad."

She huffed out a short laugh, as if it had been surprised out of her, then fell silent. Eventually, she relaxed a bit in his hold. He was just beginning to wonder if she'd fallen asleep when she said, "I suppose this is one more way that I've failed to live up to the lads. None seemed as cold or as tired as me."

He pushed himself onto his elbow and looked down at her. When she refused to meet his gaze, he nudged her onto her back. Finally, their eyes clashed. Hers flashed up at him defiantly.

Callum formulated his words with care, knowing he was at fault here—that he'd driven her to doubt herself. "Maggie, they are brawny men. You are a wee woman and not as used to grueling travel."

"I'm. Not. Wee."

He resisted looking down to see if she'd grasped her daggers in her fists and was ready to lodge a sharp point beneath his chin again. "You are compared to me and the other men. You doona have my strength or stamina—and you know it. Even Finnian, who is the smallest of us, is stronger and faster. To pretend otherwise would be addlepated. Just as it would be addlepated to believe that Finnian, Artair, or even Drustan could beat you when it came to your accuracy with arrows and daggers."

She sniffed. "I could beat all of you."

"Possibly," he said, grinning at her conceit. "I have no doubt that none of us could have made the shot into the tree like you did."

She looked a little mollified, and he pressed his advantage. "And I honestly ne'er thought we would travel as far as we did today. I didn't think we'd reach the first ridge. Would we have gone farther if you hadn't been with us? Aye. But not by nearly as much as I expected. I apologize for doubting your strength, your stamina, your determination to forge ahead. I have great admiration for your abilities."

Her eyes softened at his words—her body too. He

was hard-pressed not to lean down and steal a kiss, wanting her lips to open beneath his, to invite him in.

"Thank you," she said finally, and he could tell she meant it. "I may be slower tomorrow, and the next day too, but then I'll wake up even stronger. We'll be o'er this mountain in no time."

"Aye, we will. And then we'll be in MacLean territory and safe."

"And you willna have to worry about me anymore."

He smoothed his fingers over his top lip and lay down on his back.

"What?" she asked, sounding suspicious as *she* came up on *her* elbow this time and looked down at him.

He took another moment to craft his words, not wanting to run afoul of her again. He had to say this just right.

"Are you going to do that every time we talk?" she asked suddenly, frowning at him.

"Do what?"

"Think of the exact, perfect way to phrase something. 'Tis most annoying."

It was his turn to frown. "Well, I didn't do it this morning, and you ended up being mad at me all day."

"I'm not mad now, so just spit it out."

"Verra well. Just because we'll reach Clan MacLean doesn't mean I'll stop being concerned about you. 'Tis because I care, not because I think you're incapable. Nay, you've proven yourself more than capable in every respect, but...it's in my nature."

"You doona worry about Gavin or the others."

"I've done naught but worry about Gavin since his son disappeared—before that even, when he was so miserable in his marriage. And I worry that Finnian will make a mistake because of his youth and it will be my fault for allowing him to come with us, and that Artair will indeed slow us down because of his size, and he or someone else will get hurt because of it. I plan things and fix things and keep everyone safe and happy. I worry. 'Tis my job as laird."

"I thought Finnian and Artair were Gavin's men?"

"In all other respects, they are, but I approved them coming with us. Gavin felt they both had skills that would add to our group. And they do."

"Well, what about my skills? 'Twas me who helped us escape from Alpin and the other MacDonnells." She glared down at him indignantly.

He grasped her hand, then brought it to his mouth and kissed her palm. "Aye," he said soothingly. "And I shouldnae have doubted your skills. I'm sorry. Your foresight in planning your own escape, which aided ours, was astounding. Not to mention everything else you've done to escape Irvin and stay alive. But..."

"But what?"

"I canna lie to you, Maggie. My need to protect you is different than it is with the others. If we're in danger, I will always look to defend you first, no matter how good you are with your daggers. Maybe 'tis a failing, but I doona know how to change it. You are a woman—a skilled one—meant to be my wife, and I *want* to protect you."

Maggie flopped down on her back beside him and huffed. She sounded frustrated, and he clenched his jaw, knowing she would object. How could he possibly woo her if they were always at odds?

"All right," she said.

"All right?"

"You can worry about me and help me more than the others, and I willna take offense. And some days, *I* will take care of *you*. 'Tis a woman's right to take care of…a man too. In whatever way she sees fit. Whether it's with a dagger or in some other way."

He rose quickly onto his elbow. She looked straight past him up at the dark sky before flicking her eyes to him and away. He couldn't see her blush in the darkness, but he could feel the way her skin had heated. Had she been about to say *her man*? *'Tis a woman's right to take care of* her *man*? And what exactly did "some other way" mean?

A slow smile spread across his face. "With a kiss, perhaps?"

She huffed and rolled over on her side to face the fire. "You have to beat me at daggers first, and I doona see *that* happening any day soon."

He spooned his body around hers, excitement pulsing through him with every pound of his heart. "Is that a challenge, Maggie MacDonnell? You've thrown down the gauntlet, and you're waiting for me to pick it up?"

She scoffed. "What are you going on about?"

"A contest. You said I could woo you. Well, let me woo you with my skill at archery and tossing a dagger. We'll compete. Whoever wins gets a kiss."

She laughed, that short, sharp puff of air he'd heard before, and he knew she did it despite herself. "So you get a kiss no matter who wins?"

"Nay, *you* get a kiss no matter who wins. And I

shall give it to you with resigned acquiescence. But a kiss only, no more. No matter how much you press me to continue."

"I see," she said, sounding amused. "And is this why your foster brothers revere your sharp, analytical mind? For coming up with plans that are fail proof?"

"'Tis part of it, aye. And for finding solutions that benefit everyone—like mutually beneficial kisses. But 'twas not me who thought of it. *You* challenged *me*." By God, he loved pitting his wit against hers. She was the one with the sharp mind and the skill to back it up.

"You're an addlepated man for expecting a kiss so easily."

"Then how about this. We doona compete for kisses; those can come at any time. Like this…" He pressed his lips into the soft, exposed skin at the crook of her neck, and she shivered, gasping for breath. He was tempted to go on, but he didn't want her to refuse to sleep next to him because he couldn't keep his hands to himself. He lifted his head. "We compete for something else, something we each want. If you win, you can go to Edinburgh when it's safe to find John, and I willna protest. If I win, you will stay with me. Marry me."

"I'll go to see John whether you want me to or not, and I'll go when *I* deem it's safe."

"Aye, but the wager is that I willna fight you on your decision. Isn't that worth something? If you believe in your skills as you say you do, it's not a risk. Unless you're afraid that—"

She made a scoffing sound, and he could just imagine how she must have rolled her eyes. He couldn't hold back his grin. He knew when a negotiation was going in his favor, and he almost had this one tied up.

"You canna sway me so easily, Callum. For such a good negotiator, you're verra transparent."

"Isn't that what you wanted? No trickery. You didn't like it before when I tried to choose my words carefully, so here it is. I believe I can beat you. I'll win the wager, and you'll marry me. If you believe in your skills the same way I believe in mine, accept the wager and defeat me."

She didn't answer at first. When she did, her voice was soft. "And if we tie?"

"Then we compete again the next day, and the next." He held his breath, knowing this was it. She would agree.

"Doona expect to beat me, Callum. We will compete, just you and I, until we reach your castle. If no one has won by then, the wager is ended."

Twelve

MAGGIE TOOK A DEEP BREATH, HER FEET FIRMLY grounded on the rock, her every sense tracing the pattern of the wind. She raised her bow in one fluid motion and loosed her arrow. It flew straight and sure, and she did not need to wait to know that it hit her target dead center.

The men—*all* of them on Callum's side in their wager—muttered behind her, exclaiming over the accuracy and grace of her shot, shaking their heads at the near impossibility of matching it.

Except for Callum. He stood still…and silent.

Gill moved closer to Callum and plucked a long, black strand of hair from his head. He held it up and let it drift in the wind. "It's blowing southwest," he said, "but the current is temperamental at the tail end. Can you feel how it kicks back in the other direction just before it's done? Wait till you feel it shift, then loose your arrow immediately before the next wind hits."

Gavin stood close on Callum's other side. "And you doona need to pull the string quite so tight. The air is thinner here, and the arrow will go faster, aye?"

"Aye," the other men replied, nodding.

"But won't he have to go in hard so his shaft spears hers down the middle?" Finnian asked. The men snickered at his comment, sounding like a group of village lads standing outside the schoolhouse doors, causing her to roll her eyes.

She saw Callum's mouth open as if to say something—either to reprimand them for laughing or to add to Finnian's unintended jest—but she spoke before he did. She would use the opportunity to shake his concentration if she could.

"I wager he'll come up short and miss the mark entirely," she said. "He's feeling the pressure and will release too soon."

Silence reigned, then the men burst out laughing—all except Callum. He was still quiet and hadn't moved.

She wondered what was going on in his head. Did he know he could make the shot and was just drawing out the tension to make it more dramatic, or was he still running over all the options in his mind?

The latter, most likely. Callum was nothing if not thorough. She remembered that from his kisses three years ago—she'd felt consumed by them. When the kiss would end, her entire body would feel enlivened yet limp at the same time, the same way she felt in the tree the night she'd escaped, the night he'd kissed her, touched her. She couldn't imagine what it would feel like to make love with him.

Completely immersed in pleasure.

She shivered just thinking about it and forced her mind back to the present just in time to see Callum pulling his string back on his bow, his arrow notched.

For a second, he aimed too high, and a burst of panic exploded in her chest before he readjusted and released. The arrow shot straight and true, harder than hers had, and landed right on top of her fletching. It split her arrow in two.

The men cheered, and Callum looked over his shoulder at her. He crooked his finger, and she stepped forward until his lips touched her ear. "Doona worry, lass. I ne'er release too early, and my shaft always flies hard and true." Then he kissed her lips, softly, lightly, and walked away.

She touched her fingers to her mouth, staring after him for a moment. Her eyes fixed on the sway of the plaid that hung off his well-shaped arse and the drape of his shirt outlining his muscular shoulders and long, strong back.

With a silent sigh, she turned to find the others gathered together, watching her like a bunch of gossiping old men, sappy looks on their faces. Even Gavin, who certainly had no reason to believe in love and marriage. Yet there he was, grinning from ear to ear. A real smile too, not tinged with bitterness.

"You're definitely the better archer, lass. You feel the shot in a way Callum does not. But I think my brother is more motivated to win this game than you. He wants to marry you more than you want to leave him."

She *tched* dismissively and looped her bow over her shoulder. "You're all daft as a cloud of bats. God's truth, I doona know what you're talking about."

She and Callum hadn't been as quiet as they thought last night, and Finnian's sharp ears had heard everything—well, the wager part of it, anyway—and reported it to the rest of the men this morning.

She'd been met with smiles upon waking, and Callum had been met with much backslapping and well-meant advice.

Maggie didn't object. Oddly enough, she found it rather funny—and somewhat endearing. Every one of them wanted to see her married to Callum, not because of alliances or old contracts but because they liked her. They'd claimed her as their own—*our Maggie*, they called her—and found her a worthy match for their laird and ally.

It was actually quite sweet, even though Maggie still had no intention of becoming a MacLean. And unless her shots were disrupted by an act of God, there was no way she could lose.

Unless I want to.

The thought sent a shiver through her belly and continued down her inner thighs. She squeezed them together to stop the sensation, barely restraining a gasp. Luckily, the men had moved on, and no one noticed the heat that filled her cheeks.

Except when she glanced up, she saw Drustan standing to the side away from the group, watching her intently. Taken aback and embarrassed, even though she'd done nothing, she quickly stepped backward.

He walked toward her, reminding her of her father with his trimmed gray beard and the swath of gray at his temples. He smiled a little sadly, which also reminded her of her father—after her mother had died.

"Laird MacKinnon is right, lass," he said softly. "You are the better marksman. Markswoman, I should say.

You can beat Laird MacLean and win your freedom, if that's what you want. On the other hand, Callum's a decent man and laird. Better than his rascal father, for sure, and would make a good husband despite his treatment of you in the past. But doona let them pressure you. Be certain and stay true to what you want. Marriage isna the right choice for everyone."

Then he raised his hand and squeezed her shoulder. He held on for a bit too long, staring at her, before he nodded and let go. Slowly, he walked back to the group.

Maggie stared after him, feeling confused. It's not that he had said anything wrong. Nay, his words were touching and lovely, with a message she should ponder. Rather, it was the overwhelming feeling of sadness and loss that had emanated from Drustan as he'd spoken to her that made her want to sit and cry. Had he intended to do that? Known how his words would affect her? Or had he just revealed more about his true state than he realized? He'd been sick last night, and she suddenly wondered if there was more to his illness than met the eye.

"Drustan," she called out and took several steps before stopping about six feet away from him. Her heart raced for some reason, and her stomach had tied in knots.

He turned, his shoulders stiff and neck rigid. He smiled, but this time it didn't reach his eyes, and she found herself taking another step backward.

"Lass?" he asked.

"I... I... Are you feeling better today?"

"Feeling better?"

"From last night. You said your guts hurt. Verily, I

did pray for you that your ailment would be resolved by morning."

He raised a hand and almost appeared to be tracing the contours of her face in the air. "What ails me canna be fixed, lass, but I appreciate your prayers and concern. Thank you. I'll remember your kindness always."

He left, and she blew out a puff of air, feeling on edge and out of sorts. She turned away from the small copse of trees that hid their camp and stared out at the forest below. They'd reached the end of the ridge about midday and started the descent into the next valley. At first, she'd been relieved to be going downhill, but soon her thighs ached, and every step down was torture. When Callum stopped her without a word and lifted her onto Aristotle, she didn't protest. Nay, she'd been grateful for the reprieve. When he'd climbed up behind her on the horse as soon as the path was safe enough and ordered the others to do the same, she'd leaned her body against him and let him hold her up.

Pain and fatigue had beaten the fight right out of her.

Until they'd made camp and Callum had selected a target for them to hit—then her spirit had returned. Aye, she did not like to lose.

Now the sight of her arrow pierced by Callum's drew her, and she headed toward it. It hadn't been an easy shot—especially in this wind—but she'd had no doubt she would make it. And she'd wanted to, no matter what Gavin had said to her afterward. But then… She remembered her panic when Callum had first raised his bow and aimed too high.

Surely I didn't want him to win?

Nay, but she also hadn't wanted him to lose just yet. She was looking forward to their wager, to the excitement of pitting their skills against each other. That's *all* it was.

Upon reaching the target, she tied up her skirts and climbed the tree to reach the arrows, embedded deeply in the trunk about ten feet up. Hers had been split in two by Callum's arrow, just as Finnian had said. She pulled Callum's out and ran her fingers over the smooth shaft and soft feathers at the end, remembering what else Finnian had said. About Callum impaling her.

Not only was she thinking about it, but she'd dreamed about it last night too. And in the dream, Callum had been doing exactly that—tupping her hard, his body heavy on top of hers, splitting her legs, which she'd wrapped around him.

She'd woken with a start just as the sky had begun to lighten, snug beneath their blankets with Callum holding her tight from behind, his arm wrapped around her waist and his warm breath puffing evenly in her hair. She'd lain there for what seemed like hours, wanting him to move his hand between her legs, to stroke her slick mound like he'd almost done before, to squeeze his palm over her center and relieve some of her ache.

Aye, she wanted to be tupped by him. Hard.

"What are you thinking about up there, Maggie MacDonnell, that has your face flushed and your eyes glowing softly like the morning dew?"

Startled, Maggie tumbled off the branch right into Callum's arms. He grinned at her. "Miss me already, do you?"

She knew her face was flaming, could feel the heat burning her skin. She frowned at him fiercely, hoping he'd think her embarrassment stemmed from anger. But he looked down and saw the arrows that she'd pulled from the tree, now lying on the grass.

He kept her body flush to his as he lowered her to the ground. "Were you thinking about the arrow, Maggie? About me?"

"I was thinking that you made a lucky shot, and next time I'll let you go first, so you doona rely on me to show you how it's done."

He laughed softly, a puff of air that warmed her cheek. "I can show you how it's done." He dropped his head into the crook of her neck and kissed her, mouth open and hot, his tongue scorching her skin. Her knees softened, and her hands gripped his plaid.

After a moment, he said, "Would you like that, Maggie? Would you like me to show you how it's done?"

God's truth, she would. But instead of reaching for his cock like she wanted to—finding herself more and more curious every day to see it, to shape it with her hand, to feel it pushing inside her body and finally assuaging the ache between her legs—she pressed both palms against his chest.

He released her immediately with a soft chuckle. Capturing her hand, he kissed her palm and tugged her into step beside him, heading to the camp. Her skirts loosened from where she'd tied them up and fell into place around her ankles.

"You shouldnae be this far away from us on your own, lass, even if we can still see you." He laced their fingers together. "I doona think we've been followed by the MacDonnells, but 'tis possible we might run into another party. We could be ambushed at any moment. Or a wild animal could attack. I've seen several men injured by wild boar, and you know how dangerous a wolf can be. You may not survive an assault twice."

Part of her wanted to roll her eyes. She didn't like being told what to do. Unless, perhaps…it was while she was intimate with Callum. Then she might like receiving his direction.

She stopped suddenly as her body flooded with need. Aye, she wanted him to instruct her in lovemaking. Wanted to pleasure him too.

"Maggie?"

She raised her eyes to his. "You talk about mutual consent and carnal knowledge leading to marriage between us, but…what if…"

He stepped closer, his gaze growing hooded and the color in his skin heightening along his cheekbones and the tops of his ears. He stroked the backs of his fingers down her face. "What if…what?"

"What if…there didn't have to be marriage? What if we had carnal knowledge of each other—with mutual consent—but we didn't marry? We…pleasure each other. I allow you into my body, but nothing afterward. We walk away."

Callum stilled, and his eyes narrowed. She saw desire and lust raging there but also anger and hurt.

Oh dear God, I've hurt him.

Callum MacLean, who could choose any lass in the Highlands, wanted to be with her, married to her, and she'd just relegated him to the role of stud.

"Here then. On the ground," he said, his voice clipped. "It'll be dark soon. The men willna be able to see us." He looked up, then grabbed her hand and dragged her to the nearest tree, pushing her against it. "Or maybe here against the trunk. I'll lift your skirts, and the bark can scratch your arse as we tup." He spun her around. "Or this way. You willna even have to look at my face and *see* me. So much easier to just walk away!"

"Callum, stop," she whispered, her voice breaking, tears filling her eyes and rolling down her cheeks.

He turned her to face him, his face a mask of anger now. "Why, we're just getting started. I doona even have to swive you." He suddenly pushed on her shoulders, and she dropped to her knees on the ground with a sob, her heart broken, all of her broken— because she'd *hurt* him. "You can go on your knees and suck my cock into your mouth. That way, we'll ne'er worry about you conceiving a bairn, and I'll be pleasured without consequence. Then I'll do the same to you, all without you having to take me as your husband." He dropped on his haunches in front of her so they were eye to eye, and she could see how her words, her rejection, had ravaged him. "Or have you done that before, lass? Did I leave you alone for too long, and you found someone else to pleasure you? Are you still a maid, Maggie MacDonnell? Or did you leave a lover at your castle?"

"Aye, Callum, I'm a maid, and I have ne'er had a lover other than you. But it goes both ways, doesn't it? Are you also a virgin? Or have you lain with other women and done the things to them of which you speak to me?" She knew he'd had carnal relations with other women, and she'd felt the pain of it. She had for many years, especially when he never returned for her. She'd half convinced herself it was because he loved someone else.

He hesitated, and a look of regret crossed his face. "Nay, Maggie. I am not a virgin. I had my first woman when I was sixteen and you were nine. The same summer we were betrothed. My bedding came before our contract, but it would not have mattered. I didn't have the maturity to realize I might someday be hurting you with my actions. But I've had *none* in the last four years. None since *you* turned sixteen and you suddenly became real to me. You weren't just a lass who would grow up one day in the future, but a woman who was to be *my wife*."

He rose and walked a few feet away, his back to her, held stiffly. Maggie also rose and leaned against the tree, rubbing the tears from her face as she tried to regulate her breathing.

He half turned to her so she saw his profile—jaw clenched tight and his mouth set in a grim, hard line. "I'm sorry I frightened you. I shouldnae have been so rough under any circumstances, no matter the provocation."

"I'm sorry too," she said, voice raw. "'Twas not my intent to hurt you. I just…"

"You just doona want to marry me." He said it with a finality that shook her, and that same burst of panic she'd felt earlier exploded in her chest.

"I…I…I doona know what I want. Other than—"

"Other than carnal knowledge." He clenched his hands into fists by his sides. "And will anyone do for that, or is it just me you want?"

She pressed her fingers to her mouth to stop them trembling. "Just you," she whispered.

His fists unclenched, and his shoulders dropped as he released his breath. "Well, that's good to know."

She didn't answer. There was nothing left to say, nothing more she could do to make things right between them.

He turned to her finally, and she couldn't stop her gaze from running over his face, from drinking him in. "I suppose I should be grateful, even pleased that you want to make use of me. But know this, Maggie. If you e'er lie with me, I will consider us married." He pointed to himself. "Husband." And then to her. "Wife. There will be no reneging on our commitment, no deciding to carry on to Edinburgh by yourself. Our intent to join in matrimony will be sealed when my body enters yours, when my seed releases into your womb and we possibly bring new life into this world. I willna accept otherwise."

He turned away and started walking toward their camp. "Come. I've set out our bedrolls, and Finnian has finished with our meal. 'Twill be another hard day tomorrow."

She fell in slightly behind him. She had a lead ball in her stomach and a band around her chest that tightened with each step that he failed to take her hand like he had before. She sorely missed the way he'd linked their fingers and kissed her knuckles, the easy way he'd teased her.

Her chin dropped in misery, and her head ached with all the confused thoughts running through it. She was sick inside that she'd hurt him and wished she'd never opened her mouth, but she was scared too. Frightened that things might never be the same between them. That he might just walk away...

...or let me walk away.

She stopped abruptly at the thought. They were on the edge of the camp now, and Callum didn't wait for her, although she knew he had to be aware he'd left her behind. That hurt too, and she thought about returning to the forest to nurse her wounded heart, but she wouldn't get ten paces before someone came after her. Not that she was a prisoner, but she was under their protection, and they would never let anything happen to her, not if they could help it. And that meant keeping her close.

So she sucked in a deep breath, lifted her chin, straightened her shoulders, and crossed through the camp to her bedroll next to Callum's.

When she sat down, she picked up the bowl of oats and berries with some dried meat on the side that waited for her. Keeping her gaze lowered, she let her hair fall forward as she ate her meal, so no one would catch her eye or engage her in conversation.

The men were a little subdued, especially after the way they'd laughed with her earlier and slapped Callum's back. They sensed the tension between her and Callum, most likely. And how could they not? It was obvious something had gone wrong between them from the way they sat stiffly beside each other and barely said a word.

When she was done, she washed up her dishes in a stream that meandered through the trees not far away, and Finnian helped her hang some blankets so she could undress and clean away the sweat and dirt from the last two days.

Feeling somewhat better, she returned to camp in the dark, Finnian by her side, and found many of the men, including Callum, already lying on their bedrolls. He'd doubled up their blankets and spread them over both soft pallets, then lay down on his side, facing away from her, his eyes closed.

It was the first time he'd ever done that, and a lump formed in her throat as she stared down at him. She knew he wasn't asleep. Like her, he probably wouldn't sleep for many hours, and it tore at her. She carefully crawled under the blankets and faced the fire. It wasn't cold tonight like last night. They were lower in the valley and protected from the wind, so she didn't need his warmth.

But I want it.

Why couldn't she hold him? Comfort him and weave them back together? Last night, she'd turned away from him, and he'd made it all better between them. Maybe…maybe this was her turn to do the same.

Feeling awkward suddenly, even though she had yet to do anything, she peered around the camp in the firelight. Everyone was quiet, wrapped up in their blankets with their eyes closed. They wouldn't notice or care if she turned to Callum and spooned him in the same way he'd slept with her last night.

And it occurred to her as she looked at the other men, that no one, other than her and Callum, were lying together tonight for warmth like they had last night.

Which meant Callum may have turned away from her, but he hadn't separated completely.

She rolled to her back and let her hand rest in the spot between them, her little finger just grazing his plaid-covered arse. Holding her breath, she waited, hoping he'd roll over, too, and take her hand in his, like he so often did. When he didn't move, disappointment flooded through her. Disappointment that quickly turned to frustration and anger at her own hesitancy.

I can ride a pulley from the castle wall, but I canna wrap my arm around my...my...around Callum?

Scowling fiercely, she rolled to her other side and pressed her body against his, wrapping her arm around his waist.

"Callum," she whispered, her lips pressed close to his ear. She did not want any of the other men hearing what passed between them this time.

He took a moment to answer. "Aye."

"I'm sorry," she blurted out. "It wasn't my intent to hurt you."

Another pause, then the stiffness in his body released, and he sighed. "I know." He clasped her hand and pulled it around his body, holding it in front of his chest. "I want you too, Maggie, in that way, but I also want more than that. It worries me you still intend to leave. I'm a planner, a strategist, and methodical in my thinking. But with you, I find myself impatient. I think I was so angry, not only because you would offer yourself and then in the same breath say you would leave me, but..."

"But what?" she prompted when he failed to finish.

"But because I wanted to accept."

Her hand clenched his as a wave of heat burned through her, and he pulled her even closer. "If you offer again, Maggie, by words or by deed, I will accept. But I willna allow you to leave me afterward."

"Is that so?"

"Aye."

"And how would you keep me with you?" she asked, her heart pounding with excitement despite her cool tone.

He brought her fingers to his lips and kissed her knuckles, then gently bit one before answering. "I think you've asked the wrong question, dearling. The question you should ask is how would you get rid of me?"

Thirteen

CALLUM CLIMBED UP THE MOUNTAIN, LEADING Aristotle by the reins, while Gavin climbed by his side with his own horse. They were at a high enough elevation that the trees were sparse and spindly, and the wind had picked up, cooling his skin despite the warmth of the midafternoon sun.

They'd dropped behind to talk further about the parchments Maggie had given him, discussing any new ideas or remembrances either had had—which didn't amount to much. It was frustrating, but he suspected they wouldn't glean much more insight until all five of the foster brothers and Gregor were together.

Maggie walked ahead of them, surrounded by Finnian, Gill, and Artair and their horses, with Drustan in the lead.

It wasn't a difficult climb for the men, especially at their slower pace, but he knew Maggie struggled. It would only get harder from here on out as they left the path behind and began climbing over boulders and along narrow ledges. He wanted to make it as far as a series of caves he knew of before darkness fell.

Otherwise, they would spend a very cold, dangerous night out in the open.

Which meant Maggie was going to have to accept their help.

"I canna believe you're going to make me ask," Gavin said, making an exasperated sound in the back of his throat.

Callum faced him, his brows raised. "What in bloody hell are you talking about?"

Gavin nodded in Maggie's direction. Callum looked ahead, trying to figure out what he meant.

"Last night?" his foster brother prompted.

Understanding hit, and Callum made the same sound Gavin had seconds ago. "Och, you're naught but an old meddler."

"Well, 'twas obvious something was said last night that disturbed you both. The lads were grumbling this morning that you made *our lass* cry."

"And why am I the villain in this? Couldnae it have been Maggie who said something terrible?"

"Aye, that's what I told them, but they'd have none of it. So, what horrible thing did she say?"

Gavin looked a little too eager for Callum's liking, and suddenly, he wished he'd never started down this conversational path. He flattened his mouth, lips closed tight, and gave Gavin a stern look.

Gavin shrugged. "All right. 'Twill be more fun asking Maggie than you anyway."

"Doona you dare," Callum ordered, rounding on his foster brother, who stopped too and gave him a cocky grin. Callum considered knocking it off. A rousing fight with Gavin would be just what he needed to get rid of his pent-up frustration over Maggie. As much as he enjoyed sleeping close to her every night, the daily denial of his needs was proving more difficult than he'd anticipated.

Gavin crossed his arms over his chest and waited. When Callum didn't respond, he said, "Have you considered that I may be a good source of advice for you? I was married for almost four years, and even though 'twas a bad union, I learned a lot about women."

Callum scratched his hand over his beard. Maybe it *would* help to talk to Gavin, if nothing else than to get Maggie's hurtful remarks off his chest. "Verra well. But this stays between us and no one else. Not even Kerr, Lachlan, Darach, or Gregor."

Gavin nodded, and that eager look returned to his face.

"Maggie…Maggie…" Callum started, trying to find the words and realizing that Gavin may not be sympathetic to his plight. He tried again. "She…she…"

Gavin waited and waited, then threw up his hands and rolled his eyes. "Is that some sort of rhyme for the bairns?" He put a little sway in his hips. "*Maggie Maggie she she. Maggie Maggie she she.*"

Callum kicked out his foot and toppled the big, blond man onto his arse. Gavin burst into laughter. Callum grabbed the reins Gavin had loosed—not that he expected the stallion to bolt—and glowered down at his foster brother.

When it didn't look like Gavin was going to get up, Callum sat down heavily beside him. "Maggie suggested—asked—if we could be intimate without having to marry. She wants my body, but not my ring."

There. I've said it.

"She wants to tup you and not marry you?" Gavin asked incredulously.

"Aye." He cringed inside, waiting for his foster brother's response.

"You fortunate bastard!"

"Nay, not fortunate. I doona want Maggie for just one or two nights, or even weeks. I want her forever."

"Well, just do what Cristel did to me and refuse to tup her until she marries you. Tell her you willna lift your plaid for her until she puts her ring on *your* finger." He burst out laughing again and fell backward onto the rock, unable to muster the strength to even sit up.

"You said you would be helpful. Give me some advice."

"I just did. 'Tis what mothers have been telling their daughters for thousands of years." He shook his head. "Leave it to our Maggie to get it backward."

"She's not *your* Maggie. Or Finn's or Artair's or Gill's or Drustan's. She's *my* Maggie, and I doona intend to let her just walk away." He stood, tossed Gavin his stallion's reins, and strode up the mountain, the others a fair distance ahead now.

Gavin scrambled behind him to catch up. "Callum, wait. You're looking at this the wrong way. She's a woman."

"Aye. Thank you for that astounding insight."

"You know what I mean. Most of them have soft hearts. And that says a lot coming from me, considering the nightmare my marriage turned out to be. Maggie may pretend to be hard, but she's not. Aye, she can throw a mean dagger and hold her own among all us scoundrels, but she still wants to love and be loved like anyone. If Maggie desires intimacy with you, use that to bind her to you. Most women canna separate love and lust the way men can. She's just confused. Her heart hasn't caught up to her body yet. Or maybe I should say, her body knows what her heart and mind want before they do."

Callum grunted. Maybe Gavin had a point. "Aye. But…it's too late for that. I've already told her if she asks me again, I will consent, and in doing so, we will be married."

"Is that what made her cry? That she couldnae tup you without tying herself to you—a lack-witted ablach—for life?"

He stopped, knowing Gavin expected either a jest or a physical blow, but Callum felt shame worm itself into his heart. "Nay, I was…harsh with her. It hurt and shook me that she would crave my touch— enough to ask me for it—yet still mean to walk away."

Gavin stopped grinning and squeezed his shoulder. "But she forgave you, aye? She slept with you afterward and held you last night. I saw that."

Aye, she did.

Callum's heart lifted, and he smiled as he looked up the mountain at Maggie, who had slowed considerably since he'd last checked. "That she did." He let out a sharp whistle and jogged the rest of the way to the men, who turned and waited for him. When Maggie looked back, she appeared done in—panting, her face red, sweat trickling down her brow.

He reached her and pulled her into his side so she leaned on him, and he could feel the tremors shaking her body. "We'll rest for a bit."

He scanned the rocks, looking for a place to sit, and saw the others doing the same. Aye, she was *their* *Maggie* too.

After leading her to a flat rock, he retrieved a leather flask of water and an apple from his pack. She took the water gratefully as he began to slice the apple with his dagger, giving her the first piece.

They ate and rested in silence for a while before she asked, "How much farther today?" as she craned her neck to look up the mountain.

He pointed to the top in the distance, over rocks and shale, which could be dangerous to both them and the horses. "A few more hours to the ridge—that'll be hard going—then we'll have several more hours to the cave where we'll camp tonight. The incline will not be so bad once we're on the ridge, but the path will be rough. And the lads willna be able to help you once we reach the shale. They'll need to steady the horses."

She nodded, but he could see her eyes had dimmed.

Then she sighed heavily and struggled to her feet. "'Tis best we shoot now, then. I doona want my arms shaking so badly I canna aim straight. You'd win by default—the only way, for sure."

He let her have her fun. Although truth be told, it might not be a jest. He suspected he would beat Maggie only if she allowed him to.

And I'd take it.

Aye, Maggie letting him win would be as good as telling him she would marry him. Until then, he would fight for her hand with everything he had.

"Choose a spot, then, and I'll go first. I wouldnae want to be accused of following your arrow's path again."

She smiled, obviously enjoying herself now as she pulled out her daggers. "Not to worry. We'll use knives instead. And maybe a moving target."

The other men had also risen.

"What did you have in mind?" Finn asked, his boyish face alight with excitement.

"I'll show you," she said. "You doona mind helping, do you?"

Finn's smile faded, and he swallowed nervously. "If you think 'twill be safe."

"Well, *I* willna miss. But you may want to jump back when it's Callum's turn."

The corners of his mouth dipped down, and Callum took pity on the lad. "We willna aim at you, Finn. Maggie would ne'er risk your life that way. I'm sure she means to have you throw a target in the air."

"Aye," Maggie said, her lips twitching. "If Callum's scared he'll miss and hit you instead, we'll do it his way." She searched the ground, then picked up two flat rocks, both about the size of her palm, and held them out to him. "Choose your target."

He did, after making a show of looking them over carefully. He just liked being able to hold her hand, his fingers gliding over her soft skin, until she shivered.

And if it threw off her concentration, all the better.

"I'll take this one," he said and passed it to Finnian. He reached for his dagger as Maggie passed Finn her target, and the young man hopped across the mountain like a young goat until she whistled.

He stopped. "Right here?" he yelled.

"Aye, lad. We'll let you know when we're

ready—and keep an eye out for the daggers when they fall!" Callum said.

He turned and saw Maggie flipping her dagger in her hand—almost a ritualistic movement to help her focus. She never once looked at her blade. Instead, she stared above Finn's head in the distance, no doubt envisioning the shot in her mind's eye.

Fortunately, the wind was calm, and it would simply be a matter of anticipating and hitting the target.

"Do you want to see him toss it first?" he asked.

"Nay. Let's just do it."

His stomach tightened with anticipation—with nerves, even—and he took a deep breath to relax his muscles. The weight of what was riding on this competition sat heavily on him. He was a good shot and would pit his skills against anyone, but he was afraid Maggie might prove his better.

And this was a contest he could not afford to lose.

"I'll go first," he said. He adjusted his position, then whistled at Finn. The lad tossed Callum's target in the air. In a single motion, Callum pulled his arm back over his shoulder and loosed his dagger. It hit the rock seconds later, before the target reached the top of its arc, and the men sent up a cheer.

Callum resisted punching his fist in the air as he switched spots with Maggie, his heart conflicted. Aye, he wanted to win, but he also didn't want her to feel the shame of missing her shot.

He wondered if she felt the same.

She was grinning from ear to ear when she yelled at Finn, "Now!"

Finnian tossed her target high in the air. Callum

expected Maggie to pull her arm back and loose immediately, as he had, but she waited until the target was on its way down. The men yelled out with concern, but she waited until the very last moment. Only then did she throw the dagger, hitting the target just before it reached the ground a few feet from Finnian.

The men erupted with loud shouts of astonishment and revelry, and this time Callum couldn't stop himself from punching the air and yelling along with them. His shot had been precise; hers had been a thing of beauty.

He looked over just as she gave the men a deep curtsy. When she straightened, she looked up the mountain, hands on her hips, and blew out a heavy puff of air. "If only this mountain were so easy to beat!"

His pleasure turned to indignation. "You did not beat me!"

"Tell that to the men," she replied with a saucy grin, then cupped her hands over her mouth. "Finnian, bring my dagger. And somebody help me up this great, bloody rock!"

Wind whipped around Maggie's head, blowing tendrils of hair across her face, even though she'd tied the tangled mess into a tight braid. What she wouldn't give for a proper bath after all the days she'd been climbing over the thrice-damned mountain range with Callum and the others. They were on day five of their journey, not counting the nights spent in the glade after the wolf attack and at her grandmother's cottage.

Every night, Callum had slept wrapped around her, and she'd been grateful for the warmth, especially as the weather had turned colder and the hike more difficult. Clouds had filled the sky, and they often had to walk through fog and mist, staying tight to the path that wove along the top of the ridge. When the fog dissipated, they would pick up the pace to as fast as Maggie could go. Fortunately, today she felt a bit stronger.

The men's joviality from a few days ago had turned quieter with the dangerous weather, but Callum still insisted that he and Maggie compete with their arrows and daggers—even in the fog, which Maggie had found a real challenge. She had yet to win outright, but then neither had Callum.

Not that it mattered at this point. Maggie was just praying they'd make it out of these mountains alive— and this morning, her prayers had been half answered when dawn arrived with a bright, clear sky. It was still windy, now more so than ever. The wind bit through their plaids and threatened to push them over at times, but the damp from the last two days, the cold that soaked through to her bones, was gone.

Drustan, who was on point, let out a loud whistle up ahead.

The others around her didn't react defensively to his whistle, so she assumed they weren't being warned of danger. In fact, the men looked eager and had pleased expressions on their faces.

"What was that for?" she asked Callum, who walked by her side.

He grinned down at her, passed Aristotle's reins to Gill, and then grabbed her hand and strode quickly ahead. The others followed behind them, and she couldn't help but be caught up in their sudden good mood, even though she had no idea what they were celebrating.

She saw Drustan up ahead, sitting on a rock, and waved to him. He lifted his hand back in greeting, a small, strained smile on his lined but still handsome face.

"Callum, what's—" She let out a surprised cry as he suddenly scooped her into his arms.

He took a few steps forward then stopped. "Welcome to Clan MacLean, love. We have officially crossed the border and are on our own land."

He'd carried her over the threshold to his home. For some reason, her chest tightened and she had to blink back tears.

God's blood! I've become a Weepy Wynda.

Gill stepped over the border and let out a cry. "MacLeans! Virtue! Honor!"

"MacLeans!" both Callum and Drustan responded.

She grinned with them, remembering her own clan's battle cry, which was much more bloodthirsty. When they were young, her brothers would race to the top of the cliff over the creek or all the way from the bailey to the keep's topmost turret, shoving and laughing the entire way. The winner would shout out the MacDonnell battle cry at the top.

She'd trail behind them, occasionally winning because they'd been wrestling each other too much, and she'd squeeze past them. Sometimes they would lift her onto their shoulders and run with her instead.

If her mother had still been alive and seen how wild she'd become—her father lost to his own grief and her brothers letting her do whatever she wanted—she would have reined them all in. Maggie still missed her terribly and would do anything to have her back, but it was in the first few months after her death that Ross had first taught her how to use a bow, and John showed her how to fling a dagger. Her life would be dramatically different now if her mother hadn't died.

She fingered the dagger that she'd attached to her forearm. Her skill with knives and a bow was more than just an ability; it was a passion. One she never would have been able to experience had her mother not fallen down the well in her attempt to get Maggie out.

The joy and satisfaction the weapons gave her had come at a high price. The sadness and regret, but also the *guilt*, ate at her.

Pressure built in her chest as the conflicting emotions bubbled up from where she'd shoved them down. She resisted releasing them, not wanting to look…weak, she supposed, maybe vulnerable, in front of Callum. Still, he frowned at her as though he knew something was wrong.

"Are you well, lass?" he asked, shifting her in his arms so he could see her face—which made her realize he still held her close.

She squirmed to get down, berating herself for wanting to stay there. By the glint in his eye, he'd probably known it. When her feet touched the ground—MacLean ground—she took two steps away from him. "Aye. Just…thinking about my brothers."

He gave her an assessing look and nodded. A sharp wind blew suddenly, tossing her hair and whistling through her ears. Her blanket was little protection, and the wind pierced right through to her skin. She shivered violently, and her teeth chattered.

Callum pulled her close, opening his own blanket and tucking her inside against his body. Blessed warmth. She did sigh this time, and just let herself be held.

The men gathered around, and no one looked at them askance. Aye, they all thought of her as Callum's wife-to-be—and for Drustan and Gill, their future lady. Although Drustan had been more distant since he'd had that strange talk with her days ago.

He'd been distant from everyone, it seemed. She'd thought it was just his personality, but by the concerned looks Callum kept throwing his way, she guessed it was not. She'd added him to her list of prayers every night, hoping he was well.

"Do you want to light the pyre and announce we're coming," Gavin asked, holding the reins of his and Callum's horses, "or continue to keep our whereabouts a secret?"

Maggie scrunched her brow in confusion and looked around. "What pyre?"

Callum pointed farther up the mountain at the peak. "'Tis about an hour's hike. A great wooden pyre. Once it's lit, it can be seen from farther down the range, where another pyre sits. That one will be lit by a watcher and will be seen from an outpost that'll send a rider with word to the castle. They'll send men out to us within hours of the first pyre going up."

"And send word to our foster brothers and Gregor as well, so they know what's happened to us. If they received our earlier messages, Maggie, they should be at your castle by now. Laying siege, most likely," Gavin said.

"Well, what about Irvin's spy in your keep?" she

asked. "If you light the pyre, he or she will know and may tell Irvin where we are."

"Aye, 'tis a possibility, but 'twill also mean a message will be sent to Gregor and the lads sooner than if we waited until we arrived at the castle. We need them with us to discuss the information in the parchments you gave me. From what's written, Gavin and I both believe something else is going on that's bigger than just Irvin's desire to take over Clan MacDonnell."

Maggie's brow rose in astonishment. "Isn't that enough?"

"It's bad, Maggie. Terrible. And he'll be put on trial for what he did and plans to do, but…"

"But what?" she asked, looking up just in time to see Callum's and Gavin's eyes meet. What was in those parchments that she'd missed?

Gavin huffed out a worried breath. "That's the problem, lass. We doona know exactly. 'Tis just a feeling. From everything that's written in there, and all the clans mentioned—or whom we think Irvin is referring to—it seems more intricate than just one man's ambitions. Unless Irvin is planning to take over all of the Highlands."

Callum rested his chin on top of Maggie's head and squeezed his arms tighter around her. "We'll sort it out, sweetling. But all six of us together have a better chance of doing that than just Gavin and me."

"And you're on MacLean land now," Finnian said to her. "'Tis not like the MacDonnells can cross the border and take you without your laird knowing. They'll ne'er get through."

He sounded like a child at the adult's table. No border

was impassable, and Maggie waited for someone to tell him how wrong he was. She didn't have to wait long.

"Nay, Finn," Gavin said. "Callum protects his borders as best he can, as do we, but there is always room for error. If we understand our limitations, we'll be better prepared to deal with a breach when it occurs, aye? 'Tis why we set up our defenses in concentric circles. If one ring falls, we retreat to the next line of defense, all the way back to our castle and keep, aye?"

Finn turned a fiery red and dropped his chin. "Aye, Laird. I'm sorry."

Artair *tched* and bumped Finn with his shoulder, almost knocking him over with his great strength. Gill caught and steadied him.

"'Tis naught to be sorry for, lad," Artair said. "'Tis just one of many lessons we have to learn."

"Aye," the other men agreed.

Finn nodded, still looking red but not as crestfallen. He'd be all right.

"So we weigh the need for secrecy against the need to have your foster brothers and Gregor here sooner. Is that what you're saying?" Maggie asked.

"'Tis more than that. The flames will alert my men to our presence, and they'll follow the same route we do but travel toward us. 'Tis more protection against the MacDonnells in case they breach our borders farther down. I doona think anyone's followed us over the mountain. Or if they have, they're at least a day behind us."

"Aye. The threat will come from ahead of us, not from behind," Gavin finished. "'Twould be good to have more men."

"Well, it seems the decision is made then," Maggie said, realizing that both Callum and Gavin were of the same mind. She looked at the mountain's peak, seeing another steep and rocky climb. Lucky for her—and the men—her strength and stamina had improved over the last five days. "Let's just hope the wood will burn, or 'twill all be for naught."

Fourteen

MAGGIE STOOD, QUIETLY FUMING, AT THE BASE OF THE recently sheered cliff. The pyre still rested above her, but the route up to it would be difficult and dangerous with the unstable, fallen rock. Even more so than the path they'd already traveled to get to this point. Wind tore at her clothes and hair and threatened to blow her back down the mountain to where Drustan waited with the horses, but she'd dug her feet in and clenched her hands around her blanket to keep it in place.

And because her blood boiled, she was hot.

Five days she'd been traveling with these men, including four days of competing with Callum and besting him every time—he may not have lost, but she'd definitely won in the eyes of the men. She was the better archer, the better aim at throwing daggers. Better than him, better even than Gill. They'd seen her make the shot in the dark from the top of the keep to the tree, and they still hadn't thought about asking her opinion on this shot to the top of the cliff.

Because they couldn't do it, they assumed she couldn't either.

She looked up again at the pyre. Aye, it would be difficult, especially with the wind blowing almost constant gusts in all different directions. She'd have to feel the weather and time her shot, pulling hard enough to make the distance to the top of the pyre but soft enough that the lit arrow didn't blow out on the way there or fly past her target and land on the rocks rather than the wood.

She lifted her arms and closed her eyes, feeling the weight of the bow and learning the chaotic pattern of the wind. She pulled on the imaginary arrow, feeling the warmth of the flame near her hand before she loosed. When she opened her eyes, the men were still looking up, chattering in front of her about the best path to take to climb up the rest of the way over the dangerous, loose boulders.

All except Callum, who looked at her. Watched her. "Can you do it?" he asked.

Gavin heard and glanced over, followed by Gill and the rest of the men.

"I doona see how," Gill said. He plucked a hair from his head and held it out. The strand blew sporadically in the wind. "The arrow will be blown off course even if you do manage to get the distance right."

She studied the pyre. "The flame will have to be hot. Otherwise, the fire will be blown out."

"Too hot and the shaft will burn down too quickly," Gill said.

"Do you have a glove you can wear to protect your skin?" Callum asked.

"Nay. And even if I did, I wouldnae wear it."

His jaw clenched, and a tiny muscle jumped on the

side. She could see he wanted to deny her, wanted to end the discussion immediately.

"Maggie, there's no need for you to be hurt. We have other options. And I doona mean that we climb up to the pyre either. I willna lose men o'er this. We can turn around and make our way to the castle without alerting them. There are good reasons we should do that anyway."

She nodded. Lifting her arms again, she drew on the imaginary arrow, testing the distance to the pyre, the strength of the wind, and how close the flame would come to her hand. "I willna have to draw as far as you think. I will feel the flame, and my skin may be tender afterward, but I doona think it will be close enough or long enough to blister. 'Tis a risk worth taking, aye?"

She could see he didn't think so, but after a moment, he scrubbed his fingers through his scraggly beard, his green eyes somehow even brighter. Then he said, "Aye."

The knots in her stomach—of anger and anticipation of his denial, no, his *betrayal*, for that's how it felt—loosened. He believed in her. *Valued* her.

Their eyes met, and she could see the battle that raged within him, his need to protect her overruled by his need to *respect* her.

She smiled; she couldn't help it. It burst out of her. Wide and happy and filled with joy.

The men didn't hesitate, coming forward to light a fire and search through their packs for linen that would be cut into strips and wrapped with twine around the tip of her arrow.

Gill moved to her side and looked up at the pyre,

quietly assessing the shot. She let him, even though she knew exactly what had to be done. Finally, he said, "I have ne'er seen an archer as good as you. If anyone can make this shot, 'tis you, lassie. You doona need my advice on this."

She squeezed his arm and smiled the same luminous smile she'd given Callum. "Will you stand beside me and hand me the arrows? Four will do."

"I'd be proud to," he said, returning her smile.

The others had the fire burning now in a hole to help block the wind and were smearing the linen strips with tallow. "Your arrows, Maggie," Gavin said.

She pushed back her blanket, bracing herself for the cold, so she could unbuckle her quiver and hand it to Gavin. He took it from her, and she wrapped herself up to stay as warm as possible. She needed her muscles to remain loose—although that was almost an impossibility in this weather.

Looking up, she moved forward slowly, finding the best position to stand. Once she had it, she squatted and moved the rocks from around her feet. Callum crouched beside her to help. He took her hands when they were done, lifting the left one to his mouth to kiss it exactly where the flame might touch her skin. It felt like a seal, protecting her from fire in that spot.

She cupped his cheek and dragged her fingers through his thickening beard. Their eyes met and held. God Almighty, he was handsome—even unkempt as he was now, as they all were. He would rival the angels themselves.

The look they shared. So much emotion passed between them. So much was said through that one touch. It was chaste compared to how they'd touched before but perhaps more intimate than ever.

She rose to her feet. Callum stepped behind her and wrapped his arms and extra blanket around her. His big body protected her from the cold, and she warmed.

They stood there quietly as she listened to the blowing wind, envisioning the shot in her head, accommodating for the weight of the flame on the end of her arrow, the thinner air, and the weather. She felt the shot all the way down to her bones.

"Maggie," Gill said.

She looked over to her right and saw he held her arrow out to her, three more in his other hand.

"Do you want me to light it for you?" he asked.

"Nay. I'll do that once I have the arrow set."

"I'll light a torch and hold it on your other side," Callum said. "That way you willna have to change your position or wait too long before you loose the next arrow."

"I'll get it," Finnian said, his voice pitched high with excitement as he ran toward their pile of supplies beside a big boulder. He stopped at the fire on the way back to set the torch aflame, using his hand to shield it as he walked over.

"Ready?" Callum asked her.

She gazed up at the pyre and breathed deeply to settle her nerves. "Aye."

Callum stepped to her left side, taking his warmth with him, and held out his hand to Finn for the burning torch. Maggie pushed back her blanket so her arms were free. Clasping her bow, she took the arrow from Gill, the tip wrapped in the tallow-smeared linen and

tied in place with twine. She nocked the arrow and lit
it in the flame. The linen caught fire with a bursting
crackle, and she lifted the bow, sighted the pyre, and
drew the shaft. The flame quickly heated her hand as
the fire neared her skin. She drowned out everything
but the distance to the pyre, the weight of the arrow,
the feel and sound of the wind.

On instinct, she loosed the shot. It flew upward and
gently over the edge of the pyre, disappearing from
sight. She held out her hand and repeated the process
with the next arrow. She loosed again on instinct, not
really knowing when the next big gust of wind would
blow, feeling it in her body instead of assessing it with
her mind. Staying open to her gut feeling, her intuition.

The arrow went slightly higher this time before disappearing over the edge of the pyre. She held out her
hand for the third arrow and shot it, then the fourth,
which looked like it might have been blown slightly
wide at the end.

Callum passed off the torch to Gavin, then stepped
behind her and wrapped his arms and blanket around
her again. Until then, she hadn't felt the cold, but
suddenly, she was shivering. They stood quietly,
anticipation a breathing, living thing among them. No
one broke position, staring up at the pyre, willing it
to catch fire.

Time dragged. Seconds became hours.

"The wood may be wet," Finn said.

"Hush," Artair reprimanded him.

Hours became days.

"The wind is stronger up there. The flame may
have been blown out," Artair said.

"Hush," Gavin quieted him.

Maggie sniffed the air, hoping to smell smoke—other than that from the torch that burned not far away, of course. Surely at least one of the arrows had landed, and they'd see flames soon.

"The shots landed, Maggie. I know they did," Gill said, as if he was thinking the exact same thing.

Gavin sighed. "Maybe if we climbed halfway up, we could lob some torches over the edge. They'd hold the flame better than the arrows."

"You will hush!" Callum said. "'Twill light!"

Maggie held her breath and waited, hoping Callum was right, but when no flames appeared, disappointment seeped through her. She'd let everyone down. Worse, she'd let Callum down, and she sagged against him. She'd just opened her mouth to apologize, although she knew she'd done her best, when Callum's hands tightened on her waist. Finn yelled, "There!"

Jerking her gaze up to the pyre, she saw smoke billowing from the top and the orange glow of flames licking over the edge. A cheer went up.

Maggie screamed excitedly, her arms shooting into the air. Callum squeezed her waist from behind and lifted her off the ground, twirling her in a circle. Finnian danced a funny little Highland Fling, while Gill and Artair clapped their hands above their heads. Gavin wrapped his strong arms around Callum and Maggie and lifted them both off the ground.

She laughed as Gavin set them down and joined Finn in his dance. Turning in Callum's arms, she embraced him, her arms squeezing around his as she tilted her face up to him. "Kiss me," she said.

He dropped his head, and she could feel his smile against her lips, feel the joy humming in his big body, making hers sing along with his. The scruff of his five-day-old beard scratched her cheek and sent shivers racing along her skin. She pressed closer, rising onto her toes, seeking more of him, all of him.

He groaned and deepened the kiss as her mouth opened to his, his tongue sliding in to tangle with hers. She sucked on it, excited and thrilled, and when he drove his hand into her hair at the nape of her neck to hold her still, to devour her, she groaned too.

He withdrew slowly, and she tried to keep him close to her, chasing his mouth, her tongue sliding across the seam of his lips. He shuddered, but he held her tight in place against him as he raised his head. She opened her eyes slowly, her face turned up. He stared at her—skin flushed, lips red, and lids heavy, looking almost feral.

It made her want to bite him. Or push him over and climb on top.

"Good shot," he said with a slow grin.

She burst out laughing. "That's exactly what I was thinking."

Hearing a sound behind her, she looked over to see Gavin, Gill, and Artair lined up and watching them, indulgent smiles on their faces. Finn still danced his Highland Fling in the background, whooping and shouting out every once in a while.

"Oh look," she said. "'Tis sappy old Wynda, Glynda, and Nan, watching us young folk live our lives."

"I'm not Wynda," Gavin said, "I'm Glynda."

"And I'm Nan," Gill said. "I think 'tis obvious Artair is the Wynda of the group."

"I canna be Wynda," Artair said. "My ma was named Wynda. And she always said if she had a daughter, she'd name her Brunhild after the Viking shield-maiden. 'Tis rumored she's our kin."

"I want to be a shield-maiden too," Gavin said. "'Tis not fair Artair gets to be one and we do not."

"Aye," Gill said.

Finn had stopped his dance and listened quizzically. "What are you all going on about?" A spark floated down from above and landed on his plaid.

Artair slapped him on the shoulder and put it out. "Vikings, Finnian. And weddings."

"Naught was said about weddings, Finn." Maggie tried to scowl, but it probably looked daft when she was tucked up so tightly against Callum, who grinned again and pressed his lips to hers. She couldn't help softening under his mouth.

He pulled back almost immediately and said, "Nay, you were too busy kissing me to say aught about anything." He turned with her and headed down the mountain, keeping her under his extra plaid as the others fell in behind them, explaining to Finn, in a vague sort of way, what had happened.

Callum kissed her hand in the exact spot he had earlier. Maybe his kiss had protected it. It didn't hurt at all.

"Let's go before the whole pyre tumbles down on us," he said, "or I find myself at your mercy and suddenly married. You looked verra determined to make me yours."

Callum sighted down the arrow at the tree that blew in the wind. 'Twasn't a difficult shot, other than the fact that the target wouldn't stay still. He tried to channel Maggie, closed his eyes and opened all his senses to his surroundings. Tried to feel the wind—become the wind, as he'd heard her say—and know exactly when to loose.

"It looks like he's bloody well gone to sleep now," Artair said, and Callum opened his eyes with a scowl. Then was glad he had when he saw he was way off target. He didn't know how Maggie did it, but if he tried it her way, he'd end up alone in his keep with only Drustan for company.

"Shut it, you great giant of an ablach," he said.

Everyone laughed, and when he heard Maggie's lighter trill, not as loud as the men but still hearty and full of mirth, it sent shivers down his spine and straight to his cock. He tightened his fingers on the string, determined to hit that bloody tree. He'd end up with Maggie in his keep for good.

He drew his arrow, his jaw clenched tight, and released it toward the trunk of the tree. The wind blew the tree sideways at the last minute, and his arrow hit an outer branch—way off target.

God's blood! I missed!

No cheers or laughter sounded behind him this time. Nay, they wanted Maggie to marry him almost as much as he did. The silence was almost oppressive. He glanced over his shoulder at Maggie, his heart thudding, afraid of what he might see—her smiling or even stifling a laugh. But her face was stricken, and his heart eased.

Aye, she no more wants me to lose than I do.

"Maggie. Your turn," Gavin said, sounding clipped.

She hesitated, then stepped forward to stand beside Callum. "'Twas the wind. 'Tis blowing like a squalling bairn."

He didn't say anything—couldn't say anything. His jaw was clenched so tightly, he might never be able to separate his teeth again.

What will she do?

"Might as well get it over with, lass," Drustan said, sounding a little too cheery for Callum's liking. Wasn't Drustan supposed to be on his side?

And aye, this was a contest, but everyone knew Maggie was the better shot. The best they had all been hoping for was a tie so Callum could stay in the game, keep her by his side as long as possible.

And win her back.

Maggie lifted her arrow, and he held his breath. A moment passed, she lowered her arms, and he released the air in his lungs.

"The wind is too strong," she said. "Maybe we should choose another day. We skipped yesterday. We can miss today too."

"We missed yesterday because we lost so much time going up to the pyre," Finn said. "We've made good time so far today, haven't we?" He looked around, eyes wide and inquiring, and Callum wanted to punch him.

Maggie slowly raised her arms again. "Aye."

She chewed on her lip and never once closed her eyes to listen to the wind, which had died down considerably in the few minutes since Callum had taken his shot. She'd have no trouble hitting her mark.

"You've got it, lass. Take the shot," Drustan said, right by her shoulder.

She released her breath, centered. The tree barely moved. Still, she waited.

"Maggie," Callum said, and she loosed. At the last minute, she jerked her arms to the left, and her arrow shot wide, landing in the branches close to his.

A collective gasp went up from the men, and Callum stared at the arrow. Everything within him slowed for a moment—his pulse, his breath, every thought—before rushing back louder and stronger and faster than ever. One phrase pounded through his mind.

She missed.

For me!

"The wind took it," she said. "God above, 'tis a blustery day."

He turned slowly, looked at her. She caught his eye, and her cheeks reddened before she glanced away.

"Verily, we shouldnae have been competing today," she said, repeating herself. "'Tis as strong a wind as I've ever felt."

"Aye," he said. "The wind certainly took *my* arrow."

"What are you talking about, lass?" Finn asked, failing to see what everyone else already knew. Maggie had pulled her shot so Callum wouldn't lose. And now she was blaming the wind. She might not have said the words, but her actions had spoken loud and clear. She wanted to stay with him.

"The wind had died," Finn continued. "'Twas blowing much harder on top of the mountain yester-day, and you made all four of those shots."

This time Callum wanted to pat Finn on the back.

Not so Maggie. She scowled at the trees, her face even hotter than before, a bright, fiery red beneath all those freckles.

He wanted to kiss every one, and now he knew he would.

Aye, Maggie had just become his.

"Go, Finn," he said. "Check the arrows."

"Aye, Laird." The lad ran for the trees.

"And be careful of the wind," Gavin yelled. "'Tis blowing so hard, it might knock you o'er."

The words caused Maggie to scowl harder. The men laughed quietly. They would be excited and charmed to think Maggie had surrendered to him, the wind no stronger now than a gentle breeze. She brushed her hair away from her face and retied it at the nape of her neck, then darted a glance at him and away when she saw him looking. Her pulse beat frantically in her neck, and he marked it as a place to kiss once they were alone. Because this time when he started kissing her, he didn't intend to stop.

Maggie had pulled her shot. He needed no words for proof. She. Was. His.

A holler sounded from the trees, and she looked toward Finn. Callum continued to watch her. He couldn't—wouldn't—look away.

"'Tis Laird MacLean's arrow that's closest! Laird MacLean won!" Finnian yelled from the branches.

This time the men did cheer, and clapped Callum on the back as they walked past. Gavin shot him a huge grin, then hugged Maggie. He whispered something in her ear that made her stiffen before he picked up his horse's reins and moved on.

It didn't matter. Nothing mattered but getting Maggie alone. Finn ran up to them, both arrows in his hand. "It was close, I swear! Both arrows were on the same branch, next to each other, but Laird MacLean's was nearest to the target."

Callum reached for the arrows. "Thank you, Finn. You can go catch up with the others now."

Maggie hadn't met his eye since she'd loosed her arrow. She hesitated, then moved to dart after Finn. Callum caught her hand and pulled her into his arms. "Look at me, love."

She finally did, her face a confusing mix of belligerence, fear, and desire. He held the arrows up between their bodies. "I'm going to save these arrows, Maggie, along with the target you sent to me from before. They'll be part of the story we'll tell our bairns and grandbairns."

"Callum, you canna—"

"Aye, I can. You missed, Maggie. You *missed*."

"You didn't feel it. The wind pushed my arrow aside, just like it did yours."

He cupped his hands around her cheeks and pulled her slowly into him as she kept babbling about the wind. "It's verra unstable. It kicked the arrow aside at the last moment. 'Twas not here, but at the tree, it was a—"

"Kiss me, Maggie," he said when their lips were almost touching. "Kiss me, and I promise you'll have a warm bath tonight."

She finally stopped talking, let out a wee sob, and pressed her mouth to his.

She'd missed her shot. For him.

Fifteen

MAGGIE'S EYES WIDENED AS SHE LOOKED AROUND. THE steaming blue pool was set low in the rocks, surrounded by moss. The gloaming was upon them, and the sky had turned to amazing shades of purple, pink, and orange.

They'd ridden hard that day, covering a lot of ground. The horses were tired, but the men had an air of jubilation about them, as if they were celebrating. She refused to think what that celebration might be. She refused to admit that the heated way Callum had been looking at her all day, the way he'd held her tight against his body as they rode—a hard mass behind her, his hands caressing wherever they touched, making her daft—was anything out of the ordinary.

It did not mean that tonight she would allow Callum to tup her.

So she'd missed her shot. It hadn't *meant* anything.

Except it had. He knew it. The others knew it. She knew it.

She closed her eyes as a wave of excitement surged up through her body. She shivered, and a gasp escaped her lips. A trembling had set in along her inner thighs hours ago, and she clenched her legs together to ease the quiver, but it only increased the need for something…more. Something only Callum could give her.

God help her, she wanted his hands on her. All over her. She wanted those big, firm palms pushing her thighs wide. She wanted the heat of him there, the weight of him as his body pressed her down.

And then what?

If what Callum had said before was true, she would become his wife.

She shivered again and, for the first time, admitted that maybe that was exactly what she wanted. She had always wanted it, even when she was so hurt and angry with him for not returning. How could she be with Callum only once and then walk away, as she had suggested only a few days ago? It was nonsense to think she could let him in that far and then just leave…and forget about him.

She didn't think this ache between her legs could be so easily assuaged.

She looked over her shoulder, looked for him. He'd brought her here and then left. He'd promised her the pool was private and that the others would not come near unless there was an emergency, even the warriors who were on guard through the night. But he hadn't said if he would be back, and God help her, she wanted him with her. Now.

With a sigh, she moved to the pool's edge, toed off her shoes, undid her stockings at her knees, and stepped out of them before dipping her toes into the water. It was hot, and she groaned aloud. She took hurried steps to a rock, shed her outer layers of clothing, and laid them on it until she wore only her shift and her daggers in the leather sheath strapped to her arm. She looked over her shoulder one more time for Callum, knowing he'd already seen all of her—the last time she'd had a proper wash at her grandmother's cottage. What she couldn't decide now, though, was whether she was checking over her shoulder to make sure she was alone before she shed her shift or whether she was checking to see if he was there so he could watch her shed her shift.

Bah, she was an idiot!

She reached down to rummage in her bag for her soap—a scented thing pressed with rose petals—a wash cloth, and a linen for drying herself, then dropped her shift and marched to the water's edge, chin high and shoulders back.

She was lean and strong, and the march up the mountain had only added to her strength. But she was also endowed with full breasts and a rounded behind. Maybe not as soft and curved as many men would like, but she wouldn't change anything about herself.

Especially not if it meant she couldn't keep up with the others as well as she had this past week.

"The water will help you, lass. It'll ease any soreness in your muscles as well as leaving you as clean as a newborn bairn."

Callum's hoarse words floated over to where she stood, one foot in the water on a natural step down. The heat seeped into her skin, slightly burning at first, but she would soon be used to it. Her hair was long, down to the curve of her arse, and wildly thick and curled. She was mostly covered, but she could still feel his eyes burning through to her skin.

She glanced over her shoulder to where he stood by the entrance to their private little haven. How long had he been standing there? Had he seen her undress? The ache inside her body grew, and she knew if she slid her hands down her body and over her mound, she'd be wet with wanting him.

She'd never touched herself before he'd left her that first time, but as the months had gone by and her body had burned to see him, she'd pressed her fingers to her center. She'd found she could relieve the ache for a while by thinking of him and rubbing through her slick folds.

What would he do if she turned around and did just that? Trailed her hands over her breasts, cupped them and squeezed her nipples, then caressed down her body and through the auburn curls that hid her sex?

He'd be by her side in only a few strides, she would guess. He'd made no secret of the fact that he wanted her in that way and intended to take her if she ever offered.

Well, was she offering?

She turned back to the water, laid down her soap and cloths on the edge, unstrapped the sheath of daggers from her arm, and stepped in with her other foot. "You know naught of newly born bairns, Callum MacLean, if you think they come out of the womb shiny and clean."

When the water was up to her waist and her hair floated around her, she swam for the middle of the pool. Heat enveloped her, and she groaned in delight. All those days shivering in the wind were forgotten; the hard hikes and sore muscles were nothing but a memory. She dipped her head under, and when she surfaced, she laughed and spun in a circle, her hair slicked back from her face, her feet just touching the bottom.

"This spot is a treasure," she said. "The treasure of Clan MacLean."

"Nay, *you* are the treasure of Clan MacLean," he said.

He sounded closer to her, and she opened her eyes to see him standing naked, his plaid and shoes beside hers on the rock. He'd entered the pool, the water up to his knees, his body a sculpted mass of lean, hard muscle, and his jaw shaved clean of his beard.

So that's what he'd been doing when he'd left her here—preparing himself for her.

The thought sent a spasm of need through her belly, and she fixed her eyes on his cock—hard and sculpted just like the rest of him, jutting upward at an angle from a nest of brown curls. His sac hung heavily, swinging slightly as he stepped down, and even that was exciting, causing a pulsing in her core and a restless desire to be held in place by him.

To be held down and have him touch and lick her everywhere.

"I'm a MacLean treasure, am I? I doona recall you doing anything yet to change my clan. Perhaps in the night, by the fire, and I didn't even feel it? Nay more than a little prick, perhaps?" She raised her brow and tried to sound cool with her play on words. But he stepped to the bottom of the pool and pushed off with a laugh, swimming toward her, and she laughed too, before gawking at the muscles rippling in his chest and shoulders, her jest forgotten.

He reached her and circled his arms around her. Her legs floated up in the deeper water on either side of him. The broad head of his shaft nudged her soft, swollen center, and she bit her lip to stop herself from moaning. Nay, no small prick here.

Even though she tried to hold herself still, she jerked against him restlessly, the need in her so great, she felt like an animal in heat. But it wasn't just the physical need driving her. She found herself clenching her arms around his neck, squeezing as hard as she could. She pushed her body tightly against his, her breasts squashed against his chest, her nipples hard and erect against the soft prickle of his chest hair. And the emotions—she couldn't stop them from rioting though her, making her want to sob in his arms. Fear and uncertainty, anger and hurt, but also joy. Her heart felt full to bursting, and her breath came in short, agitated gasps.

God in heaven, she was as daft as a daylight-digging badger.

His hands rubbed up and down her back, gently soothing and whispering soft words to her. He seemed to understand, somehow, that the intensity of the moment and what they were about to do had undone her.

"It's all right, love. Hush, everything will be well. I willna let anything bad happen to you, I promise. I'm not going anywhere. I'll be right here with you. We'll take this as slow or as fast as you need to. I'll catch you, Maggie. Let yourself fall. I promise to catch you."

She was naked in his arms, her legs and arms wrapped around him, completely open for his possession. Yet he soothed her, rocked her like a bairn, helped her collect those conflicting feelings within herself that she didn't know how to handle. Those parts of who she was that fought with each other. The scared part with the brave part. The happy part with the angry part.

"Callum," she said, sounding ragged even to her own ears.

"Aye, Maggie."

"I doona know how to be with you, how to be a wife. There's…there's…something hurt inside me. Scared."

"Aye, Maggie. We're all hurt and scared in some way. Being together—making love and relying on each other—will help us heal. Help us to grieve and forgive if we need to. To believe again, trust again. Do you understand?"

She shook her head and felt tears slip down her cheek, felt like she may just break apart. It was getting dark, and with her face already wet, she knew Callum couldn't see the tears, but still she wanted to hide. She tucked her face into that spot she loved between his neck and shoulder and let out a long, shuddering breath. That spot, right there, breathing in the scent of his skin, somehow made her feel secure.

"Making love with me, in my arms, is the safest place you could ever be. I'll take care of you. Let me have you, Maggie. Please."

Her breath caught in her throat, loving that he'd asked when he could have just taken. They both knew she would have allowed it. She wanted that so much, and she nodded jerkily. She couldn't help squeezing him even closer, her ankles crossed behind him, her arms tight around his shoulders. Almost as if she wanted to push right inside his skin.

"I doona know what's the matter with me," she said. Despite the warmth of the water, she was shivering too.

"You're vulnerable, Maggie. We both are. Your walls have come down, and your heart is free."

That made her mad, and she scowled. What good was she to herself or him if she couldn't control her feelings? "Well, I doona like it. Tup me and get it o'er with."

He dropped his head into the same spot on her that she'd been snuggling into on him. Except she was pretty sure he was laughing.

Pulling back, he cupped her face with his big hands. He held her still as he looked at her, their foreheads almost touching, breathing each other's breath. "Aye, I'll tup you, Maggie. Several times, most likely. And I'll do other things too. I'll hold you down and bury my face right here." He slid his hand down her body and cupped between her legs, the heel of his hand pressing down on the nub at the top, his fingers stroking all the way along her cleft.

She let out a strangled cry and thrust her pelvis against him, her heels digging into his backside, her knees splaying wide. "Callum!"

He dragged his other hand down and roughly squeezed her breast, pinched her nipple. A streak of heat and sensation shot all the way down to her core. Her sex clenched as she rocked against him.

"I'll be rough sometimes, Maggie, if I sense you need it. Other times, I'll suckle you gently. Like this." He squeezed her breast again but in a different way, holding it up for his attention. She leaned back, her fingers digging into his shoulders as his lips closed over her swollen nipple, his mouth sucking the mound, the warmth scalding her in the same way the water had earlier. He laved with his tongue, and she felt herself close to coming apart in every way. Tears streamed from her eyes into her hair, her body winding tighter and tighter as she undulated beneath his touch.

When he lifted his head, she cried out in denial, but he replaced his mouth with his hand and rolled her nipple between his fingers as he talked.

"We can be any way we need to be together. Fast or slow, raw or gentle. Trust me to give you what you need."

"How will you…know what…I need?" Her words came out in gasps, and she couldn't quite catch her breath.

"Your body will tell me."

"What do I need right now?"

"This." He slid his palm upward and cupped the nape of her neck, anchoring her in place as he slanted his mouth over hers and took over. His tongue delved deeply, rubbing against and suckling hers. His fingers began a rhythmic stroking and circling at the heart of her womanhood, the pressure light where she needed it yet heavy when she needed more. He continued in a steady motion, and every time she pushed closer to him, his hips jerked as if he couldn't help himself. She wanted to slide her hands down and squeeze that hard length in her palm, but he was relentless in taking her up to the pinnacle of release. She broke apart within minutes, bucking and quivering, screaming into his mouth, her fingers digging into his shoulders, her legs clenching around his waist.

He held her close, his body and mouth grinding against hers, his chest heaving and legs trembling even though he hadn't been inside her yet, or spent his seed. She may be a virgin, but she wasn't ignorant, and she knew he would have softened if he had.

And he was as hard as ever, twitching against her belly.

She settled slowly, and he gentled their kiss, his lips soft, his tongue no more than a whisper against hers. He pressed his palm to her mound, not rubbing, just a firm, steady anchor that eased her down from the heights of intimacy.

She let out a shuddering breath, and he kissed across her cheek, wrapped his arms around her body, and just held her.

"Callum," she croaked.

"Aye, Maggie." His voice was still rough, filled with unreleased need. She knew they'd only touched the surface of what he wanted to do with her tonight.

"That was…" Emotion bubbled up in her throat, and her words squeaked out unintelligibly. She took a shaky breath and tried again. "I have ne'er had such pleasure before. Surely, I thought I might die from it. 'Tis no comparison to what I've felt before."

He stiffened beneath her. "And when was that, Maggie MacLean?" His voice was low and clipped.

"Doona fash, you daft man. When I've touched myself, of course." His body relaxed beneath hers, and he opened his mouth to say something, but she pressed her fingers to his lips. "And doona tell me it's unseemly or I'm not to do it again. 'Tis my body, not yours, and I shall touch it in whate'er way I want, whene'er I want. And seeing as you havenae found your own release inside me yet, you're still getting ahead of yourself by calling me a MacLean, don't you think?"

"Aye. To both. I was only going to suggest that perhaps someday, in the privacy of our marital chamber, you can touch yourself as I watch...Maggie MacLean."

It was almost dark, but she could see the flash of his teeth against his skin, and she found herself answering his grin. Did that mean she'd forgiven Callum?

She wrapped her arms around his shoulders and laid her cheek on his shoulder. He stroked his hands up her back and walked with her to the pool's edge. He let go for a moment, and then she felt the soap in his hands gliding along her skin, smelled the scent of roses. She hoped he washed her all over. Aye, for sure he would. She suspected she had only a few minutes left of being a MacDonnell.

She smiled as he retraced his steps to the middle of the pool, feeling content about their union now that she'd made up her mind. "I must say, I am happy not to have to leave the Highlands. Although we still need to find John. Can you send men to search for him, as you suggested? My clan needs him."

"Aye, we will." He rubbed the soap over her behind and down the cleft of her bottom from the back to the front. She turned her face to his skin and bit down, finding herself arching her spine and groaning, surprised at how good it felt.

He did it again. "You like that, do you, my Maggie? Well, it has been days since you've had a proper wash.

You will need lots of soap and cleaning. You are a verra dirty lass."

She had to laugh at the way he'd said the last few words, rough and guttural.

"Lean back, love. Wet your hair." She did, shuddering as his hands slid down the front of her body with the soap. He went around each breast and down over her mound to glide through her folds with broad, heavy strokes.

When he stopped, she raised her head to find him staring down at her.

"What is it?" she asked.

He raised his eyes to her face. "You are a vision, Maggie. So strong and lush and beautiful, with your hair spread out around you in the water. You shine in the moonlight. I have ne'er seen anyone—or anything—as lovely as you. My warrior faery princess, filled with such power and grace."

Her heart contracted at his words, flipped over, then expanded till it felt like it might burst from her chest. Callum found her strength beautiful.

He ran his hands down her body again and stroked his fingers through the wet curls there, spreading her folds and circling her nub with his thumb until her spine bowed. He slid his arms behind her and pulled her against his chest, the water pouring from her hair in a noisy rush as he strode with her to the pool's edge.

When he stepped out, she shivered. It was not as chilly here as it had been at the top of the mountain, but the summer nights were cooling down faster as autumn approached. Callum leaned down, still holding her up with one arm. He grabbed both their sets of knives, as well as the large linen, which he wrapped around her to keep the cold at bay.

She couldn't take her eyes off him, excited about what was to come but also uncertain. "Where?" she asked.

He knew exactly what she meant. "On the moss. I've laid my plaid there."

She looked to see his blanket covering the ground, his sword beside it. "And your sword, of course."

"Of course. To protect you with, Maggie. Always."

She snatched one of her daggers from his hand as he carried her to their makeshift bed. "I doona need protecting, remember?"

"I hope not."

"Well, I suppose you can protect me. As long as you know I'll always protect you too."

"Aye."

He stopped and knelt on his plaid, then laid her on top of it. Suddenly, she felt shy, as though the past hour in the pool had never happened and he was looking upon her naked for the first time. She pulled her knees up, hugged them to her body. He reached for her hand and she thought he would pull her legs down, but instead, he unclasped her fingers from the dagger she gripped and placed it above her head where he'd laid her other two beside his.

"Let's not bring weapons into our bed with us, aye?"

"Aye," she agreed. She rolled over onto her side, still hugging her knees to her chest.

He trailed his fingers down and up her arm, then followed her spine all the way to the tip of her tail-bone. He kept going, to glide up her inner thigh and stay there, drawing lazy circles on her skin.

"Maggie, let me in, love."

Her stomach contracted with every touch, and the ache bloomed between her legs. Still, she held tight. "Why couldn't we have done this in the water?"

He slid his fingers over her mound again, pushing slowly between the folds of her sex that protruded from between her drawn-up legs and rubbing into her slick center. The breath expelled from her lungs in a loud exhale, and her arms relaxed, her legs parting more the deeper he delved.

Her eyes had closed and her lips loosened, her pelvis already rocking to his rhythm, spiraling quickly out of control.

"The water will wash your wetness away. 'Tis what eases my entry, aye? The slicker you are from my touch, the more enjoyable it will be for both of us."

She couldn't answer, feeling like her swollen folds were almost ready to burst. His fingers just kept pushing through them in a steady, gentle rhythm. Then he slipped one palm to her inner thigh and pushed on it so she rolled onto her back, her legs spread wide and her knees pulled up, her wet, ripe center completely exposed to him.

"Keep holding your knees up and doona close them," he said almost harshly. Then his head ducked between her legs, his hands lifting her arse and his tongue sliding over the very center of her with long, flat strokes, devouring her just like he'd said he would.

She gasped as she raced toward her release, her body splintering into hundreds of pieces as he pushed his fingers inside her, first one then another, pumping and licking. Her sex clenched around him. He pushed her up to the breaking point again, clamping his lips around her nub and sucking on it hard while he flicked it with his tongue. His fingers pressed on a spot on the inside that had her splaying her knees even wider and arching her back. But when she knew she was about to burst, the biggest and loudest one yet, he took his mouth and his fingers and his tongue away.

She opened her eyes and saw him moving up her body between her spread thighs. His eyes shone wild and feral, his color high and lips parted as he panted through them. A rounded, blunt pressure at her entrance pushed slowly upward, driving her wild, and she couldn't help jerking beneath him, dislodging him.

"Maggie, for the love of all the angels in heaven, hold still or I'll lose my seed before I'm inside you."

She released her knees and wrapped them high around his hips, her hands clinging to his shoulders. She pulled him down on top of her as he repositioned himself, and the pressure at her entrance returned. He pushed forward quickly this time, and her pleasure quickly turned to a pinching pain. But he didn't give her a chance to feel it, thrusting forward through her swollen folds. The pleasure returned, and she shuddered, the hard ridge of his pelvis riding over her most sensitive spot and that nudging pressure behind on her arse from his sac swinging against her with every thrust.

He'd blanketed her with his body, his mouth open over hers, thrusting in deep with his tongue, almost dueling with her as they lost their minds to the carnality of pleasure. As though they might consume each other. His chest hair scraped over her sensitive nipples, and she rubbed against him, dragging her mouth from his. Her head tipped back as she burst around him, her inner muscles clenching and pulsing around his shaft like her body wanted to milk every last drop of his seed. He shouted out his own release, and his body jerked above her before he collapsed.

They shuddered as one, bodies moving together with the aftershocks, breath still huffing.

When the rush had subsided, she pushed on his shoulder, unable to breathe. He wedged his arms beneath him so most of his weight shifted from her to his elbows.

She gazed up at him, tracing his features with her fingers, fascinated by the look of him, the shape of him. When she reached his lips, he nibbled, then sucked the tip of one finger into his mouth, making her groan again. "We had best be truly married now, Callum MacLean, because that was far more"—she waved her other hand between them, trying to think of the word now that her mind had turned to mush— "carnal than I thought it would be. I doona know how I'll ride the rest of the way to your castle—or look Gavin and the rest of the men in the eye."

"Aye, Lady MacLean." He leaned down and kissed her before continuing to nuzzle just below her ear. "We are married. And you willna ride to my castle. You'll ride to *our* castle—or walk if 'tis necessary. Or do naught but rest here all day if you prefer. The water has restorative powers, and you'll feel better in no time."

"You'd like that, just so you can turn me into a carnal beast all o'er again."

He kissed across to the tip of her shoulder. She could feel his smile on her skin. "It willna always be so wild, Maggie. I didn't hurt you too much, did I?"

"Nay, not really. 'Twas soon forgotten among all the *carnality*." And it had been. Her restlessness had disappeared, but left in its place was an uncertainty. Not borne of the actual tupping, since she was no longer a virgin and knew she would enjoy being with her husband in that way, but an uncertainty that arose from her spirit. "Callum, you asked me to trust that you knew what I needed. You did. You do. I gave my body to you, Husband. I'm entrusting it to you, putting it in your care. But ne'er forget that my body houses my heart and mind. Take care with those too."

He lifted his head from where he'd kissed down into the valley between her breasts. "Aye, Maggie. I will take care of those always. And know that mine are in your care as well."

Tears welled, and she blinked them away as she wrapped her arms around her husband's neck. She couldn't have asked for a better answer. Her eyes filled again. She'd just sniffed and wiped them clear when a man materialized out of the darkness behind Callum, and she froze.

Sixteen

BETWEEN THE SPACE OF ONE HEARTBEAT AND THE next, Callum felt Maggie freeze beneath him and saw the look of horror in her eyes as she gazed over his shoulder. He grabbed one of the daggers lying on the ground by their heads, turned his shoulders, and flung it, shielding his wife's body with his own.

The man behind them toppled over, his hand clutching his throat where Callum's knife protruded from his windpipe.

Callum kept turning, letting out a sharp, distinctive whistle, and flung a second knife. It flew from his other hand and straight at another man just coming out of the shadows, hitting him in the chest. Blood soaked the man's dirty shirt, and he fell to his knees, dying within moments.

Callum grabbed his sword with one hand and Maggie with the other as he sprang up from their makeshift bed. She'd grabbed two daggers but hadn't used them, terror and shock clearly etched on her face.

Two more men appeared, wielding swords, and Callum backed up against the rock, Maggie behind him. No one could get to her without going through him.

"Use your daggers if you have to, Maggie," he yelled, "and if I fall, run like hell for our men. Doona try to save me."

He whistled again as he went into battle, a call to Gavin and the others to let them know he and Maggie were under attack. A whistle came back, then several others, signaling that they were also being attacked. He just hoped it hadn't been an ambush, that they'd been alerted in time either by his first whistle or one of their men on guard.

They may very well have whistled at him too, but he'd heard nothing because he'd been too busy tupping his wife, his ears filled with the sounds of her moans and the blood roaring in his veins, his heart thudding like a drum as he'd pushed into her body. He'd been utterly lost to the ecstasy of being inside Maggie. Under no circumstances would he be dying after only one time with her. And if these men who'd attacked the MacLeans on their own land thought they could get to her, they'd find out why Callum was the best sword fighter in all the Highlands.

He swung at the closest man, swinging and striking with his sword. His opponent was good but not good enough. Callum disarmed him and sliced through his belly just as the second man brought his sword down right where Callum had been standing before he'd twisted his shoulder around. The blade skimmed past harmlessly. It was a mistake on the other man's part, and Callum kept his momentum going to swing his sword up, slicing heavily through the man's groin and into his abdomen.

He pulled his sword free with a sickening sound just as Maggie yelled, "Callum, behind you!"

One last swordsman came into the glade, weapon raised. He hesitated just long enough to look at his four fallen companions, and Callum hurled his sword. It drove right through the man's gut and out the other side. He fell backward onto the ground. Callum picked up one of the attackers' swords, then sprinted to the fifth dead man and pulled his own sword free. He scanned the area as he returned to Maggie. She crouched against the rocks, trembling, her daggers gripped in her hands. He whistled out a sharp message to the others and was happy to hear their replies.

"Maggie." When she didn't respond, he called her name again, louder this time. "Maggie!"

She looked at him, and he saw the glint of tears on her cheeks. "I didn't throw my daggers. How could I not have thrown my daggers? They could have killed you, Callum, because I froze. Why couldn't I throw my daggers?"

"They're dead, Maggie. It doesn't matter."

"Aye, it does. I swore I'd protect you."

"There's a big difference between throwing your daggers into a tree and throwing them to kill a man when he's charging at you, sword in hand. My warriors train for months to overcome that alone."

"But I failed you."

"Never, Maggie. Now get up and get dressed, quickly. More may come this way at any second. If they do, you get behind me, do you understand?"

"Aye."

He helped her up, and they ran to where their clothes were draped over the rock. His shirt was wet with blood from one of the fallen men, but he didn't care. Even if the linen were clean, it would just soak up the blood already sprayed on his body.

Maggie moved fast, and he suspected she'd practiced. She'd have needed to dress quickly in the dark as part of her plans to escape Irvin and her own castle. He'd sworn to himself she'd never have to worry about that, and yet here she was, under attack and fighting to stay free and alive. Although he suspected these men would have taken Maggie, not killed her. Raped her, most likely, seeing as Irvin's plan had been to get her with bairn. He burned inside at the thought and couldn't wait to run his sword through that man's black heart.

But the men who'd attacked them didn't look like MacDonnells. They'd have to look through each man's clothing for identifying marks, perhaps even letters. He had a feeling this attack had more to do with the notes Maggie had given to him than the MacDonnells who'd been chasing them or the traitor in the MacLeans. Though something told him it was all connected.

"Hold on to my plaid at the back and doona let go unless we're attacked. If that happens, climb up the nearest tree like you did when the wolves came after you, and use your daggers and bow for defense, aye?"

"Aye."

He tugged Maggie behind him, going as quickly and quietly as he could, swords in both hands. It was about a five-minute hike from the pool to their camp during the day, without having to worry about an enemy force hiding in the dark. Now the trek was longer. They needed speed, but they also needed stealth and care. He had to trust that Gavin and the others would be able to hold their own against…how many? If five men had attacked him and Maggie, how many more had attacked the rest? They were all good fighters, even Finn. Callum had made sure of it before he'd allowed Gavin to bring him along. But too many men could overwhelm even the best fighters.

Something alerted him, a noise maybe, or the moonlight glinting off something that shouldn't be there. He stopped, and Maggie stopped behind him. She pressed her forehead into his spine for a moment before stepping back. Aye, smart lass. She'd be ready to let go if he had to fight.

He heard whispers, and he signaled for Maggie to conceal herself in the brush, then crept forward just off the path. Two men were crouched ahead, arrows notched on their bows, watching the fight in the camp down below.

The fire still burned in the middle of the glade, and relief flooded through him to see all of his companions still standing, still fighting—except Gill, who by the looks of the arrows in many of the fallen attackers, was in a tree somewhere sniping from above. Drustan stood beside Finn, his body angled protectively toward the young lad, who held his own. Artair fought beside Gavin, who did battle with a savagery Callum had seen in him only since his son was taken.

That rage boiled just beneath the surface and was

always looking for a way to come out. What better place than a battle, defending his friends?

"I doona see him," one of the men in front of Callum said to the other. "He must have moved."

"Well, unless you want him raining down arrows on us, doona shoot until you see him clearly."

"But he hasn't shot anyone in the last minute. Surely he's out of arrows by now. If Laird Mac—"

An arrow pierced the man through the eye, and Callum groaned silently. Which laird? Who had sent them?

The other man jumped and darted into the trees, right into Callum's sword. Callum pulled his weapon free and whistled to let Gill and the others know he was here, then stuck his sword out. An arrow landed two feet in front of him, Gill's signal that he understood.

Aye, if it had been his enemy standing there and not Callum, Gill wouldn't have missed.

He ran silently for Maggie to find her halfway up a tree, her bow over her shoulder. "Maggie," he whispered as softly as he could but still be heard, "come down. The trail guards are dead. I need you hidden in a safe place so I can go down and help the others."

"I saw. Gill took out one of them. I'm going to help him."

"Nay, you canna. You're not a trained marksman. There is more to what Gill does than just aim and shoot. You'll be killed."

She hesitated. "But I want to help."

"Then come down. That's the best way you can help right now. You are not prepared for battle, and I canna train you how to be a warrior in the next few minutes. Come down now. 'Tis an order, lass—from your husband and your laird. Already, you've put us in danger."

Maggie let herself drop down the trunk, her skirts tied up between her legs, just as an arrow hit the tree where she'd been clinging moments before. Callum cursed beneath his breath and dived with her into the under-brush as she let out a muffled squeak. His heart pounded with fear, as fast as when he'd watched her slide down the pulley from the castle wall. He pulled her farther away, their bellies to the ground, before he pushed her into a depression in the soil and rolled on top of her.

He heard the sound of an arrow hitting a body, then a cry as a man tumbled out of a tree on the oppo-site side of the glade. The enemy—struck down by Gill, no doubt—after he'd revealed himself by taking a shot at Maggie.

He shuddered. His wife would be the death of him yet. If something happened to her… Callum would be just like Gavin, grieving his loved one but without hope that someday Maggie would be returned to him.

The edge of the glade was just a few feet away. He grabbed some dirt and smudged it over his exposed skin before silently rolling off Maggie and laying his extra blanket over her, the dark colors blending into the night.

"Doona move until I come for you," he whispered.

He pulled the hood of his plaid up and belly crawled to the edge of the glade, careful not to make any noise or shake any foliage.

At least twelve dead or dying bodies littered the ground around them. Plus the five men he'd killed up at the spring, the two at the trailhead just now, and the marksman Gill had taken out. That made twenty. A large fighting force to keep hidden on someone else's land.

He hooted like an owl this time, to alert the others that he was there, watching, and to ask for a status report. Gill hooted in return, closer than he'd expected. Part of Gill's skill as a marksman was not only to take out the enemy with unerring aim, but also to stay hidden and move unseen to another perch and another, staying ahead of any marksmen the enemy might also have. Like the marksman who'd almost killed Maggie minutes ago.

Fear still had its roots in Callum, and he found himself furious not only at the enemy marksman, but at Maggie herself. They would have a good, long talk later, and she would listen to him. In matters of her safety, if he deemed something unsafe, she was not to do it.

He could *not* lose her.

He crawled out of the bush slowly, revealing himself, knowing Gill would have his back if anyone else appeared.

"Is Maggie all right?" Gavin asked, covered in blood. He was holding up Artair, who had a long gash down his side.

"Aye, barely," Callum said as he jogged toward them, eyes on the downed bodies and looking for survivors. "Any alive?"

Gavin jerked his chin at a man who was still moving and in obvious pain.

Callum crossed over to him. "Good. I doona think these are MacDonnells."

"Nay, me neither." Gavin helped Artair down and then followed Callum to the wounded man. "It's hard to tell in this light, but their plaids aren't right."

"Aye." He approached the man, careful to kick aside any weapons before stepping on the man's arm to restrain him. Gavin stepped on his other arm. The man had a gaping belly wound and was too weak to lift his legs. He'd been taken down by one of Gill's arrows—a killing shot that would take him hours to die and leave him in great pain all the while.

The man was nearing his middle years and had a rough countenance, with several blackened teeth and a scar down the side of his face that crossed over one eye. Callum had to remind himself that if the men had captured Maggie, this man might have waited in line to rape her.

He quelled his fury at the thought. Instead of pushing a hand into his enemy's wound and causing more pain, he crouched beside him and caressed a gentle hand down his cheek, much like a mother would do. "You're dying, lad," he said, even though the man looked older than Callum. "And not an easy death, either. I would help you with the pain, but I have no herbs with me. All I can do is end it quickly, so you suffer no longer. Would you like that?"

The man grunted and nodded.

"Aye, me too," Callum continued. "What's your name, so I can say a prayer for you?"

"They call me…Scythe." The man wheezed through the pain.

"Because you were a farmer?" Callum asked.

"Nay, because it's…how I kill…people. Doona play games…Laird MacLean. Ask your questions… and slice my throat."

Gavin knelt beside him. "Are you a MacDonnell?"

"Nay."

"A MacLean?" Callum asked.

"Nay."

"But you have men inside Clan MacLean?"

"Aye."

"And did they kill my father? The old Laird MacLean?" Callum's heart raced, wondering if he'd finally get some answers.

"Nay. I doona know who…did that, but it wasn't one…of us."

"Who is 'us'? What clan are you? Where have you been hiding?" Gavin asked.

"At a farm. Not far from here. Waiting for you."

"Working with Irvin Sinclair?" Callum asked.

"Aye. He's one…of ours."

"Your clan, Scythe. Who is your laird?"

The man didn't answer, and Gavin pressed his thumb near the open belly wound.

"Stop! Stop!" he screamed. "It's Clan—"

An arrow plunged into Scythe's chest, and blood sprayed up from the new wound. Gavin and Callum jumped back and ran for cover as a horse and rider raced into the clearing, near to where Callum had hidden Maggie. The man's arrow was sighted on Callum, and he would have loosed a killing shot, but Maggie's dagger hit the man dead center in the forehead a second before Gill's arrow hit him in the chest. He toppled off the racing stallion, whose eyes were wide with fear, ears flattened against his head.

Callum yelled at Maggie to get out of the way, but it was too late—it had been too late as soon as she'd stepped in front of the horse with her daggers in her hands. All she had time to do was spin away before the horse barreled into her and ran her down.

Yelling in terror, Callum sprinted toward her. The others closed ranks around them, weapons raised, looking for other assassins and making sure this one was dead.

He knelt beside her. She lay prone on her side, turned away from him, her body crumpled like she was dead even though he couldn't see much blood. Hadn't Drustan's wife died like this? By a horse? Aye, but she'd been kicked.

He frantically took her hand, leaned down to look at her closely. Words poured from his lips, making no sense at all. "We are married, lass. And will be for a good, long time. I tupped you hard and you liked it. I spilled my seed. You canna get out of being my wife that easily! You may have our bairn growing inside you already. Open your eyes, love."

Her eyes, those beautiful hazel eyes that had been filled with need and desire not long ago, stayed closed. Her lovely, expressive face was so pale beneath the streaks of dirt, it made his heart clench.

"Maggie, open your eyes! Look at me, dearling. Now!" He pressed his ear to her mouth, hoping to hear her breathe. Her fingers squeezed his leg, and he felt her eyelashes flutter against his skin. He cupped both hands around her cheeks, gently turned her head.

"Doona move her until we know she's all right," Drustan said at his shoulder, his voice rough, almost broken. He crouched on her other side and leaned close. "Abi," he continued. "Abi, look at me."

A chill ran down Callum's spine. What was

Drustan's dead wife's name? Abigail. The English lass who had resembled Maggie.

"Drustan," he said, his heart breaking for this man whom he considered as close as an older brother or uncle, a confidante, and a friend. "'Tis Maggie, not Abigail. Look at her red hair, man. She's Maggie MacLean. My wife."

Drustan's eyes met his, clouded with memories and stricken with grief. "Aye, Laird. I know. I'm sorry. 'Twas just a slip of the tongue. It took me back to when…" He didn't finish. He didn't need to. Callum knew what he meant.

Maggie was not Abigail! She would not die!

"Callum," Maggie whispered, and he turned to her.

"I'm here, love. Are you well?"

"Nay. My shoulder and head hurt."

He felt on the side of Maggie's head where a bump had formed, but when he pulled his hand away, only a small smear of blood coated his fingers. Still, head wounds could be serious.

Her shoulder was a different matter. It looked like it was dislocated. He'd watched Lachlan's wife, Amber, push a shoulder back into the joint several times, but the manipulation required a lot of force. It didn't look like Maggie's arm was broken, but her hand had a circular cut on her palm. That had been left behind, perhaps, after the stallion had run over it.

"Can you sit up, lass?" he asked, his arms circling her shoulders to help her.

She tried but lay down again immediately. "Nay, I feel dizzy and sick. Just let me rest for a while. Do what you have to with the bodies. You'll need to search them, aye?" When he hesitated, she squeezed his hand. "I'm not dying, Callum. I'm in pain. I think my hand is broken, but it's not my throwing hand, and I feel dizzy from banging my head. But I'm alive, and you're alive. We all are. This was a win for us. You fought well, Husband."

Pleasure surged in him at her words. He gripped her head tightly, then kissed her forehead, moved his lips down her face to her mouth, unable to stop reliving those moments. When the stallion had run her down. When the arrow had hit the tree in the exact place she'd just been. When the attackers had tried to ambush them at the pool. Not to mention the wolves, her devil of a cousin, and her ride on the pulley from the castle wall. When Callum finally withdrew, convinced she was battered but would be all right with rest, he scowled at her. "Doona think I've forgotten that I told you not to move until I returned for you."

"I heard no such thing. You put me in a hole and covered me with a blanket. I couldnae hear anything. Besides, you said I could protect you too. Well, I did. Finally. And I will do so again if the chance arises."

He sighed. Aye, she would. He'd married Maggie MacLean, a warrior faery princess who liked to throw daggers and climb out windows for fun. He'd best get used to it.

"Just so you know, Wife, you aimed well. But so do I. My seed is strong. I shall have you pregnant and surrounded by red-headed bairns in no time. You willna be able to climb out of windows for much longer."

Seventeen

CALLUM CARRIED MAGGIE THROUGH THE NARROW
passageway that led from outside the MacLean Castle
wall into his solar, lit only by the candle Gavin carried
in front of them. He carried her like a bairn, her head
resting on his shoulder, her legs wrapped around his
waist, his hands supporting her under her arse. He was
careful not to scrape Maggie's knees on the stone wall
and walked as softly as he could so as not to jar her.
She was in enough pain already.

The ride from the hot springs had been hell and
should have taken less than two days but ended up
taking almost four. They had ridden off the common
trails as much as possible and avoided any signs of
people, lest they were attacked.

They'd managed to put her shoulder into place
once she'd been able to sit up, but not without difficulty. It hadn't been easy or pain-free, and she lost
consciousness in Callum's arms soon after they'd
started manipulating the joint.

That had almost been a relief, and they were able
to shove hard to fit the shoulder into its socket.

Afterward, they'd braced her hand with sticks and linen strips around her fingers and wrapped her arm in a sling.

Upon finally reaching the castle, Callum had given Drustan and Gill strict instructions about putting the MacLeans on high alert and sent the others through the portcullis. Once they'd disappeared, he and Gavin had taken Maggie through the secret passage directly into the keep.

Her safety was paramount.

"We're here," Gavin said. "How do I open it?"

"'Tis like the one at Gregor's between the kitchens and the storage shed, except the lever is at the bottom. Push slowly. A chest sits in front on the other side. 'Tis on a cloth, but I doona want the stone scraped."

A second later, he heard a click, and the door swung open. The room beyond was cold and dark, left closed since Callum had traveled out with his men to meet Lachlan over two months ago. It had been a long two months. Both men had gotten married, and Lachlan had avenged his brother's murder and ensured his wife's protection. Callum prayed he could avenge his father's murder soon too, and keep Maggie safe from the traitor in his home.

"Once Maggie's attended to, we'll need to plan," Gavin said. "I'll warm up the room."

He went directly to the hearth and used his candle to light the kindling under the piled-up logs. They started to crackle.

Maggie lifted her head slowly from Callum's shoulder. "Are we here?" she asked.

"Aye, love. We're in my solar. Gavin's just lighting

the fire." He leaned against the secret door until he heard it click and then pushed the chest back with his foot. He'd check it later to make sure nothing remained to give the entrance away.

"Can you get the door, Gavin? The key's in my desk. Underneath where Gregor used to hide his key to keep us out of his *uisge-beatha*."

Gavin grinned as he moved to the desk and crouched in front of it, using his fingers to feel for a ledge. "I'd forgotten about that. Lot of good it did him. I doona think he thought it through when he decided to take five boys on as fosters."

"You were all terrors," Maggie said. "I remember when you'd come to visit, and the five of you, plus John and Ross, would tear up the keep. Our old steward would run around behind you pulling out his hair. Followed by our housekeeper."

It pleased Callum to hear the sleepy smile in her voice, and he squeezed her just a little tighter, rubbed his hand gently up and down her back. "You've misremembered, Wife, if you think it was just us boys running around. I remember you right there in the thick of things with the rest of us."

Maggie laid her head on his shoulder. "Probably. I gave our steward and housekeeper many bald patches as well, I'm sure."

"Found it," Gavin said. He moved ahead of them to the door and opened it, then returned to the desk to replace the key.

Callum stepped into the dimly lit hallway with Maggie still in his arms. A stooped old man in a long nightshirt stood at the opposite end of the passage, holding a candle and looking concerned. He jumped when he saw them coming out of the solar.

"Laird MacLean?" he asked.

"Aye, Donald. I'm sorry we scared you."

"For sure, my heart nearly jumped out of my throat. What's going on? Men are moving around the bailey, and the torches are lit when only sinners should be awake. And who's that with you?" he asked.

"Laird MacKinnon and Lady MacLean. We need a healer, Donald. She's hurt."

"Lady MacLean? Och, is it wee, wild Maggie MacDonnell?" Donald asked as they neared. "She's always held a special place in my heart. I'd heard Laird MacKay married, but I didn't know you had as well."

Maggie lifted her head and smiled at the steward as they passed by. "Good evening to you, Donald. I remember you well, sir. You brought me some oat cookies to fill my belly after my tutor forbade me supper for failing to attend to my studies. I apologize for all the ruckus. 'Tis not my best introduction to Clan MacLean."

"Doona worry about that, Lady MacLean. 'Tis good to finally have you here, no matter how you've arrived."

"Call for the healer, Donald," Callum said as he marched to his chamber, "then bring us some food and prepare our room and one for Laird MacKinnon. And we'll all need water for baths. We are thick with dirt from the trail."

"Aye, Laird," Donald said as he hurried to do Callum's bidding, and despite the late hour and the ruckus in the bailey, his footsteps were lively and his smile happy.

And why not? Clan MacLean finally had a lady in their castle—although Maggie wasn't like any lady they'd ever seen. Callum had no doubt she'd win over every one of them just like she'd won over his men.

He pushed into his chamber and moved immediately to the bed. It still looked fresh and clean, despite the fact that he'd been gone for so long.

"Can you sit for a minute, love, while I pull back the covers?" he asked her.

"Nay, doona put me between the linens. On top is better. I need to bathe first, or we'll have dirt throughout our bed." She stilled, then looked up at him, her skin flushing red over her pale cheeks. "I meant to say, the bed. I doona know where you intend me to sleep."

Gavin snorted from where he crouched in front of the fire. "Underneath him is my best bet, Maggie."

Callum looked for something to throw at his foster brother, but he didn't need to look long. Maggie took an acorn from her pocket and, using her good hand, nailed Gavin in the back of the head with it. Gavin yelped and loosed a string of curses, turning to glare at Callum, who grinned at him innocently.

"It wasn't me," he said.

Gavin glowered at Maggie as he rubbed his head. "Och, you're as bad as all my other sisters-in-law. Amber would twist my stones off in her grip, and Caitlin would look so lovely and confused, like a baby deer, I'd want to drown myself in the loch for being mean to her. Hurry up and get better so I can throw something back at you next time."

She lay on the pillow atop the quilt and closed her eyes. Callum leaned across her, grabbed the covers, and then pulled them over her. He could see sleep tugging her under, and when she spoke, her words were a bit slurred. "Just so you know, Gavin, I can look like a baby deer too. 'Tis part of my charm. And I'll use it if you throw anything at me. Drowning yourself in the loch is up to you."

A knock sounded at the door, and Donald entered, followed by several men who carried buckets of steaming water. They disappeared behind a screen in the corner where Callum's tub sat. Several women followed after them with trays of food and drink.

They all gawked upon seeing Maggie sleeping soundly on the bed, excited expressions crossing their faces. They broke into a flurry of whispers, and Donald silenced them with a stern look. Aye, Maggie must be tired to sleep through this noise, and without a pain draught, either.

"Laird MacKinnon, I've prepared your room and bath across the hall. Would you prefer to eat in here with our laird or over there?" Donald asked.

"Neither." Gavin swiped a full cup of mead from the tray and took it with him as he walked to the door. "I'll bathe first and then eat in the laird's solar." He looked at Callum. "You'll join me after the healer's gone? There's still much to do."

"As soon as she's been tended and is sleeping comfortably."

He nodded and left, just as the healer, Flora, a kind woman with graying hair and smiling eyes, hurried in with her satchel of tools and herbs. She looked at Maggie. "Well, would you look a' that. As lovely as a wee lamb and so brave too, if what the men are saying is true." She moved to the bedside and sat down, patting Callum's shoulder along the way like he was no bigger than a lad. "Wake up, lassie. Let's take a look at you so we can get you back to tossing daggers and protecting our laird. 'Tis good to have a smart warrior woman like you leading our clan. Just like our ancestors of old."

Maggie's eyes opened slowly, and she smiled at Flora as if she'd just found a long-lost friend, then promptly burst into tears.

"Aye, cry it out, love," the healer said. "You're safe here now, home with all the MacLeans." She'd managed to unwrap Maggie's many layers with barely a nudge to her body, and Maggie lay on the quilt in just her thin shift, her flood of tears quickly gone. And Callum stood there, helpless to do anything.

He gasped when Flora pulled Maggie's shift aside and he saw the extent of her injury. The whole side of her body and arm was black and blue, some spots already turning green.

He knelt at her head and stroked his hand over her hair. "Ah, Maggie, love. I knew you were hurt, but I had no idea it was this bad."

"I'm going to check your head and the rest of your body first, Lady MacLean, then we'll give you a pain draught and set your hand. With luck, you'll be back to saving our laird in no time."

❧

Callum walked down the passageway toward his solar. Two agonizing hours had passed while Flora worked. He'd watched her examine his wife, then massage

Maggie's shoulder to aid healing in the joint. That in itself had Maggie in tears, even though she never cried out. He'd had to hold Maggie down as Flora had worked through Maggie's hand from the heel of her palm to the tip of every finger, trying to realign every tiny bone and loosen up the hand, which had Maggie both in tears *and* crying out.

Pushing open the solar door, he found a tired-looking Gavin sitting at the desk. Drustan sat opposite him, looking like a ghost of himself—pale skin, dark-rimmed eyes, hollow-cheeked.

The same way he looked, Callum supposed. How they all looked after the last ten days.

But he couldn't repress a shiver as he remembered Drustan calling out to Maggie, thinking in that moment that she was his dead wife, Abigail…and the tormented look in his eyes when he'd returned to reality.

Drustan had always been so stoic. And now Callum had seen him crack. His heart broke for his friend, for what he'd gone through, but at the same time, it made his gut clench whenever he thought of Drustan near Maggie.

Nay, it wasn't fair of him to think that way. Drustan had survived a crushing blow that Callum couldn't fathom—losing his wife. He would show his friend some support rather than condemning him, and he squeezed Drustan's shoulder before he sat down in a chair opposite the desk.

"Is she sleeping?" Gavin asked. "We heard her cry out a few times."

"Aye. She wouldnae take the full pain draught until the very end." He shook his head. "Stubborn woman."

Drustan nodded. "The best ones always are."

"So that's why your eye is twitching and a muscle is jumping in your jaw," Gavin said.

Callum rubbed his finger and thumb over his eyes, then his palm over his jaw. "More than likely. Although having a traitor in our midst and being attacked by more than twenty brigands on my own land is enough to do it too."

Gavin grunted in agreement as Drustan nodded.

"What do we know so far?" Callum asked.

"No rider arrived from the outpost after the pyre was lit," Drustan said. "We've sent thirty men to investigate. Either they ne'er saw the fire, or the outpost was attacked and everyone killed, or the rider the outpost sent to alert the castle was killed before he arrived."

"The last option is the most likely," Gavin added, "but we decided it would be best to send more men just in case. And then they can join in the sweep of the farms and countryside looking for traces of the enemy. There may have been more than just those men who attacked us. If naught else, maybe we can track where they came from and bring relief to the MacLeans they may have hurt—or killed—during their stay."

"Agreed," Callum said. He looked at the pile of sealed letters in front of Gavin on the desk. "You've written to Gregor and the lads?"

"Aye. I told them to come here, no matter if they're at Maggie's castle already. I suggested they leave half the troops there, but to make sure they have enough men with them to fight off any ambush. We need to discuss what was written in the parchments. It's related to the group who attacked us, I think. Most importantly, we need to identify the enemy. Only then can we understand their motive and what their next step might be."

"'Tis obvious they want to stay hidden. We need to unearth them," Drustan said.

"And the traitor in our clan, along with the man who killed my father."

"Discover the identity of one, and you may discover the identity of the other. You'll have your justice, Brother," Gavin said.

Silence fell, each man lost in his own thoughts, before Drustan cleared his throat. "Was there anything else, Laird? I must confess I canna stay upright any longer."

"Aye, Drustan. Take some time for yourself tomorrow. And Finn, Gill, and Artair too. We all need time to rest and recover."

"I will. I'm...not feeling myself lately. A few days will be all I'll need." He smiled at them as he rose to leave, but it didn't reach his eyes.

When the door was firmly shut behind Drustan, Gavin caught Callum's gaze. "He needs more than a few days. Is he ill? What ails him?"

Callum shrugged, feeling protective of Drustan even though he'd wondered the same thing. "I thought you would recognize it."

"What do you mean?"

"I think he's grieving."

"Grieving whom?"

"His wife."

Gavin's eyebrows shot up. "She must have died o'er twenty years ago?"

"Aye, but..." For some reason, he didn't want to

tell Gavin what Drustan had said after Maggie was hurt. "I think Maggie reminds him of her. It's become fresh in his mind...his heart."

Gavin's eyes filled with understanding, with pity and regret. He raised his hand and rubbed his palm over his badly shorn hair. "Say no more. I know the feeling well."

Callum sighed heavily, tired beyond measure now, and wished he hadn't brought up Gavin's loss. "I do as well, but certainly not to the extent that you and Drustan do. To lose a child as you did or a beloved wife like Drustan did is a tragedy beyond compare. My father had his flaws and lacked judgment in many areas of his life, but he always loved me well. My childhood, even before I was sent to live with the four of you, was happy."

"Aye, mine too. 'Tis what I had hoped for Ewan, and then his mother had rejected him even before he was born. Now..." His voice broke, and this time, when he rubbed his palm over his hair, he grasped it and pulled it roughly away from his scalp, making Callum wonder if that was why he'd shorn it in the first place. "'Tis the unknowing. He's alive, I feel it. But is he loved? Is he safe? I willna know until I find him... and then I will kill whoever kept him from me."

They sat quietly for a moment before Gavin gathered up the letters he'd written and rose from the desk with the candle. "We should sleep," he said. "'Twill be another long day tomorrow."

"Aye." But Callum knew Gavin would work through most of the night, as he always did. Sleep brought him no relief.

Callum trailed Gavin to the door and locked the solar behind them. He slipped the key in his sporran and followed his foster brother to their rooms, where two warriors—men Callum knew well and trusted— guarded his wife. At the door to his chamber, he paused. Without looking at Gavin, he said, "'Tis time we finish this, Brother. You need your son with you, and I need my wife safe."

"Aye, Brother," Gavin responded. He sounded bleak, as if he was now doubting that he'd ever find his son. "'Tis time."

Callum pushed open the door and slid the bar across behind him, taking no chances. He stripped down to his clean shift as he approached Maggie, asleep in the middle of his...their bed. After tossing his clothes across a chair, he pulled off his boots and socks. Drawing back the covers, he crawled in beside her, thankful she'd hurt the opposite side.

He slipped his arm underneath her neck, and when she didn't seem to be in pain, he edged even closer to fit her snugly beside him. His body stirred, feeling her softness and warmth. She looked so beautiful in the firelight that his heart hurt. He let his mind wander back to their time together at the hot springs. Someday, when the dangers to her and his clan were over, he'd return with her to the pools and do all the other things he'd wanted to do to her in the water.

For now, he could wait. Aye, his wife was on his land, in his home, and in his bed. Life was good. Once she was healed and the traitor in his clan found, they had a whole lifetime for tupping.

If he could just keep her alive until then.

Eighteen

MAGGIE ROUSED FROM SLEEP SLOWLY, THE SOUND OF birds singing outside the window and Callum breathing softly in her ear bringing her to awareness. Everything still hurt, which she found most annoying, as she'd been in bed, sleeping on and off, for over two weeks. Shouldn't she be healed by now? Maybe she would be if Flora didn't keep coming in twice a day and massaging her shoulder and hand, manipulating every joint and muscle before placing the hand in freezing water.

Gah! She hated being an invalid. At least the pain and dizziness in her head and queasiness in her stomach had abated. She'd even managed to eat half her evening meal last night.

Her memories of the ride from the hot springs were a blur of pain and fear—fear that she'd slow the men down and they'd be attacked, that Callum would try to fight while holding her and he'd be killed, that they'd be hiding from the enemy, she would cry out from the pain, and they'd be found. The thoughts kept running riot in her head, mixed up with a haze of pain and sickness.

It had been torturous, nearly as bad as when her mother had been mortally injured falling into the old well. She'd died slowly, painfully, as Maggie, just seven years old, had crouched fearfully beside her in the dark, calling out for help until her voice was hoarse. Finally, her father and brothers had come, but her mother hadn't made it.

Her father had never been the same.

Even now, Maggie felt that same wave of guilt, regret, and shame well up from her belly. She'd been told many times not to go near the old well, but she'd done it anyway, chasing that beautiful butterfly. She'd never seen one that bright an orange before.

She bit her lip and tried to contain the sob that wanted to burst from her throat, trying to stay silent, to push the feelings away. What was the matter with her lately? She'd lost all control of her emotions. When she and Callum had been making love, she'd been almost frantic, not knowing what to do with the way she was feeling. He'd calmed her, said it was because she felt vulnerable.

Bah! She'd had enough of that. She needed to find her weapons and take charge of her life. Irvin might have run her out of her old home, but she refused to let the traitor in Callum's clan run her out of her new one.

Gritting her teeth, she edged slowly and silently out of the bed so as not to wake her husband. She stopped to look at him—a beautiful, warrior angel—and felt that fluttering in her chest. Like a bird was trapped inside. With a clarity she'd never known before, she knew she would do anything for him. She would put herself in any kind of danger to save him, even though he wanted to be the one saving her.

She'd start by scouting his castle, planning their escape routes, and planting her weapons. Then she'd find the bloody traitor in their midst. If Callum was right and she'd soon be surrounded by red-headed bairns, she would not abide any threat to them. She just had to look in the places Callum had missed.

She pushed herself up slowly, her arm still in a sling to keep her hand protected and to ease the strain on her shoulder. At least her breath came easier, a sign her ribs were healing, and now that she was up, she realized her shoulder felt better too.

Maybe she wouldn't stick her knife in Flora the next time the healer touched her. Not that she'd have done it anyway, of course. For some reason, Flora felt like home. Similar to how Callum felt, but different.

Spotting her daggers on the bedside table, she picked up all four of them, wondering where her fourth had come from. She hadn't seen it since she'd embedded it in one of the wolves that had attacked her. Maybe one of the other men had had it all along.

Hobbling like an old woman, she stepped behind the screen in the corner and used the clean chamber pot as quickly as she could—which wasn't very quick. If it wasn't for the fact that she didn't want Callum to find her squatting there, she might have just stayed. Instead, she took a deep breath and forced herself to stand. When she finally straightened and the pain subsided, she looked longingly at the empty tub.

But she had work to do first.

Crossing to the middle of the room, she looked

around Callum's—their—bedchamber. It was a large, richly furnished room, but it felt as though the fine quilts, intricate woodwork, soft woolen carpet under her feet, and beautiful tapestries on the wall were an afterthought. The room looked lived-in—Callum's worn-in boots lay carelessly on the rug, and his plaid was draped where he'd tossed it over one of the chairs in front of the hearth. His sword was propped up by the side of the bed, and his daggers took over the table next to it, pushing the finely wrought candleholders and cups to the side.

Even the tapestries on the walls weren't spared. His saddlebag lay against one of them, pushing it askew.

Aye, he was not a man who put much stock in fine things. Unless maybe they were books. She always remembered Callum in his younger years having a book or parchment of some kind in his possession and taking good care of it.

She looked at the door. That would be the first obvious point of entry for an attack. Where would be the best place to hide daggers to defend Callum and herself if the need arose? She gazed around the room and hobbled to the closest tapestry, lifted it away from the wall, but a sword was already hidden behind it. She looked behind the next tapestry and found two more daggers. Where hadn't Callum hid weapons?

She crossed to the hearth. If she found some there, she was going to replace his with hers. Aye, one was behind a bowl on the mantel. But had he thought to hide any down low? Or under the chair? Surely she could find a way to secure a weapon under the wooden chair.

She braced her good arm against the stone mantel

and tried to lower herself to her knees. About halfway there, her ribs pulled, and she had to let go of the mantel, crying out in pain as she tumbled to the floor.

"Maggie!" Callum yelled, jumping from the bed and racing to her side. He gently helped her into a sitting position. "For the love of Christ, lass. What are you doing?"

"I would think that was obvious, Callum MacLean."

"You're lying on the floor, writhing in pain, when you should be in bed, sleeping. How is there anything obvious about that, Maggie MacLean?"

"My daggers," she said, indicating the four knives scattered on the floor around her. "I was hiding some of them to be safe, but you used up all my spots. So I was checking to see if you'd hidden any in the hearth or under the chair. Men never think to look down low, but if someone has you trapped under them, you willna be able to reach the mantel."

Callum stared at her, a twitch in his right eyelid and a muscle jumping in his jaw. Apparently, he agreed with the necessity of hiding weapons down low.

He gathered her in his arms, mouth tight as if he was stopping himself from saying something. After carefully lifting her, he walked to the bed and laid her down. Maggie almost groaned in relief, but she didn't want him to know how much she'd needed his help.

Aye, she was a daft woman.

He sat beside her and clasped her uninjured hand. "Maggie, you doona need to worry about hiding daggers because I'll—"

"And escape routes," she interrupted.

"What?"

"Escape routes. I was going to look for them next." She held her breath and found she was actually enjoying herself, despite the ache in her ribs and hand. She wondered how long Callum could keep calm, and what she could say next to make his eyelid twitch.

He blew out a loud breath and then said something she could barely hear, cursing most likely.

"I willna convince you to let me protect you, will I?"

"Callum, why would I do that? Aren't you happy to know that I have the ability to protect you? And someday possibly our bairns? I know I froze at the hot springs, but you said you could work on that with me. And if you do, I promise to work on your aim with you." She kept her face innocent, knowing he'd catch on to what she'd said, to the two different ways her words could be interpreted.

His gaze jumped to hers, so quick and alert. It made her want to sigh and invite him between her legs, to start practicing right then despite her pain.

He leaned forward and bit her neck in retaliation, then trailed his lips upward to suck her earlobe into his mouth and nip it too. "Aye, we'll be working on my aim, Maggie. We'd start now if not for your injuries. You've already done enough damage to yourself this morning."

She lifted her good arm to pull him closer, but he clasped her hand and drew it to his mouth for a kiss before rising from the bed and retrieving her daggers. "So you want one hid in the hearth and one under the chair?"

And there she went again, wanting to cry. Because he'd put his own feelings aside and supported hers.

She nodded, unable to get words past her tight throat. Then she forgot about anything else but her husband in front of her as he leaned down on his hands and knees, head in the fireplace, and pointed his barely covered arse toward her.

Her eyes widened, especially when his shift rose up and she saw those heavy stones of his hanging down. An excited gasp escaped her lips.

"Quit staring at my arse, Maggie," he grumbled.

"Then quit waving it in my direction, you daft man."

He grunted but continued to work in the fireplace, and she continued to stare, wanting so badly to rise from her sickbed and cup those twin, muscular globes. Then slide her hand down and squeeze the other twin globes between them.

The idea filled her with yearning, her blood drumming in her veins, the softest parts of her swelling as heat and wetness gathered between her legs. She raised her hand to her mouth and bit down on her thumb so she wouldn't moan aloud. It was most unfair that she was finally married to Callum and she could do nothing to slake her need for him.

Well, she could do *that*. Her hand slid down her body of its own accord, then stopped when he suddenly backed out of the hearth, minus one dagger, and sat back on his heels. "It's near the front on the left side. Are you sure you want it inside the hearth? If the fire is burning, the metal will heat and burn your hand when you grab it."

"I'd rather my hand be burned than be dead. Or you dead."

He scowled, then grabbed one of the intricately

designed chairs and flipped it upside down. After a second, he jammed her second dagger into the wood so it lay flush against the seat.

"Use this one instead, if anything happens—not that it bloody well will. Still, I'll bring the mason in tomorrow and have him craft some hiding spots on the hearth down below. 'Tis a good idea. I should have thought of it."

"See?" she said, a smile splitting her face.

He grunted, then scanned the chamber as if taking an inventory of all the hidden weapons and hiding places in the room. "Anything else?" he asked, his back to her.

"Aye, a rope. Long and sturdy enough to climb out the window. We'll store it under the bed. In fact, have one made for every room above the second floor, just in case."

His shoulders tensed, but he didn't say no. "I'll see what we have in storage. Anything else?" He glowered at her over his shoulder. "And it better not be a crossbow, rope, or pulley."

She'd thought about all the things she'd wanted over the years. It was exciting to think that she could just ask for something and it would appear. At Clan MacDonnell, she'd had to keep everything a secret for so long. "I've always wanted a net. A big, sturdy one."

He spun around, a look of incredulity on his face. "Maggie MacLean, you've lost your bloody mind. What in heaven would you do with a net?"

"I doona know exactly, but I'm sure I could drop it on someone. Or maybe jump into it if I had need." He looked like he was going to refuse her, and she said, "'Tis customary to give your wife a gift when you marry, is it not?"

He threw his hands in the air. "And that's what you want? Not jewels or fine clothes or even land? You want a big net?"

"Aye."

He looked heavenward and muttered under his breath before shaking his head and reaching for his plaid. "You shall have your net, Maggie MacLean. My wedding gift to you. And it will be the biggest bloody net you've e'er seen."

❧

Maggie groaned in pain, her chin raised, her head pressed against the wall as Flora massaged upward from the heel of Maggie's hand and over her little finger to the very tip—the last digit to be so manipulated. For today at least.

"All done," Flora said as she reached for a pail of cold water on the floor—freshly drawn from the well and delivered only minutes ago by one of the maids, who was now busy filling Maggie's tub behind the wooden screen with hot, steaming water.

Maggie relaxed against the pillows propped up behind her and lifted her hand into the pail, which Flora had placed on the quilts. The cold water stung, and she grimaced, but she knew from experience the soaking took the swelling down and relieved her pain for a good, long while—without the use of herbs. Flora also said it quickened the healing.

"How's your stomach?" the healer asked as she prodded Maggie's shoulder, which no longer hurt.

"It's good. The sickness has abated, and the headaches and dizziness have passed. I could have eaten two of everything they brought me for breakfast this morning."

"That's good news. A serious head injury can cause lasting damage."

"And my hand?"

Flora smiled in that tender, understanding way that made Maggie want to curl up in her lap like a bairn. "A full recovery. Your ribs and shoulder too. You'll be back to tossing daggers and protecting the clan in no time, Lady MacLean."

A relieved sigh escaped Maggie's lungs. "All thanks to you, Flora. As much as I've hated your treatment at times, I can see and feel afterward how it's helped." She wriggled her hand in the water and slowly stretched out her fingers. "And please, doona call me Lady MacLean—at least not in private. It's Maggie."

"Aye, thank you, Maggie. I will." She rubbed her knuckles down Maggie's cheek. "You remind me of my own daughter. All that fire and passion in your heart and clarity and creativity in your mind. I can only imagine how you must miss your own mother at a time like this. I know she died years ago, but I can tell that she loved you well."

Emotion rushed upward from Maggie's chest at the unexpected words, said so gently and lovingly. She pressed her fingers to her mouth to contain the sob, but it was too strong and broke free anyway. Her eyes flooded with tears, and they ran down her face.

"Och, lass. I'm sorry. I didn't mean to upset you."

Maggie lowered her hand and squeezed Flora's. "Nay. 'Tis all right." She blew out a breath and tried to smile. "I…I do miss her, even though it was so long ago. She held our family together. Everything slowly unraveled when she left. First my da, then my brothers. It hasn't been easy."

"She didn't leave you, Maggie," Flora said with just a hint of chastisement. "She died. Believe me, if she could have stayed, she would have. There is no stronger, no more protective love than that of a mother for her child. Someday you'll find that out. Soon, I hope."

The tears welled again, and this time Maggie didn't raise her hand to cover the trembling of her mouth. "Aye, she died…because of me."

"Nay, not because of you. Because you were her child, a piece of her heart and soul, and it was her right and duty to protect you. Doona take that away from her."

"But if I hadn't been—"

"Nay, Maggie. You were a child, doing childish things—exactly as you were supposed to do. And she was your mother, doing everything she was supposed to do as your mother. Everything you will do one day for your child. It was an unfortunate accident, but no one was to blame. Forgive her, Maggie. And forgive yourself."

Maggie nodded. "I'll try."

"Aye, you will. And in the meantime, I will tell you all the dangerous things my children did that almost got themselves killed—and me too as I tried to save them. And all the stories of the other children I treated, and their parents—some who survived, some who didn't—and you will come to understand that carelessness and disobedience is part of childhood, and rushing to the rescue is part of parenthood. It is a miracle most of us survived."

Maggie snuffled and laughed at the same time. "Maybe I doona want to be a mother after all. Certainly not if they take after me."

"Aye, I'm afraid our laird will be assigning numerous guards to each child, and they'll still get into trouble."

A knock sounded at the door before one of the maids rushed into the chamber. She bobbed a curtsy to Maggie before turning to Flora. "There's been an accident in the stable, Flora. One of the grooms was thrown from a horse. They need you."

"I'll be right there."

The maid ran from the room, and Flora hurriedly packed up her bag. "Soak your hand for a goodly amount of time, Maggie. At least until the cold wears off. I'll return to help you in the tub if I can."

"Doona worry about that, Flora. I can manage."

It was well past midmorning by the time Maggie stood naked beside the tub, her hair a wild, knotted mess that tumbled over the curve of her behind. She'd dismissed the maids a while ago when the tub was filled, and now she wished she hadn't.

Not to worry. Maggie could climb into the tub herself, couldn't she?

She pulled the sling over her head—for the last time, if all went well today—and carefully moved her arm. Luckily, her shoulder didn't hurt, and she could raise her arm high enough to keep it out of the water. Leaning forward, she braced her hand on the tub's edge and slowly lifted her leg.

So far so good, but when she tried to swing her leg

over the top, she realized she wasn't far enough forward. She'd just decided to bring her leg down when she heard the door open. Relief flooded through her, and she called out, "I'm back here, Flora."

She knew it couldn't be Callum. He had gone to the loch with Gavin for a swim and intended afterward to go to the quarry to look at rock the mason wanted to use to resurface part of the keep. It was an ongoing project that would take years, Callum had said.

She rested her leg on the lip of the tub, knowing that Flora would be able to steady her and help her over. She looked up with a smile as the edge of a woman's skirt came into view around the corner of the screen. But it wasn't Flora. Nay, this woman was younger and quite lovely, with fair skin and black hair twisted into an intricate braid. Her age was beginning to show around her sharp, blue eyes.

Eyes that didn't reflect the cheery smile on her face.

Maggie generally had a good sense about people—although she'd had no idea about the depth of Irvin's treachery—and her hackles rose immediately. The woman's smile turned to round-eyed concern as she rushed at Maggie, and there was nothing Maggie could do about it.

"Lady MacLean, let me help you!" The woman didn't give Maggie a chance to respond as she grabbed Maggie around the ribs and pushed her leg over. Maggie gritted her teeth to stop from crying out, not wanting the woman to know just how vulnerable she was even though the fading bruises on her skin were obvious.

Why didn't I bring my daggers with me?

"Stop!" she yelled once she had both feet in the

water. She breathed deeply and tried to dredge up a smile. "Pray forgive me. I'm afraid I've hurt myself on the journey here. Perhaps just let me balance on your shoulder as I sit down."

"Aye, of course, Lady MacLean."

Maggie soon sank beneath the water and felt less vulnerable once she was covered, although she knew it was a false sense of security. If the woman intended to harm her, Maggie was at a grave disadvantage.

"I am glad to be able to help. I would have come to pay my respects sooner, but our laird, my cousin, has guarded you these past few weeks like a dragon guards his gold."

It was a good comparison, but Maggie suspected the woman used it to ingratiate herself with Maggie. What new wife wouldn't like to think of herself as being as important to her husband as a dragon's hoard?

"Your name?" she asked. "You said you were my husband's cousin?"

"Aye, Lady MacLean. My name is Glynis. I am married to Keith, the son of our laird's mother's sister." She picked up a bar of soap and a cloth and held them up for Maggie to see. "May I?" she asked.

The request to tend an invalid in the bath, or to attend one's lady, wasn't unusual, and it would have been considered rude had she not offered. But Maggie was hard-pressed to say yes.

All she could manage was a nod and smile before she drew her knees up and pulled her hair over her shoulder. She'd originally planned to wash it, but she had no intention of letting this woman dunk her head under water.

"I canna tell you how excited I am—we all are—to have you here at long last and married to our laird. I've been praying all these years for my cousin to honor your marriage contract and finally bring you into his home."

Maggie let that sit for a moment. It was a well-placed insult to both her and to Callum—bringing doubt to Callum's character and implying that she wasn't much wanted by him. "'Twas my understanding there was much distress in the clan after the old laird died. Callum made it clear he would have attended me sooner if not for that."

"Trouble, my lady? Aye, 'twas a sad day. Some suggested the old laird had jumped, but that was soon put to rest. I'm sure your husband was verra upset when it happened. Everyone grieves in their own time, be it three months or three years. He did come for you eventually. You must take pride in that."

She noted how easily the words flew off the woman's tongue, how good she was at hurting and then soothing—one then the other. Verily, Glynis was someone to watch, maybe even to add to her list of possible traitors. Most likely, she was just trying to retain her status as a high-ranking woman in the clan. She was cousin by marriage to the laird. Perhaps she'd thought of herself as the clan's lady before Maggie arrived and bumped her down the ladder. It would be reasonable to assume she was trying to reclaim her place.

But then again, maybe not. She had a cunning air about her.

Maggie needed to render her words useless and then see what else Glynis would throw at her.

"I am proud," Maggie agreed with a bright smile.

"Thank you for reaffirming how fortunate I am to be married to our laird. He has certainly blessed me by finally making me his wife."

Glynis's mouth firmed, and inside, Maggie chuckled. Aye, it would be frustrating to try to hurt someone with your words and have them take pleasure from them instead.

Dipping the cloth in the water, Glynis rubbed it in circles over Maggie's back. After a moment, she said, "Look how lovely you are, Margaret MacLean. Surely you had many fine men wanting to show you their affection these past few years. 'Tis not easy to be chaste when your betrothed keeps company with others. But that's all in the past. I'm sure he's thanking God he returned for you and you've forgiven his indiscretions."

Indiscretions?

Grasping Glynis's hand with her uninjured one, Maggie let the woman feel her strength. She met her gaze directly. "I thank you for your attentions, Glynis, but my bath is done. I have much to do now that I'm Lady MacLean. And of course, I must practice with my daggers. Did the lads tell you I killed a man who tried to kill our laird? It gave me quite a fright to see Callum so close to harm. I willna hesitate to use my weapons in defense of my family." She rose from the tub, unaided this time, her shoulders back, her body sleek and strong even though she'd been so badly hurt. "And I think you are mistaken about my husband. Callum assures me of his fidelity these last few years. I believe him."

Glynis rose as well, and Maggie could see in her eyes that her mind raced and she knew she had miscalculated. She bowed her head and dropped a small curtsy to Maggie. "I have indeed heard you are skilled. The lads talk of naught else. 'Tis a boon to our clan that you are here with us at last." She stepped to the edge of the screen and bobbed another curtsy. "I shall take my leave and hope to see you at the evening meal."

After she disappeared around the corner, Maggie moved more quickly than she would have thought possible and climbed out of the tub. She grabbed her drying towel and held it up to her body as she stepped around the edge of the screen, not wanting Glynis to be left unwatched in her bedchamber.

The sly woman was just opening the outer door. Maggie stopped her. "Glynis, have you e'er met my cousin Irvin Sinclair? He is a blackheart and a devil of the worst kind. Soon he will be taken from my castle and hanged for his crimes. 'Tis a bad day to be a traitor."

Nineteen

MAGGIE STRAIGHTENED HER PLAID AND RAN HER PALM lightly over her hair to make sure it wasn't sticking out all over the place. She'd barred the door as soon as Glynis had left and then slowly lowered herself back into the tub for a proper wash. She'd hardly been able to wait to dip her head and cleanse her hair of dirt and sweat— although it had been awkward to do with only one hand.

Afterward, she'd been exhausted but had forced herself to sit on the chair in front of the fire and brush through the tangles, working through the curling strands in sections. God's truth, it had taken her at least an hour, if not more, to finish the job with just one hand. She'd been tempted to crawl back into bed, hoping Callum might come to find her. But ever since Glynis had left, Maggie had felt an urgency to explore the castle. More than ever, she needed to know how she could escape, if need be. To plant some weapons in the castle and begin her own search and investigation for the traitor.

Just a continuation of what she'd done at her own keep, really. And she'd proven very good at that.

After making sure her two remaining daggers, plus one more Callum had given her, were properly sheathed under her arisaid along her forearm, she unbarred the door. She smiled when she met the beaming faces of her guards—Artair and Finn.

Then she scowled. "Which one of you let that awful woman into my chamber? God's truth, she tried my patience. I had to practically threaten her with my daggers to get her out." Maggie didn't want the men to know of her suspicions, but she also didn't want Glynis in her room. The news of Maggie's displeasure would spread through the guards like wildfire.

"'Twas not us, Lady MacLean. We just came on duty," Artair said, following in step behind her as Maggie swept past. "'Tis good to hear you sounding like your old self though."

"Aye," Finnian added. "We missed your sweet voice. Such a gentle sound, like a wee bairn cooing for his mother."

Maggie barked out a laugh as she glanced avidly around the passageway, counting doors and noting every nook and cranny.

"In truth, we were all so worried about you, lass," Artair said, his light tone filling with concern, "but Laird MacLean assured us you were recovering well."

"I am feeling much better, thank you." She stopped at the top of the stairs that headed to the great hall below and turned to face the men. Beside her, another staircase continued upward to the third floor, making her wonder how many floors there were in all. "I'm sorry I slowed us down on the way here. I fear I put you all in grave danger. If we'd been attacked…"

"Och, lass, doona e'er think such a—"

Artair's reply was interrupted by the sound of a woman's voice singing horribly out of tune, coming from somewhere upstairs. The song was punctuated by the sound of running feet crashing down the staircase from the upper level.

Seconds later, a lass, no more than perhaps seventeen, came barreling around the corner, her gaze fixed on a sheaf of parchments in her ink-stained hands and a lute strapped across her back. Not watching where she was headed, she was going to plow straight into Maggie.

Finnian moved to intercept her, but she caught sight of him at the last minute, squawked in alarm, and darted past, knocking him into the tapestry on the opposite wall and colliding with Maggie anyway.

The tapestry came off its moorings and fell onto Finn as Maggie groaned and stumbled backward. Luckily, Artair caught her just in time before she fell down the stairs and broke her other hand.

The lass—tall, with sandy-blond hair and intense green eyes—tumbled to the passageway floor. Her sheaf of parchments scattered into the air and fell around her.

"Lady MacLean!" Artair yelled. "Are you well, lass?"

"I will be when you stop squeezing my shoulders," she gasped.

Artair quickly released her with a mumbled apology and squeezed his hands around her middle instead.

Maggie grimaced. "Lord have mercy, that hurts too. I'm all right. Please, let go."

He did, hovering in front of her, looking stricken as she tried to breathe through the pain. Maggie peered around him, which was hard to do, considering he took up most of the passageway, and saw Finn struggling to push the wall hanging off his head. He finally untangled himself and jumped up.

"Did you kill it, Finn?" she asked, trying to keep the laughter out of her voice. "Those tapestries are deadly."

He turned bright red and glared at the poor winded lass who still lay askew on the stone floor.

"Nay, Finn," Maggie said. "'Twas an accident. Make sure she's not hurt."

Finn's face fell, and he hurried over to the lass. She jumped up, almost knocking Finn down a second time. She looked panicked, her eyes taking in the men and Maggie, then down to her parchments on the floor, then back to Maggie.

"I'm sorry," she blurted out, looking like she was about to cry. "This always happens to me. If someone is going to make a mess of things, it'll be me." She gazed at Maggie, and her lip trembled. There was a scar there, her pretty face marred slightly by the signs of a cleft lip that had been repaired when she was a bairn. "You're her, aren't you? Lady MacLean. They said you were bonny and fierce and you'd saved Laird MacLean, putting your own life in danger. And then here I go almost killing you again."

"Well, nay," Maggie said. "I doona think I could have been killed twice."

The lass laughed—more a wet, strangled sound—even though a tear had fallen down her cheek. "If anyone could have done it, it would have been me."

"Then I should know your name, aye? Best to

know the names of those who are most likely to kill you. Twice."

The lass wiped her face and gave a slow, ungainly curtsy. "I am Aileen, Lady MacLean." She sounded like a child practicing how to be a lady, her voice formal and stiff. "Cousin to your husband, Laird MacLean."

"Thank you for the clarification. I would hate to confuse Laird MacLean with my other husband."

Aileen popped up from her curtsy and gawked at her, those bright green eyes, so similar to Callum's, going wide in her face. "Two husbands? How can you have two husbands? You jest, aye?"

"Aye." She said it gravely, trying not to laugh at the younger woman. She was a bonnie relief to meet after Glynis.

Aileen's face cleared, and she burst into laughter, interspersed with wee snorts that made Maggie laugh too. "I canna wait to tell Callum you said that."

"I'm sure he willna be surprised," Artair said.

Stepping forward, Maggie very carefully leaned over to pick up the pieces of parchment from the floor—which quickly had the others bending over to help as well. She looked at the page in her hand and tried to read the words scrawled on top. A poem, perhaps? A work in progress, with words and lines scratched out and then written over.

Aileen snatched the poem from Maggie's hands, her cheeks burning. Then she bobbed a quick curtsy and mumbled an apology. "'Tis not finished, my lady. And no one but Keith has ever read my work."

"Keith?" she asked.

"My…my…your husband's other cousin on his mother's side."

"The one married to Glynis?" she asked.

Aileen's face darkened, and her mouth grew pinched. She obviously did not care for Glynis. Discerning lass.

"Aye, she is married to Keith."

Maggie knew from the tone of her voice there was a story there, and she couldn't wait to dig it out of Aileen. She might be just the source Maggie needed to ferret out the traitor in their midst.

Maggie looped their arms together on her good side, feeling a kinship to her new cousin-by-marriage that had her grinning from ear to ear. Aye, it was always best to be friends with someone who laughed at your jests and disliked the same people you did. Especially when there was a chance those people might be traitors who intended to kill you.

"Will you show me to the kitchens, Aileen, before I expire from hunger?" she asked, stepping toward the stairs that led to the main level.

"Of course, but you doona want to go that way, or you'll ne'er get out of the great hall. Everyone will want to meet you, and then when you starve to death, I will be accused of killing you a third time."

⤫

Maggie walked beside Aileen through the keep's halls and passageways, munching on her fourth honey oat square that she'd nicked from the kitchen and trying to memorize the layout of the castle.

The cook and several helpers had been overjoyed to meet their new lady, and Maggie soon had a trencher full of food in front of her. And an earful of gossip as she heard all about the MacLean families and especially about Callum. Everyone seemed to want to convince her how devastated he was when their old laird had died and how tragic an accident it had been—emphasis on accident—that had left the entire clan reeling…with Callum to pick up the pieces.

What they were really saying was "your husband didn't come for you sooner because of terrible circumstances in our clan, and please forgive him."

She sighed. Had she forgiven him? Aye, it felt like it, if the way her body wanted his touch was any indication. It would be good if she had forgiven him, as other than Glynis, she liked everyone from Clan MacLean she'd met so far. Even the brooding Drustan with his sad, strange reserve.

"Over here," Aileen said as she tugged on Maggie's sleeve.

They ducked into a stone alcove on the second floor that opened up to the most beautiful inner courtyard Maggie had ever seen.

She gasped in wonder, amazed at the craftsmanship of the stone carvings that surrounded the arches on every level. Part of the wall on the opposite side was covered in scaffolding. In front of the wooden platforms, where men were working, a net on a pulley held up several tons of stone, which were being used to repair the walls.

Maggie eyed both the net and the pulley with interest. She wondered where she could get one of those. Nay, if Callum ever found out she had a pulley, he might go a bit mad.

She stared up at the bright summer sky that shone down on the courtyard. "Can all the MacLeans come here or just the castle folk?"

"Everyone. 'Twould be a shame if the clan wasn't able to enjoy it too."

"Aye."

Several people milled in the area below, including Callum and Gavin, who talked to a man who appeared to be the mason. A few maids enjoyed the summer sun, a man sat on a bench strumming a lute similar to the one Aileen carried, and several warriors and other workers stood about in easy conversation or simply went about their days. She saw Drustan enter, and the man playing the lute stopped.

She wanted to call out to Callum, unable to take her eyes off him, but she suddenly felt shy. What if he wasn't happy to see her? She gazed down at him, remembering how he'd touched her that morning, then left her wanting, feeling like she might melt, her body flushing, her skin tingling in soft, secret places.

God's truth, he was a handsome man, so strong and well made, his body lean and defined, his short, dark hair just long enough to wave over his forehead and frame his angular face. He raised his arm and pointed to the wall as he talked to the mason, and the muscles in his shoulders bulged.

If he were to look up at her now, she just might collapse into a heap. Her bones had turned to mush along with her mind. She truly was daft.

She glanced at Aileen, expecting to see her wearing an indulgent smile at Maggie's entrancement with her new husband, but instead, Aileen stared down into the courtyard. She had the same besotted look on her face that Maggie knew she must have been wearing moments before. Following Aileen's gaze, her eyes landed on the man holding the lute on his lap.

"Who's that?" she asked with a conspiratorial smile. "The man with the lute?"

A guilty look crossed Aileen's face. "'Tis Keith, Callum's other cousin."

Maggie's stomach sank for her new friend. "The one married to Glynis?"

"Aye."

It was a curt response, but Maggie could sympathize and took no offense. "Do you play together?" she asked.

"Well, I doona play verra well—I'm still learning—but Keith plays like an angel. Mostly I strum some chords while he plays the notes, and I hum a wee bit when he's singing. But I write some of the songs. I'm good at that." She looked shy suddenly, her gaze falling from Maggie's. "I'm writing one for you, about how you saved Callum and almost died in the process."

"I didn't almost die," Maggie protested, feeling herself flush.

"According to Gill you did. And I'm starting another one about how you shot the flaming arrows into the pyre."

Maggie huffed out a surprised breath. She didn't know whether to say thank you or draw her dagger on her new friend. "And will you also write about how I just shoveled four oat squares into my mouth?"

Aileen laughed, and it suddenly seemed absurd to Maggie, and she joined in. When she returned her gaze to the courtyard, it was to find Callum staring up at her, and just like that, she was lost in the memory of their early morning kiss. She wondered if he was thinking the same thing. Unfortunately, she would never know, as Gavin smacked the back of his head to get him to pay attention. When he finally turned away, Gavin looked up at her and waved. She waved back, then waved at Drustan, who was also looking up at her. He nodded and turned away.

Such a strange man.

She turned to ask Aileen about him, but her friend was staring at Keith once more. And when Maggie looked down, Keith was also staring at Aileen.

She was just thinking what a terrible triangle had been formed when Glynis came into the courtyard. She couldn't see her husband from the direction she entered, and she headed straight for Drustan. The stiff set of Drustan's shoulders and the way Glynis swung her arm a little too closely to him when she arrived gave it away. Maggie groaned. It wasn't a triangle at all.

Four people were involved here.

"Glynis," Aileen hissed beside her.

"Aye, lass," she said. "Keith's wife."

"You should tell *her* that."

"What do you mean?"

"'Tis not for me to say." Aileen crossed her arms in front of her body. "Stay away from her, Maggie. She's a horrible person. Lower than a snake."

Maggie squeezed her hand. "But she's still married to Keith. 'Tis not something you can change, no matter how hard you may want to."

"I know." The younger woman quickly dashed a tear from the corner of her eye. "But even before she married Keith, I hated her. She's said some terrible things to me in the past. Cruel and hateful things. I was still just a child."

Maggie gasped, her blood rising with fury that someone would hurt this sweet, funny lass. "What about?" But she'd already guessed. People like Glynis always chose the easy way to damage someone.

"About my face." She cast her gaze away.

Maggie gently pulled her chin around and ran her finger over the slightly raised scar on Aileen's lip. "'Tis naught to be ashamed of, Aileen. And truly, it's not that noticeable. Many people have scars. Whoever repaired the cleft did a good job."

"Thank you. I was still teased about it as a child. And other things. But none were as cruel to me as Glynis, once she came to the castle."

"How old were you?"

"Twelve. I'd been living here since my mother died two years earlier."

"And no one stopped her mocking you?"

"Callum did once he knew. I'd never seen him so angry. But Glynis is good at hiding who she truly is. I tried to warn Keith about her, but he was too young to know any better, and she'd wormed her way into his heart. She's older than him and…had been married before."

In other words, Glynis had seduced him. It brought to mind how she'd tried several ways to manipulate Maggie earlier. A year ago, that would have shocked her, but after hearing all the things her cousin Irvin had said about people when she'd been spying on him, Maggie had not been surprised.

She looked down at the snake, who had moved closer to Drustan. Drustan had remained in place, but his arms were crossed over his chest. Maggie didn't know what exactly was going on there, but *something* was between them. And apparently, Keith knew about it. He moved up beside his wife, who now was the one to stiffen. Aye, now she'd been caught unawares.

She heard Aileen catch her breath and found herself doing the same. After just a minute, Glynis turned and fled through the archway directly beneath where Maggie and Aileen stood.

Aileen let her breath go with a loud exhale.

Maggie patted her arm. "Doona give her another thought, Aileen. People like Glynis live to inflict pain on others. Believe me, she'll get her own back."

Tears returned to Aileen's eyes, and she crushed Maggie in a tight hug. "I'm so glad you're here. Callum told me I would love you. He was so excited, we all were, that you were to be married. But then my…uncle…died. The old laird. 'Twas a terrible time for all of us, especially for Callum. People started whispering that Ivor hadn't fallen, he'd jumped. Callum had to fight the priest to have his father buried on consecrated ground."

"Who would start such a rumor, and why would the priest believe it? 'Tis not easy to have someone declared undeserving of consecrated ground. Was there any proof?"

"None that I know of. I heard tell that he wasn't a good laird, but Ivor was always kind to me. He took me in when he didn't have to and gave me a home. I'll always be grateful to him for that."

"Aye, lass. And you should be."

A creaking noise drew Maggie's attention, and she looked across the way to the scaffold and the net of rocks hanging at the top. The net shook as if someone was moving it, then it lurched and plunged toward the courtyard and all the people below. Callum yelled "Get back!" as people screamed and tried to dash out of the way. The rope above whined as it ran unhindered through the pulley, the long line going up on one side as the rocks fell down the other.

Without thought, she pulled her daggers from her sleeve and hurled one after another at the rope, piercing the hemp and nailing it to the wooden scaffold. The net halted about fifteen feet above the heads of the people scrambling to escape. It swung in place, hitting the scaffold and threatening to knock more debris down, groaning against the weight and momentum.

She held her breath, watching her daggers, praying they held until everyone was out of danger. Within seconds, the courtyard was clear, and her new clan was safe. Except for Drustan, who stood exactly where she'd seen him last, staring up at the net full of rocks that surely would have crushed him.

People began shouting orders and running to secure the net while others sobbed. Some looked at the rope and her daggers holding it to the wooden scaffold with wonder. Callum darted forward, and Maggie gasped in terror. He grabbed Drustan's arm and pulled him to safety.

"Keith!" Aileen yelled, terror in her voice.

Callum whipped his head up to them, having heard his cousin, his face a stern mask. "Stay there," he ordered, pointing his finger directly at them. "Maggie MacLean, you doona move a muscle." Then he was gone from the courtyard, Drustan at his heels.

Maggie half expected him to come to her even though she knew he would help the others secure the net first. She wanted him *there* so she could see he was safe. Her muscles began to tremble—shock and stress, she supposed—and she leaned heavily against the wall.

Finn and Artair stood guard, and when she heard running footsteps outside their alcove, both she and Aileen looked toward the door. But it wasn't Callum's voice Maggie heard demanding to be let inside.

"Aileen!" a man yelled.

"Keith!" Aileen ran to him. Maggie saw them embrace on the other side of the archway. Then Keith pulled her away, and they disappeared down the passageway.

Maggie leaned against the wall again, closing her eyes and wishing she had a chair. Hearing Callum's voice from across the courtyard roused her. She hurried to the edge of the balcony to see him at the top on the opposite side, investigating the "accident." It made her nervous to see him standing so close to the edge.

As if he sensed her watching him, he looked up. Even from where she stood, she could see he looked worried. He whistled, loud and sharp, and made a hand motion in her direction. She leaned farther over the edge, trying to understand what he meant.

He cupped his hand around his mouth and yelled, "Get back!"

Seconds later, Artair appeared at her elbow. "Maggie, lass, come away from the edge. 'Tis not safe."

She frowned at him and considered resisting, but Callum had enough on his mind right now. Best not to gesture rudely to him in public.

It was hard being a wife and a lady. But Artair knew her well, and he barely batted a lash when she let loose a string of disgruntled curses for his ears only.

Twenty

CALLUM TOOK THE STAIRS TWO AT A TIME, GAVIN AND the head stonemason, Aulay, at his heels. An urgency born of fear drove Callum to get to Maggie as fast as he could. What had he been thinking, bringing her here? Into a keep infiltrated by a viper? He needed to send her away with Gavin, to his clan, not let her stay where danger lurked around every corner.

"Why would someone do that?" the stonemason asked Callum for the tenth time in the last few minutes—ever since they'd discovered the rope that held the rocks secure had been sliced through with a knife. The question was rhetorical, of course, a sign that the man couldn't come to terms with what had just happened. That it wasn't an accident. The fall had been set in motion deliberately to kill and harm the people in the courtyard, including Gavin and himself.

Callum turned to Gavin. "We need a list of everyone who was in harm's way when the rocks came down. They can be eliminated as suspects."

"Aye," Gavin agreed.

They were almost at the alcove where Maggie

waited, and Callum had stopped to let Aulay catch up. "I want a full report by tomorrow morning. And when you finally secure that net, I want my wife's knives returned to me, do you understand? She's very particular about her weapons."

Aulay gaped at him. "Lady MacLean? That was her doing?"

"Aye," Callum said, feeling grim and elated all at once. He was filled with pride at her accomplishment but hated that it had been necessary.

"Thank God in heaven you finally brought her home with you," Aulay said, clasping his hands together as if he were praying before he hurried away.

Grimness won out over the pride Callum felt, and he could do nothing more than grunt as he turned and made his way to his wife.

Why did I bring her home with me?

Because it was safer here than where she'd been… or had planned to go. And because he'd been about to lose her. Well, he might lose her again if he didn't see to her safety immediately.

He stopped, and when Gavin stepped closer, Callum lowered his voice. "I want you to take Maggie home with you. You offered weeks ago to do that."

Gavin looked at him, his brows raised and eyes wide. "Callum, she just saved everyone. Saved us. If she hadn't been here, the traitor in your clan would have won today. Your clan needs her. You need her."

"And what if she's next? What if Maggie can save everyone but herself? What if *I* canna save her?"

"And what if she's attacked on the way to my clan? Or in my castle? You'd ne'er forgive yourself then either."

"She'd be surrounded by your warriors."

"She's surrounded by your warriors here. Put more guards on her. Take her with you where'er you go, if that's what it takes. If Maggie's reports are true, we have traitors planted in every one of our clans by now. None of us is completely safe." Gavin lifted his hand and gestured at Maggie's alcove. "Besides, it doesn't really matter what you or I want. She'll refuse to go. Guard her with your life and the lives of your men, and give her the space to be the warrior woman she truly is."

Callum gritted his teeth, shoved his hand through his hair, and pulled on the strands until it hurt.

Gah! He could understand why Gavin had shorn his head.

He turned and proceeded past Finnian and Artair into the alcove to see Maggie leaning against the stone wall, her face pale, her eyes closed. He gently lifted her into his arms.

She let out a startled sound and opened her eyes. "Callum!"

"Aye, lass," he said as he maneuvered her out of her hiding spot. Gavin, Finn, and Artair surrounded them as they walked down the passageway.

"Put me down. I can walk," she said.

"Nay. You look done in. We're going to our chamber."

"I can walk there on my own. Put me down."

His jaw set grimly. "We have enemies here, Maggie. Someone attacked us. You could have been killed."

"*You* could have been killed! But you weren't, because my daggers stopped the rocks from falling."

He came to a halt, and the others did too, all of them

scanning the passageway for danger. "You did save us. Thank you. But…you have to let me protect you now."

"And how will you do that when I am in your arms? You canna even grab your sword. I canna properly aim my daggers. Verily, Callum, you're being daft. Put. Me. Down!"

"Warrior Woman," Gavin said, just loud enough for Callum to hear. Maggie was right, of course—they were both more vulnerable with her in his arms. But it made him feel better to have her there.

He lowered her to the floor. She swayed a bit before righting herself, and he immediately regretted his decision. But when he moved to pick her up again, he felt the point of a blade under his chin—his blade, as hers were still holding up the rocks. He hadn't even felt her steal it.

"One of these days, lass, you may miscalculate. Or I will. Then how will you feel with my blood on the ground?"

The color left her face, and she tucked his blade into her sleeve. "Then doona pick me up without asking. I'm not a bairn." She turned and resumed their trek to their bedchamber. "Tell me what you discovered."

"The rope that held up the rocks was cut, not frayed," Gavin said.

"Did anyone see anything?"

"Nay, not that we know of." Callum moved slightly ahead of her, his hand on his sword hilt. "Most of the stoneworkers in the courtyard were having their midday meal."

She reached their bedchamber door and motioned him and Gavin inside. Finnian and Artair took their positions outside in the hall, and she waved goodbye to them before closing and bolting the door.

Gavin raised his brow at her.

"Sit," she said. She indicated the two chairs in front of the fire while she lowered herself onto the edge of the bed.

After a slight hesitation, he and Gavin did as she asked, turning their chairs to face her.

"It's Glynis," she said.

Callum frowned in confusion, and she elaborated. "Your cousin Keith's wife. The one who was so cruel to Aileen when she was a lass."

He resisted the urge to roll his eyes. "I know who Glynis is, Maggie. What I doona understand is your meaning. *What* is Glynis?"

"She could be the traitor." Maggie counted down on her fingers. "She's an outsider, she's tupping Drustan, which Keith knows about, and she left the courtyard moments before the rocks came down. Not to mention I doona like her. She smells rotten under her pretty clothes."

His eyes widened. "How do you know she's sleeping with Drustan?"

"I watched them in the courtyard from the balcony. All three of them. As soon as she entered, she went straight for Drustan, who stiffened at her arrival. She stood a bit too close to him and rubbed her arm against his. Then Keith, who'd seen it all, approached them. His shoulders were tense too. He said something to them, and she ran away."

Callum opened his mouth several times to speak, not knowing how to respond. "Maggie, this is all speculation. You have no proof. And just because she touched Drustan doesn't mean he's tupping her behind Keith's back." But he remembered his talk with Drustan the night they found Maggie in the tree, bloody and torn after being attacked by the wolves. Drustan had admitted he'd been with women outside of marriage—women who wouldn't want children with him.

"Aileen knows," she said, dropping that bit of information like a barrel of tar dropping through a murder hole. "Which means Keith most likely told her. Those two are as tight as Glynis's chastity belt is loose."

Gavin snorted and rubbed his palm over his jaw. He looked at Callum. "You know that's true. Glynis *is* light in her skirts."

Maggie pinned her husband with her gaze. "She tried to seduce you?"

Callum felt an uncomfortable flush burn up his neck. Glynis had indeed offered herself up to him once, and he'd said no. Not because of marriage vows—she hadn't yet been married to Keith. But something about the way she'd approached him hadn't sat right. He hadn't thought any more about it at the time.

Maggie nodded, seeing the answer in his face. She switched her attention to Gavin. "And you too?"

"Nay, not me. But she did approach Kerr and Darach," Gavin said. "Neither of them took her up on it—that I know of."

"What about Lachlan?" Callum asked.

"I doona think so. Maybe she thought he would walk away too easily. Lachlan was ne'er one to stay with a woman or to fall in love."

"Until he met Amber."

Callum grinned. "Aye."

"It makes sense Glynis wouldnae approach Lachlan. She'd have no control over him," Maggie said, "and it seems to me that's what she's all about. 'Tis what she tried to do to me. She came into the bedchamber, uninvited, when I was vulnerable and in the tub, and tried in several different ways to manipulate me. First, she tried to ingratiate herself, then to cause a breach between me and Callum, then to shake my confidence in myself—all while being seemingly helpful."

She moved and stood in front of Callum. "She's the viper you've been looking for, I know it."

Callum tapped his fingers together, not knowing whether Maggie was right or not about Glynis—it *could* all have been a misunderstanding—but Maggie was smart and not prone to fancy. He took her uninjured hand and leaned back in his chair, pulling her gently onto his lap. He liked that she went willingly and fit so snugly against him.

"Let's say all that is true," he said. "She's sleeping with Drustan, and she tried to manipulate you for whatever reason. I saw her leave the courtyard. She didn't have time to run around the perimeter and up the stairs to cut the rope."

Maggie scrunched up her face as she thought about it. What had Drustan said the other day about stubborn women being the best kind? Compliant would be nice right about now, although she felt soft and yielding in his arms.

"Maybe she had an accomplice," she said.

"Aye, maybe. I just…"

"You just what?" she asked.

"Why would a woman murder my father and attack me? It doesn't make sense. What possible motivation could she have?"

She leaned away from him, her face filled with a growing comprehension and incredulity. "Callum MacLean, do you believe women are incapable of cold-blooded murder?"

He shifted uncomfortably under her gaze, Gavin's too. "Well…yes."

"So, it has to be a man who cut that rope today? And pushed your father over the castle wall?"

He expelled a harsh breath. "Yes, Maggie, that's what I believe. You can rail at me all you want, but I believe it was a man."

"I canna believe your prejudice," Maggie said, shaking her finger at him. "Haven't I proved to you yet that women are no different than men? They can be murderers if they so choose!"

Gavin grinned. "As much as I agree with you, Maggie, I doona know that being a murderess is something a woman should strive for."

She waved him off. "You know what I mean."

They fell into silence. Callum couldn't stop his mind from wandering to what had happened between Maggie and Glynis, fury taking hold. If Glynis was indeed the traitor, she'd been inside his bedchamber with his wife, where she could have easily pushed Maggie's head under the water. He shuddered and pulled her closer.

"We'll investigate her," he said, "and we'll start by talking to Drustan."

Maggie patted her hand on his chest. "Aye, thank you."

Gavin pulled himself from the chair with a grunt. "I'll go find him. And I'll set someone to watch Glynis too. Finn maybe? People tend to overlook him because of his youth."

Callum nodded. "Finn's a good choice. But tell him to keep his distance."

"And to be careful." Maggie's voice had filled with worry. "She's smart and capable of anything."

Gavin nodded. "I will, love. Doona worry about your friend." He bent and kissed the top of her head. "And if I haven't said it yet, thank you for saving my life today."

She smiled up at him and squeezed his hand when he straightened. Her eyes shone brightly. When Gavin left, shutting the door behind him, Callum stood with Maggie in his arms. "Can I carry you *now*?" he asked her.

"Aye, where are you planning to put me?"

She looked up at him from under her lashes, and he felt that familiar stirring in his loins that was always just a breath away whenever she was near. "On the bed. You look done in."

She put her hand to her mouth and tried to stifle a yawn.

"See?" he said.

"I suppose you're right. But you doona have to rush off right away, do you?"

"I'll lie with you for a while. I'm tired too."

"And that's the only reason?" she asked, running her fingers lazily over his collarbone.

He shivered. "Nay. The only reason is because I want to be with you. But I willna touch you in that way, lass, not until I know my attentions willna cause you pain. We were…vigorous last time."

He laid her on the quilt and then crawled up beside her, stretching his body alongside hers and slipping his arm under her head for a pillow. "Even if I just kiss you down here"—he trailed his hand over her chest and down her stomach, watching with fascination as her body undulated beneath his touch—"it'll be too much strain on your ribs, no matter how good you're feeling right now. You'll forget yourself. I'll forget myself." He nuzzled along her jaw to a spot behind her ear that was soft and warm. She released a heavy breath, blowing through the strands of his hair. "I want you too much, Maggie, and I doona trust that I'll stay gentle."

She cupped his jaw, rubbing her fingers along his freshly shaved cheek. "A kiss then?" she asked, her voice unsteady.

"Aye, Maggie. A kiss."

His lips found hers. Tiny kisses at first, just savoring her mouth. Then he slid his hand up from her stomach and over her breast, the mound yielding beneath his palm. His body hardened even more as he remembered taking her breasts in his mouth, devouring them. He growled deep in his chest and forced his hand to keep moving—before he opened her dress and pushed her shift aside.

From the way Maggie panted beneath him, he knew she wouldn't make him stop. Nay, she'd probably help him lift her skirts and wrap her legs around his waist. But afterward…he had to think about afterward. About the damage he could cause to her wounded body. A body wounded saving his life. Which she'd then had to do a second time.

He threaded his hand through her hair and held her still for a firm kiss, more just a pressing of their lips together, before he lay on his pillow. He expelled the breath in his lungs with a loud *whoosh*.

Maggie let out a whimper of protest, and he smiled. Aye, he had married a warrior woman, and it would be up to him to look out for her. He could wait another few weeks until she was fully healed.

"A few weeks?" she protested, and he realized he must have said the last out loud. "I canna wait that long! We're married, Callum. 'Tis your duty as my husband to pleasure me. I promise to lie still."

He laughed and turned on his side again, wrapping her in his arms, loving that she craved him the way he did her. "'Tis my duty to keep you safe and see to your well-being first. Which means avoiding excessive movement. Can you promise you willna do that when I touch you?"

She glowered at him but did not deny it. It was going to be a happy marriage if his wife couldn't control herself during lovemaking.

After a moment, she sighed and then snuggled even closer to him. "Callum."

"Aye, lass."

"You've ne'er told me about your father. What happened the night he died?"

He fell silent, his hand stroking her hair, wondering where to begin. He hadn't spoken about this at any length for a long time, and it seemed like he had to drag his tongue through mud to form the words.

"'Twas just after the New Year. Yuletide had been good, and everyone, including me, was excited about my upcoming wedding. Believe me when I say that, Maggie. I wanted to marry you as much then as I did now. And my father and clan wanted it too."

"I believe you. I was in the kitchen today and met the cook and her helpers. They're lovely people. They all told me the same thing. How the clan was looking forward to our nuptials before tragedy struck."

He smiled, although it was tempered with sadness. "I think Cook was the most disappointed of everyone. She's had our wedding feast planned for four years, and then we went and sealed our vows without a ceremony. Although that doesn't mean we canna have one now. We'll do that after…"

He trailed off, and she looked up at him. "After your foster family arrives?"

"That too. What I meant to say was…after we find the traitor."

She pressed her lips to his arm. "Have faith, Callum. Surely we'll be able to discover who it is, especially if we doona eliminate half the clan just because they're women."

God's truth, she was right, but his heart still protested. "I think I want it to be a man because…well, I suppose I want my father's death to mean something."

She frowned in confusion. "I doona understand. Why wouldnae it mean something if he was killed by a woman?"

"'Tis just how I've imagined it, I suppose, that he was pushed off the wall to keep a great secret quiet or…as a step in a sweeping evil plan. Something that we'll soon be able to unravel. Not because he was up there tupping someone and was pushed over the edge because of it."

Maggie sat up, her mouth open and her brow wrinkled in disbelief. "Believe me, if I were to kill you now—which I may do if I e'er hear such nonsense coming from your mouth again—it would mean something. A lot of somethings to the people who love you. And it wouldnae matter that I wasn't a nefarious monster planning to take o'er the Highlands. All that *would* matter is that you would be dead for being a mewling ablach."

He winced and rubbed the nape of his neck, knowing she was right. He prided himself on his logic, yet she'd shown him that the way he thought of women clouded everything. It was a flaw Lachlan had pointed out, as well as Gavin. Aye, those two didn't put women up on a dais. Although Gavin certainly had before Cristel had come crashing down.

Where had he learned that attitude from? His father, he supposed. Ivor had always been charming with the fairer sex, treating them like angels…unless he was tupping them. And maybe that was it right there. Maybe whoever was plotting against the clans had known that and deliberately set a woman after Ivor.

God's truth, he *was* an ablach. What else had he missed?

She must have seen the realization on his face, because she said, "Are you done underestimating me and all womankind, then? Because every time you do, it diminishes me. And it makes me want to do to you as your brother's wife would do. And not the kind, sweet wife either. The one who would grab a man's stones and twist."

He couldn't help crossing his legs and shifting his sporran over top of his privates. "You mean Amber. Aye, you'll like her. You'll like them both."

She lay down again and tucked in beside him. "Go back to telling me about your father. Did anything unusual happen before he died?"

"Naught that we discovered. He'd been cheerful all through yuletide. It happened at night. Drustan came to find me, to tell me. I was in my bedchamber but not asleep. Drustan had a letter in his hand that he'd found in my father's chamber. 'Twas a note written by my father, explaining that he'd…jumped."

Callum's heart was pounding now, and he took a deep breath to settle it. "Drustan swears the letter was false, and my father would ne'er have jumped. Which means he was murdered, and the note was placed in my father's chamber to distract us from the truth. We've been searching for the murderer e'er since. We ne'er told anyone about the letter, except my foster brothers and Gregor. And now you."

"Then why did the priest try to refuse your father's burial in consecrated ground?"

"I doona know. Rumor? There was talk that he jumped rather than fell."

"Did you see the letter?" she asked.

"Aye."

"And naught struck you as odd about it? Other than the contents, of course."

"It resembled my father's hand, but wee things were different. The formation of some of the letters, some of the phrases and wording, even where he'd written the date on the page. It was subtle, but it didn't fit. Drustan agreed, and he knew Ivor even better than I did."

She grew quiet. He did too, feeling his anxiety rise. His father's death had gone unsolved for so long.

"Callum."

"Aye?" He turned his head on the pillow to find her looking at him.

"Is there *any* possibility he did jump? That he did write that letter, and you just doona want to see it?"

He took his time answering, trying to sense within himself any hidden doubt, any spark of intuition that could point to suicide. "Nay, Maggie, I doona think so. And if I had any doubts before, which I didn't, today's sabotage proves the traitor exists and has no qualms about killing."

"You believe 'tis the same person?"

He stilled. Then his fingers tapped together as he thought about it. "I'd always assumed so, but I suppose the two events may be unrelated."

"Can you tell me about him? What kind of a man was he? Was there an attempt on your life too? You doona have any brothers, do you? Besides your foster brothers, of course. No one else with any claim to the lairdship?"

"Nay, but…"

"But what?"

Callum huffed out a breath, "'Tis possible I may have a brother I doona know about. My parents did not have a love match. Maybe they tried in the beginning, but they couldnae find common ground. And I know for a fact my father had at least one lover while my mother was alive."

"How do you know that?"

"Because a bairn came out of it."

"A sister?" she asked, then gasped in realization. "Aileen?"

"Aye."

"But she said she was your cousin. Callum, why wouldnae you—"

"'Tis her choice, Maggie. Not mine. She'd rather people think she's my distant cousin than my bastard sister. She's afraid of censure, I suppose, or mockery. Even though she knows I acknowledge her and would do my utmost to protect her."

"And love her."

He smiled. "How could I not? I consider her my sister in every way. And my father did too. He visited her often when she was growing up, and brought her to the castle when her mother died. Despite his flaws, he was good to me and Aileen and not unkind to my mother. They seemed to have an understanding. I doona e'er recall hearing harsh words between them."

"So he had one lover outside of his marriage, maybe more. Is this why you didn't want the murderer to be a woman? You didn't want his death to be about his wandering eye?"

He looked up at the ceiling and expelled a breath through his teeth. "Possibly. I ne'er saw Gregor acting toward women in the way my da did. Not that Ivor hurt them, just…he enjoyed them, and they enjoyed him, you understand? Whereas Gregor had a love for his wife so great that it survived her death. That's what I thought love and marriage should be. I found my father's charm with the lasses…disquieting. After my mother died, he was more open about it, but I was long past boyhood by then. I accepted that side of him."

"And did you learn anything new when you took o'er the lairdship?"

"I'd already been laird in all but name for several years by the time my da died. He had no qualms about me taking charge, and he was happy to hand o'er the responsibility. He wasn't a good laird or husband, Maggie, but he always loved me well. And…" He found his throat tight suddenly and had to clear it before he could continue. "I miss him."

She turned on her good side and snuggled into him. "Aye. Hold on to that, Callum."

They fell silent again. Before long, Maggie's eyes grew drowsy. She blinked heavily several times, then fell asleep. He gently rolled her onto her back and slid his arm out from beneath her head, then covered her with a blanket and headed to the door. He hoped Gavin had brought Drustan to the solar so he could answer the questions Maggie had raised.

As much as he'd first doubted Maggie's assessment of Glynis, he wondered now if there was some truth to it. Or if Glynis knew something that would lead to the traitor's capture. And if Glynis was tupping Drustan—which would not surprise him, seeing as she'd approached him, Kerr, *and* Darach—what did Drustan know of her plans, if anything?

It wasn't that he condemned Drustan for bedding Glynis, but if Maggie was right and Glynis was the traitor, then his second-in-command was compromised. They all were.

He closed the door softly behind him and nodded to Gill and Artair at the door. He felt better knowing they watched Maggie. They were beyond suspicion and would give their lives to keep her safe.

"She's sleeping," he said, "and the door isna locked. Guard her well."

"Aye, Laird," they said.

He'd just turned toward his solar when the door at the end of the hall was yanked open and Gavin strode out, his usually grim countenance lightened by a smile.

"There you are," Gavin said. He punched Callum good-humoredly in the shoulder as he passed by. "Gregor and the lads are here. I canna wait to tell them you've finally married Maggie. They willna give you a moment's peace until you tell them every detail. Gregor will relish every minute."

Twenty-one

MAGGIE SAT IN THE MIDDLE OF HER QUILTS AND stared at the beautiful dress laid out on the foot of the bed. It had been placed there when she'd been sleeping, which, by the long shadows coming through the window, must have been for hours. She rose to her knees and gently ran her fingertips over the material. The wool's weave resembled that of Callum's blanket—the one she'd worn to stay warm during the trek over the mountain—except the colors were more vibrant, the wool softer, finer, and the linen shift so smooth, it almost felt like silk.

Next to the dress were several shiny ribbons that matched the green stripe in the plaid, a new pair of supple leather shoes, and some silky hose.

A gift from Callum, most likely, and she sighed in appreciation.

She rose from the bed, feeling much stronger than even this morning, her body rested, her torn muscles and broken bones almost healed, surely.

She thought back to earlier in the day when she'd thrown her daggers to stop the rocks from falling—*Was that only a few hours ago?*—and a wave of gratitude washed through her that she hadn't broken her throwing hand. Although she was fair good with her other hand too.

She'd just risen from the bed when a knock sounded at the door, and Aileen's voice came through the wood. "Maggie, are you up? May I come in?"

"Aye, of course."

The door had been left unbarred, and Aileen pushed it open with a smile on her face. Maggie hurried over and gave her a hug. "Sister," she whispered in Aileen's ear.

Aileen startled in surprise and then, after a small sob, gently returned the hug.

Maggie pulled back and looked her in the eye. "And I'll proudly call you that in front of everyone, if you'll let me. Callum too. Believe me, no one will dare cross the two of us. And if they do, you tell me." She reached for a weapon under her sleeve and found the dagger she'd taken from Callum in the leather sheath strapped to her forearm. "I'll wave this in their face and scare the wickedness right out of them."

Aileen stared at her, eyes wide, then she burst into a mixture of tears and laughter. "Well, then, you may call me sister whene'er you like. And I'll do the same to you. 'Tis my duty if it helps rid the land of wickedness." She grasped Maggie's uninjured hand and pulled her to the bed. "Come, let's get you dressed. Callum has a surprise for you."

She helped Maggie out of her clothes and then into the fine arisaid laid out for her. Picking up the end of one of Maggie's long curls, she asked, "Do you want me to weave some ribbons through it? Or braid it? I'm afraid I'm not verra good at the intricate hair styles some of the women wear."

"You mean Glynis," Maggie said with a grimace. "Doona worry about that for me. Callum wouldnae recognize me if my hair wasn't a bit wild, I'm sure."

"I can sprinkle the strands with some lavender water so the curls stay smooth and then pull it away from your face with a ribbon. My mother had hair like yours, and she swore the flower's oils stopped the curls from flying in all directions."

"Aye, that sounds perfect," Maggie said, sitting on the bed with her back to Aileen. "Can you give me a hint as to your brother's plans?"

Aileen's hands stilled in Maggie's hair. "Nay, Callum threatened to make me sing in front of everyone if I breathed even one word of it. My…brother… was most adamant that it stay a secret. I *can* say that I think you'll like it."

She brought over a vial of lavender oil that she added to a bowl already filled with a small amount of water. She mixed the two and sprinkled the water on Maggie's curls, then used a wide-toothed comb to work the oil-infused water through. It looked very pretty, and Maggie decided she would use the special water on her hair from now on to help tame it.

Which made her wonder—had she been tamed in some way too? Had Callum stroked his hand down her body and kissed her lips and changed who she really was?

She examined her hair, liking the sheen on the curls and the way her locks were drying into a glossy, curly mane. It was still her hair, just not so apt to fight her anymore. Perhaps the lavender water was like Callum's presence in her life—her hair was soothed by the oil and became its best self in the same way she was soothed by Callum. But would she become her best self, or did he want her to be someone else entirely? Someone not so apt to shoot arrows and climb out of windows?

She suppressed a sigh, not wanting to alarm Aileen. Besides, she had more important things to worry about. She could fight Callum about his expectations of her later.

"Face me now, please," Aileen said.

Maggie turned, and her sister-in-law fluffed her hair with her fingers, then picked up the matching ribbon, looped it behind Maggie's neck, and tied it on the top of her head.

She smiled. "Oh, Maggie, you look so beautiful. Come on." She took Maggie's hand and tugged her to the door. "I can hardly wait for Callum to see you."

They exited into the hallway. Artair and Gill were still there, and they beamed at her. "Och, you look like an angel, lass," Artair said.

"Aye," Gill added. "If I didn't know you were our Lady MacLean, I'd think you a lady in the Seelie Court."

She felt the heat stealing up her neck. "Being attacked by wolves and chased o'er a mountain has done wonders for my complexion. Not to mention a change of clothes and clean hair, of course."

They laughed, and then Gill said, "Wait here. I'll just let them know you're coming," before he darted ahead.

Maggie turned on Artair and pinned him with her

gaze. "Do you know what Callum has planned? My husband's sister willna tell me anything. After all we've shared, you'll tell me, aye?"

His brows raised and he glanced at Aileen, who'd flushed the color of the red berries the weaver used in her dye. "His sister, is it? Aye, I found it remarkable that for such distant cousins, you and Callum looked so similar. 'Tis the eyes. It's good to own who you are, Aileen, no matter the circumstances."

She nodded jerkily, and Maggie squeezed her arm in support.

"And I willna tell you anything," Artair continued, returning his gaze to Maggie, his huge arms crossing over his enormous chest. "Your husband would send me home to Clan MacKinnon in disgrace."

Just then, Gill appeared around the corner and waved them forward. Maggie's heart increased its rhythm in anticipation. She expected to be led down the stairs to the great hall, but instead, they proceeded to the chapel that Aileen had shown her earlier in the day. Inside was a sight to behold as the chapel opened onto a balcony that overlooked the inner courtyard, and light from above poured into the sanctuary.

Six men were in conversation in the hall outside the chapel door, including Gavin, Callum, and an older man opposite him. They were dressed in their best shirts and plaids and looked like they were fresh from a swim in the loch.

She stopped in surprise, peering at their faces. It had been years since they'd all been at her keep, running wild with her brothers, but other than the distinct differences in Gavin, they looked relatively the same.

And the older man, whom she'd never paid much attention to before—he must be Gregor MacLeod, gray streaks running through his auburn hair and beard, his face deeply lined across his forehead and down his cheeks. And he was smiling at her like a delighted old woman.

"God's truth, Callum! She's a vision." he said, coming forward to embrace her.

"She's still injured," Callum warned. "Doona squeeze her hard."

Maggie wrapped her arms slowly around Gregor's back, her fingers barely touching around that broad chest. When he pushed her to arm's length and looked at her, his eyes so happy and warm, she let go her reserve and smiled at him.

"Hello," she said, feeling like a lass of five rather than a fierce, almost-twenty-one-year-old woman who'd fought off both wolves and wicked men.

"Hello, Maggie," he said. "Welcome to the family, lass. I canna tell you how happy I am to see you here and wed to my Callum. I'm sorry to hear that circumstances in your clan are so grave, but I promise we'll do whate'er it takes to rectify the situation. Your cousin's deeds willna go unpunished. Nor any of his accomplices'. I promise you we will root them out, help Ross if we can, and find John."

"Thank you, Laird MacLeod—"

"Nay, we doona stand on formality within the family. You will call me Gregor."

"Or donkey breath, as we like to call him," one of the foster brothers said, and the others laughed.

She thought maybe it had been Kerr, the huge,

wicked-looking rogue who wore his long black hair tied in a leather thong. He also wore an expression on his face that was just a bit too innocent. She frowned in his direction and was considering what she could throw at him for his insult to Gregor and where it would hurt the most but cause the least amount of damage. Gavin interrupted her contemplations, saying, "Och, run, Kerr! Look at her face. She'll come after you now. And she willna just twist your stones like Amber did. She'll twist and then prick them with her dagger."

"My Amber's an angel! You're addled if you think otherwise," another brother said, one she recognized as Lachlan. He frowned at Gavin, but his blue eyes were filled with pride and amusement. Aye, she remembered Lachlan—always laughing and up to some mischief when he wasn't trying to tup the lasses…and succeeding more often than not.

She reached up her sleeve for her dagger, only to find her leather sheath empty. Whirling around, she saw Callum standing behind her with the dagger she'd stolen from him in his hand.

"Looking for this?" he asked.

"I thought merely to cut the long locks from Kerr's head. I think he'll fall just like Samson if I do. No matter. I'll get another blade."

Kerr raised his hands to cover his hair. "What have I done? Quickly, hide your daggers!" he said to the men.

The last brother had to be Darach, the one married to Caitlin, the innocent lass who apparently had all the men doing her bidding with a single, sweet look. He made a scoffing noise deep in his throat. "You worry for naught, Brother. I remember Maggie well.

Someone poured tar in her hair, and a chunk had to be cut out. She would ne'er commit such an atrocity on someone else. Even if 'twas you, Kerr, who did it. Would you, lass?"

Maggie's ire rose at the memory—the stickiness of the tar and her brother Ross doing a hatchet job on her hair as he cut it off to her shoulders. But she could see the laughter within Darach's brown gaze and didn't know if he told the truth. She glowered at Kerr anyway for good measure. He quickly retreated, sending the other men into gales of laughter.

Darach grasped her hand. "'Tis an honor, Maggie, to be able to call you sister. For sure, you have married the best of us." He stepped forward to embrace her, and she found his dagger pressed into her hand.

He stepped back with a wink. The remaining men hugged her after that, and by the time she reached Kerr, she had three daggers hidden in her plaid and up her sleeves. And then all five of them watched with anticipation to see what she would do next.

She faced Kerr and opened her arms wide. "Will you not embrace me as well, Kerr MacAlister?" He looked at her suspiciously, then pulled his plaid up over his head like a hood and held it tight before stepping forward. His foolishness made everyone else laugh again, including her.

"I'll call a truce, tonight, Brother, for 'tis not every day a new wife is introduced to her family." She stepped toward him, and he grasped her hands in one of his huge paws before hugging her with one arm.

"Welcome to the family, lass," he said.

She looked into his eyes and thought she detected

guilt. She would speak to Callum later and find out for certain if it had been Kerr who'd spilled the tar in her hair, and if it had been an accident. Then she'd dole out her punishment when he least expected it.

Callum's arm snaked around her waist as if he expected trouble, and he pulled her away from Kerr, who let his plaid fall down his back.

Maggie caught sight of Aileen standing behind the wall of brothers, and she reached an arm between Gregor and Lachlan to gesture for her. "I would have you greet one more sister," she said to the men. She grasped Aileen's hand and pulled her into the circle. The lass's eyes grew round, and her skin flushed pink again. "Have you all met Callum's sister, Aileen?" she asked.

Callum stilled, his eyes searching his sister's face. "Are you sure, Aileen?" he asked. "I've always told you it's your choice, and I meant it."

She hesitated, gaze darting around to the men and Maggie. Finally, she said, "Aye. It's easy being brave around my new sister-in-law."

Callum grinned, and his eyes lit with happiness. "She makes us all braver." He turned to Kerr. "Well, most of us."

Lachlan clapped Kerr on the shoulder as they walked toward the balcony. "Why doona you just cut it yourself and save yourself the aggravation, Brother?"

Kerr glowered at them. "No one is touching my hair. Isobel likes my hair, even though she'll not admit it. 'Twill be what finally wins her over." He looked at Maggie with forlorn eyes. "You wouldnae stand in the way of true love, would you, lass?"

She couldn't help laughing, but then with a quick

flick of her wrist, she tossed the dagger at Kerr's head and sliced the tie that held his gorgeous hair behind his shoulders. A few strands dropped to the floor, and the dagger embedded itself in a wooden picture frame on the stone wall.

Shocked silence reigned for a second before the men burst out laughing—all except Kerr, who felt his hair to make sure it wasn't shorn.

"Nay, I would ne'er stand in the way of love. Consider us even, Brother," she said.

He grunted and held out his hand to her. "Swear it, Maggie MacLean."

She grasped his hand. "I swear I willna touch your bonnie hair. But I may teach Isobel how to wield a dagger."

Kerr groaned. "Why couldnae I have married first? All your troublesome wives will corrupt my sweet Isobel."

"I doona think my sister cares for your hair one way or the other, Brother," Gavin said to Kerr. "But when I tell her how much *you* care, I'm sure she'll come up with several different ways to cut it."

Kerr scowled, and Darach wrapped his arm around his shoulder. "Doona worry. I'll bring Caitlin for a visit. She'll have you and Isobel married in no time."

Kerr's face lightened into a broad smile. "Aye, now *she's* a wonderful lass."

The men all said "aye" with love-filled, sappy voices, and Maggie had to restrain herself from rolling her eyes. Men really were addled.

Someone cleared their throat, and Maggie looked up to see Father Lundie standing at the chapel door.

"Father," she said, moving forward to greet him. "I didn't know you were here too."

"Aye, lass. And I couldnae be happier to be presiding o'er the ceremony, even though by canon law, you're already married."

"Ceremony?" she asked, her heart beating faster, even though she'd guessed Callum's intent.

Callum pressed a soft kiss to her lips, a touch that had her melting. When he pulled away and she opened her eyes, it was to find his foster brothers and Gregor watching them with those foolish expressions on their faces.

Gavin handed Callum a linen-wrapped package, and Callum unfolded it to reveal a stunning gold necklace set with rubies. "I know you said you didn't want jewels as a wedding gift, but this was my mother's. She'd want you to have it, as I do." He held up the necklace. "Will you do me the honor, lass?"

She bit her lip to stop it quivering and nodded, tears coming from nowhere and flooding her eyes. She lifted her hair from the nape of her neck as he looped the chain around her neck and fastened it. His fingers trembled, and his mouth pressed into the crook of her neck before he turned her around so he could see.

The necklace nestled perfectly on her arisaid, the red jewel bringing out the red stripe in the design. "It's beautiful, Callum. Thank you."

"Not as beautiful as you are, lass. I am so happy and proud to be your husband. You are truly a remarkable woman."

"Just as I am?" she asked. "Even though it's in my nature to take risks?"

"Exactly as you are, even though sometimes I may be overprotective. That's in *my* nature."

"Aye. We'll have to find a balance between the two."

"Aye." He raised her hand and kissed her knuckles. "Gregor will walk you in, and Aileen will stand with you. Is that agreeable?" On her nod, he said, "I wish your brothers could be here, and your parents."

"And yours," she added.

He smiled. "They would have loved you." He looked like he was about to say something else, and Maggie found herself holding her breath, feeling like her heart was too big for her chest.

But then his foster brothers motioned him over. Callum cupped her cheeks one last time and kissed her before he joined them, the moment lost. They disappeared through the door with Father Lundie, leaving her wondering what he'd been about to say.

Maybe that he loved her?

Was that even possible? And did she want him to love her?

A lute began playing, a beautiful melody she'd never heard before. She raised a questioning eyebrow at Aileen. "Keith?" she asked.

"Aye, he composed it for you and Callum. Didn't I tell you he was talented?"

"He is."

Gregor held his arm out to her, and she found herself shaking. She and Callum were already joined, physically by the laws of man and spiritually by the laws of God. This ceremony held no real meaning except…it did. He'd planned all this, done this for her. It was a beautiful gesture of their life together.

Making her wonder… *Can* I *love* him? *Do I already?*

Gregor and Aileen nudged her toward the chapel door. When they passed through and approached the sanctuary at the front, she was surprised to see candles, flowers, and beautiful silks draped all around the balcony, which was open to the courtyard below. The courtyard was filled with Callum's clan—her clan—dressed up in their best.

The two scaffolds still stood against the far wall, and the net, which now rested on the ground, still held some rocks, but they could barely be seen beneath all the decorations.

Father Lundie stood at the edge of the balcony with his back to the crowd, wearing a pristine white robe with a long purple stole around his neck and the holy book in his hands. Callum waited for her next to the priest, and his foster brothers lined up on either side of the balcony.

He smiled and stepped forward to take her hand, as if he couldn't wait even one more second. She leaned up and kissed him, wanting so badly to press against him.

She stayed against his side, holding his hand for the entire ceremony and mass.

Father Lundie droned on a bit, but she found herself almost giddy with happiness. The words he uttered and had them utter passed by in a blur. Then Callum faced her, her hand in his as he vowed to love and cherish her forever before sliding a beautiful silver ring, intricately woven in an eternal knot, onto her finger. It was too big for her, but that could be fixed. She liked how heavy it was, feeling as if it represented the weight of Callum's commitment to her.

Then it was her turn, and Maggie's voice thickened with emotion as she promised to love and cherish him until death did they part. And she knew with a certainty she meant it.

Aye, I love him. With everything I am.

She slid her arms around his waist as he slid his hands into her hair and pulled her close, his mouth angling over hers in a kiss that was both sweet and passionate.

The priest was speaking again, but blood was roaring so loudly in her ears that she had no idea what he said and didn't care. Even the cheer of the crowd around them wasn't loud enough to disrupt their kiss.

Only the need to breathe had them breaking apart.

Father Lundie moved behind them, and Callum stepped with Maggie to the balcony rail, sliding his arm around her shoulders. "Lady Margaret MacLean," he announced to the clan, his voice booming with pleasure around the courtyard. "My beloved wife and your cherished lady, who will fight for all of us with a strength, skill, and determination that leaves me humbled. To Lady MacLean!" Their clan cheered again.

"Maggie, look," he said, pointing upward. She looked up to see that a net had been stretched across the open space, making her gasp.

"Is that my net?"

"Aye. Is it big enough, lass?"

"Oh, Callum, it's wonderful!" She didn't know what she would do with it yet, but she'd figure out something.

Then the net released on one side, and it fell to the opposite wall from where they stood, beside the second scaffold. Masses of dried flower petals floated down to the courtyard.

"Oh!" she gasped, awed by the beauty and the sweet smell of the roses, lavender, heather, and bluebells caught in the air drafts. The sky above was streaked with vibrant pinks and oranges, changing by the second as the sun set.

A few petals drifted right to them, and Maggie caught them in her fingers and brought them to her nose, inhaling their scent. "How did you do all this?" she asked her husband.

"I didn't do all of it. Cook and our housekeeper, Linnette, have been planning for years. And they've been working constantly at it since we arrived. We have much to thank them for."

"Aye, we do."

He picked up her hand with the silver ring. "Do you like it?" he asked. "'Tis big, but we can make it fit. The ring belonged to my grandmother. My grandparents had a long, happy marriage. It's what I hope for us, Maggie. An equal union filled with caring and commitment. And bairns, of course, if we're so blessed."

"I'm sure we will be if you e'er take me to bed." She tried to sound aggrieved, but she knew her eyes were smiling at him. How could they not?

He cleared his throat. "When you're well enough."

She leaned into him, trailed her fingers along the collar of his shirt. "I'm feeling much better. You said an equal union, Callum. That means listening to me and taking my words into consideration."

He stared at her, his eyes growing wild, his skin flushing. She could see the pulse beating in his neck. She leaned up and kissed the spot, finding it smooth and warm. Her mouth opened, and her tongue pressed against it. He groaned and pulled her in for a tight hug. "God's blood, how will I make it through the wedding feast?"

He said the last loudly, and Gregor slapped him on the shoulder. "With great difficulty. Just like I did with Kellie, Darach did with Caitlin, and Lachlan did with Amber. But the wait makes it all the more sweet."

"Well, let's get started then." Callum leaned over the balcony, looked up, and whistled. Two sturdy ropes fell down from above in front of them.

He grinned and pulled Maggie to the edge. "Do you want to slide down your own rope? Or hold on to me as I slide down?"

She grasped the rope closest to her with her good hand, eyes wide in delight. "My own, for sure!"

Gregor and the lads burst out laughing.

"Aye, of course you do," Callum said, "but let me go first so I can— Maggie!"

But she'd already stepped on top of the stone bannister. The men hooted with amusement as Callum scrambled to catch up to her. With her other hand, she held her skirts tight to her body and stepped off the ledge while looping the rope around her feet to control her descent. She and Callum slid down beside each other to another loud cheer.

They walked through the crowd, receiving well wishes and congratulations before finally reaching the head table set on a dais at one end of the courtyard. Petals adorned a white linen tablecloth, and candles lit the night. She looked up to see full dark was upon them, and stars were scattered across the sky.

"Oh, Callum. It's magical! I couldnae have asked for a more perfect wedding."

He lifted her hand and kissed it.

The servers brought out dishes filled with roast quail, pickled eel, and suckling pig; greens, parsnips, and onions; and the softest loaves of bread she'd ever tasted. The mead was sweetened with honey, and the cake afterward was filled with nuts and berries.

When the meal was finished, Keith and Aileen set up their instruments and Keith sang, his voice rich and full, about Maggie and Callum—from their initial betrothal as children to their courtship and the dangers they'd faced together over the past few weeks. At first, Maggie's face flamed at the retelling, but soon she was entranced with the ballad and listened as all the others did, filled with excitement and dread, laughter and awe, almost forgetting the story was about her. When Callum finally made her his bride, she got as teary eyed as the other lasses in the courtyard. Not to mention many of Callum's brothers and great big Gregor— whom, she'd discovered, had a heart as big as the loch and a soft spot for a love story.

When the ballad ended, she stood along with everyone else and cheered Keith and Aileen. She leaned over to Callum. "Did you know that Aileen wrote that? Keith is getting all the applause, but without Aileen, there would be no song to sing."

"I've read some of her poems. This was by far her best." He whistled loudly and shouted out Aileen's name, telling those around him, "My sister wrote that!"

Keith reached for Aileen and pulled her forward so she stood beside him. He dropped her hand and bowed deeply to her. Maggie looked around curiously and saw Glynis standing stiffly at another table, her face a polite mask, her hands barely moving in appreciation.

Maggie nudged Callum, who looked over. "Not exactly a proud wife, is she?"

Glynis strode to the door as soon as the applause finished, and the tables were pushed back to make room for dancing. Several men playing bagpipes and a flute began a toe-tapping reel.

"Where do you think she's going?" she asked, her voice rising.

Callum wrapped his arm around her shoulders as they sat down. "I doona know, lass. Maybe just to her chamber. Doona worry. Gavin assigned several men and a woman to follow her. I thought on your words and took them seriously. But keep in mind, it may not lead anywhere. Remember, she didn't have enough time to run around the courtyard and up the stairs to cut the rope."

Maggie sighed. "Aye, you may be right." Still, she couldn't let it lie. "Did you speak to Drustan about her?"

"Nay, he was busy with the investigation, and I was busy with Gregor and the lads going over the parchments you gave us—all while answering a hundred last-minute questions about the wedding. I'll speak to him tonight if I can catch him alone."

She looked around the courtyard but didn't see him. "Strange. He's not here." A chill ran up her spine. "Does he know you have people following Glynis?"

"I haven't seen him since this afternoon. And the trackers are Gavin's people, so Drustan willna notice anyone pulled off duty. Maggie, he may be tupping

Glynis, but I doona think he's involved with the conspiracy. He fought beside us when we were attacked at the hot pools, and he was in the courtyard when the rocks fell. His life was in danger both times."

"I saw that. Everyone else ran for cover, and he just stared up at the rocks. You had to pull him to safety." She squeezed his leg. "I was so frightened for you."

"There was no need. I could see your daggers would hold. I doona know what's going on with him, but I think it has more to do with his late wife. He says you resemble her. I think seeing you has brought it all back to him."

She placed her hand on her heart, and a soft sob broke through her lips. "That's so sad. How did she die?"

"Kicked by a horse."

Their eyes met and held, gazes filled with the knowledge that either one of them could be taken from the other just as suddenly and as randomly.

Callum leaned forward and kissed her lips. "Come, Wife. Let's go dance and celebrate our union and our upcoming lives together. Then we'll return to our bedchamber, and I'll caress and kiss every inch of you as slowly as you walked up that mountain."

She huffed in outrage at his words, even though secretly, she was thrilled. He laughed as he pulled her up from the bench.

"Just for that, I'll expect three dances from you and one from each of your brothers and Gregor. And I canna forget Finnian, Drustan, Artair, and Gill, or any of the other men in my new clan. We may be here all night. Then we'll see just how slowly you want to pleasure me, Husband."

❦

Callum stood at the rear of the courtyard, which had emptied out considerably in the last hour. The remaining revelers had crowded around the other end where Maggie danced with the old steward, Donald, who had a surprising amount of kick in his heels for his age. She had indeed danced with all his foster brothers and Gregor, plus Artair, Gill, and what seemed like every other man in the clan.

He loved watching her, her dance steps quick, her hair flying and cheeks flushed the rosiest of reds. Gregor had called her a vision, and he was right. But Callum was ready to claim his wife, and if need be, he'd throw her over his shoulder as Lachlan had done to Amber on their wedding night and carry her to their bedchamber.

He'd just taken a step toward her when Drustan entered the courtyard, looking…off. One shoulder was raised, and his steps were almost tentative, as if he had difficulty walking.

Callum hurried past the empty tables and benches toward him, thinking maybe he was hurt—but then Drustan stopped. And he looked at the dancers…at Maggie. A frisson of trepidation ran up Callum's spine, and he clenched his hand into a fist.

Is Drustan a threat?

But when he reached his second-in-command, it was to find that the man had closed his eyes and was tapping one finger against his plaid as if he listened to the music. His shoulder had dropped so it was even with the other one.

"Drustan," Callum said.

Drustan opened his eyes and looked at him. "Laird."

"Are you well?"

He nodded. "I like the music. The rhythm…settles me."

Callum peered in the direction Drustan had been staring. Maggie wasn't there. He scanned the dance floor, and relief soared through him when he saw her dancing with Gregor.

He was seeing a problem where there wasn't one. Returning his gaze to Drustan, he found his second-in-command had twisted his head to the side and was rubbing his nape. "Drustan!"

Drustan slowly looked at him.

"Is there something wrong with your neck?" he asked.

"It hurts."

"Why?"

Drustan didn't answer right away, then he said, "The horse. In the stable."

"Did you get thrown?"

"No." He closed his eyes. "I doona remember."

Callum clenched his jaw, frustration getting the better of him. "Maybe you should go to bed. The rest might help. Doona worry about working tomorrow. Take a few days and get to your old self."

"Aye. A rest will help."

He turned away, and Callum saw Glynis watching them. When Drustan headed to the arched exit, she set a course to intercept him.

Callum scowled. "Drustan!" he called out for a third time.

The man turned around, his eyes more focused this time, looking stronger—more like his old self. "What is it, Laird?"

Callum closed the distance between them and lowered his voice. "I have to ask. Are you tupping Glynis?"

Drustan's spine went rigid, his jaw set in a hard line. "What business is it of yours?"

"She's my cousin's wife. And as her laird, she's under my protection. People know, Drustan. Keith knows. What were you thinking, getting involved with her? She's married."

"You think I'm the first man to tup a married woman? Especially one who makes herself available?"

"Of course not, but—"

"Your father did it. For years. Even when your mother was alive. Couldn't keep his hands to himself."

Callum stared at Drustan, barely recognizing him from just a few moments ago. Anger had transformed his face. "I know Aileen is my sister—"

"I'm not talking about Aileen. I'm talking about Glynis."

The blood drained from Callum's head, leaving him weak. "Glynis is my sister too?"

"Nay. I meant your father tupped Glynis—for years. Why do you think she lives in the castle?"

A coldness shivered over Callum's skin and filled his body. "She's married to Keith."

"And before that, she lived in another village and your father visited her there. She was a young, unmarried woman then, who'd caught the attention of a powerful laird. Who do you think convinced her to marry Keith?"

Callum's stomach churned like dirty, debris-filled rapids, and he could barely crack his jaw to speak. "So you took up with her after my father died? You used her too?"

Drustan's eyes clashed with his before Drustan looked away. He rubbed a hand over his neck, as if trying to massage his pain away. "Not right away, but…aye."

"Drustan, you have to stop."

"I have stopped. Before we left for Laird MacKay's. And I doona plan to resume the affair." His shoulders tightened, and he turned away from Callum. "May I leave?"

"Aye, just…be careful. Maggie believes that Glynis cut the rope that held up the rocks. She has no proof, just suspicions, and I doona believe Glynis could have made it there in time, but still…please be wary."

Drustan shrugged. "I know naught of that."

"You were underneath. You almost died. Or do you not care?" Callum asked.

A bleak look crossed Drustan's face. "Nay. I doona think I do."

Twenty-two

"In here. Quickly!" Callum grabbed Maggie's hand and pulled her into an alcove on the ground floor with a thick, velvet drape drawn across the opening. They just made it inside, trying to quiet their breathing in the dark, when some of their clan—men and women—ran past looking for them, laughing excitedly and more than a bit drunk. They had the addlepated notion their laird would allow them to undress the bride and groom for the marital bedding, but if any man or woman attempted to undo Maggie's dress, they would find themselves at the sharp end of both their daggers.

Maggie leaned her body into his and pressed her mouth to his throat, her tongue exploring his skin. Her teeth biting down, like a lioness teasing her prey. Callum groaned and rested against the stone wall in the dark, his arms around her, his knees weak as desire pounded through him. The dark added its own element of seduction as every touch and sound was enhanced and unexpected.

"Are you planning to eat me or kiss me?" he asked.

"It depends."

"On what?"

"On how hungry I am."

She'd also had a little too much to drink, and when her hands and body had begun to press into Callum's earlier, he'd known he had to get her out of the court-yard and up to their bedchamber. He hadn't thought his wife could be contained for much longer.

Seeing as he'd given her his promise to listen to her, who was he to say she wasn't ready? Besides, she'd been dancing all night. She was obviously on the mend.

"Callum," she said in the dark, kissing up his throat to nibble on his chin.

"Aye, Maggie." He wished he could see her beauti-ful face—her eyes hooded and a bit feral, skin flushed, lips plump and rosy.

And he was missing it here in the dark.

He twitched the curtain to the side so he could see if the passageway was clear enough for them to make a run for their bedchamber, and Maggie slipped her hand under his plaid and dragged it up his leg to palm his cock. It was the first time she'd touched him there, and he dropped his hand to tangle it in her hair, letting go the drape and plunging them into darkness again. He growled deep in his chest, his eyes closing, his head falling against the stone wall.

"Do you like it when I do this, Husband?" she asked, closing her fist around him and squeezing before dragging her hand up and down. He thrust his hips to sheathe himself in her hold again.

He could barely get the words out. "Aye, Maggie. I do."

"And I'm doing it right?" she asked, sounding a bit uncertain.

He half laughed, half moaned. "Maggie, you have your hand on my cock. There is no doing it wrong."

She rose on her tiptoes to press her mouth to his. "Aye, there is. I've heard others talk—men and women. Some things feel better than others. Do you like it when I do this?" She rubbed her thumb over the slit at the tip, found his drop of seed and smeared it in small circles around the opening.

He couldn't do more than grunt, feeling like his eyes had rolled back in their sockets. Cupping the back of her head, he held her tight and lifted her mouth to his. He wasn't gentle; he couldn't be gentle while she touched him like that. He could only devour her. And she liked it, opening her mouth beneath his, sucking on his tongue—just as wild and needy as he was. She pressed her body closer, turning her hand around so her palm slid against his shaft, hitting that spot right beneath the tip as her nails scraped over his sac, moving faster in her excitement. Harder.

He wrenched his head away, his breath coming in harsh gasps. Hers too. Heat flared out from his loins, sending licks of flames down his thighs and up into his belly. His stones tightened, feeling as rock hard as the mountain they'd just climbed over.

"Aye. I like that. You can do that anytime."

"Are you sure you want to grant me that freedom, Husband?" Her voice sounded sly. "Your plaid isna long. 'Twould be easy to catch you unawares."

The air huffed from his lungs—amusement, aye,

but mostly just the inability to salvage any kind of physical control over himself as she touched him.

He tried to focus, to think about what he wanted for her—a soft bed, warm quilts, the fire burning low in the background, gentle kisses—but then she pulled up her skirts with her free hand, raised onto her tiptoes, and pressed her warm skin down below to his. When she lifted her leg and wrapped it around his thigh, her slick heat scorched him, and he lost the ability to think.

"Are you sure, Maggie? Here?"

But he'd already dropped his hands, one arm wrapping beneath her bare bottom and lifting her, the other pulling her skirts and his plaid completely out of the way.

"Aye, Callum. Inside me now," she moaned, her arms circling his neck as her legs anchored around his arse. She pushed her hips against him, rubbing her mound along his hard length, driving both of them to the edge in a whirlwind of need.

He turned and pressed her against the stone wall, then tilted her hips to the angle they needed and drove through silky folds.

"God in heaven! Aye, right there," she moaned.

"'Tis heaven here with you. You take me there with every touch, lass."

He tried to go slow, to piston inside her tenderly, but she jerked down on him at the same time as he thrust up and sheathed him deeply within her body.

Her soft, wet heat tightened around him, and he dropped his head into the crook of her neck, his face contorted as he held them still for a moment. He needed some control, or it would be all over before she was ready, and he wanted her to reach the pinnacle with him—always.

But she was out of control, too, and pressed frantic kisses and tiny bites across his jaw to his earlobe, nipping it before taking it into her mouth and sucking on it.

The air whooshed from his lungs in a long shudder, and he thrust inside her again. "Ah, Maggie…what you do to me."

"What you do to me!"

He lowered his hand, wedged it between their bodies, and circled her nub with his thumb.

With a groan, she rolled her hips upward just as he withdrew, and they found a pounding rhythm. Pulling his head roughly to her, she took his mouth, biting his bottom lip just hard enough for him to growl before she laved it with her tongue.

She squeezed him tightly with her legs and arms. Down below, her muscles rippled and pulsed along the length of him. He was consumed by their kiss, not knowing where she ended and he began.

It was the most arousing, exciting experience he'd ever had. His mind, heart, and body unified—completely centered and focused on Maggie. On his *wife*.

Heat gathered at the base of his spine, in his heavy, hard stones, and his rhythm fractured. She tore her mouth from his, leaned her head against the stone wall and arched her back, screaming her release in short, keening bursts. He recaptured her mouth and tried to swallow her cries—but he shot over the edge too, and his body shattered like glass as he pumped into her, his cries loud and guttural.

Her fingers covered his mouth, and he pressed his

hand over them, holding them tight as he muffled his yells into her palm.

On his last thrust, his legs buckled, his strength draining from him along with his seed. He slumped against her, grateful for the wall that held them up as they gasped for breath. But still he stumbled and dropped to his knees. She let out a surprised shriek before she started to laugh.

"God's blood, woman," he said. "You've turned me into a lad. I canna even hold you up!"

Which only made her laugh harder. "You promised me a bed, Callum MacLean, and so far, you've tupped me in a tree, a pool, on the rocks, and against a stone wall. Is this what I have to look forward to for the next forty years?"

"I didn't tup you in the tree. But I could have, aye?" He sounded smug, and she laughed again.

"Aye, probably. But I would have regretted it afterward and maybe let you walk into one of my traps around my grandmother's cottage. And I certainly wouldnae have stayed with you after that. 'Twas good you showed some restraint, even if I wasn't able to."

"And me not having been with anyone for five years because I wanted to wait for you. Only you."

He couldn't see her expression in the dark, but he guessed from her tone of voice she'd raised one brow. "You told me 'twas four years."

He grunted. "Well, it felt like five years, especially after having been in the tree with you. Verily, I should be nominated for sainthood."

"If 'tis what you truly want, I doona feel right to stand in your way."

He grunted again before he kissed her, happy to feel the smile on her lips. "Doona listen to me. We've already established that I'm addled." Then he withdrew from her body, making them both shudder and gasp. He turned so he leaned against the wall and she sat sideways in his lap, his arms around her.

"Next time, I promise you a bed," he said.

"I'm quite comfortable. 'Twas exciting knowing we could be discovered at any minute."

"Well, doona expect me to leave our chamber door open in the future."

She huffed out a laugh as she traced her fingers along his arm, her head tucked beneath his chin. He played with the strands of her hair.

"Are you happy, Maggie?" he asked after a moment. "Have you forgiven me for leaving you in such danger for so long?"

"Aye, Callum. I am happy, and I have forgiven you even though I ne'er thought I would. I understand now the pressure you were under. You didn't want to bring me here, knowing I might be hurt."

He pulled her closer. "I still don't, sometimes. It worries me no end that you might be attacked and..."

"And?"

"And killed, love. The one thing that provides me some relief is knowing you're a fighter. You are unafraid to act, and you know how to use your weapons."

She pulled away from him, and her hands framed his face. "Truly?" she asked. "You doona want me to change?" She sounded a bit teary, and he kissed her forehead.

"Nay. I'm going to train you, however. Even

harder than you trained yourself. Fill in the gaps that were missed so you doona hesitate again, and you know your strengths and weaknesses and can use them to your advantage. You're physically strong, but I'll teach you how to use your body to kill an assailant, not just your bows and daggers."

"Callum," she said, laughing. "Such sweet words. You truly know how to woo a lass."

"I've already wooed you, Maggie. Now I'm going to teach you how to protect yourself and our bairns when they come. I willna have you defenseless. Ever. Even if we find the enemies in our ranks, I doona think it will end there. Your spying on Irvin provided us with much insight into our enemy. Your bravery will be what saves us, Maggie."

She sighed and lay back down on his chest. "Thank you. But you forgot one thing."

"What's that, sweetling?"

"I'll protect you as well as myself and our bairns."

"Aye."

A whistle sounded outside the curtain, and Callum stiffened, then stood up, putting Maggie on her feet and pressing his hands to her ears before returning the whistle.

"What's wrong?" she asked as he tweaked the curtain to give them some light. He made sure her clothes covered her before he opened the drape and stepped through, knowing Maggie would follow him.

"That's Gregor. Something's happened." He took her hand and hurried around the corner. As he suspected, his foster brothers and his foster father stood there waiting for them. Maggie's hand tightened on his.

"Tell me," he said.

Gregor passed him an unopened letter addressed to Laird MacLean, secured with the MacDonnell seal. Maggie's mouth pressed into a tight, worried line. He pulled her close and wrapped his arm around her. Her body trembled against his as Callum opened the letter.

It wasn't a surprise, but sadness still filled every corner of his heart, along with an even greater sadness for Maggie. He wrapped both arms around her and squeezed her tight. "Ah, sweetling. I'm so sorry, but according to this, Ross is dead."

Maggie cried out and buried her face in Callum's chest.

"How?" Gregor asked.

"It doesn't say, but I doona think this is from Irvin Sinclair. The writing is different from the last letter I had from him." He continued reading and stiffened. Maggie looked up at him, her face wet with tears.

"What is it?" she asked.

"The letter is signed by John…and he's demanding your return. He says he's coming to take you back."

She reached for the parchment, and Callum handed it over. "Is it from him, Maggie? Can you tell?"

She pressed her fingers against her mouth and nodded her head. "'Tis his writing, and it…sounds like him." She half laughed, half cried. "He was always short-tempered and ne'er thought anything through before he acted. Does this mean he's taken back our land and castle?"

Callum reacquired the letter and passed it to Gregor, who read it and then passed it around to the others.

"I doona know what it means," Callum continued,

"other than 'tis certain that Ross is dead and John is back…and I willna be returning you."

Maggie's face crumpled, and Callum pulled her into his arms. "I need to see him," she said, her words muffled by his shirt. "Both of them."

"Aye. We'll send men out. Our best. They'll try to speak to John directly before he gets here."

One by one, his foster brothers and Gregor came forward to give her a gentle, consoling hug and offer their condolences. She nodded at their words and gave thanks, but Callum could see in the quiver of her lip and the sorrow in those beautiful hazel eyes that she needed the freedom to release her emotions.

"Do you want to go to our room, love?" he asked.

"Aye," she replied, barely above a whisper.

"Doona worry about John right now," Gavin said to him. "Be with Maggie. I'll send a man to see if he's at his castle after all. We'll begin there."

"Let me know when you have news. I need to speak to him directly, welcome him as my brother as well as my friend, offer my help and condolences. And make sure he understands the marriage contract between our clans is fulfilled—his sister willna be going anywhere."

Twenty-three

WHEN THEY REACHED THEIR ROOM, CALLUM CURLED up with Maggie on the bed, and she wept in his arms for what seemed like hours, sobbing and talking gibberish, and he never once told her to hush or to calm herself. Nay, he'd just held her and rubbed her hair and back, pressed kisses to her brow and temple.

She'd cried for Ross, for the loss of the brother who had been as bright as the sun in her life for so many years. She'd cried for the death of his wife, Eleanor, whom Maggie had loved like a sister, and for the lost bairn whom she'd talked to and teased when he was still inside his mother's womb. She'd sobbed for John's heartbreak when Eleanor chose Ross over him and for the turmoil in her family afterward.

And she'd mourned her mother. Buckets of tears for the tragic, early loss of Margaret MacDonnell, and for the young lass Maggie had been—filled with fear, guilt, and helplessness as her mother had died slowly in the old well beside her.

And with her tears, Maggie had let her old self go, forgave the wee lass who had disobeyed and followed the butterfly toward the old well where she wasn't allowed to play. She forgave herself for the death of her mother—just as Flora had encouraged. And ultimately for the death of her father, who never forgave *himself* for not having had the well properly sealed.

She'd cried for the disappointment and feelings of rejection and worthlessness she'd felt when Callum hadn't returned for her after his father died. And she'd wept over knowing that he was here now, loving her and caring for her—and that she believed in his love and had been able to forgive him. She'd cried grateful tears for their union and the life they planned to build together.

When the torrent had subsided, she'd felt empty but full at the same time; heavy but lighter than she had in years; exhausted yet also uplifted. She stayed in Callum's arms in a strange twilight of sleep. And when a knock came on the door, she remained lying on the bed while he gently moved out from under her to answer it. She watched through half-closed eyes as Gavin entered and had a hushed conversation with Callum.

When her husband came back, she reached for his hand. He sat beside her on the bed.

"Is it John?" she asked. "He's here, isn't he? I canna imagine that he would send anyone else to get me if he feared for my safety."

"Aye. He and several of his men attempted to sneak over the castle wall rather than riding under the portcullis. Why would he think you unsafe, Maggie? John and I have always been friends. And it's not as though he wouldn't have expected our marriage. We've been betrothed for years."

She sat up, and the tears rolled down her face as she imagined the mess of emotions her brother must be experiencing right now. "He's grieving; probably angry and distrustful. And I have to believe he's feeling guilty. If he hadn't left in the first place, Irvin couldnae have done what he did. He'll be determined to get to me—save me—no matter what. And of course as much as I love him, he's still a wee ablach. John's always been reckless."

Callum nodded. "Aye. Maggie, I have to…"

When he didn't finish, obviously conflicted, she cupped his face and drew him forward for a kiss. "You have to go. I understand. Take *your* brothers and find *my* brother. Bring him back to me safely. And doona worry about me. I'm tired, Callum. I'll sleep well knowing you're a part of the search."

She knew her husband would sort it out, and when he left, she fell into a dead sleep.

Upon waking, her eyes felt gritty and heavy, almost glued shut from all her weeping. She rubbed them as she sat up, then pushed off the cover Callum had placed over her. The fire burned high, so she knew someone must have been in to check on her recently. Treading over the soft rug, she crossed to the window and opened the shutter, expecting to see the light of dawn brightening the sky, but it was still dark. Despite that, the bailey was busy with men on horses coming and going. Burning torches lit the night, and she wanted to yell out to John and tell him she was safe and happy, but she knew that was foolish. Instead, she closed the shutters and crossed to a small writing desk in the corner. She would write a letter to her brother—several of them—that could be delivered by whoever found him. A letter to ease his mind.

The words came easily to her: she loved Callum, they were happily married, and she wasn't leaving his side. She asked John to come to her so they could grieve Ross together and then, with Callum's and his allies' help, take back their clan and castle.

She'd just finished writing the last of four letters when a knock sounded at the door. She hurried over, hoping for good news as she brushed her hands down her creased arisaid and tucked her hair behind her ears.

When she opened the door, Drustan stood there, his head down and rubbing his neck.

"Drustan?" she queried when he didn't look up right away.

He dropped his hand and met her gaze. "May I come in?"

She hesitated, the tiny hairs standing up on her skin. Two guards stood behind Drustan—men she barely knew, but who wore plaids that resembled Callum's. She thought on her husband's words and remembered how Drustan had fought beside the others at the hot pool and that he'd been one of the many targets in the courtyard when the rocks had fallen. She had no reason to suspect him, and guilt flashed through her for doing so.

"Callum's not here," she said.

He looked at her blankly for a moment, then nodded. "Aye."

When he said no more yet didn't leave, she took an uncertain step back. He passed her into the chamber, eyes darting everywhere—to the rumpled bed, to her letters on the desk, to an extra pair of Callum's boots on the floor.

Maggie left the door ajar and walked toward him. "Is there news about my brother?"

He stopped in front of the hearth and turned to her, his hand tapping his leg, his brow shiny with sweat. "Your brother?"

"Aye. My brother John. 'Tis what the uproar outside is all about." She took a concerned step forward. "Drustan, are you ill? You doona seem well."

He raised his hand and wiped the sweat from his forehead. "Nay, Abi. I…I canna catch my thoughts. They keep drifting away from me."

A chill ran down Maggie's spine. She took a slow step backward. "What did you call me?" It sounded like Maggie but…not quite. Had she misheard? Or maybe he'd just mumbled?

He rubbed his neck again. "Stay away from the laird, sweetling. He has a wandering eye."

The laird? Did he mean Callum? Or perhaps Callum's father? She took another step back, now within equal distance to the door and one of Callum's daggers hidden behind the tapestry on the wall. "I canna stay away from Callum, Drustan. He's my husband."

When he didn't respond, she stepped closer to the tapestry, pulled out the dagger, and held it loosely by her side. Her heart was pounding, but she felt safer now.

She gentled her voice. "I'm Maggie, Drustan. Maybe we should wait for Callum to be here to have this conversation." She edged slowly to the door. He watched her, standing so very still. Other than his fingers tap, tap, tapping on his leg.

When she pulled the door open all the way, the two guards looked in. She held her breath as Drustan nodded then walked toward her, eyes ahead, never once glancing in her direction. She tensed, dagger at the ready, as he passed her, but he left without incident.

When he disappeared down the passageway, she said to the nearest guard, "Go get my husband. Now. And hurry." She shut and barred the door, her stomach roiling. She backed into the center of the room, her dagger trembling in her hand.

What had just happened? Had she imagined it, or was Drustan losing his mind? She turned and hurried to the bed where her arm sheath lay on a side table with several more daggers, crowding out the finely wrought candleholder and silver-backed hair brush.

She strapped on the sheath and inserted three daggers into it, then hurried to a satchel against the wall by the hearth. Inside lay her crossbow and several specially made arrows and bolts. She loaded one arrow so she'd be ready for anything, then inserted the extra arrows into another sheath she attached to her other arm.

Armed, she stood facing the door, with the crossbow ready. Several minutes of quiet later, she rolled her eyes at her own foolishness. The door was barred. What did she think was going to happen? She put the bow down on the chair in front of the fire then paced around the room a few times before she hurried to the bed and pulled up the feather mattress. Underneath was the sturdy rope Callum had promised her. She checked to see that one end was tied to the foot of the bed before she dragged the remainder of the rope to the window and readied it to be thrown out if she needed an escape route.

When she finished, she returned to pacing. Each time she neared the door, she leaned her ear against the wood and listened, but she couldn't hear anything.

Where is Callum? Why is he taking so long?

She sighed and rubbed her hand over the nape of her neck. He was out trying to track down her clever, reckless, *ablach* of a brother, that's where he was. And John would be hard to find.

The only thing she could do to help was finish her letters. With quick strides, she reached the desk, folded a piece of parchment, then poured hot wax from the candle on the overlapping edges to seal it. When she was done, she undid her mother's brooch from her *arisaid* and pushed it into the wax. John would recognize the imprint.

Her eyes fell on her hands as they lifted the brooch, and alarm skittered through her. Her fingers were bare. Where was the heavy silver ring Callum had given her? She'd barely had it half a day, and she'd lost it?

God's blood, he'll ne'er forgive me! I'll ne'er forgive myself!

She quickly searched the desk and then the bed, shaking out the linens and quilt—but she'd lifted up the mattress, so it could have flung anywhere. She crouched down on her hands and knees with the candle and began a thorough search of the floor, including the coiled rope beneath the window.

Fifteen minutes later, she sat back on her heels, empty-handed, closed her eyes, and breathed deeply to calm her racing heart and thoughts.

Where did I have it last?

Dancing with Callum just before they left the courtyard. She'd loved how her ring had shone on her hand when it was clasped with his during the reel. When they'd walked out, she'd lifted her hand to the light just for that reason, and he'd spun her in a circle.

The alcove!

Aye, she could easily have lost it there. She'd used that hand to stroke her husband, and she'd been so involved with their intimate play, she would never have noticed it coming off.

She still had on her soft leather boots, but her dress was completely askew. She quickly retrieved her mother's brooch from the desk and repinned her plaid. Then she tied the mess of her hair at the nape of her neck with a ribbon, grabbed her crossbow from the bed, and headed out. The men on guard could just follow her.

She pulled open the door, her shoulders square and chin raised in case they gave her any trouble—which they shouldn't. She was not a prisoner.

But only one man stood guard in the lit passageway, which struck Maggie as odd. She would have thought the guard she'd sent to find Callum would have passed on the message to another warrior and returned immediately.

Callum's men did not disobey orders, and with the threats looming over them, she knew he'd want at least two guards watching her at all times.

Something is wrong.

"Lady MacLean?" the guard asked, looking at her with a brow raised.

"Good morrow, Hew," she said, recognizing the warrior from her wedding feast. She'd danced a lively reel with him and clapped as he and some other warriors performed an energetic dance with his sword. "Where's the other guard?" she asked.

"You sent him to find Laird MacLean."

She nodded. He didn't seem concerned, so maybe she was overreacting. She'd been rattled by Drustan's behavior.

"No word yet about my brother, Laird MacDonnell?"

"Nay. We have men looking though. We'll find him."

"Aye, I heard the commotion in the bailey." She stepped past him into the hallway and proceeded toward the courtyard, scanning for trouble.

"Lady MacLean," he said anxiously as he hurried after her, "we should wait until we have a second guard."

"I am the second guard, Hew. No one will get past my crossbow. Callum knows I can protect myself."

Still, the guard whistled behind her, a different tone than any she'd heard before, and she half expected men to come flooding out of every nook and cranny. They didn't, which she also found odd.

"They must all be outside, then," she said to Hew.

"Aye, maybe. Keep your bow raised, Lady MacLean."

Just then, someone moved in the dark ahead of them. "Halt!" Maggie yelled, her finger on the trigger. A head poked out of an alcove. Bright green eyes, so much like Callum's, stared back at her, filled with fright.

Maggie lowered her bow a few inches. "Aileen?"

Aileen stepped slowly into the passageway, holding a lit candle in her hand. Her hair and clothes looked mussed, and a bright flush covered her cheeks.

"What are you doing out here by yourself?" Maggie asked.

"I…I was…working on a song."

She was lying. Maggie could hear it in her voice and see it in her face. *Surely she isn't…nay, it canna be. Not Aileen—anyone but Aileen!*

"'Tis not safe here. Go to your room and bar the door." Maggie put as much authority into her voice as she could. It worked. Aileen's face paled, and her eyes grew round. She bobbed a quick curtsy and ran down another corridor.

Maggie raised her bow again and hurried down the stairs to the ground level. At the bottom, she turned to the courtyard. Just around the corner from the stairs was the alcove she'd hidden in with Callum only hours before. Well, done more than hidden in.

She almost smiled, but then she saw Keith enter the passageway ahead of her. He hadn't seen them, and he headed in the opposite direction.

For some reason, she stayed quiet. Keith wasn't a trained warrior and wouldn't be able to help them if they were attacked. Nay, he'd just be someone else she'd have to worry about. And who knew what he might tell Glynis.

She took a lit candle and its holder from the wall and drew the heavy drape. "I'm going in here."

Hew approached her with his sword out. She had a moment of fright, eyes going wide and stomach dropping, but he just stepped past her and checked to make sure the alcove was empty. "I'll be right outside."

He didn't ask her for an explanation as to why she was there, and she sighed inwardly in relief. She didn't want anyone knowing she'd already lost her wedding ring—Callum's grandmother's ring!

Sending up a quick prayer for help to find it, she pulled the drape closed. But a moment later, she huffed out a resigned breath, opened the curtain, and stuck out her head. "I doona want you thinking I'm doing anything daft. I'm looking for my wedding ring. I lost it…already. Doona tell a soul, Hew MacLean, especially my husband. 'Tis not wise to be on my bad side."

He raised a brow, his lip quirking. "So I've heard. I'd help you look, but I need to be on guard. Especially if our laird comes around the corner."

She huffed out another breath and closed the curtain. Leaning her crossbow against the wall, she crouched down on her hands and knees with the candle. No rushes covered the floor in here, making her search easier. She looked on the ground beneath where she and Callum had tupped but didn't see it. Panic rose inside her again, tightening her throat, and she took a deep breath to loosen it before starting in one corner of the tiny room and very carefully going over every inch.

When she neared the opposite corner and no silver glint caught her eye, her panic returned, and tears threatened to spill down her cheeks. She wiped the wetness away and kept looking, but she soon found herself at the edge of the wall—and nothing. Maggie was staring down at the rock in the corner, willing her ring to appear, when she became aware of two things: a cold, almost indiscernible breeze blew onto her wet fingers from a tiny gap in the cornerstone on the floor, and when she dug her nails into that gap, the stone lifted.

"God's blood," she whispered. "A tunnel."

The drape swished open behind her, and she rolled and reached for her daggers in one motion. The intruder stepped into the alcove and onto her skirt, trapping her. Maggie's heart raced as she raised her daggers, one in each hand and ready to throw, when Aileen wailed, "I lied. I wasn't writing, I was with Keith. Oh, Maggie, what am I going to do? I love him so much, and he's married to Glynis. I'm just like my mother!" Then she took a gulping breath and peered closely at her sister-in-law. "What are you doing down there?"

"I'm looking for my wedding ring, and I found this." Maggie tugged her skirt free, rolled to her knees, and slid her knives into the gap between the loose stone and the next. It lifted easily. She put it to the side and lowered her candle to see five steep stairs leading into a tunnel that ran toward the courtyard.

Aileen crouched beside her and picked up something from the top stair. "Is this a clue?" she asked and handed Maggie her ring.

Joyful, Maggie cried, "Oh, thank you!"

She held it close to her heart before sliding it over her thumb, where it fit snugly. "And it is a clue. It tells us that someone has used these tunnels in the last six hours. Can you ask Hew to come in, please?"

Aileen crinkled her brow in confusion. "Hew? He's not there. No one's there."

Maggie's blood ran cold, and she readied her dagger just in case. "Then how did you know I was in here?"

"I followed the two of you. But then I lost my nerve and turned around, only to return. Maggie, what's going on?"

Maggie searched her sister-in-law's face—eyes wide, bottom lip trembling, skin blotchy from her tears—before she passed Aileen the dagger. "Take your candle and get in the tunnel." She hefted the stone into her arms and then hurled it into the hallway where it hit the opposite wall and smashed into several pieces. "We're being followed."

Twenty-four

CALLUM SLUMPED TIREDLY ON THE BACK OF HIS HORSE and rubbed his eyes with his thumb and forefinger. Dawn was on the horizon, and he needed to return to his wife. He didn't want her waking up alone. They'd thought they had John and his men an hour ago, before his crafty brother-in-law had slipped away. Once this was over, he'd sit down with John and learn whatever skill he had that allowed him and his men to avoid capture. Callum was sure he'd find it edifying.

But not right now.

"John!" he yelled suddenly, losing complete control of his temper and causing Aristotle to huff and toss his head. "Quit playing games, you wee ablach, and show yourself! She'll be awake soon and grieving—alone! I swear I'm going to beat you bloody if you cause her any more anguish!"

Gregor put his hand on Callum's arm and squeezed. "You should go to her, Son. We'll find John for you. 'Twill be light soon. He willna be able to hide forever."

Callum shoved his hand through his hair. Worry had twisted his guts, and his fear for Maggie had muddled his mind. He knew he wasn't at his best. "Aye. At least if I'm with her, I'll know she's safe."

He'd just turned his horse toward the castle when a rider galloped up to them.

"Laird MacLean! Our lady asked for you to return—and to hurry."

Panic ripped through Callum, and he urged Aristotle into a gallop, the other man by his side. "What happened?" he yelled, trying to be heard over the horses' hooves.

"I doona know. Drustan went into your bedchamber for a few minutes to talk to her. She left the door open, and we didn't hear anything untoward, but right after he left, she told us to find you."

"Was she all right?"

The other man hesitated. "She held her dagger in her hand."

Callum leaned over Aristotle and pushed his horse to go faster in the dim light.

Why hadn't he acted sooner? He'd known something was wrong with Drustan. He should have restrained him and brought Flora in to tend his ills. If something happened to Maggie, he'd never forgive himself.

"Where was she when you left?" he asked, praying his wife had stayed in their room.

"Not to worry, Laird. She locked herself in your bedchamber and barred the door."

❧

Maggie walked carefully through the dark tunnel, which was just high enough for her to stand upright, her crossbow raised in her arms. Her breath was fast yet even. Her awareness was heightened and her hands steady as she peered into the gloom.

Behind her, tall Aileen was forced to walk hunched over, carrying the candle, which threw a small pool of light around them. Her steps were erratic as she tried to keep up and occasionally broke into a sob.

"Remember," Maggie said, "if you hear a noise behind us, drop down so I'll have a clear shot."

"But shouldnae I be in the front, then? You said we're being followed. Doesn't that mean they'll come from the back?"

"Perhaps. But they may be in the tunnel ahead of us too." Aileen let out another sob, and the pool of light in front of Maggie diminished. "Keep up, Sister. Think of Keith and of what the discovery of this tunnel might mean for the two of you."

Aileen pressed up close behind her now, and Maggie was glad she'd had the sense to drag her hair forward over her shoulder so Aileen would not set the strands alight.

"I doona understand. What does the tunnel have to do with Keith?" Aileen asked, her voice sounding stronger already.

"If I'm not mistaken, this tunnel leads directly under the courtyard. Which means, if Glynis knows about it, she wouldnae have had to run all the way around that great courtyard and up the stairs in plain sight to cut the rope, as we all assumed. She could have gone through the tunnel and under the courtyard, which would have given her enough time to get there."

"But how could she have known about the tunnel?"

"I doona know...but I have my suspicions."

"What? Tell me," Aileen demanded.

"Nay. I'll discuss them with Callum first and let him ask the questions." Maggie had wondered for a while if Callum's da had been tupping Glynis.

The whole situation made Maggie's stomach sour. She didn't want to think badly of Callum's da, especially as he'd been loving and kind to his children—but not every lass would feel they had the right to say no to a man as powerful as their laird.

All Maggie could hope for was that the old laird had been respectful to the women he'd approached and made it clear no harm would come to them or their families if they refused him.

A noise sounded behind them, and Maggie spun around. "Down!" she whispered, and Aileen dropped to her knees.

Maggie waited, straining to hear. Then in the distance, Drustan called, "Abi! Love, are you down here? Abigail?"

Her guts hollowed, and she turned around, quickening her pace. "Hurry, Aileen."

"What's wrong? That sounded like Drustan. He could help us." Aileen scrambled to her feet and kept close.

"Nay. I think Drustan is the one who disposed of Hew and my other guard. Something's terribly wrong with him."

"And he's following us? Maybe to kill us?"

"'Tis possible." She didn't want to scare the lass any more than she already was, but it was important Aileen understood that Drustan was not to be trusted. "When we get out of the tunnel, I want you to run as fast as you can and find Keith—or any of the other soldiers.

Tell him to find your brother. And tell everyone you can about the tunnel. Callum needs to know."

They hurried in silence for a moment before Aileen said, "That's why you threw the stone into the passageway and broke it. To alert everyone the tunnel was here. In case...in case we ne'er made it out." Instead of faltering, her voice had steadied.

"Callum needed to know where we'd gone."

"Even though Drustan would know too?"

"Aye. A traitor is at work in the clan, Aileen, and I'm almost certain she...or he...has been using this tunnel."

"Glynis," Aileen breathed.

"Maybe. But until we catch her down here, we willna know for sure."

Maggie slowed as they reached the bottom of a spiral staircase. She pointed her crossbow upward. "Stay as close to me as you can." She felt the need for caution, but at the same time, Drustan was behind them, and she wanted to run.

They started up the stairs, and Maggie tried to keep count, to estimate how high up they were going. She peered into the thick blackness, watching for anyone ahead of them—or any weapons—while she also looked for doors or a loose stone that could be another exit. There had to be a way out, at the very least one on the highest level. She prayed they found it before Drustan found them.

As if her thoughts had summoned him, he called out again. "Abi! Abi, where are you?" He sounded closer this time, and she and Aileen crouched against the wall like mice trying to hide from a great, deranged cat. Maggie didn't know where to point her crossbow, and after a second, she urged Aileen to keep going. They were on what she thought must be the last spiral of the stone staircase when she heard the scraping of stone, followed by the sight of a familiar shape racing around the corner.

"Glynis," Aileen said, just as Maggie yelled, "Stop!" her finger on the trigger of her crossbow.

She didn't want to kill Glynis; they needed information from her. At the same time, Drustan roared behind them. He sounded close, like he was at the bottom of the steps. If she shot Glynis, she wouldn't have time to reload, which left her daggers, and she wasn't confident using them in this tight space with Aileen so near.

Glynis must have seen her hesitate and darted up the stairs two at a time. Maggie cursed and grabbed Aileen's arm. "Run!" she said. She reached the last turn and saw a door swinging shut. "Doona forget what I said, Aileen. Find Keith, Callum, anyone! Tell them what you saw! Do not wait to help me."

She burst out through the door, crossbow raised, and moved forward cautiously, peering through the dim morning light. Ahead of her was the first of two scaffolds, and beside the second one, tied to the wall, was her net.

But she couldn't see Glynis anywhere. Then something struck her hard from behind and pushed her to the edge of the balcony. Her crossbow flew from her hands, and she screamed.

~❦~

Callum ran as fast as he'd ever run in his life, through the dimly lit great hall and up the stairs to the second level, praying that Hew and another guard would be standing outside his bedchamber door. But he knew in his gut something was wrong.

He let out an anguished roar when he reached the top step and saw his bedroom door ajar with no one in sight. "Search the castle," he yelled to the man behind him. "Find Maggie, Drustan, and Glynis!"

He tore into his room, saw the rumpled quilts on the floor and the overturned mattress, and it felt as though a giant fist had punched him in the gut.

Was she forcibly taken?

He saw parchment, a quill, and ink on the desk and rushed toward them. The first one he picked up was an unsealed letter she'd written to John. His throat closed as he read her words—she loved Callum, she was happy, she would never leave him.

He closed his eyes for just a moment and held the message to his chest.

With a groan that turned into a growl, he tucked the letter into his plaid and ran for the door, filled with hope that he'd find her in time. He prayed that John had her, that he'd somehow sneaked past the guards and into the castle—and Maggie would be returned to Callum once she'd told John how she felt.

And then he could tell Maggie how he felt: I love you, you make me happy, I will never leave you.

He was at the top of the stairs when he heard a woman scream. Every hair on his body rose, and his heart began to pound.

"Maggie!"

Maggie slid toward the edge of the stone precipice. The wall up from the courtyard was still under repair, with no protective railing to stop her from going over. The scaffolding on this side had been dragged away from the wall and the structure weakened when the net of rocks had dropped and bashed into the framework, breaking some of the support beams.

She reached for anything to stop her forward momentum, but she couldn't get purchase. As she started to fall over the edge, she pushed off with her feet and lunged for a rope that was suspended over the pulley beside the scaffold. The opposite end of the rope was weighed down by a few of the remaining rocks within the heavy netting on the courtyard floor. She swung out on the rope, her tender ribs wrenching, pain shooting through her hand, and she threw her legs over the edge of the scaffold on the side. She kept hold of her lifeline as she pulled herself up to stand on the top of the wooden platform, which rocked dangerously. Once she'd steadied herself, she drew her dagger.

Glynis stood panting at the edge of the precipice, a savage look on her face, holding a heavy piece of wood that she must have used to strike Maggie. Behind Glynis, Aileen appeared from the tunnel, her skin white and eyes wide. She quietly shut the door behind her and ran as silent as a mouse down the corridor.

Maggie tossed her dagger in the air to distract Glynis, who eyed the weapon warily. She didn't want to kill Glynis. Nay, if Glynis was the traitor, she had information Callum needed. But she could scare her a little.

When the other woman lunged for Maggie's crossbow, Maggie tossed her dagger so it narrowly missed the tip of Glynis's finger, the crossbow sliding even farther away.

She pulled another dagger and said, "Try to run, Glynis, and I'll throw my knife into your leg. I'll sever the tendon so you canna walk properly again. Or maybe I'll toss it in your knee, so you'll limp for the rest of your life—if you're lucky—and you'll know exactly how Aileen felt when you taunted her about her scarred lip."

Glynis faced her, chest heaving, eyes darting around, looking for a way out. Finally, she returned her gaze to Maggie. "I'd rather be dead than look like that misshapen monster. She's a malformed demon of a lass."

"She's a sweet lass with a scar on her lip, like many people."

"She's tupping my husband."

"You're tupping Drustan. And the old laird before that. Am I right? That's how you knew about the tunnel. He used it to sneak around to tup his lasses undetected. And once you were married to Keith, he used it to go behind Keith's back."

"Did Drustan tell you that? I've seen him watching you. What will happen if I tell Callum I saw you two together? I can be verra convincing."

"He'll do naught but hang you for a traitor. It's done, Glynis. Whate'er influence you once had is lost." Maggie had been watching the other woman's eyes, hoping to make her insensible with rage so she attacked Maggie on the scaffold. She was getting close. "You canna run from this. You have nowhere to hide. Your only option is to throw yourself on Callum's mercy and tell him what you know. Starting with how you murdered his father."

Glynis's eyes widened before she burst out laughing. "I wanted him dead, that's for certain. Did you know he approached my father about courting me when I was just seventeen years old? Except he was married, of course, and courting only meant tupping. I must admit I was flattered by the attention of a laird, but in truth, I was in love with a farmer's son who lived down the lane. I ne'er thought my father would say yes."

Maggie's stomach curdled. She wanted to condemn Glynis as nothing more than a blackhearted villain, but now that was impossible. "I'm sorry that happened to you. 'Twas a betrayal of the worst kind."

Glynis shrugged as if she didn't care, but Maggie saw her lips tighten. "He had seven daughters. I guess I didn't matter. So I went to my farmer's son, and he took care of me. He said nay to the laird, and we married. I had a bairn, a sweet, wee girl who died during birth. I barely survived, and the healer said I would ne'er have another."

Maggie's fingers twisted on the rope with dread, knowing the story could only get worse. "And Laird MacLean? When did you see him again?"

"A few months later. Once I was well enough to tup, my sweet farmer's son of a grieving husband contacted him and asked if he still wanted me. In exchange for my time spent with your husband's father, Ivor, my husband and I received the best prices for our crops and animals at market. I left him the following year and went to live in another village. Ivor found me there as well."

Maggie's throat had tightened, and she swallowed twice before she could speak. "'Tis a sad story, Glynis, and I am truly sorry for you. No lass should be treated that way. But it doesn't absolve you of your crimes."

"For killing the old laird, you mean?" Glynis jumped onto the scaffold, and Maggie took a quick step to the edge. The platform swayed under their combined weight, and she heard a support beam snap. The scaffold was coming apart.

"Nay, I didn't kill Ivor," Glynis continued. "Drustan did that of his own accord when I told him about Ivor and his wife, Abigail. Now that was a truly sad story—and one you ne'er suspected, am I right?"

She laughed again at the look on Maggie's face. "I did pay to have my husband and father killed, however. By that time, I was living at the castle and betrothed to Keith. In exchange for spying on Ivor and committing acts of treason, I would be paid in gold. But I didn't want gold. I wanted revenge."

She darted at Maggie with a dagger in her hand, moving quicker than Maggie had expected. Maggie jumped off the scaffold just as Glynis's knife scraped her skin, and she swung on the rope in a half circle back to the stone floor. Quickly looping the rope around the edge of the scaffold, Maggie then tipped it backward—slowly enough so that Glynis wouldn't slide off before she grabbed an edge and held on.

Glynis's eyes changed, transformed by fear—too afraid to move lest she fall. Maggie pierced her dagger through the rope and into the scaffold's wooden frame to hold it precariously in place.

It was a victory by all accounts, but Maggie felt grim, too grim to smile at her win over a woman who had committed such vile acts as murder. Nay, she felt sick at the story Glynis had told. It was a terrible tale even if only parts of it were true.

Still, they needed information. *Who had paid her?* If Glynis refused to talk, Maggie was afraid the consequences would be dire.

A scuffing sound came from directly behind her. When Glynis smiled, Maggie knew she was too late. Turning her head, she saw Drustan reaching out for her. She did the only thing she could do. She jumped.

❧

Callum burst out onto the chapel balcony where he'd married Maggie just hours ago and saw her leap onto a precariously balanced scaffold on the opposite side of the courtyard. Drustan stood behind her, looking ready to jump himself. Glynis was already hanging off the edge of the scaffold, and if she or Maggie fell, it would mean certain death. Maggie scrambled to stay upright, and Callum clapped his hand over his mouth so he wouldn't yell out and distract her. When she leapt to the more stable platform several feet away and landed safely, he breathed a sigh of relief.

Grabbing the rope he'd slid down yesterday during their wedding ceremony, he jumped from the balcony and landed seconds later in the courtyard. "Maggie, stay there! I'm coming!" he shouted as he sprinted toward the scaffolding. He scanned the area, noting several ways up to her. Climbing the net that hung against the stone wall would be the safest way and put him closest to Maggie, but that might draw Drustan in her direction. The scaffolding looked too dangerous to mount— he'd be afraid of knocking it over. So that meant the rope hanging over the pulley that had held up the rocks earlier. It was taut and looked like it was secured at the top; otherwise, his weight would pull it down. Aye, he could climb that bloody rope to get to his wife—without fail, whether it was four stories or ten.

Maggie looked down at him. "Callum! Drustan is here. He's mad."

"Just stay there!" he repeated. He jumped up as high as he could and grabbed the end of the rope, then pulled himself up, hand over hand, ignoring the burn in his arms and shoulders. He had only one chance to save Maggie. She was vulnerable, and Drustan could get to her at any time.

"Help me, Drustan. Help me!" he heard Glynis yell.

"Callum," Maggie screamed, sounding terrified, "he's going to pull out the knife securing the rope to the scaffold—you'll fall!"

He was passing the third floor and knew he had to jump. Then he heard Maggie say, "Drustan, look at me. It's Abi, sweetling. Look at me now," and his blood ran cold.

Maggie breathed deeply and tried to gentle her voice. Drustan had his hand on her dagger, and any moment now, he would pull it out and send the scaffold and Glynis crashing to the courtyard floor. She didn't know what she wanted for Glynis, but it wasn't to die that way.

"Drustan, look at me. It's Abi, sweetling. Look at me now."

Drustan looked at her—really looked at her. "Nay. You're wee, wild Maggie MacDonnell. I knew your da."

Relief rushed through her until he looked at Glynis, and a coldness entered his eyes. "You tried to kill Maggie. I saw you."

"I'm right here, Drustan. I'm unharmed," Maggie said at the same time Glynis said, "Please, Drustan. For all the time we spent together, loving each other. Please, have mercy." It was the wrong thing to say.

"I ne'er loved you. You aren't Abi. You could ne'er be Abi." In one quick yank, Drustan pulled out the knife. The scaffold slowly tipped over backward as Glynis screamed. Maggie darted for the edge with an anguished cry and reached out for her, but the distance was too great. She reached farther, almost to the point of losing her balance, before an arm wrenched her back to safety. Maggie turned into a warm, hard chest. Behind her, she heard the scaffold crash to the ground.

"Doona look, Maggie," Callum whispered to her. "Whate'er sympathy you had for her, remember she tried to kill you."

"And you. I found a tunnel under the courtyard. She used it to race up to the rope that held the rocks and cut it."

"A tunnel? Shown to her by my father?" When Maggie nodded, he squeezed her tight. "So she killed him after all."

"Nay, Callum. At least she says she didn't. But she did say she was the traitor. I tried to trap her on the—" Maggie's voice broke.

He squeezed her even tighter. "It doesn't matter now, lass. 'Tis almost over. My brothers are here."

She looked over her shoulder to see Drustan kneeling at the edge of the precipice. Gavin and Kerr came up behind him from one side, while Gregor and Darach approached from the other. Lachlan climbed up the net.

"I killed your father," Drustan said to him suddenly.

Callum tensed beneath her, and she hugged him closer.

"Why, Drustan?" he asked. "You were his best friend."

"He wouldnae leave Abigail alone. He was always after her, cornering her, trying to get closer to her." Drustan rubbed his hand over his nape. "She was running away from him in the stable. The horse kicked her in the head. Broke her neck."

"How do you know?" he asked. "You couldnae have been there, or you would have killed him on the spot—as I would have done had it been Maggie."

"Glynis told me. She said she heard him confess it to a priest. She has a way of listening through the walls."

"The tunnel," Maggie said.

Callum nodded, but she could still feel the resistance in his body. "She may have been lying. She's a traitor to our clan."

"I asked him," Drustan said. "I caught him alone up on the wall after he was done tupping some lass. He cried and said it was true, and he was sorry. He was glad I finally knew. That it felt good to get it off his chest."

He slumped forward, and Maggie caught her breath, fearing he would tumble over the precipice.

"I pushed him after that," he said tonelessly. "Why couldn't he have left her alone? She said nay, but he didn't listen. He was laird, and he kept after her until she was dead."

"Did you write the suicide note, then?" Callum asked, his voice ragged.

"Aye. I was going to jump, but I was so angry. I wanted you to know who your father really was. I went there to tell you everything. I thought you would kill me."

"I still may, Drustan."

Drustan nodded. He pressed the heel of his hand into his forehead, rubbing it, before he wrapped his palm around the nape of his neck. "When I got there, she was still on the ground, her neck twisted, her eyes open. My wife was dead."

Gregor and Kerr had reached him and grasped under his arms to pull him away from the ledge. Drustan's head dropped forward, and his body sagged.

Callum took Maggie's hand and led her off the scaffold onto the stone floor. He stopped in front of the broken man and laid his hand on his head. "I'm sorry for your loss, Drustan. She should have been safe. My father should have kept her safe."

He raised his eyes to Gregor. "Find our healer, Flora. See what can be done. And Father Lundie too."

Gregor nodded, and Callum walked quietly with Maggie toward their bedchamber. About halfway there, he stopped and lifted her into his arms, then kept going. "I know you doona like me carrying you. Are you all out of daggers that you havenae pressed one to my jugular?"

"Nay. I have one left, but I plan to use it on— John!" she hollered when she saw her brother, bearded and dirty, standing in front of her and Callum's bedchamber door. She struggled to free herself from Callum's arms, and he lowered her slowly to the floor.

Maggie hurtled herself at her brother, barely recognizing him. His cheeks were wet, his eyes red, and he held one of Maggie's letters in his hands. She didn't care how dirty he was; he was here, and he was alive. She threw her arms around him, sobbing, and he squeezed her tight, lifting her up. "Ah, Maggie. My sweet Maggie. I missed you, love."

"*My* sweet Maggie," she heard Callum say grumpily. "And how did you all get into my castle?" She turned at his words and gasped to see four men, as dirty and bearded as John, surrounding her husband at the point of their swords and arrows.

"John," she shrieked, reaching for her last dagger, but it was gone. She looked up and saw her brother had it in his hands. "Are those your men?"

"Aye."

She marched toward them, hands balled into fists. "Och. Now you're in trouble," Callum said with a wicked grin.

John whistled, and the men backed off.

"What is it with all the whistling?" she asked. "You canna just say 'retreat' or 'come' or 'get out of my bloody way'?"

"Nay," both Callum and John said together, then scowled at each other.

Callum turned to the men behind him. "Just so you know, I'm going to smash his bloody face in. While I was outside looking for him"—he pointed to John—"his sister was in here fighting for her life."

He marched toward her brother, his hands clenched just like Maggie's had been, but now nobody was grinning. "Your wee show out there almost got her killed."

Maggie darted between them, but they each used one hand to push her against the wall, glaring at each other.

"Verra well. One punch," John said. "But I hit back after the second one."

"What is going on here?" a booming voice asked.

She turned to see Gregor standing in the hallway, scowling at them. Callum's foster brothers held the other men at the points of their swords.

Well, isn't this confusing?

She looked at Callum and saw him flash a bright grin before his smile faded under Gregor's wrath. And her brother looked cowed too. That was interesting.

"John MacDonnell. You're laird now, and family to us through our sister and daughter, Maggie MacLean. Take your men and find some rooms. And for God's sake, have a bath."

John nodded, and Maggie almost laughed. She squeezed his hand as he walked by. "John?"

"Aye, love?"

"Did you see Ross before he…?"

He squeezed her hand back. "I got there just in time."

She teared up again, and they embraced. "And Irvin?" she asked.

"He's dead, Maggie, but not by my hand. I caught the weasel trying to run and put him in the dungeon. Somebody got to him in there."

Gregor clapped John on the shoulder and nudged him down the hall toward the other men. Everyone had lowered their swords and were busy eyeing each other. "We'll talk about that later. Give your sister and her husband some time alone."

When the others disappeared down the stairs,

Maggie wrapped her arm around Callum, and he pulled her into their bedchamber. After shutting and barring the door, he lifted her again in his arms.

He dropped his head in the crook of her neck and leaned against the door, just holding her. She felt him tremble and was awed by it.

"Callum," she said, cupping his face and raising it until their eyes met. She smiled at him, feeling soft and dewy, despite what had happened to Glynis and Drustan. "I love you."

He smiled, looking just as soft and dewy as she felt. "I love you too, Maggie. So much."

She kissed him, then pointed to the bed. "Carry me there."

He did as she asked, his smile turning a wee bit sinful as he laid her on the quilt and stretched out beside her. "Surely you doona want to have your way with me in a bed?" he asked.

She rolled on her side and wrapped her leg over his hip. He wedged his hand under her knee. "Nay," she said, kissing up his neck. "I can think of several far more exciting places to tup, Husband."

"Like where?" he asked, sounding genuinely curious and excited.

She groaned inside, regretting her daft pronouncement. She didn't know enough about tupping yet to be able to list off different ways to engage in it. Although…

"Well, 'twas quite exciting sitting pressed up against you on your horse."

His eyes widened, and he sat up suddenly, his cheeks tingeing pink as his arousal and other parts of him rose.

She checked her ring on her thumb to make sure it

wouldn't come off this time. He noticed, as he always did, and kissed it. "Too loose?" he asked.

"Aye," she said, feeling guilty—which he *didn't* seem to notice.

He quickly shed his plaid, shirt, and shoes before starting on hers. She laughed as her arms got caught in her sleeves, then stopped laughing and groaned when he took advantage and sucked her nipple into his mouth.

She gasped. "How exactly…is this…like…riding a horse?"

She could feel his smile on her skin before he rolled onto his back and dragged her on top of him. Her legs slid to either side of his hips. "Consider me your horse."

She laughed, unable to stop herself, and dropped her head onto his chest. He rumbled with laughter too, and she suddenly understood the appeal of this position. Sitting up, she raised her hands to her hair and loosed it from her ribbon so it flowed around her shoulders.

She loved watching the way his eyes hooded, the feel of his hands tightening on her hips. "I think I could get used to this," she said.

"Riding me?" he asked, bucking his hips for her so his shaft rubbed along her sensitive mound.

"Aye, that too." She leaned down and kissed him. Slowly. "The bed. I think I'd like to try more tupping in our bed."

He lifted her and slowly brought her down over him. They both sighed with satisfaction when he was rooted deep within.

He undid her leather sheaths from both arms and placed them and her weapons on the bedside table, almost knocking everything else off. "As long as you doona bring your weapons to bed with you, Wife."

She unstrapped his leather sheath from his forearm and another from his calf. "As long as you doona bring yours to bed either, Husband."

Then she rolled her hips and groaned. "Other than that one, of course."

*Keep reading for an excerpt from the first book
in The Sons of Gregor MacLeod series*

HIGHLAND PROMISE

Available now from Sourcebooks Casablanca

Gleann Afraig (Fraser territory)—The Highlands, Scotland

DARACH MACKENZIE WANTED TO KILL THE FRASERS.
Slowly.

Lying on the forest floor, he peered through the
leaves as his enemy rode single file along the trail at
the bottom of the ravine. Midway down the line, a
woman, tied belly down over a swaybacked horse,
appeared to be unconscious. Rope secured her wrists,
and a gag filled her mouth. The tips of her long,
brown hair dragged on the muddy ground.

In front of her, Laird Fraser rode a white stallion
that tossed its head and rubbed against the trees in an
attempt to unseat him. The laird flailed his whip, cutting the stallion's flanks in retaliation.

To the front and behind them rode ten more men,
heavily armed.

The King had ordered the MacKenzies and Frasers
to cease hostilities two years before, and much trouble
would come of helping the lass, let alone killing the laird.
Still, the idea of doing nothing made Darach's bile rise.

"You canna rescue her without being seen."

The whispered words caused Darach's jaw to set in a stubborn line. He refused to look at his foster brother Lachlan, who'd spoken. "Maybe 'tis not the lass I want to rescue. Did you not see the fine mount under the Fraser filth?" Yet his gaze never left the swing of the lass's hair, her wee hands tied together.

"Fraser would no more appreciate you taking his horse than his woman."

"Bah! She's not his woman—not by choice, I'll wager."

They'd been reaving—a time-honored tradition the King had not mentioned in his command for peace—and could easily escape into the forest unseen with their goods. They'd perfected the procedure to a fine art, sneaking on and off Fraser land for years with bags of wheat, barrels of mead, sheep, and horses.

Never before had they stolen a woman.

He glanced at Lachlan, seeing the same anger and disgust he felt reflected in his foster brother's eyes. "You take the stallion. The laird willna recognize you. I'll get the lass."

Lachlan nodded and moved into position while Darach signaled his men with the distinctive trill of the dipper—three short bursts, high and loud pitched. The MacKenzies spread out through the heavy growth, a nearby creek muffling any sound.

The odds for a successful attack were in their favor. Ten Fraser warriors against Darach, the laird of Clan MacKenzie; his foster brother Lachlan, the laird of Clan MacKay; and three of Darach's men: Oslow,

Brodie, and Gare. Only two to one, and they'd have the element of surprise.

As his enemy entered the trap, Darach mounted his huge, dark-gray stallion named Loki, drew his sword, and let out a second, sharp trill. The men burst through the trees, their horses' hooves pounding.

Two Frasers rode near the lass. Big, dirty men. Men who might have touched her. He plunged his sword into the arm of one, almost taking it off. The man fell to the ground with a howl. The second was a better fighter but not good enough, and Darach sliced open the man's side. Blood and guts spilled out. He keeled over, clutching his body.

Farther ahead, Lachlan struggled to control the wild-eyed stallion. The Fraser laird lay on the ground in front of Darach, and Darach resisted the urge to stomp the devil. He would leave the laird alive, even though he burned to run his sword through the man's black heart. Fraser's sister's too, if she were but alive.

In front of Darach, the mare carrying the lass thrashed around, looking for a means of escape. The ropes that secured the girl loosened, and she began sliding down the beast's side.

Just as her fingers touched the ground, he leaned over and pulled her to safety. Dark, silky hair tumbled over his linen lèine. When the mare jostled them, he slapped it on the rump. The animal sprang forward, missing Fraser by inches.

Damnation.

Placing her limp body across his thighs, Darach used his knees to guide Loki out of the waning melee.

Not one Fraser was left standing.

❧

They rode hard to put as much distance as possible between them and the Frasers, and along game trails and creek beds to conceal their tracks as best they could. When Darach felt they were safe, he slowed Loki and shifted the unconscious woman so she sat across his lap. Her head tipped back into the crook of his arm, and he stilled when he saw her sleeping face, bruised but still lovely—like a wee dove.

Dark lashes fanned out against fair cheeks, and a dusting of freckles crossed her nose.

She looked soft, pure.

God knows that meant nothing. He knew better than most a bonny face could hide a black heart.

Slicing through the dirty gag, he hurled it to the ground. Welts had formed at the corners of her mouth, and her lips, red and plump, had cracked. After cutting her hands free, he sheathed his dagger and massaged her wrists. Her cheek was chafed from rubbing against the side of the mare, and a large bruise marred her temple.

His gut tightened with the same fury he'd felt earlier.

Lachlan rode up beside him, the skittish stallion tethered behind his mount. "If you continue to stare at her, I'll wager she'll ne'er wake. Women are contrary creatures, doona you know?"

Darach drew to a stop. "She sleeps too deeply, Brother. 'Tis unnatural. Do you think she'll be all right?" Oslow, Brodie, and Gare gathered 'round. It was the first time they'd seen the lass.

"Is she dead, do you think?" Gare asked, voice scarcely above a whisper. He was a tall, young warrior of seventeen, with the scrawny arms and legs of a lad still building up his muscle.

Oslow, Darach's older, gnarly lieutenant, cuffed Gare on the back of the head. "She's breathing, isna she? Look at the rise and fall of her chest, lad."

"I'll do no such thing. 'Tis not proper. She's a lady, I'll wager. Look at her fine clothes."

Lachlan snorted in amusement and picked up her hand, turning it over to run his fingers across her smooth palm. "I reckon you might be right, Gare. The lass hasn't seen hard labor. 'Tis smooth as a bairn's bottom."

Darach's chest tightened at the sight of her wee hand in Lachlan's. He fought the urge to snatch it back.

"She has stirred some, cried out in her sleep. I pray to God the damage isna permanent." Physically, at least. Emotionally, she could be scarred for life. His arm tightened around her, and she moaned.

"Pass me some water." Someone placed a leather flagon in his hand, and Darach wedged the opening between her lips. When he tilted the container, the water seeped down her cheek. He waited a moment and tried again. This time she swallowed, showing straight, white teeth. Her hand came up and closed over his, helping to steady the flask.

A peculiar feeling fluttered in Darach's chest.

When she made a choking sound, he pulled the flask away. Her body convulsed as she coughed, and he sat her up to thump her on the back. Upon settling, he laid her back down in the crook of his arm.

"Christ, we doona want to drown her, Darach—or

knock the lungs right out of her. Maybe you should give her to one of us to hold for a while?" Lachlan's laughing eyes told Darach his foster brother deliberately provoked him. Another time-honored tradition.

Gare jumped in. "Oh, aye. I'll hold the lass."

"You?" Brodie asked. "You canna even hold your own sword. Do you think those skinny arms will keep her safe? I'll hold the lass." Brodie was a few years older than Gare and had already filled out into a fine-looking man. He was a rogue with the lasses, and they all loved him for it. No way in hell would he be holding her.

"Cease. Both of you," said Oslow. "If anyone other than our laird holds the lass, it will be Laird MacKay. If she be a lady, she'll not want to be held by the likes of you."

Darach glowered at Lachlan, who grinned.

Then she stirred, drawing everyone's attention. They waited as her eyelids quivered before opening. A collective gasp went up from the men, Darach included.

He couldn't help it, for the lass staring up at him had the eyes of an angel.

They dominated her sweet face—big, round, innocent. And the color—Darach couldn't get over the color. A piercing, light blue surrounded by a rim of dark blue.

A shiver of desire, followed by unease, coursed through him. He tamped down the unwelcome feeling.

"Sweet Mary," Gare whispered. "She's a faery, aye?"

All except Lachlan looked at Darach for confirmation. He cleared his throat before speaking, trying to break the spell she'd cast over him. Not a faery, but maybe a witch.

"Nay, lad," he replied, voice rough. "She's naught but a bonny maid."

"A verra bonny maid," Lachlan agreed.

Her throat moved again, and Darach lifted the flask. Opening her mouth, she drank slowly, hand atop his, eyes never leaving his face. He couldn't look away.

When she'd had enough, she pressed his hand. He removed it, and she stared up at him, blinking slowly and licking her lips. Her pink tongue tempted him, and he quelled the urge to capture it in his mouth.

Then she raised her hand and traced her fingers over his lips and along his nose, caressed his forehead to the scar that sliced through his brow, gently scraped her nails through the whiskers on his jaw.

A more sensual act he'd never experienced, and shivers raced over his skin.

Finally, she spoke. "*Par l'amour de Dieu, etes-vous un ange?*"

Acknowledgments

I had a crazy year last year. Baptism by fire as I got swept into the world of publishing and put on my professional-writer hat. What did I discover? How much I had to learn about everything! I was no longer just sitting by myself in my chair, writing stories when I wasn't being a mom. I was writing one story, editing another, and doing a final read-through on a third; having a website built; learning about newsletters and blogs; sending a gazillion emails about everything; and attempting to conquer all things social media.

I thought my brain might explode. Especially as *Highland Betrayal* took a lot more coaxing to reveal itself to me than either *Highland Promise* or *Highland Conquest*.

But I got through the fire—maybe a little burnt but still OK—because I had people who helped me out of the flames. Not just people—teams of people! Team Sourcebooks, Team Home Front, and Team Romance Writers!

Team Sourcebooks: Cat Clyne, Rachel Gilmer, Stefani Sloma. These are my main peeps at Sourcebooks who shepherd me through editing, production, and promotion, and they do it with intelligence, professionalism, hard work, humor, kindness, and understanding. They are my first cheering squad and do whatever they can to help me make and sell the best books possible. Thanks to all three of you! There are also people at Sourcebooks with whom I don't work directly but who create my gorgeous covers, promote my books to other markets, and so much more! Thank you, Team Sourcebooks!

Team Home Front: I couldn't do this job without having help with my kids. First and foremost, hugs and kisses to my husband, Ken, who steps up whenever he can, even though he also works long, demanding hours. To my dad, Jim, who will have two five-year-olds down for breakfast so I can sleep in after a late night writing, or will pick them up from school or come upstairs just to watch them color when I'm pushing a deadline. To Courtney, my lifesaver, who put on her flip-flops, grabbed the kids, the puppy, and the car keys, and took all three of my babies on lots of summertime adventures. To Cherie, who will take on my two and never bat an eye when I only have to take on one of hers in return. Thank you, Team Home Front!

Team Romance Writers: Hey You Guys! Big thanks go out to all my fellow romance writers. They are the best group of writers evah! Here at home, I get to chat about all things publishing with the gals at GVWA and with Eileen Cook and Alexia Adams, who are always up for wine, appies, and inappropriate humor. In addition, I chat online almost daily with my fellow Mermaids and members of the Golden

Network, who offer so much support, information, and laughter. A few of these women I text with daily (sometimes hourly!) as we each race toward our deadlines, try to figure out promo or how we can possibly manage all the different hats we wear. For the past year, those women have been Layla Reyne, Melonie Faith Johnson, and Kari Cole. Love you, ladies! Lastly, a special thanks to the fellow writers who helped me in all the other aspects of being a writer this year—the brilliant Crystal Stranaghan, who created my gorgeous website and knows everything there is to know about self-publishing, and the amazingly diverse and knowledgeable Monica Burns, who held my hand, got me set up, and taught me everything else I had to know. Thank you, Team Romance Writers!